THE FEAST

MARGARET KENNEDY

THE
FEAST

faber

This edition first published in 2021
by Faber & Faber Ltd
Bloomsbury House, 74–77 Great Russell Street
London WC1B 3DA

Typeset by Faber & Faber Ltd
Printed in the UK by CPI Group (UK) Ltd, Croydon CR0 4YY

A CIP record for this book
is available from the British Library

ISBN 978–0–571–36779–5

MIX
Paper from
responsible sources
FSC® C020471

6 8 10 9 7 5

To Margot Street

Foreword
by Cathy Rentzenbrink

The Feast opens in September 1947 when the Reverend
Samuel Bott of St. Sody in North Cornwall can't play chess
with his guest, the Reverend Gerald Seddon, because he
has a funeral sermon to write. The month before, a huge
mass of cliffside collapsed into a cove, obliterating Pendizack Hotel and causing all the people inside to perish.
Seddon has read about it in the papers. Wasn't it because a
mine washed into a cave behind the house? Partly, agrees
Bott, though that had seemed to do no damage at the time.
Then cracks were found in the cliff and a survey man wrote
to the owner Mr. Siddal to say they should evacuate, but
he never did anything about it. Now Siddal is buried under
the cliff and it has been accepted that all the victims will lie
where they fell under the rocks and boulders: 'No chance
of getting them out. You should see the place; you wouldn't
know it. The cove is not there anymore. Nobody would
think a house and gardens and stables ever stood there. So
now we've got to have a ghastly sort of ceremony . . .'

Bott applies himself to his sermon. He goes to his typewriter and inexpertly hammers out 'ACTOF GOD'. Then
there is a silence for twenty minutes until Seddon remarks
that he is not getting on very fast. Bott admits he was frightened, that he is still frightened, that, yes, it should have been
nothing compared to London in the Blitz, but that when the

survivors—yes, there were survivors—came to him afterwards they said the most astonishing things. Bott abandons his typewriter and comes to take a chair opposite Seddon. 'See what you make of it . . .'

After the intriguing opening—how clever to name one victim and let us know there are lots more, but also survivors with stories to tell—the narrative unfolds in seven parts, one for each day of the week leading up to the collapse. We read on almost as we would a crime novel, with a keen curiosity to know who lives and dies as we get to know our characters via their letters, diaries, typescripts full of errors, internal monologues and scenes full of life and conversation.

Margaret Kennedy achieved stratospheric success with her second novel *The Constant Nymph* in 1924, which was much adapted and discussed for its bohemian portrayal of a teenage girl who falls in love with a family friend. Her career continued to flourish and she wrote several more novels and plays. In 1937 Kennedy was talking about the seven deadly sins with novelist friends who schemed to imagine the sins as modern characters and each write a short story. The project fell through because they felt the overall effect might be too depressing, but Kennedy continued to mull it over, envisaging the seven sins collected in an inn run by the unhappy wife of Sloth. She still worried that her cast might be too unpleasant, but when she began to think of who the other guests might be, the novel caught fire. The end result is a riveting novel, one that wears its origin and moral lightly. And what a difference those ten years made! Had Kennedy and her friends pursued the idea in 1937 they would have been exploring pre-war preoccupations; however, *The Feast* situates the age-old questions of sin, retribution and salvation against a specific post-war context of shortages and squabbling, and this is what gives the novel such immediacy and texture.

Pride, gluttony, covetousness, lechery, wrath, envy and sloth are well in evidence at the Pendizack Hotel. The first guest we encounter is Lady Gifford, who sends Mrs. Siddal a long list of all the foods her doctor says she can and can't eat and suggests that she takes her meals in her room so the other guests won't be 'selfish and inconsiderate' about her need for superior nourishment. She regrets that they have had to give up their large country house because they can't get staff: 'All spaciousness and graciousness seems to have vanished from life, doesn't it?'

Lady Gifford wants her husband, Sir Henry, to agree to move to Guernsey so that they can avoid income tax, but he is against it. 'She doesn't understand. She was in America. She wasn't in the Blitz. I was. All that suffering, all that sacrifice, all that heroism . . . I saw it.' Sir Henry is gradually coming to realize that he can't bear the way his wife values nothing more in life than her saucer of cream. 'Why shouldn't I?' she asks. 'I can afford cream. Why shouldn't I go to live where the cream is?'

The Gifford children have an air of careless arrogance and look unusually well-nourished, like they belong 'to the kind of people who feed in the Black Market, who wear smuggled nylons and who, in an epoch of shortages, do not scruple to secure more than their share'. Their pockets are full of off-ration sweets like *marrons glacés* that arrive in packages from America.

The Giffords do offer to share their spoils with the children of fellow guest Mrs. Cove, who is grim and competent with a way of saving everything for a rainy day that never dawns. She crams her family into one room at the hotel to secure a reduction, and her daughters look like 'plants that have been grown in the dark' with pudding haircuts and shabby cotton dresses that barely cover their bony knees. Mrs. Cove despatches her children to the shops to get in first with their rationed sweet points and secure the best. Turkish delight is scarce, she instructs, so get that. Or marshmallows or fudge. She then sells the sweets on without letting the children eat any.

'Fancy all these people paying six guineas a week for the chance of having half Cornwall fall on top of them one fine day!' So writes Miss Dorothy Ellis, the disgruntled housekeeper, as she delights in spreading a rumour that the cliffside is unsafe, though she doubts it is true. She complains that the hotel is 'a rotten hole, the worst I ever struck'. She dislikes everyone, especially her employers who have lost all their money and are running the boarding house badly. 'It makes me mad to see her with this huge place—I could have made my tea shop pay if I had the chances some have.' Miss Ellis loves to laugh at the misfortunes of others: 'This Socialist Government does not look after poor people like they promised but they have brought rich people down, which is one comfort.' She spends her days snooping and trying to bully Nancibel, the maid who lives locally.

Nancibel is a straight-talking delight. She falls for Bruce, who is acting as chauffeur and secretary to the peculiar-looking lady writer Anna Lechene. Bruce, too, is working on a novel, but Nancibel doesn't fancy the sound of it: 'I like books about nice people. And a story where it all comes out right in the end.' When Bruce accuses her of not wanting to face facts, she says, 'Not in story books, I don't. I face plenty between Monday and Saturday without reading about them.'

Nancibel has picked up RAF slang during her time in the ATS. Her granny doesn't like it when she says Miss Ellis is 'having kittens' because she has to empty the slops. Her granny tells the Cove children about the day the first train came to the town, driven into the station by the mayor in his golden chain, decked with garlands and boughs as the band played. There was a great feast in the town hall that day. The children want to know who gave it: 'All gave it and all came.'

The Cove children might be poor but they are rich in dreams, and their favourite game — inspired by the dormitory feasts in a book they own called *The Madcap of St. Monica's*—is to plan the feasts they would give if they were rich. As the week goes on, and after the Cove children have a narrow escape, Nancibel and some of the other characters decide that they should have their feast. They donate their sweet points, or offer to make jelly or cook lobsters, and join in with the plan to dress up. Sir Henry Gifford even provides four bottles of hock. The children create beautiful hand-painted invitations and the reader begins to grasp that there might be more than a picnic at stake as the hotel guests and staff decide whether or not to take up the offer . . .

The Feast is so full of pleasure that you could be forgiven for not seeing how clever it is. Like many of my favourite novels, it delivers an enjoyable story that can be consumed without too much strain, but also repays mulling over and re-reading in pursuit of the many and various deeper meanings. Kennedy is a playful and skilled writer and all the jokes and satisfyingly granular details of daily life coexist with a brutal ability to face unpleasant truths about humanity: four of the buried guests are parents, and it is difficult to come to any other conclusion but that their offspring are better off without them.

Like the mine that exploded in the cave and seemed at first to have done no damage, the influence and impact of this novel are greater than they at first appear. Perhaps you, dear reader, like me, will indulge in some self-assessment, nervously scanning for evidence of your own pride or gluttony or wrath. And you may find yourself categorizing your real-life acquaintances by their sins as you ponder the wider questions raised about transgression and redemption. But perhaps the biggest triumph of The Feast is that while it showcases a full range of human failure and folly, what most sticks in the mind is the dear little scruffy Cove children who have so little, but whose desire to dispense non-judgemental generosity warms the heart. Perhaps the final invitation to the reader is that salvation is always available to us, if we can recognize the offer and accept it.

PROLOGUE

The Funeral Sermon

In September 1947 the Reverend Gerald Seddon, of St. Frideswide, Roxton, paid his annual visit to the Reverend Samuel Bott, of St. Sody, North Cornwall.

They are old friends and this holiday together is the greatest pleasure they know. For Mr. Bott, though he cannot afford to go away, allows himself a kind of vacation while Mr. Seddon is staying with him. He exchanges the cassock in which he is, at all other times, to be seen, for a pair of old flannel trousers and a pullover, and he goes for birdwatching expeditions along the cliffs. In the evening they play chess. Both are in the late fifties, Anglo-Catholic, celibate, and disconcertingly sincere. They like to be called Father by their parishioners, but they do not enjoy skirmishes with Protestants as much as they did when they were young. Father Bott is grey, stocky, and hirsute; he looks rather like a Scotch terrier and he is not popular in the parish of St. Sody. Father Seddon has the dew-lapped melancholy of a bloodhound; his life is harder and more unpleasant, but his parishioners appreciate him.

He arrives in time for supper and they get out the chess board as soon as the meal is over. In London his evenings are spent in clubs and missions, so that he looks forward to this relaxation very much indeed. And he was consequently somewhat aggrieved when, on the night of his arrival in

1947, he was told to put the chess board away.

'I can't play tonight,' explained Bott. 'I'm very sorry; I have a sermon to write.'

Seddon raised his eyebrows. It was a holiday rule that Bott should get all sermons written in advance.

'It's an unexpected sermon. I tried to get it done this afternoon. But I couldn't think of anything to say.'

'Very unusual,' suggested Seddon unkindly.

'Well . . . it's a funeral sermon . . .'

Bott went across to his desk and took the cover off his typewriter.

'Not even an ordinary funeral,' he complained. 'Not a funeral at all, really. We can't bury the deceased. They're buried already. Under a cliff . . .'

'Oh? Pendizack Cove?'

Seddon never had much time for reading the newspapers, but he remembered this incident because it had been in his friend's parish. During the month of August a huge mass of cliff side had suddenly subsided. It had fallen into a small cove a couple of miles from St. Sody village, and obliterated a house which once stood on a spit of land on the east side of the cove. Every person inside the house had perished.

'It was a mine, wasn't it?' he asked. 'A mine, washed up into the cave behind the house?'

'Partly. But that was months ago, the mine,' said Bott. 'That was last winter. It went off inside the cave and seemed to do no damage. We all thought what an escape the house had had. It was a hotel, you know. Used to be a private

4

house, but they'd turned it into a guest house. The cave runs right under the cliff. The blast must have shattered the rocks in there and loosened a great slice of the cliff face. Later on, cracks were found at the top of the cliff, about a hundred yards inland. Humphrey Bevin, he's the Survey man, you know, lives over Falmouth way, heard of it and came to have a look. He was in two minds about it; thought it would have been down already if it was going to fall. But, on reflection, he wrote to Siddal to say that if those cracks got any wider he didn't think the house was safe and they'd better get out. Siddal owned the hotel. He never answered. Never did anything about it. And now he's under the cliff.'

'You mean they're all still buried?'

'No chance of getting them out. You should see the place; you wouldn't know it. The cove is not there any more. Nobody would think a house and gardens and stables ever stood there. So now we've got to have a ghastly sort of ceremony . . . Service in the church, and the rest of it as near as we can get to them . . . scrambling on the cliffs. I don't like that sort of thing, but I can't very well refuse, and we've got to give them as much of a Christian burial as we can. We'd have done it before, only there was some idea, for a time, of trying to get them out. It's tomorrow. And if I were you I'd go off for the day. We shall have all the Press over, I suppose, and car loads of sightseers . . . And I'm expected to preach about it!'

Bott addressed himself to his typewriter. He always typed his sermons because his writing was so bad that he could not read it. Nor could he always read his own typing, for that, too, was inexpert. He put a q at the top of a page, recollected himself, pulled out FIG. and put a 1. Then he pulled out GAP and made his first heading:

ACTOF GOD.

After that there was a pause of twenty minutes. Seddon settled down to a chess problem. The cheap alarm clock on the mantelpiece ticked hurriedly.

Bott drew pictures on his blotting paper. First he drew a dolphin. Then he drew some curved capitals of pillars. And then he drew Pendizack Point, standing out into the sea. That was still there. That was on the far side of the cove. It had been there for hundreds, perhaps thousands, of years. But the chaos of fallen rock and boulder, the new, raw cliff face, on the eastern side had only been there a month. He could not have drawn it; he could not accept it as having any shape at all.

For weeks that stony confusion had met him at the end of all his thoughts, blocking them with a kind of shuddering jar, as the road had been blocked on the night when he ran down to see what had happened. For he had heard, everyone in the village had heard, the roar and rumble of the falling cliff. As they ran over the fields he met people shouting that Pendizack Hotel was 'gone'. He expected to find ruins, noise, confusion, screams, corpses—any horror but that which he found.

There was a choking pall of dust which met them as they came down the hill to the cliffs, and they could see little. The hotel drive plunged downwards in steep zigzags, through trees and shrubs beside a little ravine. The silence below had already begun to chill his heart before he turned the second bend and ran into a rock. A hill rose in front of him. There was no road down any more.

At first he thought that it was a barrier of loose boulders and tried to scramble over it. But at last he was driven back by the toppling, slipping rocks, and, returning up the drive, he took a side path, a little tunnel through rhododendrons, which led him out on to the open cliff. Here, in a moonlight still hazy with dust, he could see what had happened. The fallen cliff had filled up the entire cove. No trace was left of the house, the little platform of land where it had stood, or of anything else that had ever been there.

Already the tide was lapping gently round the newly fallen boulders as if they had been there always. The coastline had settled itself to a new pattern and the cliffs had returned to their ancient and quiet solidity.

He sighed, crossed out his first heading, and typed a new one.

bE STILL ANDKNOW THAT i aM GOD.

'You aren't getting on very fast,' observed Seddon.

'I was frightened,' said Bott.

He wrote: *Sudden Death*. And added:

'I'm still frightened.'

'Nothing to North London in '41 I should have thought,' said Seddon.

'I know.'

Bott rose and went to the window. It was a fine night with a rising wind. He could see the trees waving about

7

round the church tower, a dark and moving mass against a starless sky. Soon the leaves would blow down and lie scattered on the graves until they mouldered and went back to the earth. The bare branches would thresh round the church through the winter gales, waiting for the time of new leaves. With each week and each month this remembered night of summer would slip further into the past. He felt more sure of the future. *Nothing is certain*, he thought, *but the certain Spring*.

'The survivors,' he said, 'came here. They came up here for shelter, that first night.'

'There were survivors?'

'Oh, yes. They came here and they talked. They sat here talking all night. You know how people talk when they've had a shock. They say things they wouldn't say at any other time. They said the most astonishing things. They told me how they had escaped . . . They told me a great deal too much. I wish they hadn't.'

'How did they escape?'

'I don't know what to say about it at all,' said Bott, turning from the window. 'I'm not sure what I think. They told a lot, but of course they didn't tell everything. Nobody will ever know the whole truth. But what they did tell me . . .'

He came to the fireplace and took a chair opposite Seddon.

'Now listen,' he said. 'See what you make of it . . .'

SATURDAY

1. Letter from Lady Gifford
to Mrs. Siddal

The Old House,
Queen's Walk,
Chelsea.
August 13, 1947.

Dear Mrs. Siddal,

I ought to have written before to tell you *how* much we are all looking forward to our holiday at Pendizack. But I wasn't very well in the Spring, when my husband booked the rooms, and letter writing was forbidden. Much better now. Doctors, sharpening their knives, have promised to make me *perfectly well* in the Autumn.

We shall be arriving on Saturday the 16th. The children will be coming by train and will need a car to meet them— my husband's secretary will write about this—what train and what station, etc. I shall be driving down with my husband, and we hope to arrive between tea and supper. But if we are delayed will you very kindly see to it that the children go to bed *early*? They will be tired and excited after their journey.

Our mutual friend, Sibyl Avery, has told me a great deal about Pendizack and how delightful it is. So much nicer than a regular hotel, especially for the children. She says you have several boys but could not remember what ages. If any are still in the nursery stage perhaps Michael and Luke could have meals with them as they might be rather noisy in the dining room, and I am afraid I shall have to have most of *my* meals upstairs, so cannot supervise. Will this be a great nuisance? My husband can carry the trays up, of course. I hate to give trouble. But my doctor is so very insistent upon tranquillity during meals—I get this terrible indigestion and he thinks it is because my mind is too active—I *think* and *talk* too much while I eat, so it is really better to eat alone.

Sibyl tells me you have your own farm, which should make my regime fairly simple to manage. In a regular hotel it is difficult; they won't put themselves out for an invalid. It's really not anything much, but I will just jot down now (*a*) what my doctor says I *may* eat, and (*b*) what I may *not* eat.

A.   Poultry, game, *fresh* butcher's meat, liver, kidneys, sweetbreads, etc., bacon, tongue, ham, fresh vegetables, green salads, fresh eggs, milk, butter, etc. So you see there's a wide choice.

B.   Sausage meat, twice cooked meat, margarine, and *nothing* out of a tin, i.e. no powdered eggs, dried milk, etc., and *no corned beef*.

I won't go into boring details. It's just that my metabolism has never been right since Caroline was born and the whole of Harley Street doesn't seem able to get to the bottom of it. I wouldn't mind it so much if it wasn't such a *bore*. I do hate being a nuisance, and one can't be ill without giving trouble to other people. But I know you will understand. Sibyl has told me what a wonderful person you are and how marvellously you look after your guests. She vows that I shall be a new woman after a week at Pendizack. And there is this about my having my meals upstairs: you cannot naturally, in these hard times, give everyone the food I have to have, so perhaps you would prefer that other guests do not see what I am getting. People are so selfish and inconsiderate sometimes.

I do so admire you for hitting on this means of keeping up your lovely old house. We had to give up our country home in Suffolk. No staff! All spaciousness and graciousness seems to have vanished from life, doesn't it?

Oh, and do you mind a cat? Hebe insists on bringing hers, and I hadn't the heart to say no. I'm afraid I spoil my family, but you will understand for I expect Sibyl will have told you my funny, sad little story! No more babies after Caroline, when I wanted a dozen! But I couldn't bear to let Caroline be an only child, so the little sister and the two little brothers had to be sought among the poor unwanted babes of this world, and I always feel that I have got to be *more* than a mother to them to make up for that first, dreadful misfortune. Hebe is ten, and the boys (twins) are eight years old.

I see I've said nothing about fish. I'm allowed everything except kippers, but I don't think plaice agrees with me very well, nor haddock, unless cooked with plenty of butter. Crab and lobsters are not *verboten* which is very convenient, as I expect you get plenty of them and so many people can't eat them.

It will be delightful to meet you. I shall insist that you don't spend your whole time being a wonderful house-keeper but spare some of it occasionally for a good gossip with me, for I believe we have many friends in common.

I believe you know the Grackenthorpes. I'm so fond of Veronica, and miss her so much now that they have gone to live in Guernsey. But that's where we'll all have to live if income tax doesn't come down soon.

With kindest regards,

Yours very sincerely,

EIRENE GIFFORD.

P.S.—Is there any chance of golf for my husband?

2. Unfinished Letter from Miss Dorothy Ellis to Miss Gertrude Hill

Pendizack Manor Hotel,
Porthmerryn.
Saturday Aug. 16, 1947.

Dear Gertie,

I got your P.C. last night. Yes I did get your letter alright and do not blame me if I did not answer because I literally have not been off my feet since I came here. Well, for the question you ask in your letter, no, I do not advise you to come here if you can get any other job—a cook can always get a job, not like poor I. If I could stand the heat of a kitchen I would not be where I am now—it is a rotten hole, the worst I ever struck—I shall not stay, not after I have found something else—I answered several ads—of course all the best jobs this season are gone due to me coming here—which I consider she got me under false pretences, it is not a housekeeper she needs but a maid of all work— If I was not pretty sharp at looking after Number One I should be doing every scrap of work in the place.

Well this is not a hotel at all, only a boarding house— all falling down and the roof leaking, you can see there has been nothing spent on it for years and only one bathroom. They have lost all their money, so she got the bright idea to turn this into a boarding house because of course her

darling boys have got to go to posh schools just the same—
but she does not know the first thing about running a hotel
and cant cater for toffee. It makes me mad to see her with
this huge place—I could have made my tea shop pay if I had
the chances some have.

He has never done a stroke in his life as far as I can make
out, except get himself born—they have put him to sleep in
the boot-hole and he does not count for anything more than
a sick headache in this outfit. There was a family here last
week, name of Bergman, not out of the 'top drawer'—very
common in fact—and Mr. Bergman was complaining the
water was not hot—well, it never is—and she came floating along and said she would get Gerry, that is the eldest
son, to stoke the boiler when he came in. Oh no, says Mr.
Bergman, you will do it yourself right now, Mrs. Siddal. It
is nothing to me who stokes the boiler, he said. But I pay
six guineas a week to give my bottom a rest not yours. Her
face! You ought to have seen it. I do not often laugh—not
much to laugh at—but I had a good laugh then—I was just
outside in the passage. This Socialist Government does not
look after poor people like they promised but they have
brought rich people down, which is one comfort.

It is miles from Porthmerryn and the shops so of course
she cannot get any staff. All she has got is a daily housemaid
so called and a mentally deficient youth supposed to be a
waiter. She has to do the cooking till they can get a cook.
And they have not got any boarders just now, only a barmy
old couple name of Paley—but there is supposed to be two
families coming this evening.

Well Gertie I must finish this another time because it is getting on for 8 a.m. and I can see Nancibel, the said house-maid, coming across the sands and I must get after her or nothing will be done. No rest for the wicked! . . .

3. Extract from the Diary of Mr. Paley

I have been sitting here at my window since five o'clock this morning, watching the tide go out. I can see the pretty young chambermaid . . . I forget her name . . . coming down the cliff path from Pendizack Headland. She comes this way every morning, across the sands, whenever the tide is out. It must be later than I thought.

Christina is asleep. She will not wake until the maid brings in our tea and cans of hot water. Then a new day will begin. This respite will be over. When Christina wakes I shall no longer be alone.

She will not ask why I have been sitting here half the night. She no longer asks me questions: no longer cares to know how it is with me. She passes her life, at my side, in silence. It is, no doubt, a wretched life, but I cannot help her. At least she is able to sleep. I am not. The maid has reached the sand now, but she is walking very slowly. She is a graceful young creature. She walks well. She is, I believe, quite a favourite with Christina. But my wife is always inclined to be sentimental about young girls: for her they represent the daughter we lost. The maternal instinct is a purely animal affair. A cat which has lost its kitten will suckle a puppy quite contentedly, so I have been told.

I had a talk with Siddal, our host, yesterday. He told me that Pendizack Cove used to be called Hell's Kitchen and that his sons wished to call the house Hell's Hotel. Since he seemed to regard this as a joke I made shift to laugh, and did not say, with Mephistopheles: *Why this is Hell! Nor am I out of it.* But that line, that line, haunts me wherever I am. I can never escape from it.

Let me, if I can, think of something else. Of what shall I think? *Can* I think? Sometimes it appears to me that I have lost the power. Thought travels. I remain . . . where I was.

I will think of Siddal. He is a curious fellow. Were I able to feel for any other creature I should pity him greatly. For it appears that he has never been able to support himself. And now that he has lost all his money he must live on his wife's labour—accept bread at her hands. He has no position here. He receives no respect. He lives, so they tell me, in a little room behind the kitchen, a room which, in the old days, was used by the boot-boy. All the best rooms in the house have, of course, been vacated for guests. Mrs. Siddal sleeps somewhere up in the attics and the Siddal boys in a loft over the stables.

How can Siddal endure such a life? If he must sleep in the boot hole, why does he not insist that his wife sleeps there with him? I should do so. But then I could not have acted as he has, in any particular. I should have refused to allow my house to be exploited in this manner. It is done, so I understand, in order to pay for the education of the two younger boys. If education must be bought at such a price, then, say I, it has been bought too dearly. Moreover, these boys obviously despise and ignore their father.

Yet he is not without intelligence; was, I gather, considered brilliant as a young man. He went to the Bar. Why he failed there I do not know. He had private means and this, coupled with indolence and a total lack of ambition, may have been the ruin of him.

I ought to be thankful that I never had a penny, that I have never accepted help or support from anyone. I have always had to depend entirely upon myself.

I blush when I meet him. For the most part he is invisible. But sometimes he appears on the terrace, or in the public rooms, very ready to talk to anyone who will listen to him, ill-shaven and none too clean. He has three sons who despise him. I have no child. But I would not change places with Siddal . . .

4. One Pair of Hands

Nancibel Thomas was a little late, but she walked across the sand, as Mr. Paley had noticed, very slowly. It was the same every morning. She could not hurry over this last part of the walk. As soon as she came within sight of the house her spirits sank; they sank lower with every step she took, as though she were walking into a fog of misery and depression. And every day she felt a greater reluctance to go on.

She could not tell why this should be. For the work at Pendizack was not hard or disagreeable and everybody treated her well. She did not like Miss Ellis; but life in the A.T.S. had taught her how to get on with all sorts of people, including those whom she disliked. Miss Ellis could scarcely be responsible for this aversion which assailed her whenever she approached the house, this feeling that something dreadful, something indescribably sad, was happening there.

Sometimes she thought that it might merely be a sadness which she herself had brought back to this place, where she had once been a child and happy, running errands between Pendizack and her father's cottage on the cliff. For she had come home with trouble in her heart and the winter had been a heavy one. But if it was me, she thought, as she dragged her feet across the sand, it would be getting better. Because I'm getting better. I'm getting over it. I don't think of it but two or three times in a week now. But the house gets worse.

Yet the house had an innocent and helpless appearance this morning. All the curtains were drawn and there were no bright splashes of bathing dresses hanging out of the windows, for nobody bathed now that the Bergmans had gone. And she remembered how she had once met Mr. Bergman by the rocks, as she crossed the sands. He was going down to bathe. He had looked very hard at her and hesitated, as though he might be going to make a pass at her. But he did not. He said good morning quite respectfully and went on down the rocks. Nobody now made passes at her any more. Her trouble, and the fortitude which had carried her through it, had turned her into Somebody. Even coarse Mr. Bergman could see that she was not just another girl, just another plump, pretty, black-haired girl. Even her mother seemed to see it for she had left off offering advice to Nancibel and sometimes actually asked for it.

Not all the curtains were drawn, as she saw when she got closer. Poor Mr. Paley was sitting, as usual, in the big bay window on the first floor. He looked like a statue, staring out to sea. And there was a flicker from an attic casement, just under a row of cormorants which sat on the ridge of the roof. Miss Ellis had peeped and dodged back.

Nancibel quickened her pace and ran up the steps carved in the rock. A gate at the top took her on to the garden terrace whence a path led round to the back of the house. Her white overall hung on a peg, just outside the kitchen and her working shoes stood on the floor beneath it. She put them on quickly and went into the kitchen. A kettle was already simmering on the stove. For this she knew she had to thank

Gerry Siddal and not Fred, the waiter. Work at Pendizack was always far easier when Mr. Gerry was home on his holiday. He not only did a great deal of it himself, but he saw that Fred, who also slept in the stables, got up in the morning. As she came round the house she had heard a rhythmic squeaking within, which meant that Fred was pushing his carpet-sweeper up and down the dining-room floor.

When early tea and cans of hot water had been taken upstairs she would have to do the lounge while Fred did the hall and stairs, and Mrs. Siddal cooked the breakfast. Then there would be the washing-up and the bedrooms and landings and bathroom to do. Somehow, between them, Fred and Nancibel would get it all done before lunch time.

But not if there's really ten more coming this afternoon, she thought, as she carried up the Paleys' tea. I can't do all those extra bedrooms. Ellis will have to do some.

A year ago, before she was Somebody, she would not have thought this so calmly. She would have rehearsed a heated manifesto about being put upon, she would have become flustered when she mentioned the matter to Mrs. Siddal. Now she knew how to look after herself without unpleasantness.

She knocked at the Paleys' door and was told to come in. The early light streamed through the uncurtained window. Mr. Paley still sat there, writing in an exercise book. Mrs. Paley lay in her half of the bed, her neat grey head swathed in a pink net setting-cap. There was a petrified atmosphere about the room as though something violent had been going on there, and its occupants struck into immobility only

23

by Nancibel's knock. The Paleys always gave off this suggestion of a violence momentarily suspended. They would eat their breakfast every morning in a sombre, concentrated silence, as though bracing themselves for some enormous effort to be sustained during the day. Shortly afterwards they could be seen crossing the sands, carrying books, cushions and a picnic basket. They walked in single file, Mr. Paley leading. Up the cliff path they went, and out of sight over the headland. At four o'clock, having, as the flippant Duff Siddal suggested, disposed of the corpse, they returned in the same order to take tea on the terrace. It was difficult to believe that they had done nothing all day save read and eat sandwiches.

Nancibel put the can of water on the washing-stand and took the tea tray to the bedside. Mrs. Paley, she perceived, was not really asleep. She lay tense and rigid, her eyes tightly shut. Neither Paley said anything, and all the violence no doubt broke out again as soon as the door was shut on them.

Tea for Miss Ellis came next. She never said *come in* when you knocked. She always called out:

'Who is it?'

One day, vowed Nancibel, I'll say it's the Duke of Windsor.

'Your tea, Miss Ellis.'

'Oh? Come in.'

The room was frowsty and full of cardboard boxes. It had been a nice little room before Miss Ellis came, with bright chintzes and good furniture. But she had managed to give it a poverty-stricken look. She put nothing away;

24

all her possessions lay strewn about that the world might see how shabby, soiled and broken they were. Her teeth grinned shamelessly on the dressing table beside the filthy brush and comb. But the most squalid object in the room was Miss Ellis herself, in a torn, mud-coloured dressing gown, her greasy black hair falling over her eyes.

'Have you done the lounge?'

'No, Miss Ellis.'

(A nice row there'd be if she didn't get her tea till I'd done the lounge!)

'Then you'd better do it right away, Nancibel.'

'Yes, Miss Ellis.'

'Is Fred up yet?'

'Yes, Miss Ellis.'

'Has he done the dining room?'

'He's doing it, Miss Ellis.'

'Very well. When you've done the lounge you can go and help in the kitchen. I shall be down shortly.'

This ritual conversation took place every morning and its offensiveness was deliberate. The implication was that Nancibel lacked both the wit to remember the usual routine and the conscience to follow it without a daily reminder. It was called Getting After The Girl, and constituted, in Miss Ellis's opinion, the major part of her duties: a task not to be undertaken for less than four pounds a week.

Fred was still pushing the sweeper about when Nancibel came downstairs. She took it away from him and told him to go and dust the stairs, whereat he breathed heavily and replied:

'Nancibel, you are Ree-dundant. That is to say, you are not wanted.'

This was also a formula, frequently repeated. It was Fred's one witticism and he was very fond of it. But he was a good-natured boy and always did what she told him to do.

A few minutes' break, and a cup of tea, came after the lounge was finished. Mrs. Siddal was now in the kitchen, which smelt of coffee, toast and sizzling bacon. She moved aside from the stove to let Nancibel get at the teapot, and said that a crib must be brought in from the stables and set up in the big attic.

'Mrs. Cove, who is coming this afternoon, wants to have all her three children sleeping with her. I imagine they must be quite small, as she says they won't be taking dinner.'

'It'll be a job to get four beds in there,' said Nancibel, sipping her tea.

'Yes. And we must get three other rooms ready. The sea room for Lady Gifford and her husband, and the two rooms above it for their children. Ask Miss Ellis for sheets. You'd better . . .'

Her words were drowned by the noise of the gong, hammered in the hall by Fred. Immediately she lifted the porridge pot on to the table and began to ladle out two bowls of porridge for the Paleys, who always came down the moment the gong rang. The pot was heavy and Nancibel, watching her, thought how awkward it was to have a lady working in the kitchen. Mrs. Siddal was a passable cook, but she had taken to housework too late. She had no muscle and no knack. She was clumsy and amateurish; she made many unnecessary movements. Her pretty hair was always falling into her eyes and her overalls were crumpled half an hour after she had put them on. Nancibel's mother could have done twice as much in half the time.

Poor thing! thought Nancibel. Let's hope she gets a proper cook soon. P'raps that's what's wrong with the house. P'raps I shouldn't feel so blue here if there was a cook.

5. Breakfast in the Kitchen

Duff and Robin Siddal came in from bathing, their wet towels round their necks. They were sent out into the yard again to hang the towels on a line while their mother spooned out bowls of porridge, which she set for them on a side table by the window. It had never been her intention, when she opened the hotel, to feed her family in the kitchen. The Siddals were to have had their own table in the dining room, where Fred could wait on them. But they had found that they could not talk in the dining room. The guests embarrassed them.

'Where's Gerry?' she asked, when they came back. 'Didn't he bathe with you?'

'No,' said Duff. 'He's attending to the electric light machine.'

'His porridge will get cold.'

She put Gerry's porridge bowl into the oven to keep warm and wondered who would have seen to the electric light if Gerry had not been there. Of her three sons he was the most loving and the least loved. For he had inherited none of the charm which had betrayed her into marrying Dick Siddal. Heaven knew from what plebeian strain he received his stocky build, his snub nose and his tendency to boils. Even as a baby he had bored her, though no child could have given less trouble. Low-spirited, affectionate and conscientious, he had plodded his dreary way to maturity without giving her one endearing memory. Even his letters during the war (and he had fought at Arnhem) were so flat as to be almost unreadable.

She was ashamed that this should be so and that the other two should entirely divide her disappointed heart. For Robin took after her own kin—the Trehernes. He was the picture of a brother she had lost in 1918, ruddy, comely and blythe. And Duff was the son of her dreams: he had Dick's charm, Dick's beauty, Dick's brilliance, untarnished as yet by Dick's failure. She could deny nothing to Duff. But she made a faint stand when he asked for cream with his porridge.

'Not after today,' she said. 'I shall have to keep what there is for Lady Gifford. She's going to be very difficult to feed. But I must do my best, for Sibyl Avery sent her.'

'What's the matter with her?' asked Duff. 'It sounds a very nice illness. I wish I could catch it.'

Shuffling feet were heard in the kitchen passage. The master of the house had emerged from his lair in the quondam boot-hole. He stood for a moment in the doorway, hugging his old dressing gown round him, as if uncertain of permission to come in. Duff and Robin moved their chairs to make room for him and his wife handed him a bowl of porridge, which he accepted with exaggerated humility, apologizing to his sons for giving them the trouble to move. He was in his Poor Relation mood.

After a short, embarrassed pause, Duff made an effort to resume the conversation.

'Two more families,' he said, 'will make a lot of extra work.'

'Yes,' said Mrs. Siddal. 'And Nancibel can't do it all. Miss Ellis will have to do the bedrooms. I told her so last night.'

'Mother!' cried Robin. 'How brave you are! What did she say?'

'She was shocked beyond speech. But she did manage to ask if I expected her to empty slops. I said I did.'

'Now she'll walk out,' prophesied Duff.

'I don't think so,' said Mrs. Siddal. 'I don't think she could get any other job.'

Her voice was sharp, as she said this, and a hard line appeared round her mouth. This sharpness and this hardness were not natural to her. Work she did not mind, or sacrifice of leisure, rest and comfort. But she hated having to stand up for herself when people treated her badly, and she had begun to realize that ruthless bullying was the only method likely to succeed with Miss Ellis. For Duff's sake she must learn how to hold her own, for Duff would never go to Balliol unless the hotel could be made to pay.

'I'd do it myself,' she said. 'But it doesn't do for me to be upstairs in the morning.'

Mr. Siddal ate his porridge and turned timid glances from one face to another. He was doing his silent best to make them feel uncomfortable. He was pointedly managing to be left out. Yet they knew that if they were to make any attempt to include him in the conversation he would disclaim all understanding of it. The affairs of the hotel, he would imply, were too much for the intellect of such a worm as himself.

Duff, however, ventured to address him directly.

'I don't think Ellis had better empty the slops, do you? She might empty herself out by mistake. She's very like a slop really—a human slop.'

Siddal conveyed an immense uncertainty as to the nature of slops and their place in the scheme of things. But after a while a light dawned on him.

'I begin to grasp it,' he said to Duff. 'It's the basic problem of Socialism, isn't it? As defined by the Frenchman to whom the beauties of an egalitarian society were explained. *Mais alors, qui videra le pot de chambre?*'

'That,' said Mrs. Siddal, flushing, 'is what every civilized person should do for himself. But I wish we had more bathrooms.'

'Oh I know,' said Siddal. 'I think so too. And so did Tolstoy. At least, I seem to remember that he wrote with passion on the subject. Didn't he, Duff?'

'I don't know,' said Duff sulkily.

'Oh . . . I forgot. Your generation doesn't read Tolstoy. So sorry. Old fogies shouldn't harp on books which have gone out. And anyway, our guests don't seem to be civilized. They all have a capitalist mentality and leave it to Nancibel, as we did till we became proletariat ourselves. She is beautiful and she is good and she is extremely intelligent and she is worth all the rest of us put together, but she is the only person in the house to whom we can entrust this office without a social upheaval because she is a farm labourer's daughter.'

'I do read Tolstoy,' said Duff. 'I only . . .'

'Here's your bacon,' said Mrs. Siddal, thrusting a plate under her husband's nose.

'Thank you. Is this really for me? All this? You can spare it? Well, in a truly just community (and that's what we want to secure, don't we, Duff?), this job would be given to the lowest and the last . . . the least useful, the least productive citizen. An admirable principle. I'm all for it. We have only to consider who, in this household, fills the bill. Who pulls least weight? Who can best be spared from more important tasks?'

He looked round upon his family and waited for suggestions.

'Miss Ellis,' said Robin.

'Oh, do you think so? I'm sure *she* doesn't. Now I'm much humbler. And at present I'm doing nothing to earn my keep. It's a matter of some concern to me, though your mother doesn't believe it. But there seems to be so little that I'm qualified to do. This job anyway ought not to be beyond me, and I'm perfectly willing . . .'

'Don't be silly, dear,' said Mrs. Siddal.

'Silly? Am I being silly? I'm so sorry. I didn't mean to be. I hoped, for once, to be useful.'

'You couldn't possibly . . .'

'Why not? Is it so difficult?'

'It would upset the guests.'

'You mean that Mesdames Paley, Gifford and Cove might not like it if I burst into their rooms and burrowed under their beds . . .'

Robin hooted with laughter, and Mrs. Siddal exclaimed:

'Dick! Really! That's quite enough about that.'

Mr. Siddal relapsed into a browbeaten silence, and Duff changed the subject by asking how long they could count upon keeping Nancibel.

'Only for the season, I'm afraid,' sighed his mother. 'Of course she's worth a much better job. But she wanted to be at home for a while after she got out of the A.T.S. And according to her mother . . . is Fred in the scullery?'

'Not yet,' said Robin, leaning back to look through the scullery door.

'According to Mrs. Thomas, there's been an unhappy love affair, and she's taken quite a time to get over it. She was engaged to some young man, had her trousseau all ready and everything, and he threw her over at the last moment. It seems he thought himself too good for her. His people were auctioneers in the Midlands, and they didn't like it and persuaded him to break it off. He can't have been much loss, but she cared for him, poor child. Such nonsense I never heard. How *any* family could think their son too good for Nancibel!'

'You would,' said Siddal, returning to the fray. 'If Gerry wanted to marry her you would be very much put out.'

Mrs. Siddal looked so much terrified that all three of them burst out laughing.

'Don't worry,' he consoled her. 'He won't. Unless, of course, you tell him to.'

'He could do worse,' said Mrs. Siddal, recovering. 'I don't know of a nicer girl anywhere.'

'Then why did you look so scared?' asked Duff.

'It wasn't the idea of Nancibel which scared her,' said his father. 'It was the suggestion that Gerry might marry anyone at all. He can't afford to marry. We want his money, all of it, in order to send you to Oxford, my dear boy. Gerry mustn't look at a girl for the next seven years: not until you've been called to the Bar and got a few big briefs. That's why your mother won't do anything to cure his spots. She's always worrying about those little bits of nurses at John's on the catch for a young doctor. She hopes those spots may put them off.'

This came so very near to the truth that nobody could think of anything to say.

6. The Meditations of
Sir Henry Gifford

A policeman to see Lady Gifford. That's enough about that. If I think about that any more I shall drive into a tree. I can do nothing about it. I can only wait. No use asking her. *I mustn't be upset, Harry. My heart specialist made me promise not to get upset.* And she goes very quietly out of the room. If we want to get to Pendizack tonight we must go right on. We've no time to make a detour of fifty miles because she's heard of a little inn where you get Cornish cream and lobsters. *A divine little place.* Divine my backside. They never are. She reads these ridiculous advertisements. That's how we lost mileage yesterday. *A policeman . . .* I will not live in Guernsey. When we come to the turning I shall run straight past it. Very sorry, Eirene, but I'm afraid I must have missed it. Too late to turn back now. If we want to get there tonight we must go right on. She's rustling the map back in the car there. Determined we shan't miss it. But she can't read a map. Too stupid. Not stupid at getting what she wants. If she really wants to go to that inn she'll be able to read the map. If she really wants anything . . . but not Guernsey. I won't live in Guernsey. She will only understand what she wants to understand. If we want to get there we must lunch in Okehampton. Filthy lunch I daresay. Can't help it. We must go right on. Must get there soon after the children do. Can't have them arriving in a . . . they got off all right,

35

anyway. *A policeman . . .* I rang up. Oh Mathers! Did the children get off all right at Paddington this morning? *Oh yes, Sir Henry. And a policeman called to see Her Ladyship. No, he wouldn't say. I told him she'd left for the country and he took the address.* Darling . . . a policeman called to see you. *A policeman? Why, how odd! No, darling. I haven't the faintest idea. What does a policeman call about?* Wouldn't she have looked frightened if it was . . . no! She's never frightened. She promised never to be upset, and she never is. And besides, she doesn't believe that anything disagreeable could possibly ever be allowed to happen to her. Perhaps it's nothing . . . Seventy-five pounds. Did she really stick to her allowance? But I've worked it all out a hundred times. If she was really staying with the Varens . . . *I can't think why you should call them collaborationists, Harry! As Louise said: The brutes were there and one had to be civilized.* But they don't seem to have suffered any hardships. Sat pretty all through the war; sitting pretty now. Really the French . . . and what hardships did we suffer? Eirene and I? Didn't she and the children sit pretty in Massachusetts? And now she wants to sit pretty in Guernsey and nothing to stop her except me. This war was fought by the poor and it's being paid for now by the poor . . . but if she really stayed with the Varens and had no hotel expenses she could have done it on seventy-five pounds. She promised she would. I made her promise before she went. I explained the currency regulations. I told her that if she broke them and it was found out I'd have to resign. A judge can't . . . surely even Eirene would understand that? But she only understands what she wants to understand.

Oh Lord! Sheep! If I have to crawl along behind a flock of sheep for miles it'll put us right back. It'll give her time to . . . oh no! They're going through the gate. That's better. I can't help it if she's bought a house in Guernsey. Couldn't stop it. She can do what she likes with her own money. But I won't live there, and she can't escape income tax unless I do. What about my work? *But Harry, why should you work? If you lived in Guernsey and paid no income tax you would be a rich man.* She doesn't understand. She was in America. She wasn't in the Blitz. I was. All that suffering, all that sacrifice, all that heroism . . . I saw it. I'm not going to Guernsey. If only she wasn't so ill. I wish to God they could find out what's the matter with her. One must make allowances for her, poor thing. I believe this is the turning. She's very quiet back there. Asleep? She had a bad night. Now we're past it. Yes, she had this neuralgia. I oughtn't to get so impatient. She has a lot to contend with. But I must stick to my guns about Guernsey. And if we want to get there tonight we must go right on. Lunch in Okehampton. *A policeman* . . .

7. A Windfall

Gerry Siddal's boils were always worse when he was at home. They afflicted him as they afflicted Job; they were the stigmata of a patience tried to its utmost limits.

He was an affectionate creature. He loved his mother, and he had only very recently left off loving his father. He was fond of his brothers. But things at Pendizack had got to such a point that he would do anything, invent any job, to avoid his family at meal times. With each of them separately he could still get on very well, but he could no longer bear them as a group.

So he tinkered with the electric light machine until he could be sure that breakfast was safely over and his father back in the boot-hole. Then he went into the kitchen and ate congealed porridge while his mother cut the Paleys' sandwiches. To his astonishment she gave him all the cream which she had been saving for Lady Gifford. She was suffering from one of her spasmodic fits of remorse.

'You need more fats,' she declared. 'I'm sure that's why you get those spots. I'm determined to do something about it. Darling . . . are you going over to Porthmerryn this morning?'

'I could, if you want anything got there.'

'I've a list of things . . . I don't know if I'll have time . . . but before you go, will you help Nancibel to put up those extra beds in Mrs. Cove's room?'

'I do hope you'll be firm with Mrs. Cove,' said Gerry. 'It's quite obvious from her letter that she expects you to make a reduction because they all sleep in one room.'

'Well . . . if the children are quite small . . .'

'You'll make a reduction, anyway. You mustn't come down further.'

'She seems to be so terribly hard-up. She won't have a car ordered, and said they'd wait for the station bus.'

'So are we terribly hard-up. She doesn't have to come here.'

'I'm glad to get her. We've no other bookings.'

'I know. But there's always the chance of a windfall, now that the Porthmerryn hotels are so full. People who can't get in there . . .'

'That isn't the type I want. Not like those awful Bergmans. I want nice quiet people I know something about.'

She began to wrap up the sandwiches and Gerry took his dishes into the scullery so as to save Nancibel the trouble of collecting them. She was there, washing up, and she thanked him with her warm, sweet smile. He yearned for warmth and sweetness, but he would never have dreamt of looking for them in his mother's scullery so he continued to plod his anguished way through a world which offered him none. He put up the extra beds in the big attic, collected the list of errands in Porthmerryn, and started the steep climb up the drive.

At the second turn of the zigzag road he met a tall thin woman coming down who asked him timidly if this was the way to the hotel.

'Pendizack Manor?' he said. 'Yes. Can I help you? It's my mother's hotel.'

She hesitated and murmured:

'Oh well . . . perhaps I'd better . . . I only wanted . . . I wasn't sure . . . they said there might be rooms . . .'

'Did you want rooms?'

'Oh yes . . . that is . . . I don't suppose . . . I thought I'd walk down just on the chance . . . but of course I quite understand . . .'

'How many rooms?'

To answer this was quite beyond her. Indeed, all direct questions appeared to fill her with panic. He began to wonder if she was entirely sane, for she trembled a little as she spoke and would never look at him. She kept her eyes averted and her head ducked a trifle sideways, a symptom which he had observed in lunatics.

'I'll take you down to see my mother,' he suggested at last.

At this she rallied and gave him a quick glance. Her eyes were beautiful, but a little mad.

'Oh . . .' she said. 'Thank you.'

They started back down the drive, and Gerry adopted an indirect method of getting information.

'We have three rooms vacant at present. One double, on the ground floor, and two small single on the first floor.'

'Two single? Oh . . . thank you.'

'You want two single,' he told her. 'We can have them ready at once if you'd like.'

'Oh yes. Oh, thank you.'

'Our terms are six guineas a week each.'

'Oh, thank you.'

There was a pause. Glancing at her he discovered that she was really quite young, but so thin, so worn, that her youth was not at first apparent. And she had the walk, the voice, the fidgety movements, of an ageing spinster.

'You've left your friend,' he suggested, 'over in Porthmerryn.'

This startled her greatly. She gave him a scared glance and then said:

'I . . . I have no friends.'

'But you want two rooms.'

'Yes . . . one for me as well . . . I mean it's for my . . . my father . . . he wants a room . . . and one for me as well.'

'Oh? Your father. You want two rooms. One for yourself and one for your father.'

'Oh yes. Thank you.'

'And your father is in Porthmerryn.'

'Oh no. He . . . he's here.'

'Here?'

'In the . . . at the top of the . . . at the top of the . . . at the top. In the car.'

'Your car?'

'Oh yes. I mean . . . his car.'

'Then you'll want garage room.'

'Oh yes. Thank you.'

They had reached the house by now, and he took her to the office. She seemed to become a good deal more sensible and collected when talking to his mother. She explained that her name was Wraxton; her father was a Canon Wraxton. They had been staying at the Bellevue in Porthmerryn, but had not liked their quarters there and had left that morning. They wanted two rooms for a week. Her father was waiting in the car at the top of the hill while she enquired about accommodation.

'I'll go up and tell him we have rooms,' volunteered Gerry, who thought that the poor girl really did not look fit to climb that hill again.

But she seemed to be so much disturbed at this idea, so sure that she must go back herself, and so averse from his company, that he had to let her go alone.

'I'm astonished they weren't comfortable at the Bellevue,' said Mrs. Siddal. 'It's a very nice hotel. I wonder if they're all right.'

'Ring up and find out, before they come,' suggested Gerry.

'I could do that. I could ask Mrs. Parkins, in confidence . . . one doesn't like to turn away a windfall . . .'

She rang up the Bellevue, but got no further than the name of Wraxton when a torrent of squeaks from the telephone interrupted her. Mrs. Parkins had a great deal to say about the Wraxtons.

'Well?' asked Gerry, when the colloquy was over.

'They're all right as regards money. They paid for a week in advance, though they only stayed two nights. But she says he has the most awful temper; he quarrelled with everybody and objected to cards and dancing in the lounges. And he was very rude to the staff.'

'Oh Mother . . . don't let's have them.'

'If he's a Canon they must be respectable. We can't afford to have rooms standing empty . . .'

'But if he's that sort of man . . .'

'We don't have cards or dancing . . . or much staff for him to be rude to. And it's only for a week.'

'You said yourself that you don't want windfalls.'

'It's twelve guineas.'

Outside there was a sound of wheels crunching on gravel. They looked out of the window and saw a large car cautiously nosing its way round the last bend, between the rhododendrons. It drew up before the front door.

Miss Wraxton was driving, and the Canon sat behind. He was so exactly what they had expected that both the Siddals were startled. They had imagined a man with a large nose, bushy brows, small red eyes, purplish complexion and a controversial lower lip; and here he sat. His priestly garments only made him more formidable, for they threatened eternal punishment to anyone so rash as to disagree with him.

'Oh dear . . .' whispered Mrs. Siddal. 'Oh dear. I *can't* . . .'

She went to the front door, supported by Gerry, and determined to say that she had no rooms after all.

But the Canon, who had got out of his car and was standing in the porch, was so very civil and affable, and she felt it to be so great a concession that he did not seem to be angry with her, that in a burst of gratitude she let him the rooms at once. It was, she felt, so very, very kind of him to be in such a good temper. Nothing seemed to put him out; he was positively glad to hear that there would be a number of children in the house, he did not object to small rooms, and he offered to pay for the week in advance. The bargain was concluded in a blaze of sunshine, and the only cloud came from the awkwardness of his silly daughter who could not give an intelligible answer to Gerry's question about the luggage. She twitched and muttered and grimaced until her father's attention was drawn down upon her. He gave her a glance of deep disgust and said:

'Since my daughter chooses to behave like a half-wit I must answer you myself, Mr. Siddal. The small blue suitcase is hers. All the rest of the luggage is mine.'

And he cut short further incoherencies by adding:

'That will do, Evangeline. If you can't talk sense, don't talk at all.'

Nothing else occurred to ruffle him except a little unpleasantness in the hall, where he encountered the Paleys just setting off on their day's picnic. Mrs. Siddal introduced them, and the Canon, in his sunny mood, was ready to shake hands. But they merely bowed and marched out of the door. Mrs. Siddal had become so inured to their habitual haughtiness, to the fact that they never smiled at anyone, that she did not at first estimate the impression it must make on the Canon. He stood staring after them, unable for a moment to speak.

'What intolerable insolence,' he said, after a while. 'Who *is* Mr. Paley?'

'He's an architect. You must have heard of him. He did the Wessex University buildings.'

'Oh? That man! Yes. I've heard of him. Is he always as offensive as this?'

'He . . . they're very reserved people,' quavered Mrs. Siddal. 'I don't think they meant to be rude.'

'Oh, don't you? I do. I've never been treated like that in my life.'

He continued to discourse upon the incivility of Mr. Paley while she took him upstairs and showed him his room. And the sight of the offending couple, as they crossed the sands, kept him for some time at his window, drumming on the glass and muttering:

'I foresee that I shall have a word or two to say to Mr. Paley unless he mends his manners.'

Gerry, when she went downstairs again, was reproachful.

'What have you done?' he said. 'Why did you do it?'

'Oh, I don't know. I was so frightened of him. And he was so nice, when he asked for the rooms. I couldn't face upsetting him.'

'He wasn't so amazingly nice,' said Gerry. 'Just normally polite. What did you expect him to do? Break all the furniture?'

'I'm sure I've seen him before somewhere. I wish I could remember . . . and I seem to know his name . . .'

Gerry took the Canon's baggage up in two journeys, and then carried the little blue suitcase along to Miss Wraxton's room. The girl was sitting on her bed when he went in, quite still for once, and staring straight in front of her. She did not move or thank him when he put down her suitcase. But as he went out she smiled, not at him but at something behind him. It was a very odd smile indeed, and it sent a chill down his spine.

That girl, he thought, as he went downstairs, is in a fair way to go off her rocker.

8. Feast and Fast

The train from Paddington was crowded, and many people were obliged to stand in the corridor all the way to Penzance. But the four Gifford children had seats. They had neither waited in the queue outside the barrier nor struggled on the platform. Two heavily bribed porters got the seats for them, under the generalship of a secretary and a butler, in a third-class carriage where the competition with other heavily bribed porters is not so keen. A widow with three little girls, who tried to assert a prior claim, was pushed out into the corridor, and the Giffords were installed, supplied with luncheon tickets, sweets and magazines, and instructed to apply to the guard if they wanted anything.

Sentiment among their travelling companions had been on the side of the widow, and nothing about the Giffords was likely to change it. They had an unusually well-nourished look, and no family could have been so faultlessly dressed on its legal clothing coupons. They belonged quite clearly to the kind of people who feed in the Black Market, who wear smuggled nylons and who, in an epoch of shortages, do not scruple to secure more than their share.

But mankind is strangely tolerant, especially to children, and the sins of their parents would not have been visited upon the Giffords if they had not behaved as though they owned the train. They played a very noisy game of Animal

Grab during the first part of the journey, and Hebe insisted upon letting her cat out of its basket. It was this careless arrogance which brought retribution upon her, and upon Caroline and Luke and Michael. For when they went down the train to luncheon their seats were re-occupied by the widow and her family, and nobody interfered to stop it.

There was no aroma of the Black Market, or of clothing books purchased from needy charwomen, about the new-comers. They looked like an illustration in a 'Save Europe' pamphlet. Everything they had was meagre. The three girls were tall and pallid, like plants which have been grown in the dark. Their teeth were prominent but they wore no straightening braces; their pale blue eyes were myopic, but they wore no spectacles. Their hair was home cut, in a pudding basin bob, and their shabby cotton dresses barely covered their bony knees.

The widow herself was a spare little woman, grim and competent. She whisked her family into the compartment as soon as the last Gifford had vanished down the corridor, thrust each docile child into its appointed seat, removed all the Gifford luggage from the rack and replaced it with her own. She did this with a speed and in a silence which might have daunted protest, if any had been offered.

Having taken her own seat she produced, from a string bag, a packet of dry-looking pilchard sandwiches, dealt out three apiece, and handed round water in an enamel mug. At the end of this Spartan meal she provided the children with pieces of grey knitting. But not a single word did any of them say.

A gloom settled upon the compartment and the pendulum of public sympathy swung back a little towards the handsome, noisy Giffords. It seemed that this woman was familiar. Everyone felt that they had met her before. She had appropriated something from each of them at one time or another, with the same speed and competence. She had got in front of them in the bus queue. She had snatched the last piece of fish off the slab under their noses. And her children, spiritlessly knitting, were her weapons.

But the pendulum swung back again when the Giffords, flushed with food, came hallooing back along the corridor, pushing past the standing travellers and trampling on their feet. Such a set of young hooligans could be left to fend for themselves.

There was a stupefied pause while the Giffords discovered their baggage in the corridor, and, peering through the window, identified the intruders.

'It's the orphanage,' said Hebe. 'They've pinched our seats.'

For she had noticed these thin girls in the corridor and had decided that they must be orphans travelling in charge of a matron. And she had wondered if she would have looked as awful as they did if Lady Gifford had not adopted her to be a sister to Caroline.

'What beastly cheek,' said Luke.

Caroline suggested that they should summon the guard. But Hebe had already opened the door and sailed in to do battle.

'Excuse me,' she said to the Matron-in-Charge, 'but these are our seats.'

The Matron glanced up. She scrutinized Hebe from her tawny curls to her sleek legs, and then she went on with her knitting.

'We were sitting here,' said Hebe. 'We went to lunch, but we left our luggage. You had no right to put our luggage outside.'

She looked round the compartment for support, with the confidence of a child nurtured in privilege. She encountered glances of indifference, of amusement, but not of sympathy.

'You shouldn't have let her,' she told them angrily.

At that a woman in the corner spoke up:

'They paid for their seats, same as you 'ave.'

'We got them first,' said Hebe.

She made a sudden pounce on the smallest orphan, jerked it up and was about to take its place when the Matron intervened. Smoothly and quietly she seized Hebe's arm and thrust her back into the corridor. Her hand seemed to be made of iron; it did not feel as if it had any flesh on it at all. And just before she let go she gave Hebe a savage pinch. Then she shut the door on the Giffords, returned to her seat and took up her knitting.

'I'll go down and find the guard,' said Caroline.

'No,' said Hebe, rubbing her pinched arm. 'They got in without the guard. We must retake the fortress by our own strength. We must observe the rules of warfare.'

'But Mathers tipped him ten shillings.'

'I know. But Spartans would never call in the guard.'

'I've got a water pistol,' said Michael, trying to open his attaché case. 'I can fill it in the lavatory.'

'No. The local natives are unfriendly. We mustn't use artillery. We must lay an ambush. We'll wait. Sooner or later those orphans will have to go down the corridor. When they do, we'll pop in and take our seats again.'

'She'll push us out.'

'Not if we're prepared. She took me by surprise. If she pinches, we'll pinch back.'

They waited and it was not long before one of the orphans, after a whispered colloquy with the Matron, rose and came into the corridor. Like lightning Hebe popped in and took the vacated seat. No notice was taken of her, and nothing was said until the absentee returned and stood timidly in the doorway. Then the woman leaned forward and addressed Hebe.

'Will you kindly move from my daughter's seat?'

Daughter? thought Hebe. Then they aren't orphans after all. 'No,' she said. 'I shan't move. It's mine, for I had it first. If you try to put me out again I shall have you committed for assault. My father is a judge and I know all about the law. You've given me a bruise already that I could show in court.'

She pulled up her sleeve and showed the mark of the pinch.

After a short pause her antagonist sat back and said:

'I'm afraid, Blanche, that you'll have to stand for a while, as this child does not know how to behave. Try to sit on a suitcase in the corridor. I want you to rest that poor back all you can.'

'Yes, Mother,' said Blanche.

The poor back was an unexpected thrust, and erased the impression made by Hebe's bruise.

'Been ill, has she?' asked the woman in the corner.

'Yes,' said the Enemy. 'Only just up from a bad illness.'

A murmur of sympathy went round the compartment. Hebe, blushing but defiant, asked if they all had poor backs. Opinion hardened against her.

'Pity about some children,' said the woman in the corner. 'Think they own the earth because their father is a judge. Working people's children would be ashamed to behave like that.'

Blanche in the corridor sat down upon a suitcase and returned the stares of Caroline, Luke and Michael. They, too, were impressed by the poor back. Caroline offered her a sweet, which she refused with obvious reluctance.

'Go on,' said Luke. 'We've got lots more. They're *marrons glacés*. Off the ration.'

Still she shook her head.

'Don't you like *marrons glacés*?' asked Caroline.

'I never had any,' whispered Blanche.

'Well . . . do try one.'

'N-no, thank you.'

'Are you going for a holiday?' Michael wanted to know.

'Yeth,' said Blanche, who lisped a little.

'Where?'

'Pendizack Manor Hotel.'

'Oh!' said the three Giffords.

Luke and Michael looked through the window to signal the news to Hebe. She gave them a warning scowl. One of Blanche's sisters was just about to go down the corridor, and she wanted an ally to seize the second seat. But none of them felt inclined to join her. It was more fun in the corridor. They smiled and shook their heads. Hebe glared reproachfully. But she would not come out, though they beckoned to her.

'That's where we shall be staying,' said Caroline to Blanche.

'Where is your father?' asked Michael.

'He'th dead,' said Blanche mournfully.

'Oh. I'm sorry.'

What with her dead father and her poor back they were all beginning to feel very sorry for her. Caroline again pressed her to take a sweet. But she explained that she had none to give them back.

'Oh, that doesn't matter,' said Caroline. 'We have lots. We get parcels from America.'

Blanche timidly took the sweet.

'Do you get parcels from America?' asked Michael.

'Yeth.'

'What's in them?'

'I don't know. Mother keepth them.'

'We have feasts with ours,' said Luke.

Blanche's eyes widened. She stared at him in a kind of ecstasy.

At this moment her sister returned up the corridor and was offered a sweet too, which she accepted with the same reluctance, explaining that she had none to give back. They seemed to think that all gifts must have some kind of exchange value. The newcomer told them that her name was Beatrix and that the third sister was called Maud. Their surname, they said, was Cove.

'Why don't you go back into the carriage and rest your back?' said Caroline to Blanche. 'Beatrix can stay here with us.'

'I like it here,' said Blanche, fervently.

To her sister she murmured:

'They have feasts.'

'O-o-oh!' breathed Beatrix.

Both sisters fell into a reverie, sucking sweets and staring at these wonderful Giffords.

The word *feast* had a magic significance for the little Coves. They had never been at a feast, but they had read about such doings. They had a book called *The Madcap of St. Monica's* in which dormitory feasts were held at midnight. The word conveyed to them they knew not what of hospitality and convivial enjoyment. And their favourite game was to plan feasts which they would give if they were rich. A difficulty in collecting guests (for they knew very few people) had been overcome by Beatrix, who suggested that a notice might be put up on their house door saying: A GREAT FEAST IS TO BE HELD HERE. ALL ARE INVITED. And then everybody would come.

Their ignorance of the world was fantastic, for their mother could never afford to let them do anything or have anything that they wanted. But day dreams cost nothing and in day dreams they lived, nourishing their starved imaginations upon any food that they could find. These Giffords, these madcap children who had stepped straight out of a fairy tale, were a banquet.

'Do you have a pony?' asked Blanche at last.

Yes. The Giffords had a pony apiece. But these had been lent to their cousins when their country house was given up. Michael and Luke were only too pleased to describe the glories of this house and, though Caroline felt that they were boasting, she could not stop a recital which gave such obvious pleasure. Maud, in her turn, came out, was given sweets and included in the audience. The Giffords talked and the Coves listened, without rancour and without envy, feeling themselves enriched by such an adventure. They could have knelt and worshipped the Giffords for doing and having so much.

'And we have a Secret Society,' said Luke. 'Hebe started it. It's called the Noble Covenant of Spartans. When we all get to Pendizack I daresay she'll let you join.'

Poor Hebe, sitting alone in the carriage, too proud to leave her hard-won seat, a target for adult criticism, was tantalized by all this fraternization going on in the corridor. She felt that everybody was extremely disloyal. And she knew the bitterness experienced by all leaders. She had rushed in, she had been brave, she had got herself pinched, she had gained her point—only to find that her supporters had fled.

She fished a small notebook and pencil out of her handbag. The notebook contained the rules of the Noble Covenant of Spartans. She had just decided to add a new one, although it could not become a law until the others had voted on it. After sucking her pencil for a while she wrote:

Rule 13.——When a Spartan has done a daring thing for the benefit of all Spartans, even if he is not Leader that week, everyone else must back him up.

9. The Importance of Being Somebody

Mrs. Thomas was washing up the supper dishes. Nancibel came downstairs wearing a white dress with a red belt, red sandals and a red snood. She was still saving up for a red bag.

'You going out?' said her mother, turning round.

'Yes. I'm going for a walk with Alice. But I'll help you with those first. I'm in no hurry.'

'Don't splash your dress. It looks nice. But I wish you'd wear your nylons.'

'Oh Mum! Nobody does, not in the summer. I'm saving them for dances. Give me a cloth. I'll wipe.'

'Your legs is all bruises.'

'They show through nylons. It's those coke scoops banging against my shins.'

'I meant to tell you that old Sour Puss, that Miss Ellis, came in today for the honey. Stuck here talking till I thought she'd taken root. I don't know how you stand her, really I don't.'

Nancibel laughed.

'She's been having kittens all day because Mrs. Siddal says she's got to empty slops.'

'Having kittens? Whatever d'you mean?'

'Oh, you know . . . slang! What we used to say in the war. It's R.A.F. slang really, means getting upset.'

'Sounds common to me. I can't understand half what you girls say these days. But this Miss Ellis? She strikes me as being a very nosey sort of person.'

'Nosey as they come,' agreed Nancibel. 'There's nothing she doesn't know about the guests at Pendizack, believe me. She says that clergyman's daughter that came this morning—you know, the one I told you about, supper . . . she says this girl sits in her room all the time grinding up a bit of broken glass with a nail file, and she's got the powdered glass in a pill box; and Ellis makes out she means to murder somebody. You know . . . feed it to them.'

'She would! She wanted to know every last thing about you. Wasn't I worried about you? And how thankful she is she's got no daughter because the girls don't seem to care what they do these days. And we know what men are, she says. Only want one thing from us poor women. I felt like saying rubbish! There's only one thing us poor women want from the men. But what's she know about it, anyway? I bet there was never a queue outside *her* door.'

'Oh, she knows more than you'd think,' said Nancibel, hanging up the dish cloth. 'She tells me the story of her life, sometimes, while she watches me do the work. It's a different story every time, only for one thing. That everybody has given her a raw deal. That's the same every time.'

'You don't mean to say she ever . . .'

'She did! Or she says she did. And I was quite sorry for her the first time she told me because it seems the fellow ran off. But then it came out that he was her sister's boy to start with, and she pinched him. And really, Mum, I don't want to be spiteful, but I hate to think what her sister must be like if she's less attractive than Miss Ellis. Well . . . you've seen Miss Ellis!'

'I have. And she put me in mind of nothing so much as a toad. But that's nothing,' declared Mrs. Thomas. 'Any woman can get any man she wants, for once anyway, if she's willing to lower herself enough.'

'That's quite right,' sighed Nancibel.

Something a little regretful about her sigh prompted her mother to add sharply:

'I said for once, not for keeps. And it never comes to good.'

'That's right. I know. Well, this fellow did a vanishing act. But the sister was sore about it and all the family took her part, which is why Miss Ellis quarrelled with all her relations, and why she has to work when her family is wealthy. That's what she says.'

Nancibel crossed to the mirror by the door to take a last glance at herself before she went out.

'I shan't be late,' she said. 'We're just going along the parade for a bit to listen to the band.'

Mrs. Thomas came with her to the door and watched her go down the lane.

If only she could meet Somebody, thought the mother. Some nice fellow that would appreciate her and look after her. Not too young. Somebody superior. So sweet and so pretty, my sweet Nancibel. And clever with it. Nobody's good enough, and she's well rid of that soppy Brian if she only knew it. But there's nobody good enough round here.

For Mrs. Thomas came from the Home Counties, and despised the rustic population of Porthmerryn.

At the first little terrace at the top of the hill there was a cottage with a notice on the door:

LEDDRA. CHIMNEY SWEEP.

Here Nancibel stopped to pick up her old school friend, Alice Leddra. They went down the steep hill, through the narrow streets, to the Marine Parade, where a band was playing and half the population of Porthmerryn was strolling up and down. Alice was full of a new boy whom she had picked up at the Drill Hall dance on Wednesday. He had said that he was staying at the Marine Parade Hotel, and she hoped that she might meet him again.

Nancibel was sceptical.

'Stopping at the Marine Parade? Then whatever was he doing at the Drill Hall? They've dances every night at the M.P., and a much better band.'

'Oh, he doesn't like the M.P. dances. He says the people there make him sick. Nothing but business men and their bong zammies.'

'Bong how much?'

'Bong zammies. You know . . . French for tarts. He's ever so good looking, Nance. And can he dance! But you see he doesn't feel at home anywhere because of his childhood.'

'What was the matter with his childhood?'

'Well, really, it's quite a romance. You see he was born in a slum . . . You know . . . in Limehouse. An awful place. And all his family was on the dole. But he got out of it and got himself educated and made a lot of artistic friends, and now he's a writer.'

'Good gracious! When did he tell you all this? At the Drill Hall?'

'Yes. You see he said he felt he could talk to me. He felt I was sort of different.'

'Alice, I know you never left home because you were in the net factory. But even in Porthmerryn there were the G.I.s. What's kept you so green?'

'He's not what you think,' said Alice a little crossly. 'He's not the type boy you'd have met when you were in the A.T.S.'

'I never met any type boy that didn't want to talk about himself, and they all told me I was different. But I will say I never met one that made enough money writing to stop at the M.P. Let's hope he sends some of it back to his poor family in Limehouse.'

They had moved to the sea wall and were leaning on the parapet, listening to selections from *Il Trovatore* played by the band. Dusk was falling and the lights of the harbour were beginning to shine in the water. The sea was very calm. An occasional wave fell with an indolent flop on the shingle. Across the bay Pencarrick Lighthouse sent a long beam through the air, sweeping from the horizon to the mysterious, dim mass of houses on the hill.

'There he is!' cried Alice suddenly.

She pointed out an astonishingly beautiful young man who was wandering moodily all by himself on the shingle.

Nancibel's heart missed a beat. And then it nearly stopped altogether from sheer surprise. For she had believed that such moments were over and done with for ever and ever. She had thought that her heart was broken. Nor did she want to have it mended; she had decided to get along without it.

'Isn't he lovely?' breathed Alice.

'A slum?' said Nancibel. 'What a tale! He never came out of no slum. It takes orange juice and Grade A milk to grow that sort.'

And a moment later, when he looked up, recognized Alice and flashed a dazzling smile, she added:

'Why, look at his teeth! I know slummies when I see them.'

'You know everything, don't you, Nancibel Thomas?'

'They're tough all right, some of them. But they're short, and they don't have teeth like a film star.'

He was crossing the shingle and climbing the flight of stone steps up to the parade. Alice poked a curl back under her snood.

'And what's his name?' asked Nancibel. 'You didn't say.'

'Bruce.'

He was standing before them. Alice said:

'This is my friend, Miss Thomas.'

And Nancibel was included in that brilliant smile for a couple of seconds before it vanished. The discovery that she was Somebody, not just another girl, wiped it clean off his face. He stared, hesitated, and suggested that they should all go and eat ices at the Harbour Café.

'We want to listen to the band,' Alice said.

'You can't do that,' protested Bruce. 'It's terrible. You girls can't want to listen to terrible music like this.'

'O.K.,' said Alice. 'We'll go to the harbour.'

For it had occurred to her that they would meet many more of her personal friends down that way, and she wanted to show off her new escort.

The three of them set off: and the scandalous account which he gave them of the goings on at the Marine Parade made it a very pleasant walk.

'Five thousand clothing coupons,' he assured them. 'All stolen, of course. And the thing is done quite openly. The head waiter hawks them in the dining room.'

Alice exclaimed and wanted to hear more. Nancibel said nothing, though she smiled at them both in a genial way. It's all waiters' talk, she was thinking. He pretends to have the gen on the visitors, but no visitor would know so much as that. He's some kind of servant . . .

'You don't say much,' he protested at last.

'P'raps that's a good thing,' said Nancibel.

'She's one of the quiet ones,' said Alice.

'She doesn't look it.'

But he had money. His clothes were expensive-looking, and the wallet which he produced in the Harbour Café was full of notes.

Her heart was beating quite steadily now. It had only been in that first moment, when she saw him alone on the beach, that it betrayed her. For an instant he had seemed to be some touching counterpart of herself: alone, young and unhappy. And she still felt that she could have liked him if so much had not been wrong.

His accent was wrong: a refined superstructure upon

Cockney foundations. Half the idioms which he used had evidently been picked up very recently from one person. They decorated his discourse like ornaments on a Christmas tree. And he was showing off all the time—about the Marine Parade, about his intellectual friends, about his lowly birth. Showing off to her, as she was very well aware, though the thick-headed Alice did not seem to have tumbled to it. And very awkward it was going to be, when they all went home; because he would want to escort her, and Alice would think she had poached.

But Alice had her own problem and was not anxious to let him accompany her, where he might read the notice on the gate. She had been showing off herself, to a certain extent. So, when they left the Café, she suggested that he might see Nancibel up the hill.

'I've got to meet another girl friend. So I'll say bye-bye.'

'O.K.,' exclaimed Bruce, betrayed, by alacrity, into a discarded idiom. 'I mean, I couldn't like anything more. Thank you for a delicious evening.'

'Thank *you*,' said Alice. 'Bye-bye, Nancibel.'

'Bye-bye, Alice.'

For the length of the first street the young pair walked in silence. Nancibel was a little surprised at herself for letting him come with her since she had found so much in him to dislike. But all through the evening, while he kept talking and glancing at her in hopes that she would say something and she had sat silent, she had been aware of the inevitable climax, the explanation which was bound to follow. They might as well get it over now.

62

When they got among the little narrow streets and started climbing the hill, he broke out:

'What kind of girl are you, Nancibel? Why don't you talk?'

'Because I don't like *your* way of talking,' said Nancibel.

'Ah? I thought you didn't. What's the matter with it?'

'Well . . . for one thing . . . I don't like what you said about your home.'

'Don't you? I suppose I should have concealed my slum origin.'

'Why do you keep calling it a slum?' cried Nancibel, exasperated. 'I think it's very hard on your mother.'

'What?'

'She must have been a good mother. Anyway she gave you plenty to eat, by the looks of you. Why should you tell everybody her house was a slum in that scornful sort of way? It mayn't have been much of a place, but I'm sure she worked hard to have it as nice as she could.'

There was such a long pause after this that Nancibel thought he was too much offended to say another word. They reached the top of the hill and left the houses behind them. A winding lane took them across the cliffs among little fields fenced by high stone walls. The town and its lights lay below, and they could see the great curve of the twilit ocean.

'I wasn't born in a slum,' said Bruce at last.

'What?'

'We lived in a nice Council House on a building estate. Five rooms and a bathroom and quite a big garden. Dad was very proud of the garden. He was never on the dole. He worked for the Metropolitan Water Board, and he got eight pounds a week. We had a three-piece suite in the sitting room, and my mother always had her washing out on the line on Mondays before any other women in the road.'

'My goodness gracious! You weren't born in Limehouse at all?'

'No. All lies. I tell them because Limehouse is easier to live down. People think more of you if you've risen from the gutter. But a home like mine is impossible to get away from.'

'Why should you want to? I think it sounds very nice,' said Nancibel.

'Well . . . I want to be Somebody. I . . . I don't want to be mass produced; I want to be original.'

Nancibel nodded. She understood all that very well— the need to be Somebody.

'You're not so disgusted you don't want to talk to me any more?'

'No,' she said. 'I did a little bit the same thing once myself. When I went into the A.T.S. I said my name was Rita. I hated my name: it's so sort of countrified and old-fashioned. I felt I could be a quite different person if only I was called Rita.'

He was so much reassured by her manner that he hardly listened.

'It's true about my writing,' he hastened to say. 'I've written a novel and it's to be published.'

'You mean printed?'

'Yes. And when I've got the money I shall do nothing

but write. Er . . . at present I'm a secretary . . . a chauffeur secretary.'

'What's it about? Your book?'

'I'll tell you about it, if I may,' said Bruce happily. 'It's about this kid, see? Well . . . he's a kid at the beginning of the book.'

The Christmas tree idiom was stripped off, and the native Cockney emerged as he grew excited.

'Born in a slum . . .'

'Oh help!' cried Nancibel. 'You've got slums on the brain.'

'Several distinguished writers happen to have seen the book,' said Bruce a little stiffly. 'And they think very well of it as a matter of fact.'

'Oh, I'm sure. Excuse me. Go on.'

'Some people may find it too outspoken, but if they don't like it they must lump it. I'm not writing to spare their feelings. These things should be exposed.'

'Do you begin with him being born?' asked Nancibel, craftily.

Bruce relented and continued:

'Yes. He's a bastard, you see.'

This, to Nancibel, was a reflection on the kid's character, not on his lineage, and she asked:

'Why? What did he do?'

'He didn't do anything. But he had no father. His mother was on the streets. The opening chapter, where he's born, is pretty strong. So he grows up in these terrible surroundings and then the war comes and he's evacuated to the country.'

'And a good thing too!'

'No, it wasn't. He gets sent to a terrible farm where he's treated worse than ever. It's one of these lonely farms where things go on that nobody dares write about. But I'm going to make people sit up. Well . . . then he grows up a bit more and he meets this woman . . . she's a good deal older than he is, a wealthy, aristocratic woman, and very beautiful of course, and she takes him up, just for a whim, and he becomes her lover.'

'Where does he meet her?' asked Nancibel.

'He's the Boots in a hotel where she's staying. But she takes him with her to her house in Mayfair. Of course she's terribly depraved. And when he finds out what she really is he strangles her and gets hung.'

'Is that all?'

'Yes. I wanted to call it *Waste*. But that title's been taken. So I'm calling it *Hangman's Boy*.'

There was a pause, and Nancibel felt she must say something.

'Well,' she ventured, 'I expect you'll feel better now you've got it all written out.'

'It doesn't appeal to you at all, as a story?'

'N-no. Not much. I'm afraid I don't like miserable books.'

'What kind of books do you like?'

'I like books about nice people. And a story where it all comes out right in the end.'

'But Nancibel, that's not true to life.'

'I daresay not. Why should it be?'

'You're an escapist.'

'Pardon?'

'You don't want to face facts.'

'Not in story books, I don't. I face plenty between Monday and Saturday without reading about them.'

Bruce sighed.

'I don't think a book ought to be sad,' said Nancibel, 'unless it's a great classical book, like *Wuthering Heights*.'

'Oh! You've read *Wuthering Heights*. Did you like it?'

'Yes, but I didn't think it was the right part for Merle Oberon. Running about with bare feet, well she was hobbling most of the time. You could see she wasn't used to it.'

'Oh . . . you mean the film.'

'Yes. The picture. That was a classic. Like *Pride and Prejudice*. Those Bronty sisters were classical writers.'

'Seeing the picture isn't the same as reading the book.'

'Oh, I don't know. It's the same story, isn't it? But what I mean is if you're a classical writer it's all right; you can get people so interested they don't mind its being sad.'

'And I'm not a classical writer?' suggested Bruce.

'You can't be till you're dead,' said Nancibel.

'The Brontës happened to be alive when they wrote their books. They didn't wait till they were dead.'

'Oh. I see what you mean. Well . . . it'll just depend on if you can get people interested, won't it?'

'And it doesn't interest you?'

'Not the way you tell it. Look . . . this is my home. Goodnight, Bruce.'

'Goodnight, Nancibel.'

She ran up a path and opened a cottage door. For a

moment he saw her framed in an oblong of light and got a glimpse of a family within, sitting round a table with tea cups. Faces turned to greet her. Then the door shut.

He turned and strolled back to the town. Nancibel was a stupid, almost an illiterate girl. Nancibel was unique; the most delightful girl he had ever met. *Hangman's Boy* was tripe. He would burn it. He was a great classical writer, and he might rank with 'the Bronty sisters' if only he could find something to write about. Soon, very soon, he would find something. The world was all before him. He must see her again.

He was cast down and uplifted; humble yet full of a tonic exhilaration. He knew that he had done nothing so far, but he had never been more sure that he was Somebody. He walked on air until the lane brought him within sight of the town again. Down on the Marine Parade the band was still playing.

His spirits fell to zero. He remembered who he was and what he was.

SUNDAY

1. Extract from the Diary of Mr. Paley

August 17th, 1947.

I had the Dream again last night. I came out of it sick and very cold. I could not sleep again. I do not wish to describe it, but if I have it again I will do so, here. *I am not sure that it is a dream.*

I am sitting at my usual post by the window. Christina means to go to Early Communion. She broke our contract of silence last night, and asked me if I would be so good as to wake her at seven o'clock. I undertook to do so.

I do not care for the church here. The parson is an Anglo-Catholic and calls himself, I believe, 'Father Bott'. He is in constant trouble with his Bishop; he reserves the Sacrament, hears confession and will not read what is written in the Prayer Book, but edits and alters it in a most irresponsible way. He arrogates to himself a priestly prestige and authority which would be perfectly proper in the Roman Communion, but to which the Church of England gives him, in my opinion, no claim.

Nevertheless I shall think it my duty to accompany Christina. I shall not, of course, communicate. I do not consider myself fit to take the Sacrament. When I explained this to Mallon, the Rector of Stoke, he said that nobody is fit. I completely failed to make him understand my position. He would have given me the Sacrament with no scruples whatsoever. He said that God has forgiven me. I told him that I do not forgive myself.

My wife, I told him, asserts that she has forgiven me. But I do not think she ought to do so. A stricter sense of justice, a finer appreciation of the moral values involved, would have impelled her to judge otherwise. He asked me if this criticism applied also to the Almighty. I said that I cannot suppose the Creator to be inferior to His creature. Why should I suppose He forgives me if I do not forgive myself?

I know what is in Christina's mind. Today is the child's birthday. Does she think I do not remember? She complains, or used to complain, that she cannot bear to be alone in her grief. But does she really suppose that she is alone? Is there one memory which tortures her and does not also torture me? As we kneel, side by side, in church, we shall both be recalling the same scenes. They will be clearer for me than for her, because I have a more accurate memory.

I could describe the wallpaper of the room where she lay: it had a pattern of blue ribbon on a white ground: blue ribbon crossed lattice-wise on bunches of cornflowers. We were in lodgings in Leeds. It was such a small room we scarcely knew where to put the cradle. That day was the happiest in our lives. But even then she angered me by wishing for some trifle, a pink coverlet, I think, which she had seen in some shop window. It was beyond our means at that time. She spoke thoughtlessly, not meaning to wound me. But she should not have reminded me of my poverty. I would have bought her the pink coverlet if I could. I would have given her the moon if I could. By complaining she made me feel that she regretted the luxury of the home she forsook when she married me. But she was weak and ill, so I said nothing.

Will she remember all this in church today? I shall.

2. It Takes Two to Make a Bed

Miss Ellis heard footsteps coming along the passage and hastily put Mr. Paley's diary back where she had found it. She did not want, in any case, to read much more of it. Diaries worth reading were seldom, in her experience, left lying about and Mr. Paley's was no exception to this general rule.

Nancibel came in. Mrs. Siddal had ultimately capitulated to Miss Ellis's argument that it takes two to make a bed, and had agreed that Nancibel should help with this part of the upstairs work before starting on the washing-up. But she was adamant about the slops.

'You wouldn't think,' said Miss Ellis, 'that these two had had a child, would you?'

'I don't know why not!' said Nancibel, tugging at the heavy double mattress.

'Well, they did. But it died.'

'How do you know?'

'Oh . . . I know a good bit about them.'

Nancibel left off wrestling with the mattress and stood at the side of the bed looking at Miss Ellis. It was the same in all the rooms. She did the work while the housekeeper talked. But she had had enough of it.

'It was quite a tragedy,' continued Miss Ellis. 'Her people were wealthy and he was quite poor, and they didn't want her to marry him. So she made a runaway match. But he couldn't get over it that they didn't think him good enough. Couldn't forgive the scornful things they'd said. He made her cut herself off completely; wouldn't let her write or anything.

'Well, they had an awful time. Poor as rats. And she wasn't used to that, of course. Go on, can't you? What are you waiting for?'

'I'm ready when you are, Miss Ellis.'

Miss Ellis laid reluctant hold on her side of the mattress and gave it a mild tug, complaining:

'She's no right to have these heavy things. If I get ruptured I shall sue her for compensation. Let's leave it, shall we? It's Sunday. Well . . . they had this little girl and she got ill. T.B. And they hadn't the cash for a sanatorium, and he wouldn't let her write to her people. And she said if the child died she'd never forgive him. And the child did die and she never has.'

'In her shoes,' said Nancibel, picking up a sheet, 'I'd have written all the same. Yes, I would. And got the money and carted the kid off to a sanatorium, when his back was turned, and refused to tell him where it was. Oh, I'd have been deedy, in her shoes.'

'She isn't the sort that sticks up for themselves. Not that he doesn't blame himself. He does. He knows it's his fault that child isn't alive today. And he's got plenty of money now too. He began to get on after that, and got an Art Gallery or something to build.'

'Poor things,' said Nancibel. 'No wonder they look so sad.'

Voices in the garden below drew Miss Ellis to the window. Nancibel, determined to make no more beds alone, stood still with the sheet in her hand.

'Do for goodness' sake come and look,' exclaimed Miss Ellis. 'What on earth will those children be up to next?'

Nancibel joined her in time to see the little Coves undergoing the first of seven tests imposed by the rules of the Noble Covenant of Spartans. They were walking blindfold along a stone parapet at the end of the terrace, where the rocks fell steeply away to the beach. The Giffords ran along the path beside them, shouting exhortations:

'Go on! Go on! You're nearly halfway! We'll tell you when you're there. Don't stop. You're disqualified if you stop.'

In single file they staggered and wavered, their arms stretched out, their bare feet clinging to the rough stone. But they never stopped until they reached the end of the parapet and Hebe pulled them down, one after another, to safety.

'It's that Hebe! She put them up to it,' cried Miss Ellis. 'If ever a child needed her bottom smacking, she's one. But come along; come along, Nancibel! Mrs Siddal doesn't pay you to stand gaping out of the window. No wonder the beds take such a long time!'

3. Good People Come and Pray

Pendizack Church Town stands in the bare upland fields on the top of the cliff. It consists of seven cottages, a post-office, and a public house, crouching in a fuzz of trees beneath an enormous church—the Church of St. Sody, who came long ago out of Ireland, in a stone boat, with ten thousand other saints.

For the best part of the year the services are poorly attended, for most of the cottagers go to Chapel and the better-off parishioners dislike the Anglo-Catholicism of Father Bott. But in the summer season the beauty of the cliff walk, the fame of the choir, and rumours of fantastic ritual bring a trickle of visitors from Porthmerryn. Mass at St. Sody's is attended by people from the Marine Parade Hotel who do not generally go to church at all.

Bruce, however, did not climb that steep hill for love of Plain Song, or for the sake of coastal scenery, or to see a man who was said to bring a donkey into the chancel on Palm Sunday. He went because he was told to do so. His mistress had a fancy to see the place and had ordered him to escort her. So he was waiting, rather sulkily, in the hotel lounge, conscious of critical glances from the other residents.

Presently she appeared at the top of the stairs. The cruel light of the morning sun, blazing down upon her from the staircase window, so emphasized her age, her bulk and her dowdiness that he felt considerably reassured. None but the nastiest mind, he thought, could suppose him to be more than a secretary-chauffeur to so ripe an employer.

'Don't you have to wear a hat?' he asked, as they went out of the hotel.

'My God!' said Mrs. Lechene. 'I hope not! D'you think they'll throw me out of church? I haven't got a hat.'

She couldn't get a hat if she tried, thought Bruce. No hat ever made would go on that head. I ought to be thankful her hair is up and not down.

For Anna Lechene was very proud of her hair which was true gold, very thick, quite straight, and hung to her knees. She missed no occasion for letting it so hang. But when obliged to put it up she braided it in thick cables and wound it round her head. The effect was striking though top-heavy.

'At least I'm not wearing slacks,' she said. 'I've put on a dress, haven't I?'

Yes, but what a dress! All right for a kid of thirteen. Nobody over twenty ought to wear these dirndls. Oh, all right! I know all the grandmas do in Macedonia or wherever it is you got it from. But this isn't Macedonia.

He stared venomously at Anna's broad back as he followed her along Fore Street. He was a changeable young man. Not long ago he had admired Anna's golden head and peasant embroideries. But now he was glad when he had got her out of the crowded street on to a flight of steps which led up the hill.

'Where is this church we're going to?' he asked.

'It's on the cliffs, halfway to Pendizack. You must have seen the tower.'

'Oh? Oh yes . . . I have.'

His spirits rose. For that tower was quite near Nancibel's cottage. He had noticed it last night, standing up against the evening sky. He might see her again. She might be in church.

Mrs. Lechene, panting slightly for the steps were steep, was talking about Father Bott. She had heard that he was a remarkable man.

'A celibate,' she added meditatively.

Lucky So-and-so, thought Bruce, and made vague noises of assent while Anna speculated upon the causes and effects of celibacy in Father Bott.

At the top of the hill they passed an ugly little building called Bethesda whence the first hymn of the morning already resounded:

> *Oh that will be*
> *Glory for me!*
> *Glory for me!*
> *Glory for me!*

And he reflected that he ought to be grateful to Anna for not taking him there, unaware that Nancibel was inside it, with all her family. She got time off from Pendizack on Sunday mornings to go to Chapel. But he still hoped to find her among the flock at St. Sody's, and pressed on towards that tall square tower.

What will she think, he pondered, as the great pure curve of the sea came once more into view. What will she think about me and Anna? Nothing. Why should she think anything? If I meet her again, and she asks me, I shall tell her: That's Mrs. Lechene. My boss. She's a writer. A very well-known writer. No. You wouldn't care for her books. She's been very kind to me. She got a publisher to take my novel. She's very kind to young writers. Yes, I know she looks peculiar. So do most lady writers. If you'd met as many of them as I have, Nancibel, you wouldn't think this one looks so queer. Yes, *Mrs.* Lechene. No . . . well . . . I believe she's divorced him. I type her novels and drive her car. Secretary-chauffeur.

'Pretty up here,' he said craftily. 'I think I'll take a stroll round after church and look at the cliffs.'

Anna turned and said sharply:

'I *don't* think so. After church you'll get back to the hotel and type out those three chapters of the B.B. I can't think why you didn't get them done last night.'

The B.B. was *The Bleeding Branch*, a novel based on the life of Emily Brontë upon which Anna was engaged.

'I'm out of carbons,' said Bruce.

'My God! You're always out of carbons. I never knew such a boy. Get some more.'

'I can't on Sunday. Shops shut.'

A full peal of bells rang out from the tower, over the fields and over the flat blue floor of the sea. In the distance a long procession of people was coming by a narrow path through a cornfield. Strung out, in single file, it seemed endless. Gerry Siddal led it and after him came Duff, Robin, Canon Wraxton, Evangeline Wraxton, Mrs. Cove,

Maud, Beatrix, Blanche, Michael, Luke, Hebe, Sir Henry Gifford, Caroline, a considerable gap, Mr. Paley, Mrs. Paley.

'Could it be a Butlin's Camp?' speculated Bruce.

'No,' said Anna. 'There's a little hotel down there in the cove. I hear it's most attractive and comfortable. I was thinking of going there when we leave the Marine Parade. But I'm not sure I like the look of the inmates, if these are they.'

'Pretty little girl,' said Bruce.

She thought he meant Evangeline Wraxton, and exclaimed:

'What? That skeleton in tweeds?'

'No,' he said. 'The little kid in green. Talking to her father.'

'Oh,' said Anna, slightly mollified. 'You mean Miss Bobby Sox?'

She scrutinized Hebe who was skipping along and turning to laugh at Sir Henry, and added:

'Making eyes at her father, I should say.'

'Good People come and pray,' cried the bells.

The Pendizack party climbed a stile into the churchyard. Each in turn was outlined against the sky for a moment, at the top of the stone wall, and then disappeared from view. When Anna and Bruce reached the building they were all inside. The Siddal boys had gone round to the vestry, for Duff and Robin sang in the choir and Gerry was serving at the Mass. The rest found seats in the great empty nave. As is customary among churchgoers they sat rather to the back, leaving the foremost rows of pews vacant. An old man dealt out prayer books to summer visitors who had not got any.

The chimes ceased. There was a great tramping as the eight bell-ringers came down from the tower; in that small parish everyone did double duty, and six of them were needed in the choir.

Anna and Bruce took seats in a pew just behind the Wraxtons. A faint smell of decaying wood mingled with a reek of incense. The great church was rapidly falling to pieces, and poor Father Bott could not even collect enough money to repair the pews.

'A bit niffy,' commented Anna, loudly.

Every child in the congregation turned its head to see who had said this.

'Who on earth is that supposed to be?' she continued, pointing to a banner of St. Sody, used in processions.

'I wouldn't know,' muttered Bruce.

'It's rather good,' she declared. 'A bit epicene . . . I expect one of the artists in Porthmerryn designed it for them.'

At this point she became aware of the inflamed countenance of Canon Wraxton, who had turned round and was glaring at her.

'Will you kindly make less noise?' he barked.

Anna gaped at him. She disliked parsons and was habitually rude to them. But it was not often that they were rude to her.

'Well . . .' she said at last, 'you quite startled me.'

'I mean it,' thundered the Canon. 'If you can't behave decently I shall have you turned out.'

'You're making a terrible noise yourself,' retorted Anna.

'Hush!' whispered Bruce, scandalized in spite of himself.

'Why should I hush? This isn't his church. Or if it is, I can well understand why it's so empty.'

The Canon was now surveying Bruce.

'If you've any decency,' he said, 'you'll go, and induce your mother to go with you.'

Nothing could have silenced Anna more effectively. She could, for some seconds, think of no retort. And the appearance of Gerry in the chancel, carrying a taper, created a diversion. Candle after candle was lit. The Canon, looking like a bull in a field, turned to survey this fresh enormity. Anna giggled but did not venture to speak again. The congregation had left off staring before the cross preceding the choir appeared, and Father Bott, surrounded by servers and acolytes, emerged from the vestry.

4. Typescript Notes for a Sermon preached by the Rev. S. Bott.

Sunday, August 17, 1947

——"deLIVER JS FORM EVIL"

q1 Fear. insecurty. Atom bomb.£Heplessness

2 Nothingnew abt Eveil. Causes old as Adam.
Effects merely more spe ctacular. Sin.

e 3 Sin isolates the soul z(@) frim God. (b) from
fellowmen. Mutual generosity, willingness to give
and accet, essential condition of Salvation.

4 Teaching of Church. 7 deadly froms of spiritual
isolation. Vices which destroy gratutude and
generosity.

prIDE accepts nothing.

E

ENVY guves nothing.

sloTH accidie especially insidious to the
intellectual.

   xxxxxxxxxx substitues speculation for
   action.

xxxxx24@5£ WRATH lust for power.

S LECHERY Sexual expliotation. "Hardensall
within and petrifies the feelins"

X GLN. GLOT/. GLUTTONY Their God is in ther
belly.

7 COVETOUSNESS Financial exploitation.
  These sins the most deadly weapons of the Enemy.
  We should fear them more than any waepons of
  man.
  Grace is our only protection.
  £Hence importance of last petition in the Lord's
  Prayer.

5. The Canon Testifies

Yes, thought Sir Henry Gifford, as he got to his feet for the Offertory hymn. But where do I come in? I'm a sinner, I suppose. We all are. But which of this little list is mine, and what do I do about it? Number 4. I know this. A nice easy tune. I really don't think I'm proud. I know I'm not envious.

New every morning is the love
Our wakening and uprising prove;

I'm not slothful. I work very hard. And I've plenty of practice in keeping my temper.

Through sleep and darkness safely brought,
Restored to life and power, and thought.

Nor am I particularly covetous, lecherous or gluttonous.

New mercies each returning day . . .

If I were covetous I'd go to the Channel Isles and dodge income tax. But I'm standing out about that. And if I do, if she wears me down, it won't be because of pride or envy or any of the list. It'll be sheer exhaustion. Here comes the plate. Good Lord! Michael's going to drop it! No . . . all safe. Hebe needn't have pushed him like that. She's unbearably bossy. Do I hand it back or pass it to the Coves?

A pound seems a lot, but I have no change. Must get some tomorrow. My sin is weakness. And I believe that goes for most of us here. We don't do evil, but we consent . . . we let ourselves be pushed about.

> The trivial round, the common task,
> Will furnish all we need to ask,
> Room to deny ourselves, a road . . .

It was years before I noticed the comma there. Thought it was *Room to deny ourselves a road* . . . a sort of contortionist's feat. Yes, sheer spinelessness. Very few entirely evil people in the world really; but we let them run us. Eirene . . . do I really think she's evil?

> And help us, this and every day,
> To live more nearly as we pray. Amen.

Yes, I do. Sometimes I do.

The Giffords had expected the service to end after the Offertory. But it went on. Everybody knelt down, and Father Bott prayed for the Church Militant. Then, turning to the congregation, he muttered an Invocation unfamiliar to many of them. All the little Giffords began to rustle the pages of their prayer books. So did Beatrix, Blanche and Maud, who were eager to do everything the Giffords did, until their mother took her face out of her black gloved hands and scowled at them. Whereat the three Coves became immobile, their foreheads pressed against the ledge of the pew in front, and the tender infantile backs of their necks exposed to the world.

'It's the Communion Service,' whispered Sir Henry.

Hebe looked shocked and protested:

'We oughtn't to be here. We aren't confirmed.'

'I know. But you must just stay and kneel quietly.'

He felt more than a little embarrassed himself, since it was years since he had heard this Service. He was not much of a churchgoer, but he considered that children should be brought up with a religious background and if no one else was available to take them he accompanied them himself. He, too, had merely expected Matins, at which a decorous demeanour would be all that he need offer. He tried to remember the details of the coming ritual, and then he tried to compose his wandering thoughts to some mood of sincere gravity, as he did at funerals. For it would be indecent, he felt, to dwell upon trivial subjects at a moment which was, to his neighbours, of the highest importance.

But at funerals he could always think about death, which dignifies life and abolishes triviality. While here no suitable topic occurred to him. His reflections during the hymn had been too detached, too flippant. He wanted to *feel*, if he could. He stared at the top of the pew in front of him and tried to clear his mind of the petty traffic which daily swarmed through it, as a street might be cleared for a procession. No procession arrived.

I must think about people I love, he decided, and then could not think of any. The children . . . He glanced at the little creatures on either side of him. Caroline had her head buried in her arms. Luke was following the Service in his Prayer Book. Michael was twisting a button off his jacket.

Hebe knelt erect, staring avidly at Father Bott. They meant very little to him. They were Eirene's affair. Only one of them was his, and she was the least attractive. For five years, during the war, they had been in America. And even at home he seldom saw them. Were they all right? Were they happy? Were they growing up as they ought?

These uneasy speculations were not quite suitable. He must postpone them to a less sacred moment. He would do better to think of his own childhood, of people whom he had loved and who were gone now, of remembered places and happy moments. He looked across the years and sought a way back.

Evangeline's sick feelings were beginning to subside. Nothing dreadful was going to happen. That little disturbance before the Service started had been nothing: those people really deserved it. The thing she most dreaded had not befallen, in spite of the incense and the genuflections and the candles. God had prevented it.

Her father took, it was true, no part in the Service. He sat with folded arms, looking on with an expression of grim amusement, as though he had been told in advance of some well-merited retribution which was going to overtake Father Bott. And that was bad enough, for people stared when he did not stand up for the Creed. But she was used to staring people, and if he would only keep quiet she would believe that God did really listen to prayer. She would show her gratitude. She would give up her sin, although nobody could really call it a sin because it did not hurt anyone.

Perhaps it was a waste of time to grind up glass with a nail file, but surely nothing worse? Because she would never use it, she would never do anything wicked with it. And that little pill box full of powdered glass was such a relief to possess. They said it could never be detected in a person's food. If she were a wicked woman it could free her from this martyrdom. It was a very powerful little treasure, that box. She kissed it sometimes. But if God kept the Canon quiet, then God was really there and she would placate Him by throwing the box into the sea. For He would know all about that box.

When I am confirmed, thought Caroline, I shall be religious. The Bishop will put his hand on my head and the Holy Ghost will go all through me like an electric shock, and I shall be religious. But Hebe will be wishing she was the Bishop.

'It is very meet, right, and our bounden du-uty . . .' intoned Father Bott.

The Lord's Supper! thought Beatrix Cove. I am at the Lord's Supper with Hebe and all the people. Her heart swelled with ecstasy. She lifted her head and looked at the dazzling candlelight, half expecting to see a long table with all the disciples round it and the Divine Presence in the midst. But she only saw Father Bott and Gerry Siddal. It had been so nice when young Mr. Siddal waved the incense at all the people and bowed, and all the people bowed back politely. These gracious courtesies were the very essence of a Feast. She looked round to see if Blanche was as happy as she was. But Blanche, white and rigid, had tears on her cheeks, not of bliss but of pain. Kneeling had brought on the agonizing ache in her back, and she was entirely concentrated upon enduring it. But she caught her sister's eye and gave a faint smile.

'Evermore praising Thee and sa-a-aying . . .'

Duff and Robin fixed their eyes upon their parts in the Sanctus and drew deep breaths.

'Holy! Holy! Holy!' sang the choir of St. Sody's.

I became dumb, prayed Christina Paley, and opened not my mouth. For it was Thy doing . . . Hear my prayer Oh Lord, and let Thine ear consider my calling. Hold not Thy peace at my tears. For I am a stranger with Thee and a sojourner, as all my fathers were. Oh spare me a little that I may recover my strength . . . before I go hence and be no more seen.

Father Bott was speaking in a whisper and when he paused three soft, clear notes from a bell filled up the silence, just before the incredible horror fell upon them. A kind of bellow rose up from the nave. A great voice was howling:

'I denounce this mummery!'

The shock was so great that everyone recoiled, as though struck. Still upon their knees they turned to see the Canon coming out of his pew.

'This is a Protestant Church . . .' he began.

He was interrupted by an excruciating scream from his

daughter. Evangeline's nerves had snapped. She was not only shrieking, she was banging her Prayer Book on the ledge of the pew.

'No!' she yelled. 'No . . . no . . . no! I can't bear it. I can't . . . ahoo! Ahoo! Ahoo!'

This attack from the rear seemed to confuse the Canon. He had meant to march up to the altar and attack Father Bott. But he now turned round and ordered the girl to be quiet. She only screamed louder. He seized her arm and tried to drag her up from her knees whereat she laughed insanely and hit him with her Prayer Book.

'Help me, somebody,' he said, almost humbly.

The paralyzed congregation bestirred itself. Bruce and Sir Henry went to help him and between them they carried the laughing, screaming girl out of church. The verger shut the door upon the noise, but there was still a sound of sobbing for several of the children had begun to cry. It was some minutes before these gasps of woe subsided and Father Bott was able to finish the Consecration.

6. Dost Thou Well to Be Angry?

'But you've no idea,' said Gerry, 'how utterly disgusting it was. What an outrage . . . One reads about that sort of thing in the papers and it sounds shocking enough then. But to be there . . . they *must* go. We can't keep them. I told Father Bott . . . I said we'll turn them out immediately.'

'We can't make them go,' sighed Mrs. Siddal. 'I spoke to Canon Wraxton. I explained how embarrassing it is for us. But he simply said he'd paid for a week and should stay for a week.'

'What about the girl? She was worse than he was . . . the ghastly noise she made.'

'I don't know where she is. She wasn't at lunch, and she's not in her room.'

'Would Father . . . ?'

'Gerry, you know he wouldn't.'

'Very well, then. I must. I'll go and speak to the old brute now. I'll tell him to clear out. Give me the money they paid, and I'll return it.'

Gerry marched upstairs, determined to have a fight with somebody. He was not naturally pugnacious, but he felt that the morning's outrage demanded action of some kind. The Wraxtons must be demolished. He did not distinguish much between them, nor was he quite clear about the facts. They had created a most blasphemous disturbance, shouting and laughing, until they were turned out. From his place, up by the altar, he had seen very little. He had tried to rush down and hit Canon Wraxton, but Father Bott had restrained him. He did not realize that Evangeline's laughter proceeded from hysteria, not from mockery, and he believed that the interruption had been deliberately planned by both the offenders.

The Canon was lying on his bed having forty winks. But when Gerry came in he sat up and swung his legs to the floor.

'Well?' he demanded. 'And what can I do for *you*?'

Gerry put twelve guineas on the bedside table.

'You must go, please,' he said. 'At once. Here is the money you paid.'

'Are you,' asked the Canon, 'the proprietor of this hotel?'

'No. I'm speaking for my mother.'

'Why doesn't she speak for herself?'

'Because you won't listen to her.'

'I listened to her. It's she who didn't listen to me, or she'd have told you what I said.'

And the Canon flung himself back on his bed.

'She told me you wouldn't go.'

'And I told her that if she wants me out she'll have to send for the police to put me out. Let nobody make any mistake about that.'

'All right!' said Gerry.

'I also told her that, if I'm put out, I shall sue her for breach of contract. She agreed to take me in and to render certain services for which I paid.'

'No hotel is expected to keep people who cause a public scandal,' said Gerry.

'No scandal, as you call it, occurred on your mother's premises. But if she wants a fight she can have it. I don't mind a fight. If Mister Bott wants a fight he can have one too. He'll have it whether he wants it or not. I'm writing to his Bishop. I shall see that the facts are known.'

'So shall we,' declared Gerry

'And if I'm turned out of this hotel for doing my duty as a Minister of the Church of England, I shall see that that's known too. I shall write to every newspaper in the country.'

'You must do as you please about that,' said Gerry. 'As long as you go.'

'I'll go if I'm flung out by force. Not otherwise.'

Gerry went off to find his mother, but could not persuade her to send for the police. She said that she would rather put up with the Canon for a week, nor would she agree that loyalty to their Parish Church demanded extreme measures. When he persisted, she even said that it was partly Father Bott's fault, for being so High Church. 'He's not High Church,' explained Gerry. 'He's Anglo-Catholic.'

'Which is worse,' said Mrs. Siddal. 'I'm sure I sympathize with people who don't like it. What did we have the Reformation for?'

'I'm an Anglo-Catholic myself,' said Gerry.

'I know. But I'm not. I'm a Protestant and I don't like all these goings on in my Parish Church. It's six of one and half a dozen of the other, and I won't have the police brought into it.'

95

In despair Gerry took an unusual step. He decided to consult his father, hoping to get some kind of parental encouragement in pursuing the vendetta. For Dick Siddal had often annoyed his wife by professing considerable admiration for Father Bott. It was not to be hoped that he would do anything energetic himself, but he might say something which could be construed as authority to ring up the police.

He, too, was taking a little nap when Gerry arrived, in a boot-hole strewn with Sunday newspapers. He had just finished the crossword in the *Observer* and was collecting his resources before attempting that in the *Sunday Express*. But he opened one eye and looked at his son good-humouredly.

'Well?' he asked. 'How's Martin Luther?'

'He won't go.'

'Why should he go?'

'We can't have people of that sort here.'

'Then why did you take them?'

'We didn't know what they were like.'

'But you must have known. Do you never read the newspapers? He's always doing this sort of thing; his name's a household word. Why . . . only last month he started a free fight somewhere down in Dorset. He's been suspended, or whatever it is they do to parsons who won't behave, but he goes on doing it.'

Gerry gaped at his father and presently asked:

'Did you know all about him, then, yesterday?'

'Naturally,' said Siddal, 'when I heard we'd got a Canon Wraxton I supposed it must be *the* Canon Wraxton.'

'But why didn't you tell us?'

'I wasn't asked.'

'But, Father, you must have known . . . that we wouldn't . . . if we'd had the slightest idea . . .'

'Not a bit of it. I didn't like to interfere. Advice from me is seldom appreciated. I don't pretend for a minute to understand how or why your mother chooses her inmates.'

'Then you knew . . . when we all went to church . . . you knew this would probably happen?'

'I thought it likely. And when I saw you all coming back I knew I was right. I've never laughed so much since your mother opened this hotel. I wish you could have seen yourselves.'

No help was coming from this quarter, so Gerry climbed the hill in search of Father Bott, hoping to be told that it was his duty, as a good Churchman, to use physical violence on the Canon. But the Vicar, whom he met in the churchyard, was discouraging.

'Oh leave it, leave it,' said Father Bott. 'He can't do more harm than he's done already. If he tries to get into my church again, *I'll* deal with him.'

'But for us to harbour such people!' cried Gerry. 'I won't have it.'

'My dear boy, that's for your parents to decide. It's their hotel, not yours.'

'But I'm so angry,' protested Gerry. 'I can't bear to let them get away with it. It was so . . . so vile . . . so obscene . . . it made me sick.'

'It made me sick too,' agreed Father Bott. 'But there you are.'

And he sighed. He was feeling very old and discouraged that afternoon. As a younger man he had enjoyed tussles with Protestants, but he had come to regard his own pugnacity with suspicion as a vice rather than a virtue, and he knew that a fresh scandal at St. Sody's would do his church no good. He looked up at the sky and down at the grass and then he looked at Gerry's irate face.

'Dost thou well to be angry?' he asked, smiling suddenly.

'Yes,' said Gerry. 'I really think there are occasions when anger is justified.'

'There may be,' agreed Father Bott. 'But I've never been able to make up my mind which they are.'

'He insulted God,' said Gerry.

'Oh no, no, no! Oh no. He couldn't do that, could he?'

'He tried to.'

The Rector sighed again, looked at his watch, and said impatiently:

'We don't have to make all this fuss about God.'

Then, trying not to laugh at Gerry's shocked expression, he added:

'God can look after Himself. And He's told us not to make a fuss. *Be still and know that I am God.* Now excuse me . . . I have to take a children's service.'

'Then you mean . . . do nothing?'

'Not now. Anything you do just now will probably be wrong. I must admit I'm extremely angry myself. But I doubt if I do well.'

He turned away and strode across the grass, his old cassock flapping about his thin legs.

Baffled, the good Churchman returned to Pendizack. He was not going to be allowed to fight anybody though his fury was unabated. The Wraxtons were not entirely responsible for his frame of mind; the long trial to his patience, his father's spite, his mother's partiality, and his own frustrated existence were getting to be more than he could bear. So that it was a relief to feel that his wrath was righteous.

On the doorstep, unfortunately, he encountered Evangeline. She had been hiding for hours in some lair on the cliffs, unable to endure her disgrace, and was now hoping to creep back to her room unnoticed. Gerry stood aside, grimly, to let her pass. But at the sight of him the silly creature dodged and swerved and waited for him to precede her. For a few seconds they danced about on the doorstep.

'Please go in,' said Gerry, with freezing politeness.

She gulped and began to mutter. He caught the words:

'So very sorry . . . apologize . . .'

'Don't speak of it,' he said. 'If you were really sorry you wouldn't insist on staying here when we've asked you to go.'

He watched her cross the lobby and crawl up the stairs. It should have been a satisfaction to see her so brought down. But it was not, and he felt more miserable than ever. He had never before in his life spoken to anyone so unkindly.

7. Old Acquaintance

The whole house was suffering from moral shock. The hideous scene in church weighed upon the spirits of all who had been there, and there was a tendency among the adults to sit alone in their rooms.

The children vanished, rising up like a flock of starlings immediately after luncheon and betaking themselves to some hidden place. They retired into their own world, as children will when their elders misbehave. Bewildered, unable to judge, they turned their backs upon the ugly memory.

At supper time they reappeared and, as one child, refused the dessert of loganberries and ice-cream with which Mrs. Siddal had hoped to cheer them. The Giffords waved it away grimly. The Coves, who were dining, after all, downstairs since Mrs. Siddal had insisted upon charging full rates for them, declined it with a devotional enthusiasm. Fred brought a whole dish back into the kitchen, and Siddal consoled his wife by suggesting that Duff could eat it.

'It will melt unless he comes in soon,' she said. 'He and Robin went over to Porthmerryn. I'll put it in the larder.'

'Yes . . . do,' said Siddal. 'Gerry and I don't want any, either.'

Blushing a little she exclaimed:

'Oh . . . I meant after you'd had some.'

And began to help them, while Gerry tactfully diverted his father's attention by passing him a piece of paper.

'I picked this up in the hall,' he said. 'It looks like a cypher.'

On a page torn from an exercise book a message was printed in capitals:

BBM TQBSUBOT XJMM SFGVTF
EFTFSU UPOJHIU CZ PSEFS

Siddal, who liked puzzles, took it and put on his spectacles. When Duff and Robin came in he was so intent that he hardly looked up.

It was at once apparent to Mrs. Siddal that Duff had been up to something. He was flushed, excited and unusually silent. She was so much disturbed by his looks that she scarcely noticed Robin's boisterous swagger. But Gerry did, and thanked heaven that his father's attention should be engaged elsewhere. He hoped that the cypher would take a long time to solve. Later on, in the privacy of the stable loft, he would doubtless hear all about it.

Robin, however, had no wish to conceal his condition.

'We've been drinking!' he announced. 'We've been drinking old fashioneds in the bar of the M.P.'

'*Robin!*' cried Mrs. Siddal.

'Who paid?' asked Gerry.

Duff looked up and asked why they should not have paid for themselves.

'Because you've got no cash, either of you.'

'A strange lady paid for us,' said Robin. 'So what?'

He teased his mother for a little while, and then he explained:

'We met her on the Parade. She couldn't make her cigarette lighter work. So Duff gave her a light. And we talked a bit and she asked us into the M.P. for a drink. She's staying there.'

'Oh well . . .' said Mrs. Siddal unhappily, 'I suppose girls do that sort of thing nowadays.'

'She wasn't a girl,' said Robin. 'She was older than you I should think, wouldn't you, Duff?'

'No,' said Duff. 'A bit younger than Mother.'

'It's quite easy,' said Siddal. 'It reads: "All Spartans will refuse desert tonight by order." I think desert means dessert.'

He sat back and smiled triumphantly at his family.

'So that explains it,' said Mrs. Siddal. 'Some game of the children's.'

'She's a lady authoress,' said Robin. 'I never met one before. She says she knows Father.'

'What's that?' asked Siddal.

'A lady we met in Porthmerryn. Her name is Mrs. Lechene.'

Siddal gave a joyous squeak.

'Good old Anna! Fat old Anna! You don't mean to say she's still above ground?'

'Of course she is,' said Mrs. Siddal, who did not look pleased at the news. 'She's not old . . . only my age, as Duff says. And she's always writing books. You see them in the library.'

'I don't,' said Siddal, 'because I never go to the library. And all my old friends have dropped me. They might be dead for anything I know. But is Anna in Porthmerryn then?'

'She's staying at the M.P.,' said Robin.

'Oh? At the M.P.? Who with?'

Duff and Robin looked at one another.

'She didn't say,' said Duff. 'We thought she was alone there.'

'Not very likely,' said Siddal.

Duff gave his father a quick, sharp glance and said:

'She's writing a book about Emily Brontë.'

'Oh my Lord! She would! She *would*! The only wonder is that she hasn't done it before. Poor Emily! What a shame! Why can't they leave that unfortunate girl alone?'

'Is she a good writer?' asked Robin.

'She writes well. Everybody does nowadays. She writes this biographical fiction, or fictional biography, whichever you like to call it. She takes some juicy scandal from the life of a famous person, and writes a novel round it. Any facts that don't suit her go out. Any details she wants to invent come in. She's saved the trouble of creating plot and characters, and she doesn't have to be accurate because it's only a novel, you know.'

'You don't sound,' said Duff, 'as if you liked her very much.'

'Don't I? I'm talking about her books. I hate 'em. But that doesn't mean I've any personal animus against the poor girl. You think one shouldn't criticize the work of a friend? Disloyal? Isn't that rather suburban of you?'

'I only read one of Anna's books,' put in Mrs. Siddal hastily. '*The Lost Pleiad*. I couldn't bear it.'

'Oh yes . . . the one about Augusta Leigh. "Like the Lost Pleiad, seen no more below!" That made her name. A huge success. You'd have thought that stale old bone had had all the meat pecked off it. But no! It seems that in Cardiff and Wimbledon and Tunbridge Wells and Palm Beach and Milwaukee they still *didn't know*. So they all lapped up *The Lost Pleiad*. There was an unforgettable chapter about Byron and Augusta being snowed up . . . I believe they actually were snowed up. Anna didn't invent that. But oh, bless you, she knew everything they did and said and thought from the first snowflake to the thaw. What's she like to look at now? I haven't seen her for . . . it must be at least ten years.'

Duff and Robin looked vague.

'She's fat and rather pale,' said Robin at last. 'And she doesn't look as if she makes up, except her hair which is peroxide.'

'Oh no, it's not. It's true, Teutonic gold, and she's very proud of it. Lets it down on the slightest provocation. She hasn't changed apparently. She was a fat, pale girl twenty or thirty years ago, and whatever she wore looked as if she'd slept in it. She used to let her hair down at the dinner table and lean confidentially towards her neighbour till it trailed in his soup. If he blenched she said he had repressions.'

Robin guffawed and said that Anna had told them a limerick about repressions.

'Limericks!' cried Mr. Siddal. 'How crude she must be getting! But I suppose she mistook you for schoolboys.'

'Who is Mr. Lechene?' asked Duff, ignoring this dig.

'Haven't an idea. She'd finished with him long before I knew her. She used to say she was married at fifteen, and I daresay she was. But I expect there's a current Mister of sorts. There always is. You didn't see him? Perhaps he was taking a little time off.'

'She wants to come here,' said Robin. 'She asked if we had room.'

'Oh no . . . we haven't,' exclaimed Mrs. Siddal.

'Why Mother? We've got the garden room still unlet.'

'I couldn't possibly have Anna here. The Wraxtons are bad enough.'

'Well, she might upset people,' agreed Robin. 'She says such . . . she doesn't seem to mind what she says, does she, Duff?'

Duff made a non-committal noise. He did not know whether he wanted Anna to come or not. She had upset him. He had been quite ashamed of the ideas which she managed to put into his head; and then she had stared at him, smiling, as though perfectly aware of what she was doing.

'Duff,' said Mr. Siddal, 'had better be careful. She is older than the rocks on which she sits and she eats a young man every morning for breakfast. Her ash can is full of skulls and bones.'

'Not now, surely!' said Robin.

'Oh yes. Every word she says, every look she gives, is a most powerful aphrodisiac; after a sufficient dose of it they don't know that she's fat and old and an ogress. They think she's going to teach them some wonderful secret.'

'And does she?' asked Duff, with another of those keen looks.

'That,' confessed Siddal, 'I don't know. I'm not in a position to tell you. And if she has suggested anything to the contrary it's just a little lapse of memory on her part. She finds it difficult, I daresay, to believe that any old acquaintance escaped her ash can. But I, whatever my faults, have never looked at any other woman since I married your mother. I'm what they call a happily married man.'

8. Starting Hares

The hotel got its first glimpse of Lady Gifford at Sunday supper, for she had kept her bed ever since her arrival the evening before. Some curiosity was felt when at last she appeared. Her pallor, her emaciation, and her faint voice bore witness to her ill-health, and nobody felt able to protest when she asked for a fire in the lounge, though the night was very warm. Gerry took up logs and she sat close to the blaze, warming her delicate hands and looking round her with a faint, triumphant smile, as if expecting to be congratulated upon her gallantry in getting downstairs at all.

But nobody said the right things except Dick Siddal, whose custom it was to clean up and join his guests in the lounge in the evenings. And even he found the heat of the fire intolerable. He was obliged to go and sit at the other end of the room, beyond the range of her plaintive whispers. The room had several occupants, and all of them were suffocated. Sir Henry was writing letters at a desk in the bay window. The Paleys sat side by side on a sofa reading the Sunday papers. Upon another sofa sat Miss Ellis who was not supposed to use the lounge, but had done so as a protest against emptying slops. Nobody sat near the fire except Mrs. Cove who had left her knitting in the most comfortable chair before supper and chose to stay there in spite of its subsequent disadvantages.

Between these two ladies, crouching in their private inferno, a desultory conversation sprang up. Lady Gifford whispered questions to which Mrs. Cove gave terse replies in a singularly disagreeable voice. It was cold and sharp and it had a subtly common overtone, not innate, but acquired in the course of many battles with the grasping mob. She said that she was taking this holiday because she had recently sold her 'haouse' in the south of London. A mere house, as Siddal said afterwards to his family, would not, probably, have fetched half so much as a 'haouse' could. Houses are sold through estate agents who take commission. 'Haouses' are disposed of by their owners, who always get the best of the bargain.

This one, explained Mrs. Cove, had doubled in value since she bought it, for the flying bombs had created a scarcity in that district.

'Oh terrible!' agreed Lady Gifford. 'So much worse than the Blitz! More of a nervous strain, weren't they?'

'Were you in London through the Blitz, Lady Gifford?'

This was from Miss Ellis, chirping up from her sofa, reminding them that she not only had the right to sit but might talk if she liked.

'No,' breathed Lady Gifford. 'No . . . actually I was there very little. But my husband was all through the worst of it. And naturally I was very anxious. For I felt I had to be with the children. Where,' she asked Mrs. Cove, 'did you send yours?'

'Nowhere,' snapped Mrs. Cove. 'We stayed in London. We had an Anderson shelter. I wasn't nervous.'

'Weren't they?' asked Lady Gifford.

'No.'

Mrs. Cove pursed her lips as if to say that her children knew better than to be nervous.

'How lucky. Mine would have been shattered. They're all so highly strung. I'm thankful to say not one of them ever heard a bomb.'

'In America weren't you, Lady Gifford?' suggested Miss Ellis.

Lady Gifford ignored her and continued to address Mrs. Cove.

'We had a kind invitation from a friend in Massachusetts. They had a wonderful time. But I didn't, naturally, want them to become Americanized. So I felt I must go with them.'

'Why?' asked Mrs. Cove, looking up from her knitting. 'Don't you like Americans?'

'Oh yes, I love them. So wonderfully kind and hospitable.'

'Then why didn't you want your children to be Americanized? When you accepted all this hospitality?'

'Oh well . . .' Lady Gifford made a helpless little gesture. 'One does want them to be British, doesn't one?'

'Yes,' agreed Mrs. Cove. 'Which is why I kept mine in Britain. I had invitations for my children. But I don't like cadging.'

Lady Gifford flushed slightly.

'Naturally one disliked that part of it,' she said. 'I always thought it quite ridiculous that one wasn't allowed to pay for them. But personally I think we owed it to our children to put them in safety, whatever the sacrifice. Don't you?'

She turned her haggard gaze upon the Paleys as if asking for their support. Mrs. Paley looked flustered and made no reply. Mr. Paley stared at his boots and said:

'I agree with Mrs. Cove. If I had had children I should have kept them in England. I should not have allowed them to live on charity.'

'Plenty of places in the British Isles were fairly safe,' said Sir Henry, turning round. 'Many people here never heard a bomb.'

'Oh, but one couldn't know that,' said Lady Gifford. 'And I don't think innocent little children ought to suffer. I always say that. The innocent oughtn't to suffer.'

'They invariably do,' said Mr. Siddal. 'They always have.'

'But why? Why?'

Dick Siddal leant back upon his sofa and stared at three flies circling round the chandelier. He was getting bored with Lady Gifford.

'Perhaps,' he suggested, 'the sufferings of the innocent are useful. That idea first occurred to me when one of my children said how unkind it was of Lot to leave Sodom, since, as long as he stayed there, the city was safe. The presence of one righteous man preserved it. I shouldn't wonder if the entire human race isn't tolerated simply for its innocent minority.'

'What a sweet idea,' said Lady Gifford.

He lowered his eyes for a moment and gave her a look. Then he raised them again and pursued the hare he had started. She was an intolerably stupid woman and could not understand a word he said. But he enjoyed the sound of his own voice, and nobody was likely to interrupt him.

'I daresay,' he said, 'that mankind is protected and sustained by undeserved suffering; by all those millions of helpless people who pay for the evil we do and who shield us simply by being there, as Lot was in the doomed city. If any community of people were to be purely evil, were to have no element of innocence among them at all, the earth would probably open and swallow them up. Such a community would split the moral atom.'

He sat up straight and addressed his remarks to Paley, who might be able to follow them.

'It's the innocent who integrate the whole concern. Their agony is dreadful, but:

> Their shoulders hold the sky suspended.
> They stand, and earth's foundations stay.

Why didn't the earth open to swallow Delson? Even in the bunkers of the Berlin Chancellery you might find the innocent children of Dr. Goebbels. Where you have the suffering innocent, the crucified victim, there you have the redeemer who secures for us all a continual reprieve. The oppressed preserve the oppressors. If the innocent did not suffer we should all go pop.'

Lady Gifford looked a little bewildered.

'But surely,' she said, 'there were babies in Sodom, even after Lot went out.'

Siddal shook his head.

'Weren't there? Surely . . .'

'Not one.'

'Really? I never knew that. Does it say so?'

The door opened and Canon Wraxton stood upon the threshold. All conversation died down at once.

'It's insufferably hot in here,' he announced.

'I'm afraid that's on my account,' sighed Lady Gifford. 'I have to be very careful not to catch a chill.'

'To roast yourself will be the surest way to do it, Madam. If I'm to sit in here I really must ask for some of the windows to be opened.'

'Then I can't sit here,' she pointed out.

'You must judge for yourself about that,' said the Canon.

He made a tour of the windows, opening them all, before he sat down at the other desk to write a letter. Lady Gifford was obliged to go back to bed, and departed on the arm of her husband.

9. In the Deep Night

The murmur of the sea came in through the opened windows. A breath of cool air fanned Christina Paley's cheek. She looked out and saw a gull so high up in the sky that a beam from the sun, already set, caught its wings.

The heat and the darkness of the room were stifling her. She glanced at her husband. He was not reading. He was not thinking. She was sure that when he sat huddled up like this he was not thinking of anything at all; he was simply existing inside his shell. Of late he had seemed to shrink, as if the brain behind his skull was shrivelling.

She wished that somebody would say something, and peered through the stifling dusk at her companions. There were only four of them now. They were all withdrawn, all heavily silent. Mrs. Cove knitted in the firelight. Mr. Siddal stared at the chandelier. Canon Wraxton drew circles on his blotting paper. Miss Ellis seemed to be examining a hole in the carpet. She got the impression that none of them were thinking, that nothing was passing through their minds from the outer world. Each had retired, as an animal retires with a bone to the back of its cage, to chew over some single obsession. And this frightened her. She could no longer bear to be shut up in this murky den of strange beasts. She must get out, right out of the hotel, and away to the safety of the cliffs. She rose and slipped out of the room. Nobody noticed her departure.

Her panic did not subside till she was across the sands and halfway up to the headland. She mastered it only to discover that her misery had returned. Despair broke over her so irresistibly that she wondered how she could still observe the pure peace and beauty of the scene. But her senses continued to tell her that the sky, sea, cliffs and sands were lovely, that there was music in the murmur of the waves, and that the evening airs smelt of gorse blossom. To that message her mind replied: No good any more. It might have helped me once.

For she loved natural beauty, and in the earlier stages of her struggle had often found consolation in a country walk. But this was a late stage, the final stage. Now she merely felt a clearer conviction that life was over for her, the last ano-dyne gone. If this fair prospect could not tempt her to stay, then nothing could and she might go when she pleased.

She went to the end of the headland and sat on a rock looking out to sea. The water was flat and pale, paler than the sky, except at the horizon where a dark blue pencil had sketched a great curve. On her left, behind the dusky mass of the next point, an after-sunset light still burned. On her right, over Pendizack Cove, fell the shadow of advancing night. She thought that she would rest for a little while and then go back to the sand. She would wade out into that warm, flat sea, wade as far as she could and then swim. It was years since she had swum but she supposed she still could, for how far she did not know, but far enough. She would swim straight out towards that thin blue line of the horizon, on and on, until the end. A time would come when she could swim no more. And then there might be some moments of panic. The wish to live might reassert itself before she went under the choking water. But it would soon be over. And no one would be hurt by it, for she had given up all hope of helping Paul. Her life was useless and a burden.

So much suffering, she thought. So much suffering everywhere. And as long as I live I merely add to it. I am not strong. I can do nothing. I'm simply another hopeless, helpless person.

A faint wind sighed in the dead thrift beside the rock, and a longer wave than usual fell upon the beach below her. Decision had relaxed her nerves. She leant her back against the rock and closed her eyes, her mind vacant and open to any vision that might drift through it. Suddenly and vividly she saw a deep pit from which many faces peered up at her. It came and went so quickly that she could recognize none of them although she was sure that some were familiar; a girl's face and three pale children distinct among millions and seen by a lightning flash. At the same time a voice said in her ear: *Their shoulders hold the sky suspended. They stand and earth's foundations stay.*

Mr. Siddal had said that. Mr. Siddal had said some very strange things, sitting in the lounge and staring at the ceiling. She was not sure that she understood them. He had said that the innocent save the world and that their suffering is necessary. He said that the victims, the helpless, hopeless people everywhere, are the redeemers who sustain and protect mankind. She could not remember his words exactly. But she had felt very strange for a moment, while he was talking, as though she might be on the verge of some enormous discovery. Crucified, he had said. The Lord was crucified. He was innocent and He redeemed mankind. But Mr. Siddal said *redeems*, as if it was all still going on. And did he mean, she asked herself, that we are all . . . all the oppressed . . . and the poor people in China . . . and the homeless . . . the poor little Jewish babies born in ships . . . no home, no country, turned away everywhere . . . Oh, I do think that is the worst of all, for a poor baby to be born with no country even . . . but did he mean that we are all one person, innocent and crucified and redeeming the world . . . always? Is that what he meant?

Another wave fell on the beach, and before its reverberation had died away she knew that, whatever Mr. Siddal had meant, she herself had arrived at a certainty. She had made her discovery and knew that she was no longer alone. The chain of her solitude had been broken, that solitude, forced upon her by Paul's cruelty, which she had been unable to endure. Her pain was not entirely her own, and it had transported her into an existence outside and beyond her own, into a mind, an endurance, from which she could never again be separated.

They endure for me and I for them, she thought, and strove to summon before her inward eye those pale faces peering from the pit. But the glimpse was gone and she could not bring it back. She could only speculate upon their familiarity and wonder if the girl she saw had not been

Evangeline Wraxton, who was shut up now, somewhere in the hotel, among those wild beasts in their dens. And who must be brought out, out of the pit, before she sank.

'At once! Immediately!' exclaimed Mrs. Paley aloud, as she sprang to her feet. 'Not a minute to be lost.'

She set off as fast as she could, down the path to the cove.

Night had almost fallen when, half an hour later, she returned with Evangeline. She had marched into the girl's room without any prepared plan and had suggested a walk on the cliff as calmly as though it had been a long-standing habit. Evangeline had looked startled, but she rose obediently and put away in a drawer some objects on her dressing table—a piece of glass, a file and a little box.

'Shall I need a coat?' she asked.

'Better bring one,' advised Mrs. Paley, 'and then we needn't come back if it gets cold. We can stay as long as we like. My coat is downstairs. I'll get it as we go out.'

They had also got two cushions from the lobby settle lest sitting about on rocks should give them rheumatism.

'Because that hotel isn't a nice place at all,' said Mrs. Paley. 'It's not nice at night.'

'No,' agreed Evangeline. 'I can't sleep there.'

'I can't either. With coats and cushions we can sleep on the cliff if we like.'

'Unless it rains.'

'It won't. And there's a sort of shelter, anyway, up on Pendizack Point.'

They found a comfortable little hollow in some heather close to the shelter and lay upon their backs, side by side, watching the stars come out and discussing the best way to make the tea ration last. Neither felt the least impulse, just then, to confide in the other. But they knew what united them. They were a little astonished at themselves and inclined to giggle, as women will, when they embark upon some daring adventure.

'I infuse,' said Mrs. Paley. 'I just cover the leaves with boiling water and leave it for five minutes before I fill up the pot.'

'You make me feel quite thirsty,' said Evangeline.

'I've got a picnic basket and a kettle and spirit lamp. If we come up here tomorrow night we'll make ourselves some.'

'That will be nice,' said Evangeline. 'I should like to come here every night till the week is over. I wish I didn't have to stay. They've asked us to go.'

'They know it's not your fault.'

'Do they? Mr. Gerry Siddal . . . Do you know him?'

'Hardly at all. I've just seen him about.'

'He's nice, I think,' said Evangeline, wistfully.

'Is he?'

'He's very considerate to his mother. But . . . I tried to speak to him . . . to apologize . . . and he wouldn't listen.'

'I'll have a word with him tomorrow,' promised Mrs. Paley. 'I daresay he didn't understand. I expect you muttered at him.'

'Yes . . . I did. I can't help it. People frighten me. Do beg him not to be angry.'

'I will.'

'If only people wouldn't be angry . . . if only they wouldn't . . .' sighed Evangeline.

Very soon afterwards she fell asleep. But Mrs. Paley lay for a long time staring at the stars, very small and pale in the summer sky. The thin girl beside her filled her with an immense tenderness and compassion, a love beyond any she had ever felt before. She thought of the child she had lost, whose birthday this was, who had been put into her waiting arms for the first time just twenty-three years ago. But it seemed to her as if the child had been sent in place of Evangeline, because at that time her heart had been smaller and could not have accommodated a creature in no sense her own. Nor could she have borne to know as much about that child as she knew about this one, to be aware of all that life with Canon Wraxton must entail, to guess at the significance of that box and nail file on the dressing table.

Presently she dozed a little, waking to find many more stars in a darker sky. The spaces between the stars looked very black and the wind whispered in the heather, and she murmured sleepily a line learnt in her forgotten childhood: *and whispers to the worlds of space . . . a sentinel . . . I hear at times a sentinel, Who moves about from place to place, And whispers to the worlds of space, In the deep night, that all is well.*

MONDAY

1. The Omniscience of Miss Ellis

Miss Ellis had much to say on Monday morning about the beds of Mrs. Paley and Miss Wraxton. But her speculations were conducted without any help from Nancibel, who had caught sight of the truants on the cliff as she came to work and decided to hold her tongue. It was not safe to say anything about anyone to Miss Ellis.

'Not touched since we made them yesterday,' declared Miss Ellis. 'Whatever does it mean? If it was only Mr. Paley I wouldn't be surprised. He often sits up all night.'

'All the less work for me,' said Nancibel.

'For us both. We'd better do Lady Guzzle.'

'We can't. She's still in her bed.'

'My patience! Where would this house be if I lay in bed all day?'

Pretty much where it's always been, thought Nancibel and followed Miss Ellis upstairs to the Coves' dormitory. This was a quick room to do as its occupants had neat habits. All the four beds were stripped and the sheets hung over the rails at the end.

'Look at that!' cried Miss Ellis in disgust. 'Shows they don't trust us, doesn't it? Shows they think we just turn back the sheets.'

'We do it at home,' said Nancibel, turning the first mattress. 'Our mum always makes us hang the sheets over a chair. She says it's a dirty habit to throw them on the floor.'

'In a cottage,' said Miss Ellis loftily, 'that might be necessary. But here it's an insult to the staff. Will you kindly look at their nightgowns? You'd think she'd be ashamed.'

'Dressing three children costs money,' said Nancibel.

'She can afford it. She's got plenty. The stories I've heard about her! I thought I knew the name. Cove! I said to myself. Where did I hear that name before? But I couldn't remember till it came out the children were called Maud and Blanche and Beatrix. Then it all came back to me. She had these three old aunts, well great-aunts really, and of course she hoped for legacies . . .'

'Would you mind,' asked Nancibel, 'sitting on a bed I've made? I want to turn this mattress.'

Miss Ellis changed her seat and resumed:

'Of course she wanted a son because of the title. And wasn't she wild when she only had daughters? And then *he* died before his uncle did, and the title and property went to another nephew. That's how I came to know about her. They've a place in Dorsetshire—the baronet, I mean. The uncle. And I lived quite near there for a while. Well, I accepted a post as housekeeper in a small nursing home for a few months. And I got quite friendly with a Mrs . . . a Mrs . . . oh, what was her name? Well, it doesn't matter. Anyway she'd been a governess or something at the Court before she married, and the tales she told us about *this* Mrs. Cove, this niece, and her mean ways . . . they all used to laugh about it. And the last straw was that all the money was left to those children. She's only got a life interest. Unless they die, of course. And they wouldn't *all* die. Not likely! If they did people would think it funny. But she expected to get a big fortune and a title and this old family mansion, and when she didn't get it she went on as if she'd been left without a penny. And all this scrimping and starving is just because she wants to make a purse for herself before those children grow up. Where are you off to?'

'I've done all these beds,' said Nancibel. 'I'm going to the little boys' room.'

Luke and Michael slept next to the Coves, and their sheets were scarcely turned back.

'What's the idea?' said Miss Ellis, when she joined Nancibel, 'giving us all the trouble of stripping the beds as well as making them. I never knew a family give so much trouble. Have you heard the latest? Lady Guzzle's got to have coffee with an egg beaten up in it, in the middle of the morning!'

'I can't think,' said Nancibel, 'how she can eat all she does and stay so thin. She's nothing but a skeleton.'

'Ah! I've my own ideas about that. I shouldn't wonder if she didn't put on a lot of weight, one time, and got it off the Hollywood way. *You* know. Like the film stars do.'

'No,' said Nancibel. 'I don't know. What?'

She regretted the question a moment later, for she saw by her companion's expression that the answer would be unsavoury. But she was not to be spared. Miss Ellis came round Luke's bed and whispered two words in her ear.

'No!' cried Nancibel, turning pale. '*No!* I don't believe it. How awful!'

'They do,' said Miss Ellis, nodding sagely. 'I worked once with a girl who'd been a dresser in one of these studios, and she told me a lot.'

'But how could they?'

'In a little pill,' sniggered Miss Ellis. 'I daresay it's not so bad in a glass of champagne.'

'But doesn't it make them terribly ill? Why . . . it might kill them.'

'Of course it might. But they can eat all they want and not worry about weight.'

'I don't believe it,' repeated Nancibel. 'Nobody could.'

'They have to. They have to keep their figures or go out on their ear.'

'But she's not a film star. She hasn't her living to earn.'

'I daresay she didn't know what she'd taken. Somebody told her about a wonderful doctor who'd work a miracle for £500 and she took his pill and asked no questions.'

Miss Ellis chuckled and added:

'I'd like to have seen her face when she found out.'

'Well,' said Nancibel, 'it makes me urge. It does. It fairly makes me urge.'

'When you've seen all I've seen of the seamy side of life,' said Miss Ellis, 'you won't be so easily upset.'

They finished Michael's bed in silence. Then Nancibel exclaimed:

'It's a pity you can't say anything about anybody but only what's disgusting.'

'Are you speaking to me, Nancibel Thomas?'

'Certainly I'm speaking to you, Miss Ellis.'

'Then you're a very impertinent girl, and I've a good mind to complain of you to Mrs. Siddal.'

'O.K., Miss Ellis.'

'This is what comes of talking to you as if you were an equal. You think you can take liberties.'

'I'd ever so much rather you didn't talk, Miss Ellis. If it was true it would still be disgusting. And I don't believe half of it. Nothing but servants' gossip, all said and done.'

'I've never been so insulted in my life.'

Nancibel turned her back and stalked off to Hebe and Caroline's bedroom, which was next down the passage. She had decided that she would make no further efforts to keep on good terms with Miss Ellis. But she did not like quarrelling with people, and made no answer when the housekeeper came to offer a piece of her mind.

'I never expected to have to work,' said Miss Ellis, standing in the doorway. 'I was not brought up to earn my own living. My father was a wealthy man. We kept five servants; not rough girls out of cottages but nice, superior, well-trained girls. And it's the bitterest of all to me, now, that I have to mix with low, common people who think they can insult me because I have had misfortunes and nobody to protect me. There's nothing a certain type of person likes better than to see their superiors brought down . . .'

Nancibel picked up Hebe's dressing gown which was lying on the floor, and took it to the wardrobe. Her gasp of surprise, when she opened the cupboard door, checked the stream of Miss Ellis's indignation.

'Well . . . I never!' she said.

'What is it?' asked Miss Ellis, hastening to look.

Inside the door a large notice was fastened with drawing pins. It was printed in capitals on a sheet of poster paper, and it read:

THE NOBLE COVENANT OF SPARTANS

OBJICT.　　To raise up a band of Spartans to rule England and eventaully to rule the world.

MOTTO.　　Everything nice is Bad.
Everything nasty is Good.

(1)　Always obey the Leader.

(2)　Never give away Spartan secrets.

(3)　Never flinch from hardship.

(4)　Never endulge yourself.

(5)　Never eat your sweet ration.

(6)　Never kiss anybody. If somebody kisses you and you cannot help it mutter the folling silent curse: CURSED BE THY FLESH AND BONES MARROW LIVER AND LIGHTS FOR THAT THOU KISSEST ME AGAINST MY WILL.

(7)　Never praise except ironicly.

(8)　If they make you utter non-Spartan ideas say 'not' under your breth.

(9)　A new Leader is ellected every week. Everyone is to have their turn.

(10)　The Leader may not order trials which leave a scar or bruise which non-Spartans might notice.

(11)　Not more than three trials in one week.

(12) No new rules unless there is a meeting.

(13) When a Spartan has done a daring thing for the benefit of all Spartans even if he is not Leader that week everyone else must back him up.

TESTS FOR NEW SPARTANS

(1) *Fear.* Do something that frightens you.

(2) *Food.* (a) Eat something that makes you sick (eg. chocolat eclare and sardine) and not be sick.
(b) Eat nothing for 24 hours.

(3) *Smell.* Smell a bad smell for 10 minutes. Eg. talk to Miss Rigby. wretching is not allowed.

(4) *Sight.* Look at the annatomy pictures.

(5) *Hearing.* A squeaky slate pencil, if you don't like it.

(6) *Cold.* Sleep one week on the floor without any blanket.

(7) *Touch.* Lie still and let yourself be tickled.

(8) *Pain.* Little finger pinched.

(9) A specially brave deed to be chosen by the Leader. Really dangerous.

When Junior Spartans have passed all nine tests they get their membership card and can be leaders. While they are passing they can attend meetings but not vote and use all the privylege of the society including the Spartan code. But they must obey all rules.

This manifesto so much astonished Miss Ellis and Nancibel that they buried the hatchet for a while.

'It seems so unnatural somehow,' complained Nancibel. 'I mean it's unnatural. Everything nice is bad! Fancy a kiddie getting an idea like that!'

'P'raps it's because of all the guzzling she sees going on,' suggested Miss Ellis. 'Supposing she knows something . . . well . . . like I said just now! A thing like that might give her an awful shock. Enough to start any amount of funny ideas.'

'But she wouldn't know. How'd she know?'

'Might have heard servants talking. You mark my words: it's something of that sort behind it.'

Steps were heard running along the passage, and Miss Ellis hastily shut the cupboard door. It was Hebe. When she saw them she paused in the doorway and said, with abrupt haughtiness:

'Oh . . . Haven't you finished?'

Turning and tossing her curls she ran off.

'Someday,' vowed Miss Ellis, 'I'll tell young Hebe Gifford just who she is and what she is. Gifford! Her name's no more Gifford than mine is. They adopted her. She's a love child, a servant's child most likely. And I have to empty her slops!'

2. The Ship in the Bottle

'Porthmerryn is such a little place,' said Mrs. Cove, as she hurried her family over the cliffs. 'And full of extra visitors. If we don't get in first with our points all the best sweets will be gone. So don't dawdle. Blanche, can't you walk faster?'

'Her back is hurting,' said Beatrix.

'Walking is good for it.'

Blanche broke into a lopsided trot, helped along by her sisters. Their errand did not interest them for it was unlikely that they would eat any of the sweets thus promptly secured. Their mother had a habit of saving such things for a rainy day which never dawned. But they knew how important it was to possess goods which other people would be likely to want, since value depends upon scarcity.

At the top of the hill, just by Bethesda, Mrs. Cove paused for a moment to give final instructions:

'We'd better split up. If we all go into the same shop they might see we were one family and make us take a mixed selection. I believe there are several shops. Blanche! You go along Marine Parade. Beatrix can do Church Street. I'll do Fore Street. Maud can do Market Street. Here is half a crown for each of you, in case you can get Turkish delight. Go for that if you can; it's very scarce. If not, get marshmallows or fudge. Don't get boiled sweets or bars; there are always plenty of those. And if there's any nonsense about not selling to visitors tell them that you will report it to the Food Office. We'll all meet outside the post office in half an hour.'

They separated and Mrs. Cove hurried down to Fore Street. But Blanche's back had delayed them, and they were not first in the shops as she had intended. There was a considerable queue in the largest confectioners. She joined it and took her place just behind Robin Siddal and Sir Henry Gifford.

'You're early,' she said sourly, when they greeted her.

'I'm after marshmallows,' said Gifford. 'My wife charged me to get her some before they all disappear. They've got some here, I see.'

'I want butterscotch,' said Robin. 'There's none on the Parade. I saw Blanche there, Mrs. Cove, and she wants to know if she and the other girls can come with me to see a ship in a bottle that I told her about. I said if I saw you I'd ask.'

'Where is it?' asked Mrs. Cove.

'In a cottage, just off the harbour. It's Nancibel's great-grandmother's, as a matter of fact. She's got a lot of interesting old things.'

Mrs. Cove pondered and then said, rather grudgingly, that the girls might go if they liked; but they must be back at Pendizack by lunch time.

'She's a very old woman,' said Robin, turning to Sir Henry, 'and almost blind and they think she ought to go to the workhouse. She's awfully upset about it. They all are.

But there's no room for her at the Thomases', and she needs to be looked after. I can't help wondering if some of her old things mightn't bring in a bit—enough to keep her more comfortably. Do you, sir, by any chance, know anything about black amber? You said you liked amber yesterday.'

'I know a little about it,' said Sir Henry cautiously. 'It's very rare.'

'I think she has a piece. Her sailor son brought it home, ages ago. He's been dead for years. He got it somewhere out in the East.'

'What is it like?' asked Sir Henry.

'A little carved figure, so big,' said Robin, holding his fingers about four inches apart. 'It looks and feels like amber to me. She has it sitting on the dresser.'

'But that would be worth at least a thousand pounds!'

'I know. I know black amber is very valuable. If it *was*, she needn't go to the workhouse.'

The queue moved up, but neither Robin nor Sir Henry noticed this. Mrs. Cove waited for a few seconds and then took the vacant place in front of them.

'I didn't tell her what I thought,' said Robin; 'I don't want to raise her hopes. But I would like to get an expert to look at it.'

'I should think it's extremely unlikely,' said Sir Henry.

'I expect so. But it would be just worth finding out, and I don't know who to ask.'

'I could look at it,' volunteered Sir Henry. 'If that would be any help.'

'Oh, sir! Would you?'

The queue moved again, and Mrs. Cove took her place at the counter.

'Marshmallows,' she said firmly.

Sir Henry and Robin looked round, surprised, wondering how she could have got in front of them. But they realized that it had been their own fault.

'And if, by any chance, you're right,' said Sir Henry, 'I could help her to sell it and see that she got a fair price.'

'I say, that's frightfully good of you. I'm going there this morning. Could you come?'

'No. I can't now. My wife expects me back. But I'll go with you some other day if you like.'

The queue moved again and it was Sir Henry's turn. But he could not get marshmallows, for Mrs. Cove had just bought the last. He bought nougat and Robin got his butterscotch.

'That was a mean trick,' said Robin, as they went out of the shop. 'She pushed in front of us. Did you see?'

'We let her. You know, if I were you I shouldn't talk about that piece of black amber, if it is black amber, quite so publicly. Not in a Porthmerryn shop. Anybody might hear. And the sooner it's put away safely, the better. Can't you drop her just a hint to look after it carefully?'

'I don't want to disappoint her, in case I'm mistaken.'

'Tell her it might be worth five pounds. It would probably fetch that, whatever it is. And get her to put it away.'

Robin agreed to do this, and they parted. He did a few errands for his mother and then went to the post office where the three little girls were waiting for him. They said that their mother had gone home and that they all wanted to see the ship in the bottle.

'Come along, then,' said Robin. 'Have some butter-scotch.'

He proffered a paper bag. But they all shook their heads, explaining, as usual, that they had none to give him back.

'None?' he exclaimed. 'But you've all been buying sweets, haven't you?'

'Our mother has them,' explained Beatrix.

'Oh, I see. Well, have some of mine, anyway.'

Eventually they each accepted a small piece, without much enthusiasm. They would so much rather have dispensed bounty than accepted it. Had they been allowed to keep their sweets they would have run round Porthmerryn offering a free treat to everybody.

Robin conducted them towards the harbour by a side street, for he was not anxious to meet any of his cronies while he had these queer girls tailing after him. At moments he was astonished at himself for embarking on such an expedition, for he did not usually take notice of any little girls between the ages of seven and seventeen, and these were singularly lacking in charm. But the smiles of Blanche had involved him. She had such a radiant expression, when pleased, that it was impossible not to go on pleasing her. She had been gazing, in the purest delight, at some cheap little mass-produced boats in bottles, in a shop on the Parade. This delight had soared to ecstasy when he told her about old Mrs. Pearce's boat. She was all radiance, all gratitude to him, merely because he had described it. Before he knew what he was saying, he had offered to show it to her, some day, and this offer so plainly carried her into the sixth heaven that he felt compelled to unlock the seventh and suggested they should go immediately.

'This boat,' he told them, 'might be a hundred and fifty years old, for it was made by Mrs. Pearce's grandfather. It's a five-masted schooner and it's in a long, thin bottle, not a fat one like the imitation ones. Here we are. Up these steps.'

The stone steps led to a green door on the upper floor, for the lower part of the house was a fish store. Robin knocked at the door, which was open, and ushered them into a room full of furniture, potted ferns and cats. Nancibel's great-grandmother, a tiny old woman, was rustling and poking about on the hearth. She turned to look at them, rubbing her bleared eyes.

'It's Robin Siddal,' he shouted. 'I've brought three young ladies to look at your ship, Mrs. Pearce. May they see it?'

Mrs. Pearce chewed upon this news for some time and asked if it was the young ladies up to Tregoylan.

'No. No. They're from London.'

'London? I don't see so well as I used. The maids from Tregoylan, they come sometimes. But I don't expect them in August month. London?'

Blanche moved forward and put her hand into the gnarled old fingers.

'I'm Blanche Cove,' she said, low but clearly. 'And these are my sisters, Maud and Beatrix. We are staying at Pendizack with Mrs. Siddal.'

'Staying to Pendizack, are ee? That's a whisht old place, Pendizack Manor. My grandson, Barny Thomas, he lives up to St. Sody Church Town. But I don't get up there now. Not since my old leg swole up so bad. Sit down, m'dears. You, Robin! Find chairs for the maids.'

The whole party sat down. Robin was struck by the good manners of the Coves who said no more about the ship though their eyes often strayed towards it, where it stood on the mantelshelf, as they made polite enquiries after Mrs. Pearce's leg. After a time he explained the real object of the visit and this time the old woman took it in.

'My ship? Oh my dear soul yes. The maids shall see it. Give it into my hand now. You know where it is? Over the slab?'

He gave it to her and she held it out for them to admire.

'This little old ship,' she told them, 'have been on that very same shelf since the time you see written in the bottle. If you look sharp and close you'll see a name wrote: Phineas Pearce. Which is the name, m'dears, of my old grandfather. And after the name you'll see figures: one, seven, nine, five—seventeen hundred and ninety-five, which is the figures for the year the ship was made . . .'

Robin had heard this recital many times, and he strolled away to the dresser to have another look at the piece of black amber. He had seen it last on the second shelf, standing next to the bottle of ink. But it was not there now.

'There wasn't no Marine Parade in them days,' Mrs. Pearce was saying, 'nor there wasn't in my young days neither. It was wholly a pull up for pilchard boats . . .'

'Mrs. Pearce,' he broke in, 'where's the little black figure? The one that stood on the dresser?'

'Inside the tureen,' said Mrs. Pearce. 'I put 'un there for safety when I were dusting.'

He looked in the tureen and found it. His heart stopped pounding.

'Why,' she went on, 'I saw the railway come. I saw the first train that come to our town and the flags and the cheers and the band so sweetly playing. It was a feast that day in our Church Town. A feast for one and all.'

A thrill ran through the Coves. Maud asked if all the people came, and who had given the feast.

'All gave it and all came,' said Mrs. Pearce. 'Every man, woman and child in the town was there, and the farmers from up along, they come too, for miles round. Some said it were five thousand, some ten. It were a great big old crowd, that I do know, being there; such a crowd as I never seen before nor after. And the station so green as a forest with boughs and garlands. And one would shout: Here she come! Here she come! I hear the whistle! And such a pushing and a shoving, oh my dear soul, like a herd of bullocks. And then another: That's no train. That were me awhistling for my dog. And everyone laugh so loud as a clap of thunder. Such a laugh I never heard before nor after. But she come at last, all hung with garlands, and the mayor in his golden chain adriving of her. And the bands they struck up and one and all we sang Old Hundred.'

'How *lovely!*' cried Maud.

They took their leave reluctantly, with wistful glances at

the little ship as it went back on to its shelf. And Robin, as he thanked her, ventured upon a word of caution to Mrs. Pearce about the amber, hinting that it might be valuable.

'It's worth more than a pound I b'lieve,' agreed the old woman.

'More like five pounds, Mrs. Pearce, so keep it safe.'

'It's safe enough in the tureen. Goodbye, m'dear. Goodbye, you maids. Any time you're down along and like to come in you'll be very welcome.'

Robin had to go round by the road with a message, so the three girls walked home alone over the cliffs. They went slowly, for Blanche was tired, and they had to drag her up the hill. Their heads were so full of feasts, trains and ships that they said very little. But when they got out of the fields, on to the turf and gorse of the cliff top, Maud began to sing in a tuneless chirp. The others took up the chant, their faint notes scattered by the salt breeze.

All people that on earth do dwell,
Sing to the Lord with cheerful voice!

When alone they were usually very happy, though their pallor, gravity and forlorn shabbiness gave them a deceptive pathos. They had so little, knew so little, had been to so few places and met so few people, their lives were so entirely bare that they had never learnt to want much. During the war their school had been evacuated to the country. But they had not gone with it, and their mother had taught them. She boasted, with some justice, that they knew more history, geography and mathematics and Scripture than they would

have learnt at any school. But there had been no other children left in that neighbourhood, so for amusement they had
learnt to rely entirely upon themselves. They never disputed
or quarrelled and they seldom disagreed. Blanche was the
most intelligent, but so much of her energy was absorbed
in enduring pain that she was behind Beatrix in her lessons.
Maud, the youngest, was the most worldly wise and the
least content. Maud was sometimes naughty.

This trip to Pendizack was the supreme adventure of
their lives. They were all a little stunned by it. It was as if
a story book had suddenly become real. A week ago they
would have thought it impossible that they should ever have
friends like the Giffords. Now the barrier between possible
and impossible things seemed to have disappeared.

'Hebe will give us our specially brave thing tomorrow,'
said Beatrix, when they had done singing. 'I wonder what
she will decide.'

'We've not done half the tests yet,' said Maud. 'We
haven't smelt a smell or slept on the floor.'

'She says those can wait,' said Beatrix. 'I explained we
couldn't sleep on the floor here because Mummy is in the
room.'

'I hope it won't be a train,' said Blanche nervously. 'Lying
between the rails and letting a train go over us. I should be
too frightened. I don't think I could.'

'Did Hebe do that?' cried Maud.

'No. They couldn't, in London. You can't get on to a railway line in London. But she thought we might.'

'What did Hebe do?' asked Beatrix avidly.

'She stayed in St. Paul's Cathedral all night. She hid, when they shut it up. She said she saw the ghost of Henry the Eighth.'

'What a story!' cried Maud. 'St. Paul's wasn't built till after the fire of London.'

'New buildings don't stop a ghost,' said Blanche. 'There's a house in London that was once a road and a man on horseback gallops through it. But if we have to lie under a train I really can't. Just think of hearing it come roaring along!'

'I don't think it will be a train,' said Beatrix. 'Caroline says she thinks it will be swimming.'

'But we can't swim!' protested the others.

'I know. I told her. But Hebe says the Spartan way is to learn by jumping into deep water.'

'But supposing we didn't learn?' asked Maud.

'That's what Caroline said. She told me that if Hebe makes us swim she will stop it.'

'How can she?'

'I don't know. But she was quite angry. She said the Spartans is only a game, and we mustn't take it too seriously. She said she didn't do a brave thing. She only pretended.'

'How very disloyal!' said Blanche.

When they came within sight of the cove Blanche suddenly sank down upon the grass saying that she must rest for a minute. They all lay on the short turf, rubbing wild thyme between their fingers. Beatrix said dreamily:

'If we had something to make small things big . . . a sort of magnifying glass, and took that ship out of the bottle, and made it big, we'd have a schooner.'

'How would you get it out of the bottle?' said Maud.

'I would find out. Phineas Pearce put it in.'

'Why not make the bottle large, too?' said Blanche. 'And crawl down the neck and live on the ship. If it was inside the bottle we could sit on the deck even if it rained.'

'Where would you put it?' asked Maud.

'On the headland,' decided Beatrix, 'where it could be seen for miles . . . a huge bottle with a ship inside it. Great crowds would collect every day round the bottle, singing Old Hundred.'

'But nobody would be allowed inside except loyal Spartans,' said Maud.

'And Robin,' said Blanche. 'And Nancibel. I do wish we could do it. Hebe would be so surprised.'

'I think everybody would be surprised,' said Maud. 'But I suppose it's not possible. There can't be such a glass.'

'There was a telescope once,' asserted Beatrix, 'and if you looked through it you saw the past.'

'Beatrix! Was there? Who told you?'

'In the *Strand Magazine*. A man looked through it at his house and it wasn't there. So he focused it nearer to his own time and saw it being built.'

'That *must* have been made up,' said Blanche.

'No. It said Science.'

Blanche looked unconvinced and tried to get up, for she felt it was time they were moving again. But her back hurt so much that she fell down again gasping.

'Is it very bad?' asked Beatrix anxiously.

Blanche nodded. Tears began to roll down her cheeks, a

thing which hardly ever happened.

'Shall we rub it?'

'You might try.'

With an effort she got on to her face. Beatrix pulled up her cotton frock and pulled down her faded pants and began to knead her spine. But the pain got no better. All three of them were crying now.

Presently a voice said:

'Has she hurt herself?'

They looked up to find old Mrs. Paley standing beside them on the path.

'It's only her back,' explained Beatrix. 'It always hurts. We rub it when it gets very bad.'

'Let me try,' said Mrs. Paley. 'I'm rather good at rubbing.'

She knelt beside Blanche and began to massage gently. As she worked she asked questions. How long had this back been bad? Always, they said: but amended this to 'ever since Blanche had diphtheria'. Did their mother know? Yes, she knew. Maud volunteered that their mother thought it must be growing pains.

'Did the doctor say it was all right to rub it?' asked Mrs. Paley. 'Some bad backs shouldn't be rubbed.'

'Oh, the doctor didn't see it,' said Beatrix. 'It's not an illness; only a pain. We always rub it when she can't sleep at night.'

After a while Blanche declared that the pain was better and, between them, they got her to her feet. Going down hill, she explained, was especially difficult, but she could manage if the others helped her and she was sure that it must be late.

The three set off, Beatrix and Maud supporting Blanche, each with an arm round her waist. They seemed to be in quite good spirits again, and as they staggered down the cliff path they began to pipe once more their tuneless anthem:

> *O enter then His gates with praise!*
> *Approach with joy His courts unto!*

Mrs. Paley watched them anxiously until they got to the level sands.

3. No Lady

Nancibel, going down to the garden to get some mint, thought she saw a stranger hiding among the loganberries.

'Who's that?' she called.

He straightened up and came towards her, smiling broadly.

'Why Bruce! Whatever are you doing here?'

'I'm looking for the stables. What are *you* doing here?'

'I work here. And this isn't the way to the stables. Who said you could eat our loganberries?'

'What do you mean . . . you work here?' asked Bruce, with some agitation.

'I'm housemaid.'

'But I thought you lived up the cliff.'

'I come in daily.'

'Oh? I see.'

He looked relieved, and picked up a cardboard suitcase which was left on the path, adding:

'I wasn't eating loganberries because there weren't any. Do you know where the stables are?'

'Through the door in the wall. Why?'

'I'm to sleep in them.'

'Oh! You're stopping here? Your people are stopping here?'

'That's right,' said Bruce.

'Funny! Mrs. Siddal never said anything, breakfast, about a new party coming.'

'I don't expect she knows. She was out when we came. The old man let us the rooms.'

'Mr. Siddal! Well, I never!'

'He's an old boy friend of my . . . boss. So we asked for him at the door.'

'Who opened the door then?'

'A youth with adenoids.'

'Oh *him*!'

'Yes *him*! I'm glad you feel that way about him.'

'Why?'

'Because I don't have to be jealous.'

'Be your age. What happened?'

'Well, we waited in the hall for a thousand years while adenoids went to wake Mr. Siddal. But at last he came and let the garden room to my boss. But there was no room for me in the Inn and so . . .'

'Don't be irreverent. You'll be in the small loft, I expect. The Siddal boys and Fred have the other two.'

'Lead me to it, then. Up the garden path!'

'Lead yourself!' said Nancibel. 'It's only through that door. You can't miss it.'

'Aren't you glad I've come?' he called after her, as she turned away.

'Sure,' she cried, over her shoulder. 'I haven't had a good laugh, not since Saturday.'

She ran off, hoping that she had not betrayed her pleasure in seeing him again. For she had thought a lot about him since Saturday night and had decided that he must really be very nice, in spite of his silly ways. Not every boy would take a telling off as good-humouredly as he had. And it would be amusing to have somebody young about the place: somebody lively, to make a change from Fred and his heavy breathing. 'Nancibel! You are redundant!' She would go bats if she heard that crack much oftener. And he's a bit gone on me, she thought, which is good for my morale All winter I haven't cared if the fellows were gone on me or not, but I'm getting better now.

She pranced into the house with the light step and bright eye of a successful girl. *I'll see you again,* she carolled at the sink, *whenever the Spring breaks through again!*

'Have you got to make that shocking row?' asked Fred. 'What you singing anyway?'

'It's a very old-fashioned song,' said Nancibel. 'My mum used to sing it.'

Miss Ellis came into the scullery, looking important.

'There's a new party come,' she announced. 'With a chauffeur. He'll be sleeping in the stables. You'd better take out sheets and make up his bed, Nancibel.'

'Yes, Miss Ellis.'

Bruce had found the small loft and was surveying it gloomily when she arrived with the sheets. It had wooden walls and ceiling, no rugs, and no furniture save a broken chair and a folding bed.

'Austerity is our watchword,' he said. 'Am I allowed sheets on the bed?'

'Yes. I've brought you some. And now listen! Don't ever

sit on that bed. If you do it shuts up with you in it, and it's quite a job to get out. Fred had it at first and he got shut in it and if somebody hadn't heard him yelling he'd be inside it still.'

'How long was he there, actually?'

'Oh . . . two or three days,' said Nancibel, solemnly, spreading the sheets on the bed.

'But how do I get in,' asked Bruce, when they had both giggled a good deal, 'when I go to bye-bye?'

'You get in at the end and creep up it. You have to get out the same way.'

'I'll get into training. Tell me about the Siddal boys. There seem to be three, by the look of their room.'

'Well, there's Gerry. He's the eldest. He's *very* nice.'

'Oh, is he? And good looking, I suppose?'

'No. Nothing to write home about. Duff . . . that's the second one . . . he's a dream.'

'Better looking than me?'

'No. But he doesn't shoot a line about Limehouse.'

'Oh Nancibel! Must you bring that up? Is it fair?'

'P'raps not,' she agreed. 'I won't again unless you annoy me.'

'Oh, I'll never annoy you any more. You've changed my life.'

'You don't look a bit changed, to me.'

'Oh, but I am. You can't think.'

He opened his suitcase and began to take out his possessions.

'I've been thinking about you ever since Saturday,' he

148

told her. 'Wondering if I should see you again.'

'What a lovely dressing gown,' exclaimed Nancibel.

'Sweet, isn't it?'

'What's all that typewriting?'

'That's part of my boss's new book.'

'Who is your boss?'

Now for it, thought Bruce, hanging his dressing gown on a nail. But it might have come at a worse moment.

'Mrs. Lechene,' he said airily.

'*Mrs.* Lechene?'

'Yes. I told you. She's an authoress.'

Had he told her? Nancibel could not remember. Surely she would remember if he had said he was working for a lady?

'How did you get that job?' she asked.

Bruce hesitated, and remembered his vow to shoot no more lines.

'I was Boots in a hotel where she . . .' he began.

'*Oh*,' cried Nancibel. 'Like in your book, you mean? That boy, he was Boots in a hotel, wasn't he?'

'You remember a lot about my book, considering you didn't like it,' said Bruce crossly.

'Well, it's funny him being a Boots and you being a Boots.'

'I don't see. One has to use one's own experience.'

'And this lady . . .'

'*She's* nothing to do with the woman in the book. It's not autobiographical.'

'Pardon?'

'It's not the story of *my* life,' said Bruce hotly. 'That's all I mean.'

'Well. I should hope not.'

'We've had that out before. And anyway that book's no good. I'm going to burn it and write another.'

'Good for the fuel shortage.'

'I'm going to write a book about a boy who got shut up inside a bed. And nobody knew where he was, because he was too proud to yell.'

He paused.

'Go on,' said Nancibel.

'I can't. It's so miserable. And you don't like miserable books.'

Heavy steps creaked on the loft ladder and a voice called sharply. His expression changed.

'Bruce,' said the voice again.

A woman appeared in the loft doorway and stood there surveying them. Nancibel realized that this must be the lady authoress. An old friend of Mr. Siddal's! Nothing surprising about that; boy and girl they must have been, sometime in the year dot. Authoress if you like, but no lady, poking her nose into the chauffeur's room and staring in that funny way. What if she had caught him laughing with the house-maid? Ladies are careful not to notice that sort of thing. Mrs. Siddal never would.

The seconds passed and the stare became an insult. Nancibel lifted her eyes and looked full at Anna, obscurely aware that it would not do to mutter *excuse me* and slip out. She must stand her ground and vindicate her right to be there. Like a big old white slug, she thought. Only slugs have the sense not to wear slacks. I shan't say anything. I'll let her feel she's the one to intrude. She can speak first. Let's hope Bruce has the sense to keep quiet.

Bruce had not. He found Anna's stare unendurable, as it slid, with meditative deliberation, over the curves of Nancibel. He broke in nervously:

'We were just . . .'

The eyes slid round to him. The pale mouth smiled slyly.

'So I see,' said Anna.

Two can play at that game, thought Nancibel, and began an equally deliberate scrutiny of the enemy. No bra and no girdle, and if I had toes like that I wouldn't wear sandals. We can play statues till the cows come home, duckie, if that's your idea of fun and games.

'Miss Thomas kindly . . .' jabbered Bruce, 'she brought my sheets.'

Anna's slow gaze shifted to the bed.

'I . . . I'd better put the car away, hadn't I?'

'No hurry,' said Anna, 'if you've got anything better to do.'

'Nothing! I've nothing better to do,' he declared.

Pushing past Anna, he rushed downstairs.

Nancibel had finished making the bed, but she thought it better to do one or two trifling tasks about the room before she left it, so as to emphasize the fact that it was her job to be in it. So she picked up the typewritten sheets which Bruce had spilled out on the floor and put them on the window ledge.

'I'm afraid I interrupted,' observed Anna. 'Has Bruce been telling you the story of his life?'

'Oh no,' said Nancibel, smiling. 'He told me that on Saturday.'

'Saturday?' said Anna. 'Saturday?'

She crossed the room to sit on the bed, meaning obviously to get the whole story. But Nancibel saw that the moment for a strategic retreat had arrived.

'Excuse me!' she muttered, and rushed from the room.

As she scrambled down the ladder she heard a crash and an oath. Anna had sat upon the Pendizack booby trap and was now sharing Fred's fate. But she can get herself out, thought Nancibel, scurrying across the stable yard. She's not a little skinny thing like Fred. Gracious! What language! Whatever she is, she's no lady.

4. Marshmallows

Lady Gifford could not believe that a big place like Porth-merryn was really barren of marshmallows on the first day of a new ration period. She was sure that a thorough search might have produced them.

'Did you explain it was for an invalid?' she asked.

'It wouldn't have made any difference,' said Sir Henry. 'There just were none. I tried everywhere.'

'I expect there were plenty under the counter. All you mean is that you saw none.'

'I saw some at Saundry's, but Mrs. Cove bought the last before I could get to the counter.'

'Mrs. Cove! I'm not surprised. Why did you let her get in front of you?'

'I'm very sorry, Eirene.'

'No, dear. I don't think so. If you were really sorry for me you'd try to make things easier instead of more diffi-cult.'

'I do all I can,' he muttered.

She flushed, sat up in bed, and spoke with unusual energy.

'How can you say that when you force me to live in this horrible way when we could be perfectly comfortable? I heard from Veronica this morning. She says there's plenty of everything in the Channel Islands if you've got the money to pay for it.'

'Eirene, we've been into all this before . . .'

'You force me to live in these coolie conditions . . .'

'They are not coolie conditions. You know nothing whatever about coolie conditions . . .'

'Don't shout, Harry. Please don't shout. You know how any kind of a scene upsets me. Can't we discuss this quietly?'

Sir Henry lowered his voice and stated that coolies eat nothing but rice.

'Which we can't get,' said Eirene Gifford triumphantly. 'So we're worse off than coolies. I'm sure I should be only too glad to eat rice . . . I love risotto . . . but Mr. Strachey won't let me have it because the workers don't care for it. All my friends in America say they do not know how we manage on our rations. Everybody who can get out is getting out, except us.'

'I've told you before, Eirene, that there's nothing to stop you going to Guernsey if you want to.'

'But it's no good unless you come too. I'd have to pay income tax. We can't get off income tax unless we both go.'

'I've told you I'm not going, and I've told you why.'

'You think it's unpatriotic. You think patriotism matters more than your wife and family.'

'Well . . . yes. I suppose I do.'

'Then don't pretend you're sorry for me. If you want to see me starve for the sake of a Government you never voted for . . . a Government that says you aren't worth a tinker's curse . . .'

'It didn't.'

'Yes, it did. You aren't Organized Labour. Mr. Shinwell

said that everyone who isn't Organized Labour is not worth a tinker's curse.'

'Shinwell isn't the entire Government.'

'I'm not so sure. Mr. Attlee daren't sack him, though he can't get us any coal.'

'Well, Eirene, if Shinwell called me his blue-eyed boy, would you be content to let me stay on the Bench and do my job?'

'Don't be stupid, Harry. You know he never would.'

'I must admit it's not very likely.'

'And for the sake of these people, who only want to li-quidate you, the children are to be undernourished . . .'

'I really don't think they are.'

'Of course they are. They're only getting fifteen hundred calories when they ought to get three thousand.'

'A day or a week?'

She was silent for a moment, and he was sure that she did not know.

'They don't look undernourished,' he said. 'Compared with the Coves . . .'

'The Coves,' said Eirene, 'are apparently going to get all the marshmallows in Porthmerryn.'

'Too bad. Did Shinwell arrange that or Strachey?'

'Both,' said Lady Gifford. 'If the Conservatives had got in we shouldn't have had these shortages. Look, Harry: per-haps Mrs. Cove might be willing to exchange. She might like some of my nougat instead.'

'If she'd wanted nougat she'd have bought it. There was plenty.'

'You could tell her how ill I am. But don't worry. Just go on saying you're sorry, and don't make the slightest effort to help me.'

She fell back upon her pillows again and her eyes filled with tears.

Sir Henry hesitated and then stole out of the room. In a quarter of an hour he was back again with a bag of marshmallows which he put upon the table beside her bed.

'Harry! Where did you get them?'

She took one and tasted it critically, wrinkling up her nose.

'Mrs. Cove.'

'She exchanged them for mine?'

'Er . . . no. She sold them to me.'

'Good heavens!'

She tasted another and added:

'They aren't very nice. Did she offer or did you ask?'

'I offered an exchange and she refused. Then she mentioned that her children don't care much for sweets. They prefer books. She said they often sell their sweets to buy books. So then I offered to buy their marshmallows.'

'How much did you give?'

'Eight and six.'

'But Harry! That's fantastic. More than three times what she gave.'

'I thought it pretty stiff, but she said they couldn't get a decent book for less. And I knew you wanted the sweets.'

There was a tap on the door and Hebe appeared, also carrying a paper bag.

'Why darling,' exclaimed Lady Gifford. 'Good morning! Have you been having a good time? What have you been doing? Give me a kiss.'

Hebe extended her cheek and, as she received the caress, her lips moved in the silent curse of the Spartans.

'We went into Porthmerryn for our sweets,' she said, putting her bag on the counterpane. 'These are marshmallows. I got them because I know you like them best.'

'Why . . . how darling of you! But I can't take them, you know. Not your sweet ration.'

'You always do,' said Hebe coldly. 'I don't care for sweets.'

She gave a hard glance at the bag already in Lady Gifford's hands, and ran off.

'Hebe's austerity,' said Lady Gifford, 'is really formidable.'

'H'm,' said Sir Henry.

The undisguised contempt in Hebe's manner had shocked him.

'Is she often like that?' he asked.

'Like what?'

'So much . . . so very much with her nose in the air?'

'She's very reserved. Sensitive children often are.'

'She's not our child, after all. One wonders . . .'

'What?'

'If she's all right . . . with us . . .'

'My dear Harry! Where could she have got a better home? She has everything a child could want; or would have if we weren't obliged to live in this God-forgotten country.'

Perceiving Guernsey once more upon the map he made

his escape. Hebe's expression still disquieted him. It was not right that any child should look so at her mother, or speak so either. Somebody ought to reprove her for it, and the obvious person to do so was himself. He had not wanted to adopt her, or the twins. He had done so merely to please Eirene. But he had signed papers and agreed to act the part of a father to them, and he could not feel that he had ever done very much to fulfil this promise.

He supposed that they were all bound, as they grew older, to criticize Eirene to a certain extent. He did so himself, and faults which were apparent to him could not be hidden from their sharp young eyes. But they must also learn, as he had, to tolerate and excuse her, or life would become impossible.

He went downstairs and wandered about the beach for a while, aghast at the discovery that life could really become more impossible than it was already. For nine years he had been resigned to the fact that his marriage was a disaster and had tried to make the best of a bad job. But he had thought of it as a calamity which could only affect Eirene and himself. He had never perceived that it might involve the children. Nor had it, as long as they were babies, tended by nurses on the upper floors of Queen's Walk.

And babies they had still been when he saw them all off for the United States in 1940. Caroline had been five, Hebe three and the twins were little more than a year old. He had been a trifle uneasy over the adoption of Luke and Michael, in the Spring of 1939, foreseeing the outbreak of war in a near future and fearing a period of domestic upheavals. But

Eirene had been set on it. An obstinate optimism was one of her strongest characteristics. She would never believe that anything unpleasant was going to happen; she condemned anyone who did. Her tranquillity remained unshaken until the fall of France in 1940 threw her into a corresponding panic and sent her scuttling across the Atlantic.

For five years he had lived his solitary life in the basement of Queen's Walk, working as best he could, eating when and where he could, through the raids of '40 and '41, through the flying bombs and through the rockets. To some extent he had relished it. Release from the constant irritation of listening to Eirene compensated for a great deal of material discomfort. He was active in Civil Defence and enjoyed the grim good fellowship of the Wardens' Post. In many ways he felt that his life was more satisfactory than it had been for some years past.

In the early months of 1941 he acquired a mistress, a step which he would never have been allowed to take had Eirene been at home. He was a little surprised at himself but was, at that time, discovering a great many other things at which to be surprised. She was a red-haired girl, one of the women wardens, and neither in the pre-war nor in the post-war world would he have found her attractive. Her name was Billie. She had a slight Cockney accent. He used to patrol the streets with her on noisy nights. Her stock of limericks was inexhaustible, and when a bomb fell she invariably told him a new one. He remembered her best in a tin hat, grasping the business end of a fire hose—a gallant trollop demanding nothing and giving what she had, with careless hospitality. After some months she joined the Wrens and vanished from his life. But in a very short while she taught him several things about women which he had never known before.

He realized that Eirene could never, at any time, have loved him. This, according to Billie, was probably his own fault. He had not, she said, 'educated the poor girl up to it'. She also told him that where the bedroom is wrong the whole house is wrong. She was a coarse creature, but he took some of her maxims to heart. Only he felt that, in his own case, the converse might be true: at Queen's Walk the whole house was wrong and the bedroom, therefore, would never be right. A submissive husband cannot be a successful lover.

Gradually his bitterness towards Eirene melted away. He made resolutions for the future, vowing that when she and the babies came home he would make a fresh start. He would rule his wife and she would love him. In the excitement of reunion some tender link might be forged. For he expected them all to come back quite unchanged.

They returned in the summer of 1945, changed beyond recognition. The babies had become people—they asked questions, they had points of view. And Eirene was an invalid, feeble, emaciated, unfit for any normal life. She needed a nurse rather than a husband, and he was obliged to postpone his plans for a better life. There was some talk of her ultimate recovery, though nobody seemed to be able to tell him what ailed her.

On his way back from the beach at lunch time he

encountered Hebe again. She was sitting on the terrace parapet, her cat on her shoulder. If she was to be reprimanded, now was the time.

'Hebe,' he said severely. 'I want a word with you.'

She lifted her lovely eyes to him and waited.

He took her to task for her manner to her mother. Eirene, he reminded her, was very ill and suffered a great deal.

'What's the matter with her?' asked Hebe.

'She . . . we aren't quite sure. Unluckily they can't find out.'

Hebe gave him a searching look and her expression changed. He could have sworn there was at last a touch of compassion in it, but he had the oddest impression that this pity was not for Eirene.

'She's loved you,' he said, 'ever since you were a little baby. She's done everything for you.'

'Who was my real mother?' interrupted Hebe, with some urgency.

'Eh . . . er . . . I don't know her name, my dear.'

'Don't you know anything about her?'

'I . . . we know some of the circumstances. You'll know them some day . . . when you're older.'

'Why not now?'

'We think you're still too young.'

'A child's questions ought always to be answered honestly and sincerely or else it gets a compress.'

'Complex. I am answering you honestly.'

'Am I a bastard?'

Sir Henry was startled, but after a moment's thought said:

'Yes. But that's not a word you should use. Where did you learn it?'

'Shakespeare. Are Luke and Michael . . . ?'

'What they are is none of your business.'

'Just tell me one thing. Did I belong to poor people? Working people?'

'No.'

Her face fell.

'I wish I had,' she said.

'Why?'

'I think they're nicer.'

'Often they are,' he agreed.

'But if I belonged to rich people, how did I come to be adopted?'

'They didn't want you. We did.'

'Why didn't they want me?'

He hesitated again, but decided she had better have it.

'You'd have been in their way.'

'Oh!'

She looked down at the flagstones and kicked her bare heels against the wall. He felt sorry for her. And he remembered that when they had taken her as a baby he had raised this point with Eirene: how would the child feel when she learnt, as she must learn some day, that her own mother did not want her? That it had been no case of necessity or hardship which had thrown her on the chance kindness of strangers? To learn this, at any age, might, he suggested, be a shock. But Eirene had assured him that she would never ask.

And now he had dealt the blow; dealt it carelessly, without any tender preparation. She had asked for it, but she was only ten, and he should have put her off. It was not to do this that he had sought her, but to act the part of a good father.

'Was my mother a virgin?' asked Hebe suddenly.

'No. Of course not.'

'Are you sure? How can you be sure?'

'Don't talk nonsense. A virgin can't have children.'

'One did,' said Hebe darkly, jumping off the parapet.

He could think of no reply to that and let her run off. He felt that she could give as many shocks as she got, and ceased to reproach himself quite so bitterly.

5. Love's a Man-of-War

Evangeline Wraxton was coming on nicely. Her improvement was not apparent at meal times; huddled into a chair opposite her father she twitched and muttered as before. But she no longer sat in her room all day. She bathed with the Giffords and played rounders with them on the sands. She ran well and her laugh, heard for the first time at Pendizack, was pretty.

After tea she walked with Mrs. Paley up to the post office to buy stamps. They had scarcely left the house before she burst suddenly into all those confidences which had been left unspoken the night before. She poured out the whole story of her life with many exclamations and repetitions. When, for the tenth time, she announced that nobody would ever know how awful it all was Mrs. Paley cut it short.

'Don't keep saying the same thing over and over again, Angie. It's a bad habit. And plenty of people can guess how awful it is. You're not the only person with an odious father. Gerry Siddal, as far as I can see, has a stiff row to hoe.'

'Yes. I suppose so. Er . . . have you spoken to him yet?'

'No. I've not seen him today. But I will. Now tell me: how on earth did your father ever get to be a Canon? What do you suppose induced anyone to ordain him at all?'

Evangeline had no ideas about this. But from her vague

reminiscences it emerged that the Canon had not always been so impossible. His ill-temper had grown on him. He had been a notable preacher and successful in any kind of controversy. The Low Church party had hoped to make use of him and the old Bishop, the Bishop who gave him the living of Great Mossbury, had admired him.

'But he quarrelled with everyone,' she said. 'And at last nobody came to church. Nobody at all. For a whole year he read the services just to our family. You can't think how awful . . . sorry!'

'How many were there in your family?'

'Oh, there were six of us; I've three brothers and two sisters. But he's broken with all of them so I never see them. Well, so the parishioners asked the Bishop—the new Bishop—to get them another Rector. But Father wouldn't resign, though they broke his windows and all sorts of things. You can't think . . . You see I stayed at home, when the others went, because of Mother. I couldn't bear to leave her alone. Well, so the Bishop sent for Father one day to the Palace, and Father found he had resigned. He'd flown into such a rage he didn't know what he was saying till he heard the Bishop accepting his resignation. He said it was a trap and he wouldn't go, and he barricaded the Rectory. And none of the tradesmen would sell us anything. It was in all the papers; the reporters stayed at the inn. They called it the Siege of Mossbury. I was twelve. You can't think . . . well, so he gave in at last; I don't know why. And he never got another living. Only luckily he had some money of his own, and he does locum sometimes in a parish. But we've never had a home since Mossbury. And he was forbidden to preach after one sermon he preached . . . that was all in the papers. Everywhere it's been awful. You can't . . . Mother died three years ago. She was ill for a long time. Always in pain. You can't think . . . Mrs. Paley, it was awful and I must say so. And when she was dying she asked me to promise never to leave Father. I couldn't refuse. It was the last thing she said. She was worried over what would happen to him. So you see!'

'How could she condemn you to such a life?'

'Well, you see, she had rather a gloomy idea of life. She thought we are all born to suffer, and the more we suffer now the less we shall hereafter. She thought it was wrong to be happy. I expect she worked all that out because she was married to Father.'

'And you feel you must keep your promise?'

'Oh yes. Yes, I do.'

'Even if you end by going crazy or murdering him?'

'Mother said God would give me grace to endure it.'

'And does He?'

'No.'

'I thought He didn't. Here's the post office. Go in and ask for your stamps, just once, not several times. But try to be audible. The postmistress does not eat human flesh. Say: four twopenny halfpenny stamps, please.'

Evangeline obeyed and returned in triumph. On the walk home she told the whole story over again, in fuller detail, while Mrs. Paley let her talk and pondered upon schemes for freeing the girl from her rash vow. The most obvious would be that of the astute Bishop. Canon Wraxton, if suf-ficiently enraged, might be manœuvred into dismissing his daughter of his own accord. He might cut her off with a shilling and turn her out into the snow. But he must not do this until some refuge had been found for the girl. Some friend must be waiting in the snow who would snatch Evangeline away before the Canon changed his mind. And she has no friends, reflected Mrs. Paley, except me. She must have other friends. I must see to it, and I must do something about Blanche Cove's back.

She had been worrying about Blanche Cove's back ever since the forenoon. Yesterday she would have sighed and dismissed the matter as being none of her business. But today she was convinced that such pain must not be per-mitted, if anyone could do anything to relieve it. Today she was a new woman, changed in the twinkling of an eye, be-tween the fall of two waves. So far as her own problems were concerned she was still a helpless, hopeless being: the deadlock with Paul continued. But, in the case of Evangel-ine and Blanche, who were equally oppressed, her natural energy—frustrated for years—gushed out in a torrent.

She hobbled briskly down the hill, for sleeping in the heather had given her a touch of rheumatism, and went in search of Blanche's mother.

Mrs. Cove was sitting, as usual, upon the terrace, knit-ting for dear life. But she looked a little less grim than usual, and almost smiled when Mrs. Paley came to sit be-side her. It was not quite a smile, but the small straight line of her mouth relaxed a little and she said that it had been a beautiful day. Something must have happened to please her.

She made short work, however, of enquiries about Blanche and intimated plainly that she thought them impertinent. The pains, she said, were growing pains such as all children had. Blanche was tall for her age. She was not in the least disturbed, and she thought it a mistake to encourage complaints.

Mrs. Paley accepted the rebuff and spoke of Dorsetshire. Her father had known a Cove, Sir Adrian Cove, of Swan Court. Was he, by any chance, a connection?

'My husband's uncle,' said Mrs. Cove.

'Was he really? He's dead now, isn't he? Who has the place now?'

'Another nephew. Gerald Cove.'

'And he's able to live there? So many people nowadays . . .'

'I believe so,' said Mrs. Cove. 'But I really don't know.'

The fate of landed proprietors was mourned for a while by Mrs. Paley before she hobbled away to look up Sir Gerald Cove in Burke's *Landed Gentry*, which she had noticed on the bottom shelf of the lounge bookcase. She discovered that he had succeeded Sir Adrian five years ago, and that his wife had been a Miss Evelyn Chadwick, elder daughter of Guy Chadwick, Esq., of Grainsbridge. This was unhelpful, for she knew nothing of the Chadwicks. But she could, at least, find out from the little Coves the Christian name of their father, and then, when next in London, she could go to Somerset House and look up any wills that might be relevant—his will and Sir Adrian's will. She wanted very much to know how much money Mrs. Cove had got, and from whom she had got it. If she had none, and she presented every appearance of having none, an allowance from her husband's relatives might be inferred. They might not, perhaps, give her enough to cure Blanche's back. But if they paid the piper they could call the tune, and it would do no harm if they should come to know about Blanche's back. The world is full of busy bodies, of gossiping old ladies. It was not impossible that the tale of Blanche, groaning on the cliffs of Pendizack, might some day find its way to Swan Court.

If, on the other hand, it should appear that Mrs. Cove possessed an independent income the problem would be greater. Nobody can force a mother to cherish her children. Unless, thought Mrs. Paley, with rising spirits, it should turn out that the children themselves had been beneficiaries. Pressure might be brought to bear on their mother if she was mismanaging an allowance intended for their maintenance. There might be trustees or other guardians. She would find out. She would poke her nose into other people's business and she would make an intolerable nuisance of herself, and she would go on and on doing this until a doctor had looked at Blanche's back.

Her next task must be to tackle Gerry Siddal, while she was in this deedy mood. She had promised that she would, and he was nearly always to be found pumping water, between tea and dinner, since Pendizack depended on a well.

The pump was close to the drive, hidden in a clump of rhododendrons. She went to the front door and listened.

She could hear it creaking, but not so steadily as usual. There were pauses, as though Gerry's mind was not entirely on his work. And as she took the narrow path between the bushes she heard a burst of laughter. Two people seemed to be pumping; two young voices, a tenor and a treble, were raised in song as the creaking was resumed:

> There was meat . . . meat . . . never fit to eat,
> In the stores! In the stores!
> There were eggs . . . eggs . . . nearly growing legs,
> In the quar . . . ter . . . mast . . . er's stores!

Peeping through the branches she saw Nancibel, who had just gone off duty, with a strange young man—a very handsome young man. They were enjoying themselves enormously, and Mrs. Paley would have retreated if Nancibel had not turned and caught sight of her. She explained her errand, and Nancibel said:

'I think Mr. Gerry is chopping wood, Mrs. Paley. In the stable yard. We offered to do the pumping tonight.'

Mrs. Paley retraced her steps, glad to think that Nancibel had got such a well-favoured boy. Poor Gerry, chopping wood in the stable yard, had no lovely girl to sing with him. He smiled when he saw Mrs. Paley, but he did not expect her to speak because he did not know that she could. Few people at Pendizack had ever heard her do so. Changed she might be, but she did not look it, and to Gerry's eyes she appeared as grey, as pinched, as unsmiling as ever. He was quite astonished when she came up and asked if he would do her a favour. Might she borrow two lilo mattresses from the garden shed for herself and Miss Wraxton. They were planning, she explained, to sleep out in the cliff shelter.

'Of course,' said Gerry. 'I'll take them up for you. Will after supper do?'

'Oh no. You mustn't trouble to do that,' said Mrs. Paley, who had every intention that he should. 'We can carry them.'

'They're quite heavy. I'll take them. Anything else you'd like? Rugs? Cushions?'

'We've taken up rugs and cushions. Mr. Siddal . . . I think that Miss Wraxton is very much worried about staying here. Naturally she wants to go, but she can't when her father won't. I told her I was sure that you understood.'

Gerry looked sulky, for he had Evangeline on his conscience.

'I don't,' he said. 'In her shoes I should go, whatever my father did.'

'She has no money. Only half a crown.'

'Oh!' said Gerry.

'She feels she ought not to have had hysterics, but one can't wonder, can one? The shock of her father's behaviour made a good many people behave . . . as they wouldn't otherwise have done. Personally I think we should be grateful to her, for she did get him out of church, even if she was noisy. Nothing else would have got him out, and I hate to think what would have happened if he'd stayed.'

'You mean . . .' said Gerry, 'she wasn't laughing deliberately?'

Mrs. Paley opened her eyes.

'But of course not. You're a doctor. You must know hysterics when you hear them.'

'I didn't realize,' he muttered.

'You were some distance away. I was quite close.'

'I'm afraid I was rude to her, yesterday afternoon.'

'That doesn't matter, as long as I can tell her that you—that you feel differently now.'

'Oh I do,' said Gerry. 'Indeed I do.'

Mrs. Paley gave him her pinched smile and departed.

He went back to his chopping with a lighter heart. The memory of Evangeline's stricken face as she crawled up the stairs would no longer torment him. Mrs. Paley had put it right. She might look like a sour lemon, but she wasn't a bad old trout when you came to talk to her. He would take the mattresses up to the shelter for them, and he would make a point of saying something friendly to that unfortunate girl. Half a crown! Somebody ought to do something about a thing like that!

6. The Bleeding Branch

There had been no overt explosion when Mrs. Siddal came back from her shopping expedition to find that the garden room had been let to Anna Lechene. It had been done, as she well knew, to annoy her; but she held her peace and asked mildly where the chauffeur was to eat. With Fred or in the dining room?

'In the dining room,' said Siddal. 'At a cosy little table with Anna. He's a secretary-chauffeur. Very high class.'

'Very refined, except when he forgets,' said Duff, who had taken a dislike to Bruce. 'And he looks like a bit part actor.'

'He's done all the pumping for us,' said Gerry.

'Well, that was nice of him,' conceded Mrs. Siddal.

'It was for love of Nancibel,' said Robin. 'He's fallen for her in a big way. He peeled the potatoes for her this afternoon. And now she's taken him home to supper.'

'Has she?' exclaimed Mr. Siddal. 'But how intriguing! Where was Anna?'

'She was in her room writing her book.'

'What fun! I think I'll join the company tonight and see how they are all getting on.'

Shaving always took Siddal a long time, and when he went to find Anna she was already established on the terrace, with Duff, Robin and Bruce sitting on cushions at her feet. None of them much wanted to be there, but she wished it and her will was stronger than theirs.

'I've come to chaperone the boys,' said Siddal, pulling up a deck chair, 'and to ask what your new book is called, Anna.'

'*The Bleeding Branch*,' said Anna, in her slow, deep voice.

'Thank you. It was the only detail I wasn't sure of, and even that I should have guessed: *There! Let thy bleeding branch atone, For every tortured tear! Shall my young sins* . . . Now I know exactly what your book will be, as well as if I'd written it myself.'

'Really,' said Anna. 'Then how does it begin?'

'It begins with the innocent, or quasi-innocent (because you couldn't depict true innocence, Anna) little Brontës carving their names on trees. I don't know why they chose branches rather than trunks, but they did. It's possible they then climbed the trees and sat in them, playing Gondals.'

'Dick! What a devil you are!'

'And it ends with a moribund and remorseful Emily hacking a branch out with an axe. And in between we have "a wildering maze of mad years left behind", in which Bramwell writes *Wuthering Heights* and she pinches it and rewrites it. Bramwell's was a far greater book, but she murders it because she can't stand the Truth. She will not allow Cathy to be Heathcliff's mistress. She will not allow the young Catherine to be their daughter, palmed off on Linton. Young Catherine, of course, was the heroine of Bramwell's book and her half-brother, young Linton, the hero. But Emily changed all that. She pushed him right out of the picture, because of course he was a self-portrait.'

'There's plenty of evidence,' began Anna.

'Oh, plenty. The build-up of young Catherine in the opening chapter, for instance. But you see, my dear Anna, I know it all. I know exactly what poor Emily's young sins are going to be, and you shan't tell me about them.'

'I blame her for nothing,' said Anna sententiously, 'except for murdering that book. If there is a Last Judgment she'll have to answer for that.'

'I do hope there will be,' said Siddal. 'I shall enjoy hearing you answering for your books, Anna.'

'I know you hate them. At heart you know, Dick, you're a bit of a Puritan.'

'And what do you mean by a Puritan?' enquired Siddal.

'You hate Sex.'

'No, I don't. I think sex is very funny.'

'That's a sign of frustration.'

'Maybe. But I don't think food is funny, and I don't get enough of it nowadays.'

'We all talk about food a great deal,' said Robin.

'Oh yes,' said his father, 'we are immensely preoccupied with it. And sex-starved people are immensely preoccupied with sex. Much cry, little wool. I always suspect people who boast of their rich and various sexual experiences. I find myself doubting if they ever had any worth speaking of. Satisfied people hold their tongues. They know it's an unlucky subject to discuss.'

'What do you mean? Unlucky!' asked Anna.

'Terribly unlucky. When Psyche turned on the light,

Eros flew out of the window. He's a very touchy god and he can't bear publicity. And that,' he said to the three young men, 'is why you boys will never be able to pick up much information at second hand. Those who know won't talk. Those who talk don't know.'

'I talk,' boomed Anna, 'and I know. I've never rejected an experience.'

'I never rejected a brief,' said Siddal, getting up.

He shuffled over to the terrace parapet to look at the sunset on the water. The tide was half out and the sea as calm as glass, flecked here and there with gulls who seemed to sleep as they floated. In the wide tracts of wet sand the rosy sky was reflected. Nearer the cliffs, where it was dry, three figures crossed the bay. Gerry was staggering under a load of two mattresses, Evangeline carried a picnic basket, Mrs. Paley some pillows. They took the path up to the headland.

A cormorant came flying low over the water, its long neck outstretched. It flew inland, and Robin turned to watch it.

'Look!' he said. 'It's perched on the roof! There's a whole row of them. Six or seven!'

But Anna was not interested in birds.

'You know,' she said, 'I think your father would have been perfectly different if that affair with Phœbe Mason hadn't ended so unhappily. He was so astonishingly brilliant, as a young man. Everyone thought he'd set the Thames on fire. And then, when he didn't, you'd hear all sorts of explanations. People said he shouldn't have gone in for the law, that it wasn't the right profession, and he should have stayed in Oxford. But everyone knew it was that he couldn't be bothered to do any work. Now why?'

'Who's Phœbe Mason?' asked Robin, pop-eyed.

'Didn't you know?'

'Never heard of her,' declared Robin.

'How queer! It just shows what a queer frustrated family yours is. Everything hushed up, I suppose. But that's probably Barbara's . . . your mother's doing.'

Duff stirred uneasily on his cushion. He had at last made up his mind what he thought of Anna.

'If only she'd had more generosity . . . more frankness . . . if she'd let the affair run its course instead of parting them . . .'

At this point Siddal returned from his stroll and passed them, observing:

'Whatever you're saying, Anna, it's a lie. No. I overheard nothing, but I protest that I wasn't and I didn't. And if you write books about me before I die I shall sue you for libel.'

7. From Mr. Paley's Diary

I wrote nothing this morning, and I have been able to write nothing all day. Christina is to blame for this. Last night, when we were sitting in the lounge, she rose suddenly and went away. I did not see her again until eight o'clock this morning. I went to our room, at the usual hour, but she was not there. I sat up all night waiting for her. She did not return. She came in just before Nancibel brought our early tea. She did not tell me where she had been, and I did not ask. I dislike having to ask questions, a fact of which she is perfectly aware.

We went, with our lunch, to our usual place over Rosigraille Bay. She continued to act strangely. She left me for a while to talk to the Cove children who were crossing the cliff. And after lunch she lay down in the bracken and slept all the afternoon. She has never done so before. At four o'clock, our hour for return, I was obliged to wake her. Some pieces of bracken were caught in her hair which made her look very foolish; but she did not seem to mind this when I told her of it. She then said casually that she had not slept much last night because she had been on the cliff with Miss Wraxton. This was not said in any tone of apology. On the contrary: she gave me to understand that she means to repeat this performance again tonight.

I told her, quite plainly, that I don't choose she should do this. It is an affront to me. Her place is with me, not with Miss Wraxton. Her reply was curious. I will try to report our conversation *verbatim*, as far as I can recollect it. But Christina is difficult to report. Her ideas are confused and her powers of expression are limited. It may be that I shall give her credit for better arguments than she really produced. I find it hard not to make some sense out of the silliest reasoning.

Christina:	I cannot stay beside you, Paul, because I now believe what you have been saying for the last twenty years.
Myself:	And what is that?
Christina:	I believe that you are in Hell. You have often told me that you were, but I would not believe it.
Myself:	Wherever I may be, you are my wife. Your place is with me.
Christina:	My place is not in Hell. It is not my duty to be there with you. I used to think you were mad, and I was very sorry for you. But now I know that it is in your power to recover and you will not.
Myself:	Do I understand from this that you wish to leave me?
Christina:	I will do all I can to make life comfortable for you. And I shall be at hand if ever you

	want me. But I will not share your prison
	any more, for it is a bad prison which you
	have made for yourself.
Myself:	You have never understood. My integrity
	means more to me than happiness.
Christina:	You have none. There is no such thing.
	You are not a whole person. Nobody
	is. We are members one of another. An
	arm has no integrity if it is amputated.
	It is nothing unless it is part of a body,
	with a heart to pump the blood through it
	and a brain to guide it. You have no more
	integrity than a severed arm might have.

This reply surprised me. She does not usually express herself so clearly. I told her that, by integrity, I mean self-respect.

I do not know how this will affect me. She has changed. I must have wished her to do so, since I have consistently rejected all her attempts at reconciliation.

We were late for tea.

8. Strange Beds

The Pendizack booby trap shut up with a crash, and Bruce's oaths rang across the stable yard. He had forgotten Nancibel's warning.

The noise woke the occupants of the big loft. Robin sat up with a start to hear chuckles from Duff's bed.

'It's the high-class chauffeur,' said Duff. 'He didn't know . . . or else he forgot.'

'But what time is it?' asked Robin, looking at the luminous dial of his watch. 'Why . . . it's half-past four!'

'I know.'

'Where on earth can he have been?'

'I can guess.'

Robin reflected.

'Not,' he said at last, '. . . not with . . . ?'

'Of course. It's obvious.'

'Well! I call it pretty thick.'

There were violent bumps next door as Bruce extricated himself from the bed, opened it out again, and climbed in the proper way. Then there was silence.

'It puts me,' said Robin at last, 'off the whole idea.'

Duff grunted non-committally and turned on his hard mattress. He disliked Anna, but he could understand her attraction and in part he responded to it. Her lure was that of Circe. In her company a man had leave to be as big a brute as he liked. She imposed no sanctions, asked for no loyalty, no delicacy, no tender considerations. She offered freedom of a sort. The brute in Duff yawned hungrily.

'I say,' exclaimed Robin, 'where's Gerry?'

'Isn't he here?'

Robin flashed a torch for a minute on Gerry's bed. It was empty.

'This,' he said, 'is a much stiffer guess.'

'I shouldn't wonder,' said Duff, 'if he's cleared out. He was in a black rage before supper. I expect he's so furious he's just gone.'

'What happened?'

'He had a row with Mother.'

'*Gerry* did?'

'Mother gets a bit tired of advice from Gerry. He's always telling her what she ought to do.'

'Tells all of us,' agreed Robin.

'He was trying to dictate about Father's Law Library. Mother got a letter from the people in his old Chambers. It seems it's still there, and they've been writing and writing to know what he wants done with it. But you know him. He never even opens his letters. So at last they wrote to her. It was none of Gerry's business. Mother was livid.'

'Do they want it moved?'

'Yes. They've no room for it. He just left it there when he gave up practice. Mother's giving orders to have it stored. She would before if she'd known anything about it. But Gerry wants to sell it. A good Law Library is very valuable nowadays, and it's worth about five hundred pounds.

Somebody did offer to buy it, apparently, but that's off, because Father never answered the letters.'

'Five hundred pounds would be very useful,' said Robin.

'If I go to the Bar I might like to have it myself. It's no concern of Gerry's. Infernal cheek of him to say what's to be done with Father's books. Mother told him she's storing it for me, and he proceeded to go right off the deep end. Just because he gives her fourpence half-penny a week out of his screw he thinks he's got the right to boss the whole family. He said he should go to South Africa and never come back.'

Robin considered this, and then said:

'We should be in quite a hole if he did.'

But Duff was growing sleepy again, and did not answer.

'I don't see why you should have five hundred pounds,' said Robin more loudly.

'Wha-at?' said Duff, rousing.

'If all this family has left is books worth five hundred pounds, I don't see why you should get it all.'

'I'll have to have a library if I go to the Bar.'

'What about me?'

'You aren't going to the Bar.'

'How am I to get educated?'

'Get a brain specialist to operate on you, I should think. Do shut up. I want to go to sleep.'

'I think Gerry's absolutely right.'

'You take a flying . . .'

There were thumps on the wall from Bruce, who was trying to go to sleep.

'Thump back,' said Duff indignantly. 'What blasted cheek! He wakes us all up falling about in his bloody bed.'

Robin thumped and yelled: '*Shut up!*' through the wood partition.

'Shut up yourself,' came in a faint answering yell from Bruce.

Robin and Duff continued to talk in voices aggressively raised until Bruce, losing patience, got out of his bed. There was another crash as it shut up. Yells of laughter came through the partition. Gerry, who was cautiously climbing the ladder, thought that everybody in the loft must have gone mad.

But the noise died down when he joined his brothers. Duff and Robin stopped laughing and stared at him.

'What is all this?' he asked.

'Bed fun,' said Duff, indicating the renewed bumps next door, as Bruce once more struggled into freedom. 'He's a very restless sleeper, poor chap. But what about *you*? Where have you been? Africa?'

Gerry, who had switched on the light, sat down upon his bed and began to take off his shoes.

'I've been up on the cliff,' he said, 'with Mrs. Paley and Angie.'

'With who?'

'Angie Wraxton. They wanted to sleep out, and I took up mattresses for them and then they made tea, and we stayed talking for quite a long time. And then, when they turned in, it was so pleasant I stayed a bit and fell asleep.'

'Angie Wraxton? You mean the maniac?' asked Robin.

'She's not a maniac. She's a very intelligent girl.'

'What in heaven's name did you talk about?' asked Duff.

'About Africa. I told them about the Kenya opening, and they both thought it sounded marvellous. They couldn't think why I didn't jump at it.'

Gerry pulled his shirt over his head with a very well-satisfied expression. Never before in his life had he been allowed to talk so much about himself, and it had been pleasant to have two women fussing over him.

'I told them I haven't finally turned it down,' he added.

Robin and Duff became pensive. They both knew that the African post—that of medical officer in a big district—would not bring enough to pay their school fees, though it had good prospects of future advancement. And for that reason the whole family had assumed that Gerry would certainly refuse it.

Neither of them spoke another word. Gerry finished undressing, put on his pyjamas, switched off the light and got into bed. Silence fell upon the stables.

TUESDAY

1. Stubs

The garden room was on the ground floor and had French windows opening into a small rose garden. Miss Ellis said that she could not fancy it. Anybody might walk in.

Next thing, thought Nancibel, stripping the bed, she'll be saying that somebody *has* walked in.

Miss Ellis did so, and Nancibel laughed.

'You think it's a laughing matter, do you?' said Miss Ellis. 'I don't. I think it's disgusting. If you knew the world like I do, if you'd seen as much of the seamy side . . . women of that age can be *awful*.'

'Making hay in the twilight,' agreed Nancibel. 'That's what Mum calls it.'

'That's her typewriter,' said Miss Ellis, peering at it. 'Supposed to write books or something, isn't she?'

'She does write books. She's a famous authoress. Didn't you know?'

'Who told you?'

'Everybody knows. My sister Myra read one of her books. *The Lost Plaid* it was called. She was all excited last night when I told them at home we've got Mrs. Lechene stopping here.'

'*The Lost Plaid*? That's a funny name.'

'They do have funny names.'

'Is it Scotch, then?'

'I wouldn't know. It was Myra read it. But it's a bestseller. She said it was a bit . . . you know . . . blue. But a fascinating story.'

'Blue?' said Miss Ellis. 'I'm not surprised. A bestseller is always like that, or else it attacks somebody.'

'Well,' said Nancibel, 'I read a bestseller once, *The Good Companions*, and it wasn't blue and it didn't attack anybody either. It was lovely.'

'That just shows how ignorant you are, Nancibel. Everybody knows that's an attack on J. B. Priestley. It was written simply to show him up. You're putting that counterpane on crooked.'

'It's not easy for one person to get it straight.'

Miss Ellis ignored the hint and stared enviously at the typewriter.

'Some people have all the luck,' she said. 'Fancy her making thousands and thousands of pounds, just for writing nonsense. What can she want with all that money? I've a good mind to write a book myself.'

'Why don't you, then?'

'When do I get the time?'

She turned away and picked up the ash tray from the bed table. After one glance at it her expression changed from disgust to something very like pleasure. She carried it across to the window, scrutinized its contents, and exclaimed:

'I thought as much! Look at that!'

She held it out to Nancibel, who only saw a lot of cigarette stubs.

'Haven't you eyes, Nancibel?'

'She smokes a terrible lot.'

'Yes, but look! Don't you see something funny about these stubs?'

'Some's yellow and some's white.'

'The yellow ones are her special brand of Egyptian. Like those in that box on the mantelpiece. She gets them from some place in London. She never smokes anything else. She said so in the dining room last night. The white ones are Player's Weights. Look! You can see . . . here's one only half smoked.'

There was a pause. Nancibel grew very pale. Miss Ellis continued:

'I emptied that tray last night, when I took round the hot-water cans. After ten o'clock. Somebody's been in here for hours on end since then. Know anybody who smokes Player's Weights?'

'Lots of people do.'

'Not here. But I'm not surprised. I knew it when I saw them together at dinner. Chauffeur! I thought. That's very likely. Come along, we've all the upstairs beds to make.'

'I haven't,' said Nancibel. 'I'll make no more beds with you, Miss Ellis. I've had enough. I warned you yesterday. I can't stand your way of talking. I'm going to Mrs. Siddal.'

'If anybody goes to Mrs. Siddal, I shall. There are limits . . .'

'There certainly are. I'm tired of hearing everybody scandalized behind their back. You're nothing but a mean, spiteful old woman that's got your knife into everybody better than yourself, and that means everybody in the house, because you're the lowest class of person in it. You never did a decent job of work in your life, I believe. You couldn't if you tried; you're so dumb you couldn't put a kettle on the fire without spilling half of it and blacking your nose. It burns me all up . . .'

'Straight to Mrs. Siddal. I go straight to Mrs. Siddal. Either you leave this house or I do.'

'O.K. Trot along and see which of us she can spare best.'

Miss Ellis rushed out of the room.

As soon as she had gone Nancibel burst into desolate tears. She knew who smoked Player's Weights. And she knew, now, what Anna had meant to convey by that long stare yesterday. There had been so many little things which she had thought funny: now she understood them all. Bruce was a rotten bad lot. He was living on this horrible old woman, whom he did not love, did not even desire in the most perfunctory way. He had sold himself for a silk dressing gown and that wallet full of notes which he brandished at the Harbour Café.

There were all the upstairs bedrooms still to be done, but for the moment she could not face them. She ran out through the French windows into the garden and hid herself among the rhododendrons until she could control her tears, a little astonished at the immensity of her own bitterness. For she had not taken him very seriously; they had only been acquainted for three days, and she had begun by disliking him. But yesterday he had been so nice, helping with the potatoes and the pumping. He had made her feel young and merry again. When she went off duty he had walked home with her, and her mother had asked him in for a cup of tea. Everyone had been charmed with him. His manner to her parents had been perfect—friendly and cheerful, with just the right hint of respect. He had made them all laugh with a story of his own mother's retort to the girl in the Food Office. There had been no nonsense about slums. No young man could have made a better impression, and Nancibel's only trouble had been a fear lest her mother's satisfaction might be too obviously displayed. As soon as he had gone she had been quite sharp with poor Mrs. Thomas for making such a fuss of him, and had shrugged derisively at the suggestion that he might take her out dancing on Saturday night. But in her heart she had already determined that he should and on Thursday, which was her half day, she meant to have a perm in honour of it.

Beyond Saturday she had not allowed herself to think. There would be time enough, later, to get serious, if her liking for him increased at its present impetus. It was quite enough to want to go dancing once more, to be looking forward to Saturday, and to think a new perm worth while. Yet now she was crying as she had never cried in her life, even for Brian. For she had always known that she would in time recover from the pain that Brian had caused her. But this wound had poison in it. In getting used to the idea that Bruce was a rotten bad lot she must become a harder, colder person. So she went and sobbed among the rhododendrons, not for him, but for the Nancibel of yesterday.

2. Black Amber

Sir Henry kept his promise and went over to Porthmerryn with Robin immediately after breakfast to look at Mrs. Pearce's carved figure. But a disappointment awaited them. The trinket had been sold. A lady had called and bought it on Monday afternoon—a foreign lady, a Mrs. Smith, who said that she was passing through the town and that another lady had told her of Mrs. Pearce's curio. Only three guineas had she offered at first, but Mrs. Pearce had been too sharp for her and had stood out for five pounds ten shillings.

'For Robin, he told me it were worth five pounds,' she chuckled, 'and I got ten shillings over and above that. I was too sharp for her, I b'lieve.'

She was unable to describe the lady, not being able to see so well as she used.

'But she had a short way of speaking. I didn't take to her, and that's the truth. But five pound ten is a lot of money . . . I'm very sorry, I'm sure, sir, that you should have come too late to see it.'

'So am I,' said Sir Henry. 'What made you think she was foreign?'

'Mrs. Pearce means that she wasn't Cornish,' explained Robin mournfully.

'She was from London Church Town,' said Mrs. Pearce. 'She said she come from London. And gone back there today. For I had it in mind, first of all, to wait until I could ask my grandson, Barny Thomas, up to Pendizack, if he'd be agreeable, seeing as it's he that'll get my bits of things when I'm gone. But no, she couldn't wait for that. It's take it or leave it, says she, for I'm going back to London tomorrow, she says. And five pound ten is a deal of money.'

Robin's lamentations broke out as soon as they had left the cottage. He was heartbroken. His ruddy face was quite pale. He would not console himself with the hope, suggested by Sir Henry, that the piece might not, after all, have been black amber. He was quite sure that it was and that Mrs. Pearce had lost a thousand pounds.

'Do you think,' he asked, 'that it would be any good to advertise? If this Mrs. Smith knew what it's worth . . . she probably hasn't the least idea . . .'

'I shouldn't be too sure of that,' said Sir Henry.

'Oh, but she couldn't! Nobody could be so mean. A poor old woman, afraid of having to go to the workhouse!'

'I don't suppose Mrs. Smith knew that.'

'I can't think how she knew anything about it at all. Who can have told her that Mrs. Pearce had this piece?'

'Plenty of people heard you talking about it in the shop yesterday.'

'I never said where she lived.'

Sir Henry tried to remember who had been in the sweet shop, and a sudden suspicion flickered across his mind. But it shocked him so much that he hastily dismissed it and concentrated upon other possibilities. He remembered that Robin had taken the three little Coves to see Mrs. Pearce.

It was possible that they had talked about the carving. He suggested this to Robin, who agreed that they had seen it and said he would question them as soon as he got home.

They walked back over the cliffs to Pendizack, each occupied with his own thoughts. Robin meditated an enquiry at all the hotels in Porthmerryn for a Mrs. Smith, returned that day to London. He was determined to get the carving back, for his mind misgave him that his own indiscretion had been inexcusable. He would track this woman down. If she was honest he would buy the piece back from her; he had seven pounds in his Savings Bank account. If she was dishonest he would write a letter to *John Bull* about it. He would proclaim her infamy to the uttermost ends of the earth.

Sir Henry was trying not to think that Mrs. Cove probably had it. She had overheard Robin in the sweet shop. She had a short way of speaking. She was a mean, grasping woman; the episode of the marshmallows proved that. He did not like her at all. But he felt that he had no business to suspect her of anything quite so outrageous; the use of a false name, and the lie about her return to London, would preclude all hope that she had been acting in good faith.

'There are the Coves,' said Robin suddenly.

He pointed to Pendizack sands which had just come into view. Blanche, Maud and Beatrix were kneeling in a bunch, their heads close together, intent upon some game.

'It looks like them,' agreed Sir Henry, peering.

'It is them. Nobody else wears gym tunics on the beach.'

They turned off the cliff and went down towards the

beach. As they got nearer they saw that the girls were busy on a sand castle. It was not a mere mound but an exquisitely finished little fairy tale castle of a peculiar triangular shape, with tall, thin towers. They were carving a long causeway over a moat with an old table knife, working very swiftly and in complete silence. It seemed as though their bony little hands were impelled by some communal inspiration, for there was no discussion or consultation, and no one child appeared to be the architect; yet their creation was perfect—in detail, proportion and design.

'How lovely!' said Sir Henry.

The Coves, startled, sat back on their haunches and looked at him. Their castle was much more real to them than he was.

'French, isn't it?'

'Poitiers,' said Blanche, nodding.

'Have you been there?'

'No. It's in a book.'

'*The Very Rich Hours of the Duke of Berry*,' said Maud.

'Oh yes, of course! I thought I recognized it. There's a very good Vernet book of reproductions. Have you got it, then?'

'We wanted to ask you . . .' began Robin.

But Sir Henry checked him and pursued an oblique approach. For there was something which he wanted to find out on his own account.

'You're very fond of books, aren't you?' he said.

The three fair heads nodded.

'Have you got many?'

They looked doubtful.

'We have seventeen books,' said Beatrix at last.

'Do you often buy them?'

They had no difficulty in answering this. They had never, they assured him, bought a book.

'But we would if we had the money,' said Maud.

'Your mother buys them for you?'

No. They were quite sure that she did not.

'When did you last get a new book?'

'When we had measles,' said Blanche, after some pondering. 'The doctor gave us *Uncle Tom's Cabin*.'

'When was that? How long ago?'

'It was when peace broke out,' said Maud. 'We couldn't go to the rejoicings because we had measles.'

Two years! So much, he thought, for that woman's story of selling sweets to buy books. The mean liar!

'We got *The Very Rich Hours* because of the Flying Bomb,' said Blanche. 'An old gentleman gave it to us. He had a book shop.'

'Yes,' said Maud. 'We were sent on a walk to the Common and we heard it coming so we ran into his shop and got under the counter. We heard it cut out and it came down just outside. And the next thing we were all buried under books. So we stayed all the afternoon helping him get it straight. And he gave us *The Very Rich Hours* because the back was torn off.'

'And he gave us sherry,' said Blanche. 'Oh, he was nice. But the milkman told our mother we were dead. He was further down the road and he saw us just before; and he flattened out when he heard it coming and didn't see us run into the shop. So afterwards when he looked and we weren't there he thought we'd all been blown to bits.'

'He went off and told our mother we'd been blown to bits,' said Beatrix. 'And of course we didn't come home, because we stayed so late helping with the books; we didn't realize how late it was. So she thought it was true and went in a taxi to the Town Hall. So it was a waste of three shillings.'

Robin and Sir Henry were so stunned by this narrative that they almost forgot why they had come.

'It was more than three shillings,' said Maud solemnly. 'There was the fare back, when she had notified the Town Hall.'

'That was only twopence,' said Beatrix. 'She came back in a bus.'

'Of course the Town Hall couldn't tell her anything about us,' explained Maud. 'We weren't in the mortuary.'

'But wasn't your mother frightfully upset?' asked Robin.

'Oh very!' said Maud. 'You see she was still out when we got back so we couldn't get into the house. And the people next door saw us on the doorstep. And the milkman had told them we were dead too. So they came rushing out and quite a crowd collected. And when she came back there was quite a crowd, and when they saw her they started yelling: "It's all right! They're safe!" And she doesn't like the people next door; they're very inquisitive. So she couldn't get the door unlocked, because her key stuck. And a man took a photograph of her and sent it to the newspaper.'

'And she said,' continued Beatrix, 'would they kindly go away and cease from trespassing in her garden. So the people from next door started to be very rude. But just then another fly bomb came over and everybody did go away as fast as they could.'

'But it was one of the very happiest days in our lives,' said Blanche, 'because we got *The Very Rich Hours*.'

The more I hear of that woman, thought Sir Henry, the less I like her.

'We've just been to see old Mrs. Pearce,' he said.

They all beamed at him, and Blanche asked if he had seen the little ship.

'Yes. It's beautiful, isn't it? But I had very much wanted to see another treasure she had.'

'Did you . . . ?' interrupted Robin.

Sir Henry again silenced him with a gesture, and continued:

'A little black carved figure. Did you see it when you were there?'

'The one she kept in the tureen?' asked Maud.

'Yes. I wanted to see it, but I couldn't, because she sold it yesterday afternoon.'

'It wasn't as pretty as the ship,' said Blanche consolingly.

'No. But I'm sorry she sold it because it might have been very valuable, and the person who bought it gave very little for it.'

'I'm sure she'll never sell the ship,' said Blanche.

'I hope she won't. Robin and I both think that it would be better not to talk about it too much. It isn't a good thing if an old woman, living alone, is known to have valuable things.'

They all nodded wisely at this, and Maud whispered:

'Robbers!'

'So don't tell anyone about Mrs. Pearce's things, will you?'

They promised that they never would.

'Did you mention the ship or the little figure to anyone yesterday?'

'Lots of people . . .' began Blanche, looking concerned.

'But only the ship,' put in Maud. 'We forgot about the little figure.'

'Yes,' said Blanche, 'I only remembered that when you said about it. But we told everyone about the ship . . . the Giffords, and Mrs. Paley and Miss Wraxton and our mother, and we wrote a description of it in our diary. We never thought of robbers. Shall we tell everyone not to tell?'

'No,' said Sir Henry. 'Don't worry. But don't mention it to anyone else.'

He walked off, followed by Robin.

'I think they were speaking the truth,' he said, as soon as they were out of earshot.

'I'm sure they were,' said Robin. 'But I had an idea . . . when they were talking . . . you don't think . . . could it possibly be Mrs. Cove herself?'

'I think it's more than likely,' said Sir Henry. 'But I don't see how in the world it's ever going to be brought home to her.'

3. Getting Experience

Half the morning went by and Nancibel did not appear in the stables to make Bruce's bed. He had hung about in the yard, after he had washed the car, in the hope of a pleasant interlude. But she did not come, and at last he went in search of her. He looked in at the kitchen window and saw her standing by the table, peeling potatoes in an oddly dispirited way. To his gay greeting she made no reply.

'When are you coming to do my room?' he asked.

'Fred will do it,' she replied coldly, her face still averted. 'The work has been rearranged.'

'What's the matter?'

She did not answer. So he went round through the back door and the scullery into the kitchen, and planted himself in front of her.

'What's happened?'

She looked at him then. She gave him one brief glance before returning to the potatoes.

'Oh,' he said, 'I see.'

There was a long silence which neither of them was willing to break. Nancibel dared not speak lest she should burst out crying again. Bruce found himself, unexpectedly, with very little to say. He had thought that he was prepared for this crisis, and he had already rehearsed his own defence. For he had known that it was inevitable, sooner or later.

She was bound to find out, and when she did she was bound to be angry. But he had expected a tirade of reproach and abuse, and this mournful silence was disconcerting. It stung him at last into saying the worst thing he could possibly have said.

'Jealous?' he enquired.

He would have done anything to recall the word as soon as it was out of his mouth. Only a thorough-paced rotter would have made such a suggestion. And his whole intention had been to convince her that he was not a rotter but an artist getting experience.

It galvanized Nancibel, however. It dried her tears and loosened her tongue.

'Please get out of this kitchen,' she commanded. 'You've no business here, and Mrs. Siddal wouldn't like it.'

'I'm a servant, aren't I? The kitchen's my place, isn't it?'

'No. You eat in the dining room, so your place is in the lounge.'

'You let me sit in here yesterday.'

'I didn't know you were that kind of boy.'

'What kind of boy?'

'You get off to the lounge and tell them how you rose up out of a slum. Ladies may stand for it. I don't have to. I think you are disgusting.'

'You've got very old-fashioned ideas, Nancibel.'

'No, I haven't. Some things don't go out of fashion. Everybody has always despised a boy that lives off an old woman, and they always will.'

'She's not old.'

'Twenty years older than you, if she's a day. You wouldn't look at her if she didn't pay you.'

'I drive her car.'

'Very hard work, I'm sure. Well . . . if you drove a bus you could sit in this kitchen. There's a shortage of bus drivers. I don't wonder you were ashamed to say you came from a decent home.'

'You don't understand,' protested Bruce. 'A writer has to have experiences . . .'

'I daresay. Well, you're having one now. You're getting the experience that a girl like me doesn't have any use for a boy like you. If you didn't know that before you've learnt something useful, and you can put it in a book.'

'I damn well will put it in a book.'

'Yes. When you've altered it a bit so's to make it sound better. You'd never dare to put anything in a book that was quite true. Look what you've put in your book about you and her! That she was beautiful and aristocratic! *Her* beautiful and aristocratic! It's enough to make a cat laugh!'

'You're plain, downright jealous and that's all there is to it.'

'You say you want to be somebody. You'll never be anything but a wretched little show-off that everybody despises and laughs at behind your back.'

Mr. Siddal appeared at the kitchen door, plaintively demanding his elevenses. Perceiving that some drama was afoot he came into the room and sat down at the table. His innocent eye strayed from one furious young face to the other, and he concluded that the boy had been getting the worst of the argument.

Nancibel went to the teapot on the stove and brought him a cup. He told her to give Bruce one too, which she did before taking herself off, with her potatoes, to the scullery.

'I hear you're writing a book,' said Siddal genially, as he pushed the sugar bowl across to Bruce. 'A novel. Mainly autobiographical, I suppose?'

'No,' said Bruce loudly.

'No? That's unusual. That's interesting. Anna's young . . . *protégés* generally write three books. The first is on the little victim theme. It has promise. It is well written. It gets astonishingly good reviews. It is very frank and tells how their childhood has been warped, either in a preparatory school or a public school, or both, or else in Wapping or on Cold Comfort Farm. At secondary and grammar schools they don't seem to go in for warping children nearly so extensively. I don't know why. The hero of your novel now . . . was he warped at Eton or in Stepney?'

'Stepney.'

'H'm . . . yes. I see. Well . . . the next book on the list doesn't have to be so tragic. It's a comedy, a bitter comedy, and very *mondain*. With a continental background. It deals with the vicious and corrupt lives led by expatriots in Capri or Majorca or the Maritime Alps. The hero is the biggest bum of the lot, but he has the saving grace of being able to despise himself nearly as much as he despises everyone else. The heroine is the only woman in the book with whom the hero does not sleep. She sometimes dies rather pathetically.'

Siddal paused to stir his tea, and Bruce could not restrain himself from asking what the third book was about.

'The third book?' Siddal seemed to start out of a reverie. 'Nobody knows. Nobody has ever read it. One hears that it has been written. I think it gets published. But I've never been able to get hold of one. So I can't tell you. It's one of the things I hope to do before I die—to read a third book by one of Anna's young friends. I can't think what they can be about; religion, possibly. If you ever get as far as a third book, I do hope you'll send it to me. More tea?'

'No, thank you,' said Bruce.

4. The Other Cliffs

A frieze of Gifford children appeared for a moment on the skyline. They were running across the cliffs which rose immediately behind the house, and this glimpse of them reminded Sir Henry of a question he had been meaning to ask ever since Sunday afternoon, when he had been up there himself.

This part of the coast, known locally as The Other Cliffs, and on the Ordnance Survey map as Tregoylan Rocks, was much less frequented than the more accessible slopes leading to Pendizack Point, Rosigraille Cove and Porthmerryn. To reach them it was necessary to go far inland, almost to the village, in order to skirt the deep ravine which ran down beside the Pendizack drive. The ravine ended in a narrow creek, immediately below the back of the house, and the Other Cliffs rose to a great height on the far side of this creek so that the back windows looked out upon an overhanging wall of rock. The whole peninsular, upon which the house was built, must have fallen from this rock face into the bay in some prehistoric time.

The cliffs, at the top, were covered with a mass of blackthorn, bramble and gorse which had quite obliterated the old coastguards' paths, so that walking there was not pleasant. But Sir Henry had gone there in order to escape from the atmosphere of catastrophe which had enveloped

Pendizack on Sunday afternoon; and, while he was fighting his way through the gorse, he came upon some curious cracks and fissures in the ground. They were quite far inland, but they had raised in his mind a doubt as to the safety of the whole area, and he now asked Robin about it.

Robin said that they had been there since the mine exploded, the mine which had been washed up into the cave at the end of the creek, just before Christmas. He could not say if the cracks had appeared immediately, for he had not seen them himself until the Easter holidays, when he and Duff discovered them. He fancied that somebody had been to inspect them; his mother had mentioned in a letter, during the summer term, that somebody had appeared and asked the way to the cracks. He did not know what the verdict had been, and when they reached the terrace he asked Gerry, who was mending a striped umbrella.

'What cracks?' asked Gerry, lifting a crimson face from his task.

The cause of his embarrassment was obvious, for an angry roar, proceeding from an open window on the first floor, made conversation on the terrace quite difficult.

'. . . Do you realize that I've been waiting for you all the morning? I want to dictate some letters. Where have you been? Oh! . . . For heaven's sake, speak up! *Where have you been?*'

'You know!' shouted Robin. 'The mine cracks. On the Other Cliffs.'

'. . . Can't answer the simplest question. I tell you plainly I sometimes think I ought to have you certified . . .'

'Never heard of them,' shouted Gerry.

'Didn't Mother write about them? We found them at Easter. They're up among the brambles . . . long cracks about six inches wide . . .'

'Six inches?' put in Sir Henry. 'Why . . . the ones I saw were a yard wide or more. And seemed to go very deep.'

'Then they must have grown,' said Robin. 'I've not been up there since Easter.'

'. . . Well, never mind! Never mind! You're back now. And you'll oblige me by a prompt answer to this question: *Where did you sleep last night* . . . ?'

Gerry began to look quite agonized and made no further attempt to understand about the cracks.

'Ask Mother,' he said, 'I know nothing about it.'

'. . . Who told me? That slut of a housekeeper told me . . . What's her name . . . Ellis. I'd hoped she was lying . . .'

'Sir Somebody Bevin came over, or somebody like that. Surely Mother told you,' persisted Robin.

'. . . Been at it again, have you? I thought I'd put a stop to that sort of thing. While you live in my house you'll behave decently. Yes, even if I have to lock you up! Creeping out of the house at night like a . . .'

'Mother never tells me anything,' yelled Gerry furiously. 'Ask Duff. Perhaps he'll know. She writes to him.'

'. . . Who is it this time? I mean to find out. Make no mistake about that. So you might as well save time by speaking up. Who is he? . . . *Mrs. Paley?* . . . You're a fool, Evangeline, as I know to my cost. But you can't be quite such a fool as to expect me to believe that . . .'

'I'll ask your mother some time, when she's not busy,' said Sir Henry, retreating into the house.

Gerry abandoned the umbrella and began to collect his tools. He felt that the terrace was unbearable. He scowled at Robin, who was listening with horrified attention.

'. . . Ask her? I certainly shall ask her. And I shall tell her what she ought to have seen for herself . . . I'd have thought it was only too apparent to everybody, after the exhibition you made of yourself in church . . .'

'I say, Gerry! He *is* an old . . .'

'Shut up and come away.'

As they left the terrace the voice pursued them:

'. . . Only one alternative . . . to put you under some kind of restraint . . .'

Robin went to the kitchen, where he found his mother and Duff. He began immediately to tell the sad story of the black amber and he was in the middle of it when Gerry, who had gone to put away the tools, joined them in a belated fit of anxiety about the cracks on the Other Cliffs.

'What cracks are they?' demanded Gerry. 'Where are they? Why wasn't I told?'

He had to repeat these questions several times before anyone would listen to him. But at last Mrs. Siddal said:

'They're all right. Sir Humphrey Bevin heard about them and came to look at them.'

'When?'

'Some time in May, I think.'

'Why wasn't I told?'

'Why should you be told?' said Robin, who was annoyed at the interruption to his story.

'Did he say the cliff was safe?' asked Gerry.

'He'd surely have said if it wasn't,' said Mrs. Siddal.

But Gerry was not satisfied.

'He mightn't have said so to us. We don't own those cliffs. How do we know it's safe to walk on them? Perhaps we ought to warn people not to go up there. I think we ought to find out.'

'Old fuss pot,' muttered Robin.

And Mrs. Siddal exclaimed:

'I do wish you wouldn't fuss about everything so, Gerry. I've got quite enough on my mind as it is. Miss Ellis has gone on strike because I won't sack Nancibel.'

Gerry shrugged his shoulders and went out to oil the engine of the boat. This was kept at the top of a slipway cut in the rocks above the creek at the back of the house, and it could be launched when the tide was high, on a calm day.

Nobody ever went to the creek unless they wanted the boat, for it was not attractive. The towering mass of cliff kept it in shadow for the greater part of the day, even in summer. The rocks, never dried by the sun, were slippery and slimy, and covered with bright green weed where the little stream came down. Occasional spaces of coarse sand were always dimpled, at low tide, by great drops of moisture falling at regular intervals from the cliff above. And there was a smell of rotting weed.

Gerry shivered as he pulled the boat out from under its little tarpaulin roof. He had never liked the Other Cliffs, and today it seemed to him that they were looking un-usually black and grim. He supposed at first that this must be a fancy, but, when he took a second glance at them, he realized it to be a fact. They were blacker than they had ever been before because there were no gulls there. In other years this whole cliff face had been a famous nesting place; every crevice and ledge had been splashed white with their droppings. Generations of chicks had taken their first swim in the creek, pushed callously off the lower rocks by their parents. Now there was not a gull to be seen. Patches of discoloration showed where former nests had been, but there were no recent ones.

He could not remember that such a thing had ever hap-pened before. And an uneasy inference was beginning to take shape in his mind when the door from the house flew open and Evangeline Wraxton came running down the steps to the creek.

Had he not known the cause of her distress he must have thought her crazy, for she was grimacing and muttering to herself like a lunatic. She did not see him until she was half-way down the steps; when she did she turned and started to run up again. But he called to her to stop. He did not want her to go rushing about the house in this manner, giving further proofs of mental instability to anyone who should catch sight of her.

'Stay here,' he commanded. 'Sit on the doorstep where it's sunny. I'm only oiling the boat. I shan't be a minute. And then you can have the place to yourself.'

She obeyed him. He turned his back on her and busied

himself with his oil can, but he could feel that her agitation was subsiding. Presently she sighed and said:

'I didn't know the boat had an engine.'

She pronounced it *ingine*, like a little girl, and Gerry smiled. He had already been aware of a touchingly childish quality that she had; he had felt it during the tea party in the shelter last night on the cliffs. Encouraged by Mrs. Paley she had been happy and at ease; the spinsterish mannerisms, the jerky movements, had vanished. She talked and laughed freely, and did not mind when they teased her. But she was like a very charming little girl—a child who had never been allowed to grow up. This tender creature had remained hidden and protected behind the battered front which she presented to an unkind world. And he had felt, dimly, that there was a certain valour in this refusal, at any rate, to grow up crooked. It was as though she was still wisely waiting for the climate to grow more propitious.

'I thought you were on the terrace,' she said presently.

'I was,' he agreed. 'I was mending the umbrella.'

He paused, pondered, and then added:

'I couldn't help hearing some of what your father was saying. I'm so very sorry.'

She made a variety of grimaces before she could reply. But at last she burst out:

'It's not true! I used to sleep badly, and I felt better if I got up and went for a walk. He found out and thought I was going to meet some . . . some man. But it's not true. I wasn't. I . . . I don't know any men.'

'Has he forbidden you to go out with Mrs. Paley again?'

'Oh yes. And he says he'll shut me up in an asylum if I do.'

'That's rot, you know. He can't, without a doctor's certificate.'

'He might get one. If he brought a doctor to me I should be so frightened I should be sure to do something silly. And a lot of people do think I'm mad.'

'No qualified doctor would,' declared Gerry.

'You're a qualified doctor, and I'm sure you did . . . on Sunday.'

This was disconcerting. The dangers of her situation began to be more clearly apparent to him.

'You should get away,' he said. 'Why do you stay with him?'

Evangeline explained her rash vow. He argued with her until the luncheon gong roared inside the house. Evangeline grew very white.

'I can't go in,' she whispered. 'I can't go into the dining room. Everybody heard. I'm sure they did.'

Gerry stood up and wiped his oily hands on a piece of rag.

'Wait a minute,' he said, 'and I'll bring you some lunch out here.'

He ran up into the house. In a few minutes he was back again with a tray. He had snatched up two plates of cold tongue and salad, two rolls and four large plums from the serving-room hatch.

'We can eat our lunch here,' he said, sitting down beside her on the sunny step. 'And then we'll go fishing. Would you like to go fishing?'

Evangeline's heart leapt with pleasure and then sank to extreme depths, as she became convinced that he had only asked her because he was sorry for her. She said mournfully that she would like to go fishing very much indeed. Gerry's heart sank too, for he regretted the invitation even as he gave it. He had meant to get an afternoon in the boat, all by himself, away from his exasperating family; and now he had saddled himself with this depressing girl. He was extremely sorry for her, but he had, after all, troubles enough of his own. Sometimes he felt that his father would drive him crazy, and *he* did not rush about making faces.

He grew more and more morose as the meal proceeded. Evangeline's timid little attempts at gaiety were not encouraged. As they finished their plums she said:

'I think, perhaps, that I won't come after all. Thank you very much for asking me. The . . . the sun on the water might make my head ache.'

Gerry knew that this was a lie and that she wanted to come. But he was, by now, so sulky that he made no attempt to dissuade her.

'I'll take the tray in,' she said, getting up.

She sounded so meek and humble that Gerry was infuriated. He said certainly not, snatched it from her, and hurried into the house. Evangeline followed him, protesting miserably:

'I could perfectly well . . . it's silly . . . I don't see why I shouldn't . . .'

In the kitchen passage they met Mrs. Siddal, who looked at them as though they were the last straw. When Gerry explained what they had been doing, she exclaimed:

'So that's where those two helpings went! And I've been scolding poor Fred. Really, Gerry . . . I can't think what possessed you to do such a thing. To take the dining room lunches . . .'

'One of them was Angie's anyhow,' protested Gerry.

'*Whose?*'

'Miss Wraxton's! One of them would eventually have been given to her in the dining room, wouldn't it?'

Angie? thought Mrs. Siddal. He calls her Angie? Oh, the sly creature! And she glared at Evangeline.

'I really can't have people walking off with their lunches like that,' she told them. 'I'm always ready to cut sandwiches if I'm asked.'

'I'm so sorry, Mrs. Siddal . . .'

'I'm very sorry, Mother. It was entirely my fault. I suggested we should have lunch on the rocks. I didn't know there was any rule against it.'

'But you weren't having tongue for lunch, Gerry. That was only for the dining room. You've eaten Canon Wraxton's tongue. What can I give him for lunch?'

'Can't you give him whatever I was going to have?'

'No. It was only bread and cheese.'

Mr. Siddal, who had been listening to all this from behind the boot-room door, now intervened and called out:

'Duff's getting tongue, Gerry. Give the Canon Duff's tongue.'

'There wasn't enough for everybody,' explained Mrs. Siddal. 'And it's all very hard on poor Fred. I blamed him.'

'Fred's getting tongue,' cried the voice from the boot room. 'And Nancibel is getting tongue.'

'Well, I'm very sorry,' said Gerry again. 'We were going fishing, and . . .'

'Going fishing? In the boat?'

'Of course we're going in the boat, Mother. And Angie . . .'

'But not this afternoon, surely, dear. I . . . I really can't spare you. Miss Ellis has given notice. Perhaps . . . some other day, if Miss Wraxton really wants you to take her in the boat . . .'

'I don't,' muttered Evangeline.

'You asked me yourself,' protested Gerry, 'to try and catch you some mackerel for supper.'

'I know. But I can manage. I'd rather you stayed here.'

'But what do you want me for?'

There was a pause. Mrs. Siddal could not, for the moment, think of anything, though she was determined to stop the fishing scheme. The voice from the boot-hole was heard to suggest that she wanted Gerry to catch a mouse, and she was too much flurried to be aware of any sarcasm.

'Yes,' she said, brightening. 'There has been a mouse. In the pantry.'

Gerry lost his temper.

'Borrow Hebe's cat,' he said. 'Come along, Angie. The tide will be just right by now.'

He strode out of the house and down the steps followed by Evangeline, who saw that now he really wanted her to come.

'I'm getting just about sick of it,' he muttered as they pushed the boat down the slipway.

'You can't think . . .' he exclaimed, as they went chugging out of the creek, '. . . nobody could ever imagine what I have to put up with. All this fuss because I want to take you out fishing.'

'You didn't want to,' said Evangeline, 'until there was a fuss.'

He looked at her, a little startled.

'Well,' he said at last, 'I do now.'

'So you really ought to be grateful for the fuss,' she pointed out. 'But we'd better fish, hadn't we? I mean, if we don't catch enough mackerel for supper I don't see how we can ever dare to come back.'

They fished, cruising up and down outside Pendizack and Rosigraille coves. In less than two hours they had caught twenty-seven mackerel.

5. Dead Man's Rock

Their progress was observed by the Paleys, who were sitting in their usual niche, a hollow on the headland looking towards Rosigraille Point. Nothing could have pleased Mrs. Paley more, for it was plain, even at that distance, that they were enjoying themselves. She had already wondered if she could not persuade them to take some little jaunt together, and now they had done so without any persuasion, apparently, from anybody. For it did not occur to her that Gerry's mother might have supplied the impetus.

And in Africa, she surmised (for in her opinion they were already as good as married and despatched overseas), in Africa they will get a lot of fishing, so the sooner she learns how to manage a motor boat the better. But will they? Why do I think that Africa is full of enormous rivers? The Zambesi . . . Perhaps their part will be swamps and crocodiles; too dangerous. And then there is the veldt. That's dry. We must get him to tell us some more about Kenya. But whatever it's like they'll enjoy it. Neither of them has ever had any fun. They'll never get over the pleasure of being first with somebody . . . of being cherished and considered . . .

The boat chugged out of sight round Rosigraille Point. But she did not think that it had gone far for she could hear the noise of the engine now and then.

She asked her husband for information about Kenya. He looked up from the *Times Literary Supplement* and gave it to her. It was the sort of thing which he could be relied upon to do, for he had a retentive memory and he liked to accumulate facts. He gave her a concise account of Kenya, its history, geography, fauna, flora, products and population.

'It sounds nice,' said Mrs. Paley when he had finished.

He waited for a moment in case she should wish to know anything more, and then went back to his paper.

'Gerry Siddal thinks of going there,' she explained. 'He's been offered a job there.'

Mr. Paley looked up, but said nothing, though his expression conveyed a faint bewilderment, as if wondering what he was expected to say.

'Don't you think he'd better go?' asked Mrs. Paley.

'I'm not sure which one he is. Not the one who has just got a Balliol scholarship?'

'No. That's Duff; the good-looking one. Gerry is the little spotty one who does all the chores. He's a doctor.'

'How should I know whether he'd better go or not?' demanded Mr. Paley. 'I expect he had. England is no place nowadays for a young man who wants to stand on his own feet. If I were his age I should emigrate.'

'Where to?' asked Mrs. Paley, pleased at having established something so nearly resembling a conversation.

But he did not seem to know. It was easier to him to speak of shaking the dust of Britain off his feet than to accept the dust of any other country.

'I think China would be rather nice,' mused Mrs. Paley.

'Not just now, I expect. But I've always liked the idea of China.'

And she sat for a while in the sunshine smiling at her idea of China. For she knew it to be fantastic and ridiculous, founded upon the memory of a screen which she had admired as a small child. At the bottom of China there was a lake and people fishing from frail boats amid curiously curved rocks. Then, after a layer of clouds, another landscape began. A procession went up a mountain path towards a kind of shrine. After more clouds the mountain tops emerged and some birds flying.

The afternoon sun sparkled in a myriad diamonds on the sea in Rosigraille Cove, so that she had to shut her eyes against the glare. It was very quiet. No waves fell on the beach and round the rocks there was only the faintest whisper and gurgle of water. For twenty minutes or more this murmurous peace was unbroken save for the occasional scream of a gull, and then she heard voices calling on the beach. She opened her eyes and saw some children scrambling over the boulders towards Rosigraille Point. It was the three Coves and Hebe, and they were all carrying bathing towels.

They had chosen a bad time to bathe, she thought, for the tide was rising and the hard sandy floor would be out of their depth. They would have to splash about among the boulders at high water mark, since the little Coves could not swim.

She watched them as they scrambled steadily along towards the far side of Rosigraille, and then, glancing up at the cliff, she saw that somebody else was watching. A small, active, dark-clad person was standing on the path which led over to Porthmerryn. Mrs. Paley had good eyes, but she picked up her husband's field glasses to make sure.

Yes, it was Mrs. Cove. The glasses revealed her face distinctly—they even revealed her expression which was, in itself, a revelation. Its uncontrolled bitterness, as she watched the children down on the beach, gave Mrs. Paley quite a shock. For the face which she showed to the world, though disagreeable, was watchful and guarded. Now that she was alone, now that she believed herself to be unobserved, the guard was lowered. She was looking at Blanche, Maud and Beatrix, not with her customary calm indifference, but with unmistakable dislike.

After a few seconds Mrs. Paley turned her glasses upon the children. They had not paused upon the beach, but were climbing the rocks at the foot of the point and making their way towards a long ledge called Dead Man's Rock which ran out into the sea at the extreme end of it. Blanche was finding it difficult to get up, but the others were pulling her along.

A first faint qualm of uneasiness assailed Mrs. Paley. But she told herself that they could not possibly be meaning to bathe from there. The water off Dead Man's Rock would be completely out of their depth. And a notice, pinned up in the hall at Pendizack, warned all visitors never to bathe from any of the rocks because the currents were dangerous.

She looked quickly again at Mrs. Cove, who had not moved. And she thought that a shout from the path would reach them, if they tried to do anything silly. It was lucky that Mrs. Cove should be so near. The Paleys up on the headland could never have been heard.

Now the children were collected in a little group on Dead Man's Rock. Her uneasiness changed swiftly into real terror when she saw that they were stripping off their dresses. All four emerged in bathing suits.

'But they can't . . . they mustn't . . .' she exclaimed aloud.

'What's that?' asked Mr. Paley, rousing.

'Those children. They seem to be going to bathe off Dead Man's Rock.'

He sat up to look and reached for the glasses.

The three Coves were standing in a timid row on the edge of the rock. They seemed to be receiving some kind of harangue from Hebe.

'They'll be drowned if they do,' he said.

'But their mother! Why doesn't she stop them?'

'Their mother?'

'Mrs. Cove. She's up on the cliff.'

She snatched the glasses from him. But she could not, immediately, find Mrs. Cove, who seemed to have left the path.

'Oh, there she is,' she exclaimed after a few seconds. 'She's going down. Thank goodness. But I wish she'd shout.'

'Good God!' cried Mr. Paley.

She lowered the glasses and looked at the rock. Hebe, dancing up and down excitedly, was now the only child to be seen. The Coves had vanished.

'But where are they? Where are they?'

'They all jumped in together. On the far side of the rock. The current is probably taking them round the point.'

Hebe had stopped dancing. She was shouting now, so loudly that the echo of her cries rang across the bay. Then she too vanished.

'Gone in after them,' commented Mr. Paley. 'Much good that will do.'

'But their mother . . . their mother . . .'

Mrs. Cove was not scrambling down any more. She had stopped dead in her tracks and was staring, as they had stared, at the empty rock.

'She saw. She must have seen.'

'Where is she?'

'Just a bit below the path. By that big patch of bracken. Oh, why doesn't she go on?'

'Not much use if she does,' said Mr. Paley. 'They'll all be round the point by this time.'

Mrs. Paley picked up the glasses again and focused them on Mrs. Cove. The pale square face came into view. It looked blank and uncertain.

'We'd better go round to her,' said Mr. Paley, getting up.

'She's . . . going away . . .'

Mrs. Cove had turned and was scrambling up to the path again. She did not seem to be in any great hurry. When she reached the path she paused for a moment, as if undecided whether to continue towards Pendizack or return towards Porthmerryn. Then she made up her mind, apparently, and left it altogether. She went higher up the cliff slope and vanished behind a stone wall.

'There's nothing in the world that she or we can do,' Mr. Paley was declaring. 'By the time we could get to the rock they'd be half a mile away. We'd better go back to the hotel and raise the alarm. If they can swim they might manage to get on to some of those rocks far out . . .'

'But they can't. The Coves can't swim.'

'Then it's hopeless.'

They were both hurrying back across the headland, and they now came in sight of Pendizack Cove which was unexpectedly full of people. Nearly everybody from the hotel seemed to be running and shouting. Robin and Duff, closely followed by the Gifford boys, had almost reached the top of the path. Halfway up were Sir Henry and Caroline. Strung out across the narrow strip of sand left by the tide were Mrs. Siddal, Bruce, Nancibel and Fred, while Miss Ellis and Mrs. Lechene were scrambling down the rock pathway from the house. Mr. Siddal was on the terrace.

'Boat!' shouted Mr. Paley. 'Get a boat!'

Duff turned and yelled to the people on the sand:

'Boat! Boat! Get the boat!'

But nobody seemed to understand except Nancibel, who turned and began to run back. Whereat Bruce turned too and followed her.

Robin had reached the headland and was panting out questions to the Paleys. Had they seen the Coves? When he heard what they had to tell he groaned and Duff, joining them, exclaimed:

'Off Dead Man's Rock? Then it's hopeless. The current is wicked. That bloody Hebe . . .'

But he started to run round Rosigraille, followed by the other boys.

The next to arrive was Sir Henry, so badly winded by an attempt to run uphill that he had to sit for a while on a rock. Caroline, who was with him, explained to the Paleys the cause of this panic-stricken pursuit. It was she who had raised the alarm, as soon as she discovered that Hebe and the Coves were missing. She had warned Hebe that she would do so, unless the swimming ordeal was abandoned.

'And I thought she'd given it up,' wailed Caroline. 'I'd have told before, if I'd thought she was really going to do it!'

Cries and shouts of *Stop them! Oh, stop them!* interrupted her. They came from Mrs. Siddal who had now gained the top of the hill and was running and shouting with but one purpose: Robin and Duff were not to go in off Dead Man's Rock. They would save nobody, and they would only be drowned themselves.

'Hush!' said Mrs. Paley, suddenly. 'Listen!'

They all fell silent.

'Don't you hear it?'

The faint chugging of a boat was certainly audible, though none was to be seen.

'It's Gerry and Angie,' said Mrs. Paley. 'They're behind the point. I saw them go round. They must be quite near . . .'

'Then perhaps . . .' began Sir Henry.

'Call to Duff. Call to Robin. Stop them! Duff . . .'

'Look! Oh, look!' Caroline pointed. 'They're coming . . .'

The nose of the boat appeared from behind the rocks. As it came into full view Mrs. Paley raked it with her glasses.

'I think they've got the children,' she said. 'Yes . . . yes, they have. All four.'

'Shout to the boys. Robin! Duff! Duff!' repeated Mrs. Siddal.

Mrs. Paley handed the glasses to Sir Henry. Gerry was steering the boat. Hebe and Evangeline were pummelling two Coves who lay inert amidships. A third was being sick over the side.

'I think it's all right,' said Sir Henry, after a long look. 'One of them is certainly . . . yes . . . and another one is moving . . .'

Caroline snatched the glasses and identified the moving Cove as Beatrix and the sick one as Maud. Blanche, she said, had not stirred. But, while she was looking, Evangeline, who had been busy with Beatrix, pushed Hebe aside and began work on Blanche.

The continued shouts and cries of Mrs. Siddal had halted the boys, who now turned and saw the boat. Hebe's attention was also attracted. She looked up, saw the group on the headland, and began to wave her arms in a semaphore message which Caroline interpreted.

'She says: All Safe!'

'Oh, does she,' said Mrs. Siddal. 'How very kind of her.'

She spoke so bitterly that Sir Henry began to apologize, promising that Hebe should be brought to book. But Mrs. Siddal was not to be easily placated. She had run very fast uphill expecting to see two of her sons drowned. And the appearance of the boat, though it allayed her fears, had not relieved her anxieties. She very much disliked the cosy tone in which Mrs. Paley talked of Gerry and Angie as though their names might naturally be coupled.

'I hope,' she said coldly, 'that Hebe will be forbidden to bathe again, while she's here. A really sharp lesson is what she needs.'

Caroline, uneasily aware of all the trouble brewing for Hebe, interposed to point out that the Coves had jumped into the sea of their own accord. But nobody listened to her, for the Coves were popular and Hebe was not. A universal sense of irritation pervaded Pendizack, and a scapegoat had become a necessity. By unanimous and instinctive choice the lot had fallen upon Hebe. Nobody understood, nobody wanted to understand, why she had lured the little Coves to Dead Man's Rock and persuaded them to attempt *Hara-kiri*. It seemed that she must have been prompted purely by the devil and, since the devil had been loose among them ever since Sunday morning, it was a relief to be able to locate him in a single agent. They turned against her with the fury which succeeds a panic.

'My wife will be very much distressed,' pleaded Sir Henry. 'She'll speak to Hebe.'

'I should hope so, Sir Henry. And I think Mrs. Cove will have something to say to Hebe too. I really don't know what Mrs. Cove will do when she hears of this.'

'She'll take a taxi to the Town Hall,' said Robin, who had returned and was listening. 'That's what she did when all her children were nearly killed by a flying bomb, wasn't it, sir?'

Sir Henry shook his head reprovingly.

'But it's true,' protested Robin. 'They . . . the little girls . . . told us so this morning. She sent them for a walk with flying bombs dropping all round them, and when the milkman told her he'd seen them blown to bits she hopped into a taxi and drove to the Town Hall, not to the scene of the incident. So they were all in dog house for making her waste three shillings.'

Everybody told him to hush, but a sort of smile went round the group, and the tension slackened. It was felt that Mrs. Cove could stand the news of this near fatality better than most mothers.

There was a general move back to the hotel, and the Paleys were once more left in possession of the headland. They sought their hollow again and Mrs. Paley said, as she took up her knitting, that she would be interested to hear how Mrs. Cove took the news.

'She can't have seen the boat,' said Mr. Paley. 'So she must think they are all drowned. What can she be doing?'

'I think she means to come in, later on, and be told about it.'

'But why?'

The strangeness of Mrs. Cove was too much, even for Mr. Paley, and he spoke with unusual interest.

'I'm not quite sure,' said Mrs. Paley slowly, 'I think . . . I think it's just an impulse. I don't think she often acts on impulse. But this afternoon . . . well . . . an impulse made her run down to them when she saw the danger. But then when it was hopeless, as she thought, she didn't know what to do. She seemed to be hesitating for quite a while.'

'But surely her natural impulse would have been to rush off and tell somebody?'

'I don't think she could trust herself to tell anybody. She feels it's better that somebody else should tell her. She's afraid of her own voice saying it.'

'But why?'

'Because,' said Mrs. Paley earnestly, 'I think she would really rather they were dead.'

'Oh, nonsense, Christina!'

'You didn't see her face. I did.'

6. Loaves and Fishes

'What is it? Why are you coming back?' cried Anna, as Bruce and Nancibel passed her on the sands.

'Boat,' panted Bruce.

She asked Miss Ellis, who was waddling along behind her, what boat that might be. Miss Ellis explained, adding gleefully:

'But they won't find it, for it's out. Gerry Siddal and Miss Wraxton took it. I saw them from my window.'

'But why do they want it? What's it all about?'

Anna had seen everybody running past her window and shouting, and so she had run out too. But she had not, so far, been able to discover what had happened.

'Some of the children have gone bathing in a dangerous place,' said Miss Ellis. 'A storm in a teacup probably. But those two will get a shock when they find the boat gone. We'll see them coming back ever so down in the mouth.'

'Why on earth couldn't you have told them?' asked Anna sharply.

'I don't care to speak to Nancibel,' explained Miss Ellis. 'She's a very impertinent girl. Refused to empty your ash tray this morning, Mrs. Lechene. Said it was too full.'

Anna reflected upon this information, saw the point of it, and grinned.

'Perhaps it was fuller than it should have been,' she

agreed. 'But who did you say had taken the boat?'

'Gerry Siddal and that Miss Wraxton. Sneaked off at lunch time when they thought nobody'd notice. Now there'll be a fussification, I shouldn't wonder; it's bad luck on them to be caught like this. Nobody takes that boat out in a donkey's years, but just the one day they slip off on the Q.T. it turns out to be wanted.'

Anna looked interested.

'I didn't know,' she said. 'Are they . . . ?'

'Why . . . didn't you hear the Canon going on at her this morning, Mrs. Lechene? You could hear him a mile off.'

'No. What happened?'

'Why . . . it seems that ever since Sunday night . . .' began Miss Ellis, settling down to it.

Her story was so absorbing that Anna could not tear herself away, though she was aware that Bruce and Nancibel had not returned, as prophesied, from their search for the boat and she did not like to leave them long together.

They had stayed on in the kitchen, when they found the boat gone, because there seemed to be no point in rushing again to the top of the cliff. Everything would be over, one way or another, long before they got there.

'We don't know for sure that they ever went in the sea at all,' said Nancibel. 'Let's hope somebody got there in time to stop them. I'll get the kettle on for when they come back, for I'm sure they'll all be glad of a cup of tea.'

She seemed quite to have forgotten that she had ever quarrelled with Bruce, and he found himself wishing that this panic might go on for a long time provided that it proved groundless in the end.

'Anything I can do?' he asked.

'Yes. Put the cups out. And then look to see if anyone's coming back. If there's anybody looks to be injured you can ring up the doctor. It's Dr. Peters, Porthmerryn 215. But we'd better make sure he's wanted before we do that.'

She sat down and leant her elbows on the kitchen table. Her kind eyes were full of distress.

'Oh dear,' she said, 'I do hope nothing's happened to them, poor little dears. They're such funny little things, the Coves. Very old-fashioned somehow. You know . . . babies for their age. Well . . . they've been kept back so. They don't know a thing about anything. They wanted to catch a lobster and feed it to the whole hotel.'

'What for?' asked Bruce, revelling in this genial interlude.

'That's just what I said. Whatever for, I said. Oh, they wanted to give a party. A feast! And ask *everybody*. And they didn't have any money to buy anything so they planned to catch a lobster and asked me if I knew how to do it. Well, I said I didn't think they could. And if they could, they couldn't cook it. And if they could cook it, one lobster wouldn't go far. So the little one, Maud, she said, What about the loaves and fishes? That was Jesus, I said. So then Blanche, she said, He *might* do it again for us. Just like a kid of five. So I said, you wait till Christmas and then p'raps your mother will let you give a party. But no, it seems they've never given a party in their lives. And they're just mad to give one here.'

233

'Poor kids! What a shame.'

'That's what I felt. There's something sort of . . . pathetic about them, if you know what I mean. That Hebe . . . she ought to be smacked. Oh dear! I do hope they're all right.'

'Sure to be,' consoled Bruce. 'Duff Siddal's gone. He's a fine swimmer. They'll be all right.'

'I could easily get some lobsters. And I could cook 'em. And I thought p'raps Mrs. Siddal would let me make some jelly. I could get some cream too, and I've still got some sweet points. It does seem a shame they shouldn't have their feast, poor little loves.'

'I've got all my sweet points,' said Bruce. 'They could have them. And there are peaches in Porthmerryn. I would like to help.'

'They could ask the little Giffords, and make quite a party of it . . . if . . . if they get home all right. Oh dear!'

'Don't worry. Have a cig. It'll all come right.'

Poor Bruce pulled a packet of Player's Weights out of his pocket, and the truce was over. He did not know what he had done wrong, but he saw her expression change.

'No thanks,' she said coldly.

'Nancibel!'

He got up and tried to go round the table to her, but she waved him off, saying drearily:

'It's no use. I can't ever feel any different to what I do feel, Bruce. But this isn't a proper time for us to quarrel and be angry. There's other things more important than our affairs. P'raps we'd better look out and see if anyone's coming.'

Bruce took some comfort, as well he might, in the

allusion to 'our affairs'. It seemed to admit some tie between them, and he was not absolutely without hope of
winning her round.

He followed her into the garden where a glimpse of the
boat coming into the creek put an end to their anxieties.
With cries of relief they ran to the slipway to help the party
ashore.

Blanche and Beatrix, the most nearly drowned of the
Coves, were sufficiently restored to be getting a severe lecture from Hebe upon their want of resource.

'You just went down like stones,' she was saying. 'If you
couldn't swim you could have floated. If I hadn't gone in
. . .'

Gerry told her to hold her tongue. They would all have
been drowned if he had not brought the boat in close to the
rock, when he saw what they were going to do.

'Oh, I could have managed quite well without the boat,'
boasted Hebe airily, 'if I hadn't had three fat-heads to save
at once.'

She had had a shattering fright, and she was trying to
work it off.

'You saved nobody,' said Gerry severely. 'You had to be
saved yourself.'

'And you gave more trouble than anyone,' said Evangeline. 'You struggled. The Coves had the sense not to.'

Gerry looked at her anxiously, for her voice had an overtone of exhaustion. He was still transported with amazement at her courage and judgment during the critical five
minutes. She had gone into the sea at the very moment

when the Coves had jumped, and as she dived she told him to take the boat back. He saw what she meant. She was afraid that the current might carry them all past him and that he would never catch them up. So he raced round in a wide circle and picked up Maud, who was floating. Then he came in to meet Evangeline. She had got Blanche by the hair and Beatrix by one foot, but could do no more than hold on to them until he came up. Hebe was carried right past the boat and they had to chase her. She could swim a little but lost her head and sank as the boat came up, so that Evangeline had to go in again to fetch her. He had been obliged to allow it, for no one else could manage the boat, but he very much disliked taking the safer role, and he had been furious when she was forced to go in a second time. If it had not been for her persistence, her intrepidity and her accuracy in gauging the direction of the current, he would have been helpless. Not a word had passed between them, from the moment she went in, but he had always managed to meet her at the point for which she was making, and he felt that her sense had been as valuable as her courage.

'You're all in,' he said. 'You must have a hot drink the moment we get back, and go to bed with a hot bottle.'

She looked up and met, for the first time in her life, a glance of unqualified admiration. It was so new and so agreeable that she smiled broadly, as if he was handing her a prize.

'Danger,' said Hebe, 'is good for people.'

This was really too much for Gerry.

'You don't know very much about it, do you?' he said. 'You've had less of it than most of us. You were kept in cotton wool in America, weren't you, while the Coves went all through the London Blitz?'

Hebe grew pale with mortification.

The boat bumped up against the slipway where Bruce and Nancibel were waiting. Maud, when lifted out, could walk, but Blanche and Beatrix had to be carried. Bruce took one and Nancibel the other, while Gerry helped Evangeline on to dry land.

'I haven't said . . . I haven't begun to say . . . how wonderful you were,' he told her. 'Go along, Hebe. Go into the house.'

'Why should I?' protested Hebe. 'I don't need hot drinks and hot bottles. I'm not frightened of a little sea water.'

'You need a whipping,' declared Evangeline fiercely.

For it was too bad of this horrible child to spoil everything and interrupt Gerry just when he was saying such delightful things.

'That's very old-fashioned,' said Hebe. 'Modern parents don't whip their children.'

'Perhaps not. But modern children aren't generally quite as spoilt and pampered as you are.'

'Pampered?' howled Hebe. 'I am *not*. I am not pampered. I am not pampered. I am not pampered. I can't help it if they adopted me so Caroline shouldn't get an only child compress. I'm a homeless waif. I'm a bastard.'

Gerry and Evangeline were obliged to laugh, but they went into the house with the delightful things unsaid and with little charity in their hearts for Hebe.

7. The Mothers

'You wouldn't think it, to look at her, would you?' said Miss Ellis.

'Yes, I would,' said Anna. 'It's exactly what I'd think. The first time I ever saw her, when she made that scene in church, I said to myself that girl is a nymphomaniac. I know all the signs. But how do you know it's Gerry Siddal she's meeting?'

'Fred,' said Miss Ellis. 'I asked him if he'd heard anything in the stables last night—anybody coming in late, I mean.'

'Yes, of course,' said Anna smoothly. 'You would be anxious to know about that.'

Miss Ellis gave her a sharp look and continued:

'Poor Fred complained he couldn't sleep at all. Such a racket going on! First there was your chauffeur; he came in and got shut in that awful camp bed. And then it was Gerry. He'd been on the tiles too. So I put two and two together. I knew her bed hadn't been slept in, and I didn't think it was the chauffeur somehow.'

'Fascinating,' agreed Anna. 'Hullo! They're all coming back. It must have been a false alarm.'

The panic party from the cliff was strolling back across the beach. Well in advance came Fred, not because he was in any hurry to get back to his work but because he wanted to be first with the news and to startle the few people who had remained at Pendizack. He had quite a little success with Anna and Miss Ellis, for they had been talking so eagerly that they had not seen the boat go past to the creek, and knew nothing of the rescue. Fred, who liked news to be bad, made it as little of a rescue as he could.

'They've just brought the bodies in,' he said solemnly. 'See the boat? It's gone round to the creek.'

'Bodies?' cried Anna and Miss Ellis.

They had not understood that there was any serious danger, and they were both shocked.

'The Cove kids,' explained Fred, 'and Hebe. S'awful!'

'But not drowned? Not dead?' cried Anna.

Fred breathed heavily and said:

'They're trying that artificial prespiration.'

There was a gloomy pause, broken by Anna.

'Oh my God,' she said. 'What a bloody nice holiday!'

Turning abruptly, she went through the garden and up the drive, away from the stricken house. She caught a bus at the cross roads into Porthmerryn where she sought the bar at the Marine Parade.

Miss Ellis pursued Fred into the house asking for details. But he could tell her no more.

'But where's their mothers?' demanded Miss Ellis. 'Do they know? Were they there? Has anybody broken it to them?'

Fred shook his head. Neither Lady Gifford nor Mrs. Cove had been up on the cliff, that he did know.

'Lady Gifford's asleep in her room,' said Miss Ellis eagerly. 'Had no idea of it probably. Somebody really ought . . .'

'S'awful!' said Fred again.

'I'd better go myself,' decided Miss Ellis, with some satisfaction. 'Since nobody else seems to have thought of the poor thing.'

She solemnly mounted the stairs and Fred went to the kitchen, where all the Coves and Evangeline were drinking hot tea. He took a cup himself and felt no qualms at having described them as bodies. When he had seen them in the boat they had looked like bodies.

Nancibel took the Coves upstairs to bed as soon as they had had a hot drink. But Evangeline stayed in the kitchen with Gerry and Bruce to dispense tea to anyone who came. Mrs. Siddal, Sir Henry, Caroline, and all the boys appeared, and they lingered for a while, drinking and chattering in the idle mood which succeeds tension. Caroline was questioned more closely about the Covenant of Spartans and her embarrassed reticence intensified the general impression that Hebe had been bullying the other children in a most reprehensible way.

'But it's a secret society,' she protested. 'We promised we'd never give away its secrets. I wouldn't have told today if I hadn't thought it was too dangerous.'

'Hebe made us promise,' said Luke. 'We all hated having to be Spartans, but Hebe made us do it.'

And Michael obliged the company with the most horrifying details.

'I think you're both very unloyal,' said Caroline hotly. 'You enjoyed a great deal of it. You both begged Hebe to let you be Spartans when she started it.'

'But why do you let her boss you all like that?' asked Robin. 'You're three to one.'

Sir Henry said despondently that Hebe should be reprimanded. His wife would . . . But he was interrupted by Mrs. Siddal, who said sharply that Lady Gifford and Mrs. Cove were apparently the only people in the house who had, so far, suffered no alarm whatever. Where were they, and why were they not looking after their own children?

'My wife is upstairs,' he said. 'She's having her afternoon rest. I'd better go up and tell her.'

He hurried up and knocked at Eirene's door. A harsh, unexpected voice told him to come in. He did so and was confronted by Mrs. Cove, who told him grimly that his wife had fainted.

'She's heard, then?' he said, looking at Eirene, who lay senseless upon the bed.

'Yes, I suppose so,' said Mrs. Cove. 'I rang the bell repeatedly, but nobody came. I dashed water in her face.'

He went to get brandy from the flask in Eirene's dressing-case. Mrs. Cove had certainly dashed water. She must have dashed a whole jugful, for when he tried to administer the brandy he found the bed was soaked.

'How long has she been like this?' he asked.

'I really don't know. She was like this when I got here. I was just coming in from my walk when that stupid house-keeper called over the bannisters, shouting for help, so I came up. She told me . . . what has happened, but beyond that she wasn't the slightest use, so I sent her off to get someone. I've been here ever since. I didn't like to leave your wife, but I think somebody should have come.'

'I'm very sorry. It must have been the shock. Could you hold her up a little?'

Mrs. Cove roughly jerked Eirene up while he gave her the brandy, and then let her fall back again. A faint flush lit up in the ashy cheeks.

'It's a good thing I'm not given to fainting,' muttered Mrs. Cove.

'Yes, indeed,' he agreed. 'It must have been quite a shock for you too.'

'Quite a shock?' she repeated, staring at him.

There was in her gaze such a strange mixture of alarm, suspicion and defiance that he was puzzled. She plainly thought that he had meant to insult her. He remembered the taxi ride and realized that she might be vulnerable to an accusation of callousness.

'An awful shock,' he amended. 'But they're really quite all right, you know. Blanche and Beatrix are still a bit shaky, but Hebe and Maud don't seem to be a penny the worse.'

'*What?*'

Her expression changed. It dissolved into blank astonishment.

'Then they're not . . . they're not . . .' she whispered.

'Didn't Miss Ellis tell you that? What did she say?'

She did not answer. She dropped her eyes and a slow crimson spread all over her square, pale face, up to the roots of her hair.

'What did she tell you?' he repeated.

'She said they were drowned,' muttered Mrs. Cove in a thick voice. 'All four of them.'

'Drowned? Good God? No wonder Eirene fainted!'

He seized his wife's hands and began to call to her eagerly:

'Eirene! Eirene! It's all right, darling! It's all right! Hebe is quite all right. They're all safe . . .'

The long eyelashes fluttered and Eirene moaned faintly.

'It was all a mistake. Hebe is safe. She's safe, darling. I'll bring her to you . . .'

He ran to the door and told Fred, who was listening outside, to find Hebe and send her up. Then he returned to the bed.

'Oh, Harry . . .'

'I know, darling. I know. But it's quite all right. She's safe. Young Siddal saved them. He had a boat out there . . .'

'They said she was . . . oh . . .'

'Oh, my poor darling! My poor, poor darling!'

'And what about me?'

Mrs. Cove's voice was not loud, but it broke on them like a scream.

'Hebe is only one child, and not your own either. I was told that all mine were lost. Where are they?'

'They're in their beds. Nancibel is seeing to them. Yes, darling . . . Hebe is coming . . .'

Mrs. Cove went towards the door. But her rage was too much for her. She turned, came to the foot of the bed, and addressed Lady Gifford.

'Stop that whimpering, you silly creature. You've nothing to cry for.'

Astonishment silenced Eirene. She stared at Mrs. Cove, who went on:

'There's nothing in the world the matter with you except overeating and no exercise. If you'd been left as I was, a penniless widow, with three children to fend for, you'd be as strong as a horse. You'd have to be. You wouldn't be able to afford these fainting fits.'

'You know nothing about it,' cried Eirene, finding her tongue. 'I happen to love Hebe. You don't love your children so, of course, it wasn't such a shock to you.'

'Why do you suggest I don't love my children?'

'Anybody can see you don't. You neglect them. You sell their sweets.'

'Which you aren't ashamed to eat.'

There was a tap at the door and Hebe looked in, half frightened, half impish.

'Fred sent me up,' she said. 'What's the matter? Am I wanted?'

'No,' said Sir Henry, crossing the room, 'you aren't. Go to bed.'

He pushed her out and slammed the door. Neither lady had noticed her brief appearance. They were too deeply absorbed in their battle, each intent upon an utter condemnation of the other. But neither listened much to what the other said.

8. Solitude

Beatrix and Maud were asleep. Blanche lay awake, staring at the sunset hues on the ceiling. Their mother had gone down to dinner. She was very angry but she had not whipped them because they were still unwell. They were, however, to be punished. They were never to play with any of the Giffords again.

But it was not this woe which kept Blanche awake after her sisters had sobbed themselves into a doze. It was something much more dreadful—a discovery so terrifying that, for the first time in her life, she felt no impulse to share it with the others.

Mrs. Pearce's little carving was locked up in the suitcase under the bed.

Not many of their possessions were left in the wardrobe or the chest of drawers for fear that Nancibel or Fred or Miss Ellis might be thieves. As much as possible was kept locked up in the suitcases, the keys of which lived in Mrs. Cove's handbag. Just before supper she had pulled this particular suitcase out and unlocked it, in order to find a pair of stockings. Maud was suddenly sick again, so that it had been left on the floor with all its contents displayed, while Mrs. Cove jumped up to fetch a basin. Blanche, peering over the edge of her bed, had caught a glimpse of the little carving, where it lay in a tumble of handkerchiefs and gloves. She recognized it at once.

She said nothing, but she was profoundly shocked.

She did not love her mother. None of them did, nor had it ever occurred to them that they ought to do so. She had never asked for their affection. But neither did they criticize or rebel against her. She pervaded and ruled their lives like some unpropitious climate, and they accepted her rule as inevitable, evading its harshness by instinct rather than by reason. For she only dominated their outward and material existences; over their minds she had no sway. She never invaded their imaginations or attempted to impart to them any ideas. The very aridity of her character had been their salvation. Nothing of importance had ever been said to them in their mother's voice, and many characters in their favourite books were more real to them than she was. They seldom thought about her.

But Blanche was thinking now. At the sight of that dark little lump among the handkerchiefs a sudden illumination had come to her. For she had already decided that the person who bought Mrs. Pearce's carving must be very cruel and wicked.

Her thoughts were oppressed by a frightening sense of solitude. She felt as though she had been transported to some strange desert where she was completely lost. In the past she had always shared any new idea with her sisters. She hardly knew how to make any decision quite alone. Yet she flinched from the thought of telling them, or of putting her discovery into words.

Footsteps came softly along the passage and Nancibel

looked in. She had stayed over time that evening until supper was served in order to oblige Mrs. Siddal, for the household was still disorganized.

Catching the watchful sparkle of Blanche's eyes she came on tiptoe and knelt by the bed.

'All right, ducks?' she whispered.

'Yes,' breathed Blanche.

'Thought I'd just look in before I went home. You don't look too grand, I must say. What is it, dear?'

She leant over and saw traces of tears on Blanche's cheeks.

'I'm frightened.'

'I don't wonder. We've all been frightened. But you'd better forget all about it now. Only you mustn't be so silly another time.'

'We'll try not to. But we're rather . . . queer children, aren't we?'

Nancibel was taken aback.

'I don't know,' she hedged. 'Why do you think so?'

'Our family is queer, don't you think?' whispered Blanche. 'We have no friends. We don't know any people. We don't live like other people, do we?'

She gave Nancibel a straight, enquiring look, and Nancibel blushed.

'Listen, Blanche! I've been thinking. I believe you could give that feast. I could get you some lobsters and cream and sweets if you like.'

'Oh, Nancibel! How good you are! But it's no use. We mayn't play with the Giffords any more, so we couldn't ask them.'

'Well, then, ask somebody else. Ask me. I'll come.'

'And Angie and Gerry Siddal . . . all the Siddals. We could ask them. They're so kind. And the chauffeur and Mrs. Paley . . . and Fred . . .'

'That's right,' said Nancibel, laughing. 'Ask the whole hotel, I would.'

Blanche glowed with pleasure.

'The Giffords would have to come if we asked the whole hotel, wouldn't they?'

'You'd need a lot of lobsters, duckie.'

'How much do they cost?'

'You don't get them for nothing. But you shall have your feast, I promise. Just a nice little feast. Now give me a kiss and go to sleep, and you'll feel quite well tomorrow.'

Blanche flung her skinny arms round Nancibel and hugged her.

'I wish you were our sister, Nancibel!'

'Do you?'

'I expect you have lovely times at your home.'

'We have good times and bad times,' said Nancibel, smiling. 'Everybody has. Your good times are all coming.'

'Are they? How do you know?'

'The cat told me.'

'What cat?' cried Blanche, astonished. 'Hebe's cat?'

'No. My great-grandmother's cat. *Now* what's the matter?'

For Blanche, reminded of old Mrs. Pearce, had looked woebegone.

'Mrs. Pearce's cat?'

'No, no. It's just a saying . . . what people say. It doesn't mean anything. It means I've a sort of guess.'

She lingered for a while, wondering what had upset the child again, but Blanche would say no more; and at last she went off to climb the hill and tell the tale of the day's adventure to her family at supper.

If she knew, thought Blanche, if she knew what's in our suitcase! Mother will sell it to get a lot of money. She needs money because she is so poor. But Nancibel is poor and she is going to give us a feast. And Mrs. Pearce is poor, poorer than anybody.

The light faded and the noise of the sea grew fainter as the tide went out. At the last low tide she had been on the sands with her sisters, making their little castle. And she remembered how suddenly Sir Henry had appeared with a warning about old Mrs. Pearce. She fell into her usual habit of narrating the incident to herself as though it had been in a book.

And, all unknowing, footsteps were approaching across the sand, dear reader, the footsteps of the one who was to give us a warning. Give them a warning. Because the three sisters had been so intent upon their castle that they did not hear the rapid approach of the . . . of the baronet . . . until they were startled by his voice speaking in a fashionable drawl. *Beautiful. French, is it not?* For he was a man of great culture and good taste, and the *Très Riches Heures* was a household word in his mouth. But after paying some florid compliments, he revealed the true purpose of his . . . his . . . his errand to that lonely spot. It was to give a warning.

Do not, he whispered, *breathe a word about Mrs. Pearce's treasures. There are some very wicked people in the world.* We thought he meant robbers. They thought he meant robbers.

But what did he mean? This is not a book. Does he guess? Does he know? Why did he ask us? Does everybody know?

At ten o'clock Mrs. Cove came up to bed. Blanche pretended to be asleep. She heard her mother's movements, rapid and decisive, the opening and shutting of drawers, the creak of the wardrobe door. And then Mrs. Cove went to have a bath, leaving her handbag on the dressing table.

Blanche sat up. She slipped out of bed, took the keys from the bag, and opened the suitcase. Taking the carved figure she flung it out of the window as far as she could, on to the grass terrace. Then she locked the suitcase, returned the keys and went back to bed.

It was the first time that she had ever taken a decision without consulting her sisters. The idea of returning the piece to Mrs. Pearce never occurred to her, though it would probably have occurred to Maud. She merely wished to put it out of her mother's possession.

9. Voices in the Night

'What on earth is the matter, Bruce?'

'Nothing's the matter with *me*.'

'What d'you mean by that?'

'My dear Mrs. Bassington Gore . . .'

'You filthy little twerp. Get out!'

'All right. I'm getting out.'

'If Nancibel has this effect on you . . .'

'You shut your trap about Nancibel.'

'Amuse yourself with her as much as you like. But . . .'

'Did you hear what I said? Another word about her and I'll shut your mouth for you.'

'Nancibel . . .'

'All right!'

'Oh, you filthy brute!'

'I warned you.'

'My lip's bleeding. It's bleeding all over the pillow. Just look at it. What will Miss Ellis say? . . . You're rather exciting when you lose your temper. I wish you'd do it oftener. I didn't realize you'd fallen for Nancibel in a big way. What are you crawling about for?'

'I'm looking for my shoes.'

'You're not really angry, are you?'

'Yes.'

'But why? I think I've been very nice about Nancibel.

Can't I even mention her without getting my face slapped?'

'No.'

'Well, you'd better take care, Bruce. There's a point beyond which you can't depend on me to be nice. I'll forget
the face slapping and I'll advise you to forget Nancibel.'

'Or you'll tell the police I pinched that car?'

'I didn't say that. I'm only reminding you that we'd better not quarrel. Come here . . . Bruce! Come here! Oh,
very well. Go if you like. But don't say I didn't warn you.'

The night was vast and cool. All Pendizack Cove lay in a
gulf of shadow, but the cliffs stood bare in the starlight.
Bruce did not go back to the stables and his precarious bed.
He went down on to the dim sands and walked about, trying to make up his mind what to do next. He was sick of
Anna but he was afraid of breaking with her. For it was she
who had introduced him to literary people, the friends of
whom he had boasted to Alice and Nancibel. He did not
like them much, but they were a step on the ladder which
he wished to climb. As soon as his book was published and
his genius recognized he could be independent of her and
of them. If he left her now it might never be published, for
he had overstepped the truth when he described this event
as a certainty. Anna was bringing pressure upon a publisher
friend of hers to accept it.

And then there was that little matter of the car which
he had stolen when he was Boots in the South Coast hotel
last summer. He had borrowed it to take a girl to a dance,
smashed it up in a ditch, and killed a cyclist. Anna knew

about that. She had supplied him with an alibi when he was questioned. She had rescued him from the police and his blacking brushes, and taken him back with her to London. She had encouraged him to write and taken him to cocktail parties. He certainly owed her a great deal, though he felt that he had paid for it.

He disliked his position, and at intervals he despised himself for it. But he would have been content to stay on with Anna until his book was published if it had not been for Nancibel, and the fact that such a choice would cut him off for ever from Nancibel's regard. He had an idea that she might, in time, forgive the past, but he was sure that she would stand no compromise in the future.

It was nonsense. It was Nancibel against his whole career; not even her love either, merely her respect. Who was she, and what was she, he wondered angrily, to overset his life like this? A servant, a village girl, not outstandingly pretty. She had no brains either, and but a poor education. With his intelligence and his looks he could do much better for himself. He must get over his infatuation. On Monday he would be leaving Pendizack. He would never see her again, and in a year's time, when his book was out, he would thank his stars that he had avoided this pitfall. She did not care for him. The rift would mean nothing to her.

She must be asleep by now, in that little cottage up among the stony fields where he had been given a cup of tea last night. He had enjoyed himself there. He had been happy. But that sort of happiness was, he felt, too easy. He might just as well have stayed at home, and taken on his father's job at the waterworks, if that was all he wanted. Surely it was no crime to wish for distinction, to want to be Somebody?

She was asleep now, with her mother and father, and all her brothers and sisters, packed together in that little house, sleeping soundly after their hard day's work. While he, in Anna's bed, had been working his way towards distinction. But his next book . . . *a comedy, very corrupt and mondain, with a continental background . . . nobody ever reads the third book . . .*

He had turned to go back to his bed in the stables, but the memory of Mr. Siddal's speculations about that third book frightened him so much that he swerved aside and began to climb the path to the headland. Suppose there never was any distinction? Suppose he never arrived at being Somebody?

When he first went with Anna to London he had known nothing of his predecessors. Anna had referred to them freely and had spoken of them as if they were all important people, but he had never met any of them, seldom heard them mentioned. He had supposed this to be an accident. But now he began to wonder if there was not some truth in Siddal's implication and that oblivion was the sure lot of any man by the time that Anna had done with him.

He wished very much that he could consult somebody —frankly, and without shame, confide his dilemma. But it must be some person whose judgment he could respect and to no such person could he tell the exact truth. Besides, how could anybody else tell him what he was worth?

And what had the others been worth, potentially? Did Anna specialize in nonentities or in young men of promise whom she ruined? Only Mr. Siddal would be likely to know about that, and Mr. Siddal was a disagreeable old tom cat.

He had been striding along very fast, unconscious of his direction, when he became aware of voices in the night. He was not alone upon the headland. People were talking, in low tones, quite close by. He drew up and approached more quietly.

It sounded like a couple of lovers hidden among the boulders. He could not see them but he could hear a man's voice telling some long story. As he drew nearer words became audible. The story seemed to be some kind of lecture on biology.

'Tarsals,' said the voice, 'and metatarsals. Is that clear?'

There was no answer, and the voice said:

'Angie! Are you asleep?'

'No,' replied another soft little voice, 'no . . . I'm not asleep. Who did you say met a tarsal?'

The night rang with Gerry Siddal's laughter, and Bruce strolled away. He had caught sight of a third person, some little distance off, sitting outlined against the stars on the topmost rocks of the point. The place, he thought, was as populous as Piccadilly. Who were they? What was going on?

At the sound of his feet upon the rocks Mrs. Paley turned round.

'Oh,' she said pleasantly, 'have you come to join us?'

WEDNESDAY

1. Soapstone

Miss Ellis was sitting in the office. She was doing nothing, for there was nothing to do. But she had grown tired of sitting in her bedroom. Officially she was on strike and under notice, but she did not intend to leave Pendizack until she had found another job.

Presently Mrs. Cove looked in and asked for Mrs. Siddal.

'Out,' said Miss Ellis.

'Are you in charge?'

'No,' said Miss Ellis, with a titter. 'I believe I'm sacked.'

'What a place,' muttered Mrs. Cove, retreating. 'First I'm robbed and then . . .'

'Robbed?' cried Miss Ellis, galvanized into interest. 'Have you missed something?'

'Yes. Something has been stolen from my room.'

'Tck! Tck! You'd better give me the particulars, Mrs. Cove.'

'If you are not in charge I don't see . . .'

'Oh, I'd better look into it, I suppose. Mrs. Siddal would probably expect it. What have you lost?'

Mrs. Cove gave the details in as few words as possible.

'I saw it in my suitcase last night,' she said. 'That was the last time I had it unlocked until five minutes ago, when I opened it to get a handkerchief. I missed the carving at once. I always carry my keys. But it's a cheap suitcase. Most keys would open it, I'm afraid.'

'Had your room been done?' asked Miss Ellis.

'Yes, as much as any room ever gets done here. The beds were made.'

'Hmph! And the room has never been empty since you saw your carving last night until you all went down to breakfast this morning?'

'That is so. It must have been taken this morning, within the last hour. I should like Nancibel to be questioned.'

'Certainly, Mrs. Cove. I'll call her.'

Miss Ellis, with lofty satisfaction, rang a bell which was supposed to summon Fred. But nobody had ever dreamed of calling him in this way and, though he heard it, he did not realize that it was for him. So the bell remained unanswered.

'You'd better go and find somebody,' suggested Mrs. Cove contemptuously.

Miss Ellis went to the door into the kitchen passage and yelled orders that Nancibel was to be sent immediately to the office.

'It's what I've never been accustomed to,' she said to Mrs. Cove when she came back. 'Servants living out. In a good hotel you don't find that sort of thing. It gives them so much more opportunity . . .'

'Has anything else been missed?' asked Mrs. Cove.

'Not that I've heard of. But people don't always find out at once,' said Miss Ellis.

'Is she a good servant?'

'Very bad. Quite untrained. And very lazy and impertinent. I don't think she had a reference. She came here straight out of the A.T.S. I may say that *I* thought certain things disappeared in a mysterious way. Soap, for instance. And a roller towel was missing. And I never could make out what became of all the jam. Of course, nowadays, when everything is so valuable . . . ah . . . here she is.'

Nancibel appeared and stood by the office door. She was surprised at this summons, and showed it.

'Now, Nancibel,' began Miss Ellis. 'Please answer truthfully.'

The girl flushed, but she controlled her tongue and waited.

'Did you take anything out of Mrs. Cove's room this morning?'

'I took the slops, Miss Ellis.'

'We don't mean the slops. A valuable ornament has been stolen from Mrs. Cove's room during the last hour. You were the only person known to have entered that room. Can you tell us anything about it?'

'No.'

'Are you sure?'

'Quite sure.'

Miss Ellis looked at Nancibel and smiled.

'Because,' she said, 'if you did yield to a sudden temptation it would be very much better to confess to it now. In that case, provided you give back what you took, I daresay Mrs. Cove will overlook the theft.'

Nancibel did not reply. She turned and marched off to the kitchen where Duff and Robin were finishing a very late breakfast.

'Will you tell Mrs. Siddal I've gone home,' she said to them. 'And I'm afraid I can't come back here till Miss Ellis has gone. Miss Ellis will explain why.'

She went to the peg by the back door where her bag and her outdoor shoes were kept. Robin and Duff, horror-struck at the thought of losing her, came out too, entreating her to think better of it and wait till their mother came home.

'I can't,' she said, changing her shoes. 'Miss Ellis has as good as called me a thief. I don't stand for that from anybody.'

Voices were heard at the end of the passage. Miss Ellis was unctuously reassuring Mrs. Cove.

'But, of course, that goes without saying. She shan't leave the house . . . why, Nancibel . . . what are you doing?'

'I'm going home, Miss Ellis.'

'What's in that bag?' put in Mrs. Cove, sharply.

'That's where I put my overall.'

'A very large bag for such a purpose, don't you think, Miss Ellis?'

'It is indeed, Mrs. Cove. I've always thought so, but of course my opinion was never asked. How can one check up on what goes out of the house . . .'

'You're welcome to search it,' said Nancibel contemptuously.

She held it out and Mrs. Cove took it. Duff, unable to contain his indignation, stepped forward.

'This is perfectly monstrous,' he said. 'We've known Nancibel all our lives . . .'

'Ah,' exclaimed Mrs. Cove. 'Here it is.'

She held up a small dark object.

'Here is the piece I lost.'

'That!' exclaimed Nancibel in astonishment. 'Why . . . that's my great-grannie's. It belongs to her.'

'I say . . .' burst out Robin.

'It's mine,' said Mrs. Cove. 'I bought it in Porthmerryn. It was in my suitcase last night. This morning it was gone. How does it come to be in your bag?'

'I found it on the grass outside the house when I came to work this morning,' said Nancibel. 'And I picked it up and put it in my bag. I forgot about it till this minute. I thought you said it was a valuable ornament you'd lost.'

'It's very valuable. It's black amber.'

'*I say!*'

'Is it a habit of yours to pocket any little things you find lying about?' asked Mrs. Cove. 'Why didn't you hand it in to the office?'

'Found it on the grass! She never! What a tale . . .' cried Miss Ellis.

'I meant to ask Mrs. Siddal, but I forgot. I thought it was my great-grannie's. It is too. It is hers. I'd know it anywhere.'

'And why, pray,' asked Miss Ellis, 'should your great-grannie's junk be lying on Pendizack lawn?'

'It is hers. It's got my uncle Ned's initials scratched on the bottom. I looked to see, and you can look too if you like.'

Here Robin emerged from his first exclamatory surprise.

'Then it was you,' he said fiercely to Mrs. Cove. 'You did buy that poor old woman's carving. You knew it was valuable, and you only gave her five pounds ten.'

But Mrs. Cove ignored him.

'It vanished from my suitcase and now I find it in your bag,' she said to Nancibel. 'That's all I know. I've a very good mind to send for the police.'

'I shall fetch Sir Henry,' declared Robin. 'He knows all about it. He knows how she's cheated poor old Mrs. Pearce.'

He rushed off just as Nancibel burst into tears.

'It was on the grass,' she sobbed. 'I don't know how it came there, but it was.'

'Nobody's going to believe that,' Miss Ellis proclaimed. 'You've been caught this time, my lady.'

Duff advanced and took Nancibel by the arm.

'Don't cry,' he adjured her. 'Everybody will believe you. Everybody knows you. If you say it was on the grass, then it was.'

'I shall charge her with the theft,' said Mrs. Cove.

'I really think you ought,' agreed Miss Ellis, 'if only for the sake of other visitors. If it's known that Mrs. Siddal is deliberately sheltering a dishonest servant . . . well . . . people will know to be careful of their things.'

'*You'd* better be careful what you say,' Duff warned them. 'Nancibel could have you up for slander.'

Sir Henry and Robin here appeared, and Sir Henry at once asked Mrs. Cove if it was true that she had bought the piece in dispute from Mrs. Pearce on Monday afternoon.

'I don't really see that it's anyone's business where I bought it,' said Mrs. Cove. 'It certainly belongs to me.'

'I only ask because I was particularly anxious to look at that piece. I was very much disappointed when I heard that it had been sold. I was hoping you would allow me to see it.'

'Why?' asked Mrs. Cove suspiciously.

'I collect amber. If it's really black amber it must be a find. I . . . I suppose you wouldn't sell it . . .'

There was a pause and Mrs. Cove looked thoughtful. Duff, who had taken the sobbing Nancibel into the kitchen, could be heard saying:

'Let her send for the police. Everyone will believe you. And all the newspapers will get the story of how she cheated your great-grandmother.'

'Suppose we go somewhere quieter,' suggested Sir Henry.

Still a little doubtfully, Mrs. Cove agreed. She went with him and Robin into the lounge. Miss Ellis, her eyes popping, tried to follow them, but Mrs. Cove said coldly:

'Thank you, Miss Ellis. That will do. I shall take no proceedings against Nancibel this time, as I have my carving back.'

In order to emphasize the dismissal she shut Miss Ellis out of the lounge. Half eagerly, half reluctantly, she handed the piece to Sir Henry, who examined it carefully.

'You know, Mrs. Cove,' he said at last, 'I really think that old lady ought to have this back. I should like to buy it and give it back to her. What will you take?'

'A thousand guineas,' said Mrs. Cove.

'You think it's worth that?'

'That's what it's worth to me.'

'Yet you bought it for five pounds ten,' he pointed out. 'This old woman is almost destitute. She's threatened with the workhouse. She's very ignorant. She has no idea of the value of a thing like this. Do you really think it's . . .'

Mrs. Cove interrupted him, her eyes blazing.

'And who will pay for her in the workhouse? Who pays her old age pension? Who pays for all these wretched improvident people who haven't troubled to save for their old age? Their children? The people who ought to look after them? Oh no, I have to. Three-quarters of my income is taken from me for people like that. I've not the slightest sympathy for the so-called poor, Sir Henry. They get everything done for them, their children educated, doctors, hospitals, everything. Just because they're too lazy to work and earn enough to keep themselves decently. I think that nowadays people in our class are justified in looking after themselves. We know very well they'd take every penny from us if they could.'

'My wife would agree with you,' said Sir Henry. 'But are you really taxed seventy-five per cent? Of course, super-tax is pretty steep nowadays but . . . oh, well, that's not the point. About this object . . . will you take ten pounds for it?'

He held up the carved figure.

'Ten pounds!' exclaimed Mrs. Cove. 'You must think I'm feeble-minded. Give it back, please.'

In spite of a gesture from Robin, Sir Henry gave it back saying:

'You really won't take ten pounds?'

'Certainly not.'

'Well . . . I thought you probably wouldn't. I'd have been stung if you had. The thing isn't amber. It's only soapstone, and I doubt if it's worth a guinea.'

2. The Resistance Movement

'Mr. Siddal,' reported Fred, 'sends his compliments, and he's not dressed yet.'

'That doesn't matter,' said Anna impatiently. 'I must see somebody, and there's no one in the office. Either take me to him or tell him to put on a dressing gown and come to me.'

Fred departed. After a considerable interval Mr. Siddal, in his dressing gown, came to her room.

'It's no use sending for me, Anna,' he protested. 'I'm nothing in this hotel.'

'You let me the rooms on Monday.'

'Yes. And a nice hullabaloo there was about it too.'

'I don't wonder. You only did it to annoy Barbara. Well, all I want is to find somebody capable of giving her a message. She seems to be out and Ellis has gone to ground and Fred is wanting.'

'You could have given it to Nancibel.'

'No, I couldn't. She's the last person I could have given it to, as a matter of fact. There's only you. Will you tell Barbara that I'm going away for a night or two, but will be back before the end of the week?'

'If I remember. But you'd much better write her a note. Is Antinous going too?'

'Bruce? Of course he's going too. Who'll drive the car if he doesn't go?'

'Who indeed. Does he know he's going?'

'Not yet.'

'Very wise. May one ask where you're taking him?'

'Up the coast to St. Merricks. Polly's got a house there for the summer, and I promised I'd spend a couple of nights there before I went back to London. I might as well go now.'

'Polly? Not Polly Palmer? I thought she was dead.'

'Why should she be dead?'

'I'm sure it's time she was.'

'My dear Dick! She's not old.'

'No. But most of her circle are dead, aren't they? She's got no business to survive them like this. I thought they all died on the coal boats coming home in 1940.'

'Some did. But the rest are still alive.'

'Then where are they? One never hears of them. How do they live? They can't go back because their relations can't send any remittances to them. Where do they live now?'

'With Polly mostly,' said Anna. 'She has money.'

'Still?'

'She had an awful lot of it to begin with, you remember? And she still has some left, I believe. You never hear of any of them because in this benighted country they can only hope to survive by keeping quiet.'

'Poor Poll. I suppose she now supports the whole damned crew. I must say for her, she was always generous. And a very lovely girl . . . once. What's she like now? Pretty *délabrée*, I suppose.'

'What you'd expect.'

'But why St. Merricks?'

'She must live somewhere.'

'Very little drink there, I should have thought, and no golliwogs.'

'She's finished with men, and she doesn't drink much. I don't know what she takes, but it has limited her interests.'

'Poor Polly. At the best she was a sad little mess. I thought you'd dropped her ages ago.'

'I'm rather sorry for her.'

'You're *what*? D'you mean to offer her the reversion of Antinous?'

'I've told you. She doesn't want any more men. When she talks at all she talks about *St. John of the Cross*.'

'But why take him there?'

'One usually takes one's chauffeur.'

'Not to Polly's, one doesn't, unless one wants to lose him. Somebody's sure to make a pass at him.'

Anna laughed.

'We dropped in for an afternoon on the way down,' she confided, 'and somebody did. He was furious.'

'I should think so. He's very middle class, that young man. Never been to a public school. You'd better take care or he'll be joining the resistance movement.'

'The what? What do you mean?'

'An underground resistance movement has been started in this hotel,' explained Mr. Siddal, sitting down on Anna's bed. 'I think Mrs. Paley and Miss Wraxton started it, and then they nobbled my son Gerry. They're hand-in-glove with Nancibel, and she might rope in your boy friend. The thing is spreading.'

'But what resistance? What against?'

'That I don't know. But I do know that a great deal is going on. All sorts of people are getting together. They meet on the cliff at night. Canon Wraxton forbade his daughter to attend these agapemones, but she defies him. Gerry talks of going to Kenya and leaving us to support ourselves. And I think there is a junior branch which writes messages in code. Nancibel means to provide a feast for the little Coves, and my wife has promised jelly. Mrs. Paley laughs in the lounge. All these are straws in the wind.'

'But what's it all for? What is it all about?'

'When I know that I shall be a wiser man . . .'

At this moment Fred rushed in with his eyes starting from his head. He told them that a policeman was coming across the sand.

3. The Law

He was coming across the sand because his bicycle had punctured just as he left Porthmerryn and, being obliged to walk, he came the quickest way, by the cliffs, instead of going all the way round by the road. But he felt himself that the Law should have arrived in state along the drive, not scrambling up the rocks like a tripper. So he did his best to march across the cove in an official and menacing manner. And his advance, observed by the inmates of Pendizack, caused widespread alarm, before ever he reached the front door. Bruce thought he must have come about that stolen car and slipped away to hide in the creek. Miss Ellis thought that the Siddals had sent him to turn her out, for she had had a scene with Mrs. Siddal that morning when she had explained her intention to remain a full month at Pendizack although she refused to do any more work. Canon Wraxton thought that his own eviction was impending and prepared for battle. Fred thought Nancibel was going to be arrested for stealing the carved stone. He rushed to warn her. But Nancibel only said:

'Rats! He wouldn't dare. He's my cousin.'

She had been persuaded to abandon her threat of going home. She was a reasonable, kind-hearted girl, and she very quickly saw that the only person to suffer would be poor Mrs. Siddal, who had not been to blame. Moreover the story, gleefully brought to the kitchen by Robin, of Mrs. Cove and the soapstone, had restored her spirits. She was now inclined to regard the whole thing as a joke, and when the policeman rang the bell she went gaily to the front door.

'Morning, Sam,' she said.

Sam Peters was a very young policeman and he had never served a summons before. He ignored her genial greeting and asked solemnly:

'Is this the Pendizack Hotel?'

'No, it's St. Paul's Cathedral,' said Nancibel. 'Have you lost your memory or what?'

'We have to begin by asking that,' explained Sam. 'It's merely a matter of form.'

'I should hope so, considering you were born in Pendizack village I'd be sorry if you hadn't found out where this is by now. How's Auntie?'

'Off the record,' said Sam, 'Ma's got kidney trouble again. Is there a party residing here name of Gifford?'

'That's right. Sir Henry Gifford.'

'It's not him I want. It's a lady. Lady Gifford.'

'Well, that's his wife. Whatever do you . . . ?'

'I got to see her.'

'What about?'

'Don't you be so nosey, young Nancibel.'

'Well, you can't see her. She's in bed still.'

'When does she get up?'

'Never.'

'I got to see her if I wait here for ever.'

'Won't the gentleman do?'

272

'No, he won't. I got to hand her this personally.'

He indicated an envelope which he held.

'Come in,' said Nancibel. 'I'll find Mrs. Siddal. I think she's back.'

Sam came in and sat on a chair in the hall. Nancibel went in search of Mrs. Siddal, who was counting the laundry with Gerry. She explained Sam's errand.

'A summons,' said Gerry.

'But she doesn't drive a car,' said Mrs. Siddal, who could imagine but one reason for a summons. 'Are you sure it's not Sir Henry?'

She went out to the hall to confer with Sam, and then she went up to Lady Gifford's room.

'I can't possibly see him,' declared Lady Gifford.

'He won't go till you do,' said Mrs. Siddal. 'Shall I bring him up or will you come down?'

'Mrs. Siddal, I can't possibly. I'm much too ill.'

'He'll simply sit in the hall till you get up.'

'I shan't be getting up today.'

'I can't have a policeman sitting in my hall indefinitely,' declared Mrs. Siddal.

'Then tell him to go away. I absolutely refuse to see him.'

'One can't treat the police like that.'

'I don't see why not. Who pays their wages? We do.'

Mrs. Siddal went downstairs and reported all this to Sam. But he was obdurate. His instructions were to put the document in the lady's own hands, and he would not quit the house till he had done so. He remained on the chair in the hall and Nancibel brought him a cup of tea.

The news spread gradually over Pendizack that he had come for Lady Gifford. Bruce came back from the creek and Miss Ellis unlocked her door. But nobody told the Canon, who grew tired of waiting for the assault and came down to confront the enemy.

'I believe,' he said to Sam in the hall, 'that I am the person you wish to see. Very well. Here I am.'

Sam gaped and asked if he was Sir Henry Gifford.

'Certainly not. I am Canon Wraxton. And I warn you that if you attempt to molest me in any way I shall make a great deal of trouble for you. What's that you're holding? A summons?'

'It's not for you,' said Sam. 'It's for a lady.'

'A lady? My daughter, I suppose. That's the game, is it? They're going to put it all on to her? Let me see it.'

'It's got to be put into her own hands,' said Sam, withholding it.

'Not before I've seen it. I'm acting for her.'

'Then you'd better bring her here, sir. I'm waiting here till I see her.'

'She's out. She's gone to Porthmerryn.'

'They said she was in bed.'

'Oh, they did, did they? Then they were lying. I ask you once again to let me see that document.'

'Not till I see Lady Gifford,' declared Sam.

'Lady Gifford? What in heaven has she to do with it?'

'She's the lady it's for.'

'That's impossible. Lady Gifford is not my daughter. What do you mean by all this nonsense?'

'I never said she was,' cried the badgered Sam. 'It was you said she was.'

'I said nothing of the kind.'

They were interrupted by Sir Henry, who had just come in from his walk and had been told by Mrs. Siddal of Sam's presence in the hall.

'I understand,' he said to Sam, 'that you have been instructed to see my wife. I am Sir Henry Gifford.'

'That's right,' agreed Sam.

'The man's a fool,' interrupted the Canon. 'This has nothing to do with your wife, Sir Henry. It's my daughter he's come to see. It's part of a trick to get us out of here.'

A momentary relief flashed across Sir Henry's harassed face. When he heard of a policeman in the hall he had been so sure that the blow had fallen. Subconsciously he had been waiting for it ever since they arrived. But Sam soon dashed his hopes. The document was for Lady Gifford and for nobody else.

'She's upstairs in bed,' said Sir Henry heavily. 'I'd better take you up. You can hand it to her in bed, can't you?'

'That'll be all right, sir,' said Sam gratefully.

'Then this,' exclaimed the Canon, 'has nothing whatever to do with me? . . . Why was I brought down?'

Nobody could determine why he had been brought down, and he was left to decide the matter for himself while Sir Henry took Sam upstairs.

'I can't,' cried Lady Gifford, as they trooped into her room.

Sam clattered across to the bed and asked if she was Lady Gifford.

'I refuse,' she said. 'I utterly refuse . . . my doctor ordered me . . .'

'This,' said Sir Henry, 'is Lady Gifford.'

Sam offered the envelope but she would not take it. So he laid it upon the counterpane and withdrew.

'I shall never forgive you for this,' said Lady Gifford to her husband. 'Bringing that brute here! You! Who have sworn to love and protect me.'

'Let me look at that summons.'

'How do you know it is a summons?'

'Of course it is. What else could it be?'

She seized upon the paper and tore it up before he could stop her.

'Eirene! You fool! If you behave like that you'll be sent to prison.'

'No. No, I shan't. Sir Giles will give me a certificate. He knows how ill I am, even if you won't believe it.'

'That summons means you have to appear before a certain court on a certain date. You'll have to be there.'

'Not if I'm ill.'

'What is it about? Why are you summonsed?'

'How should I know? It's ridiculous.'

'If you won't answer me I shall take steps to learn the particulars elsewhere. I'll go to the police station. I shall undertake to see that you appear.'

'Is this loving me? Is this protecting me?'

'I can't protect you unless I know how matters stand.'

'I tell you, I don't know what it's all about.'

'A policeman called to see you in London, after we'd

left. They told us on the telephone. Do you remember?'

'No. I don't remember anything.'

'They must have got your address and sent the summons to be delivered here.'

'Instead of guarding our house from being burgled. No wonder there is this crime wave if that is how they waste their time.'

'Have you ever had a letter from the Treasury?'

'No, I don't think so. Why should I?'

He turned away in exasperation.

'It's a waste of time talking to you,' he declared. 'I'll go to the police station.'

'No, no . . . Harry! Don't do that. I remember now . . . I did get a letter. Perhaps it was from the Treasury.'

'And what did it say?'

'I've forgotten . . . no . . . no . . . Don't go. It was to ask me to explain something or other.'

'Explain what?'

'I couldn't understand.'

'So what did you do?'

'I tore it up.'

'You didn't answer it?'

'Oh, no.'

'Why did you not show it to me?'

'I didn't think it was important.'

'What . . . roughly . . . was it about?'

'About Mr. Perkins.'

'Who is he?'

'I don't know. He was a man I met at the hotel.'

'What hotel?'

'A hotel at Cannes.'

'But you weren't staying in a hotel. You were with the Varens.'

'Y-yes. Most of the time.'

'Did you, by any chance, give a cheque to this man Perkins?'

'Yes.'

'And what did he give you? Francs?'

'Yes.'

'What was the cheque for?'

'I forget. I think . . . four hundred pounds.'

'But don't you know that's a breach of the currency regulations? You promised me you wouldn't . . .'

'I didn't. I promised I wouldn't take more than seventy-five pounds out and I didn't. But one can't stay at Cannes indefinitely for seventy-five pounds. Of course I needed more money . . .'

'You told me, when you got back, that you'd managed it on seventy-five pounds.'

'I suppose I forgot. Mr. Perkins was an Englishman.'

'I told you . . . I explained to you . . .'

'Everybody was doing it. Everybody gave him cheques.'

'If you read the newspapers you'll find that people who have done this sort of thing are heavily fined.'

'Well, if I am fined, I can afford it. I don't see why you are making all this fuss.'

'I've told you. It'll be more than a fine if you go on like this. It will be prison.'

'No, Harry. People in our class don't get sent to prison. I have several friends who have been fined. Nobody sent them to prison.'

'And another thing. This is the end of my career. If this comes out and there is a public scandal, I shall have to resign. I've too much respect for the law to stay on the Bench when my wife has so flagrantly broken it.'

'Oh? So it's your career you're really fussing about?'

'I know you have always wanted me to resign, so that we might live in Guernsey.'

'Yes, I have. And now we can. I must say, Harry, I can't see that there's anything so very terrible about all this. If we could get off income tax, living in Guernsey, the fine would be nothing.'

For a few minutes he could not reply. At last he said:

'I shall never live with you again. There's nothing in life you value more than your saucer of cream.'

'Why shouldn't I? I can afford cream. Why shouldn't I go to live where the cream is?'

'I won't live with you any more. You're not human.'

Lady Gifford closed her eyes and lay back upon her pillows. Hard words break no bones, as both of them knew very well. He left her and went downstairs.

4. The Scapegoat

The little Coves, though much restored, were still shattered by yesterday's experiences. They sat about on the terrace in deck chairs, with an invalidish air, and there was a tendency to make much of them. Public opinion had fastened all blame for the incident upon Hebe, who met black looks wherever she went and snubs whenever she opened her mouth.

The only smiles she had had were from the Coves, who had waved to her wistfully when their mother's back was turned. She knew that they were loyal and friendly, but she was not grateful and she resented the fuss which everyone made over them. Nor would she accept the timid apologies of Caroline, who had betrayed the Spartan secrets.

To efface herself until the storm of disapproval should have blown over was a precaution which never occurred to Hebe. With each snub she grew more aggressive and more determined to fight the entire hotel. She played selections from 'Sunny Hours' on the lounge piano until Mrs. Siddal came and locked it. She took her cat into the dining room for lunch. She drew a picture of Mr. Chad on the terrace wall saying: 'Wot? No black amber?' And finally, finding Mrs. Lechene's French window open and the room empty, she strolled in. An uncovered typewriter stood on the table, with a clean sheet of paper in it. She began to experiment.

th3 HorRIBL3E HOTeL

Onceupon a time ther was ahotel inhabited by devils dressed up to look like ladys and Gentlemen . . .

Anna came In and caught her. But for once there was no lecture. All that Anna did was to smile in a queer sort of way and say:

'Well! You're a one, aren't you?'

Hebe nodded.

'Do you realize you've set the whole place by the ears?'

Hebe nodded again, with some pride.

'Suppose you sit down and tell me all about it?'

Anna took the cigarette box from the mantelpiece and proffered it.

'Smoke?'

'Oh, thanks!' said the ravished Hebe.

They lighted their cigarettes and Anna dropped into a chair.

'You'll go far,' she prophesied. 'At your age I was meekly hemming handkerchiefs.'

Hebe cautiously ate the end of her cigarette and tried to think of Anna hemming handkerchiefs. In her ignorance she supposed that Anna must have worn a crinoline.

'You'll always be in hot water, you know. Always!' Anna continued. 'But don't worry. It's worth it. Live your own life, and you'll never regret it.'

She looked Hebe up and down and muttered:

'Coined in nature's mint in ecstasy. One can see that. Who were your real parents? Do you know?'

Hebe obliged with all the details she could give, and Anna listened with flattering interest. It was very agreeable to Hebe. Yet, although her spirits rose, she had an odd sense of insincerity and dissatisfaction. She was far from sure that she really liked Anna and wondered at herself for these confidences.

'So they adopted you,' concluded Anna, 'and now they want to turn you into a bread-and-butter miss. Why don't you run away from it all?'

'I've often thought about it,' said Hebe, who had.

'They'll be furious, mind. But you might as well be hanged for a sheep as a lamb. I'm going up to St. Merricks this afternoon to stay with some friends. I think you'd amuse them and they'd amuse you. Like to come along?'

'Oh, Mrs. Lechene!'

'My name is Anna.'

'Oh, Anna! It's very kind of you . . .'

'Not at all. I happen to like naughty girls. I was one myself, once. But, as I say, I was a Sunday School prizewinner compared with you.'

'But won't they miss me?'

'Let 'em. Teach 'em a lesson. Now go and find Bruce and tell him I want him. Bring him back with you. But don't tell him a word about our plot.'

Hebe ran off and found Bruce hanging gloomily about in the yard. He gave her the scowl which she now got from everybody, and told her to hop it. But he had to come with her when she haughtily gave him her message.

'Oh, Bruce,' said Anna, when they reached her room, 'will you bring the car round and pack yourself a bag? We're going up to St. Merricks, to Mrs. Palmer, for a night or so. I've told them in the office.'

Bruce looked at Hebe and did not know what to say. If she had not been there he might very well have refused to drive Anna up to St. Merricks, for he had been considering how to give her notice all the morning.

'I felt an impulse to get out of here,' added Anna blandly. 'A policeman sitting in the hall this morning quite put me off my lunch.'

That sent him off to get the car.

'Now,' she said to Hebe, 'pop up to the top of the drive and hide among the bushes there. When he gets out to open the gate, and his back is turned, nip out and get in with me. I'll have the door open.'

'But hadn't I better pack a . . . ?'

'No. Don't bother to pack anything.'

'Or put on a dress?'

'No. Come just as you are.'

Hebe wore shorts and a pullover. Her face was very dirty. This reversal of all visiting rules entranced her, and she felt that Anna's friends would certainly be amusing. She sped off to hide among the bushes by the top of the drive.

How frightened they would be, she thought, when they found her gone! A search would be made. Everybody would be sorry. Their faces would grow more and more haggard as the days passed and no trace could be found of the poor child whom they had persecuted. All attention would be diverted from the Coves. She would return a heroine, with Anna, and Anna's prestige as a grown-up, to shield her from reproof. She giggled as she squatted among the bushes. And yet there was still this uneasiness, this nagging dissatisfaction. She did not really like Anna.

Presently she heard the car coming up the zigzags of the drive. It rounded the top corner and crunched to a standstill by the gate. Bruce got out. At the same time a door opened at the back and she saw Anna beckoning. In three seconds she was nestling on a heap of rugs at Anna's feet.

'Lie low,' whispered Anna.

Bruce returned and drove them through. Then he got out again to shut the gate. After that they went on, their pace quickening when they reached the high road.

Hebe soon grew bored, crouching there among the rugs and unable to see out of the window. It was very stuffy and the smell of petrol made her sick. She began to understand why so many dogs hate travelling in a car, and why they are always so anxious to get up on to a seat. But after a while she fell asleep.

She woke up to hear Anna talking.

'Nobody's forcing you to stay there if you don't like it. You can get yourself a room at the inn.'

'I damn well will,' came the voice of Bruce from the front. 'I don't want ever to see any of that lot again. How you can . . .'

Anna saw that Hebe was awake and said quickly:

'That's enough. I've told you to please yourself.'

Hebe made signs of enquiry, but Anna shook her head and motioned to her to remain hidden. They seemed to be going very slowly down a long hill. And then they were in a town, winding through narrow streets. Then they went up a hill and at last they stopped.

'Here we are,' said Anna, getting out. 'Leave the car here, and garage it later. Go and get yourself a room. Come along, Hebe.'

Hebe skipped out and laughed when she saw the amazement of Bruce. So did Anna, who explained:

'I've kidnapped her. She's a kindred spirit, I feel, and they don't appreciate her properly at Pendizack.'

'Anna! You can't dream of . . . a kid like her . . .'

'Don't fuss. I'll look after her. We'll take her back on Friday.'

'But Mrs. Palmer . . . a kid of that age . . . you know perfectly well that they're . . .'

'It's no affair of yours, is it? Come, Hebe!'

Anna pushed open a green door in a very tall white wall, took Hebe through it and shut it in his face.

The garden went uphill in a steep succession of grass terraces and a flight of stone steps up the middle. At the top stood the house. And on the bottom terrace two people were lying on the grass, sunbathing. They lay on their faces and they wore slacks. They had such curly hair and such round bottoms that Hebe supposed they were girls, until, as she and Anna went past, they sat up, revealing masculine torsos.

'Oh, Anna,' said one of them. 'Have you got any cigarettes? We've run out.'

'Only enough for myself,' said Anna. 'Is Polly up at the house?'

'I expect so. Where's Bruce?'

Anna laughed and took Hebe up the steps to the house. At the top they had a fine view of the harbour and the roofs of lower houses. And then they walked through a long window into a room full of people who looked all alike to Hebe, until she had begun to sort them out. They were not young and they were not old. Most of them wore slacks so that it was difficult to tell, in several cases, whether they were men or women. They did not seem to be particularly pleased to see Anna, but they stared at Hebe.

Presently Polly, who had red hair and was unmistakably female, asked who she was.

'This,' said Anna, pulling her forward, 'is Hebe. She's staying at my hotel and I brought her along because she's in dog house over a slight case of murder.'

This was received with some animation and an old gentleman, who was quite certainly not an old lady, came forward and shook Hebe by the hand. Hebe made the little curtsey she had learnt in America, but could not get her hand away until Anna intervened and told him that Hebe was only there to be looked at.

'Oh, my God,' said Polly crossly, 'I draw the line at infant murderesses.'

'Who did she murder?' asked several voices.

And somebody gave Hebe a drink.

'She'll be no trouble,' declared Anna. 'She can play with Nicolette.'

'Nicolette's not here. Her father has got her. Listen, Anna, I've had a letter from the landlord . . .'

The drink was like nothing Hebe had ever tasted. Her head spun after a couple of sips. Their voices became booming and indistinct so that she could not be quite sure of what she heard. But it seemed to her that Polly had used one of THE WORDS. There were three or four of them, and she had seen them written up on walls but had never been able to find out what they meant—only that nobody ever used them, and that the people who wrote them up were not agreed as to spelling.

Presently Polly used it again, quite unmistakably, and then she used another. By the time that she had finished describing her landlord's letter she had used them all and several which Hebe had never seen written up. But nobody seemed to be surprised and presently someone asked again about the murder.

'Three adenoidal brats, staying at the hotel,' explained Anna. 'She took them to the top of an exceeding high cliff and pushed them into the sea. But unluckily some busybody came and fished them out again.'

'Anna! You're making this up.'

'No,' said Hebe loudly. 'It's true. Their names are Blanche, and Maud and Beatrix.'

This was received with applause, and enquiries as to who Hebe was, anyway.

'Nobody knows,' said Anna. 'Born on the wrong side of the blanket. But her mother . . .'

'I won't have her here. There's no room. You seem to think I keep a bloody hotel . . .'

'Never mind Polly, Hebe. Have another drink and tell us why you did it.'

Somebody pushed her into a chair, saying:

'Tell us about Blanche and Maud and Beatrix. Why did you do it?'

'They wear combinations,' giggled Hebe, starting on a second drink.

This went down well.

'And their teeth stick out.'

More laughter.

'And they believe in fairies.'

This was the best joke of all. There was a concerted screech. A wave of nausea went over Hebe, but she could not tell if this was the drink or because she hated herself for jeering at the gentle and loyal Coves. She felt an impulse to sing, and did so, waving her glass:

> There are fairies at the bottom of our garden.
> They're not so very, very far away . . .

Her voice was drowned in a roar of laughter. Even the morose Polly was laughing and asking:

'How old did you say it is?'

Hebe stopped singing and stared at her owlishly.

'I don't like you,' she said. 'You're awful. You're a . . . a . . . harridan. My friends the Coves are very nice.'

Soon after that she must have fallen asleep in the chair, for she lost the thread of what they were saying, though she could hear their booming, screeching voices. But somebody kept poking her and patting and stroking her, which she did not like, so at last she cried out violently:

'Oh, get *away*!'

There was a sudden silence and then Anna said angrily:

'Bonnett, you old goat. Leave the child alone. I told you . . .'

'Why in hell did you bring her,' interrupted Polly. 'She's pickled.'

'She'll sleep it off if she's left alone.'

'Better put her outside for a bit,' said another voice, 'with Bint and Eggie. She'll be safe as houses with *them*.'

Somebody picked her up and dragged her out into the fresh air and down to the bottom lawn where the voices of the sunbathers were raised in protest.

'Polly says you've to look after her,' said Hebe's escort. 'You must do something occasionally for your keep.'

'How can Polly be so unkind? We're not Sitters In.'

'I'm going to be sick,' said Hebe.

And was, amid angry squeals from Bint and Eggie who removed themselves and their mattresses on to a higher terrace and left her lying, exhausted and miserable, on the grass.

How long she lay there she did not know. But at last she was aroused by someone exclaiming:

'Oh, Hebe!'

With difficulty she turned her head and opened her smarting eyes. Bruce was bending over her.

'I felt I must know . . . I was worried . . . are you all right?'

'Oh, Bruce, do take me home. I'm so sick and they don't want me, and there was a horrible old man . . .'

'That's all right. Don't cry. I'll take you right back. Can you walk?'

'No. I should fall down.'

He picked her up and carried her through the gate in the garden wall to the car.

5. Siddal's Hour

'Is the chauffeur joining us again tonight?' asked Evangeline, as she sat on the terrace with Mrs. Paley after dinner.

They were waiting for Gerry to bring out the tea basket before adjourning to their night's quarters on the cliff.

'No,' said Mrs. Paley. 'I believe he's gone to St. Mer ricks with Mrs. Lechene. But Duff and Robin are coming, I think.'

Evangeline made a face. She did not much want Duff and Robin.

'What were you and the chauffeur talking about so late?' she asked.

'A lot of things. He told me about Nancibel's plan for a party for the Coves. I've promised to help with it.'

'What sort of party?'

'A kind of universal beano, as far as I can make out. That's what they want. But they've got no money, poor chicks. However . . . that can be remedied. It's collecting the food . . .'

'Perhaps I could help,' said Angie. 'I've some sweet points. When is it to be?'

'As soon as they are quite well again. I think Friday would be a good day. And it has to be in the evening, because they want to invite the staff.'

'I hope it will be outside,' said Evangeline. 'I hate this hotel. It's so shut in, with the cliffs hanging over it. Mrs.

Paley! I . . . I want to talk to you. I can't make up my mind
. . . about . . . if only . . . Gerry Siddal is so nice . . . but of
course there's . . .'

'Talk connectedly or not at all,' commanded Mrs. Paley.

'Well . . . my father says I run after men.'

'You don't, I'm afraid. I wish you did.'

'Oh, Mrs. Paley!'

'A girl who runs away from men is a fool, Angie.'

'But he says . . . he's often said, that I'd snatch at anything
in trousers, just to get away from home.'

'Very natural if you did. I know I would.'

'Yes. But I wouldn't want to snatch at Gerry. He's so
nice. I'd want to be sure I really . . . I mean, I believe I could
make him so sorry for me that . . . but it wouldn't be fair.
He ought to get somebody who really . . . who really . . .
I'd never feel sure that I hadn't just snatched . . .'

'Are you worrying about your feeling for Gerry, or his
for you?'

'Mine for him, I suppose. Do I really . . . or is he just a
harbour?'

'You'll have to fight like the devil to get him, Angie. Only
a very determined girl could face it. I think by the time
you're through you'll find that you're very sure of yourself.
You've got to rescue him from his family.'

'Yes,' said Evangeline, flushing. 'It's abominable . . .'

'You're not good at fighting for your own rights. You are
more likely to become obstinate about his rights. And why
should you do that, unless you care for him? Here's Mr.
Siddal. Now don't get up and rush away. Stay and talk to

him. He may be your father-in-law one of these days, and he has no idea what you are like.'

Evangeline subsided, trembling, on to the swing seat beside Mrs. Paley, and watched the approach of Mr. Siddal, who had washed and dressed and come out of the boot-hole to mix with the visitors. He had looked into the lounge but found nobody there except Sir Henry, listening morosely to the wireless. So he strolled out on to the terrace where Mrs. Paley and Miss Wraxton greeted him with inviting faces.

He took a seat in a deck chair beside them and prepared to talk, to lecture indeed, upon any subject they should choose. Once launched, he seldom allowed anyone else to get a word in, but he always left the selection of a topic to his victims.

'So what,' he said to them, 'shall we discuss tonight?'

Mrs. Paley was obligingly ready with a subject.

'There was something I wanted to ask you,' she said.

'I'm always at your service, Mrs. Paley.'

'What is the difference between pride and self-respect?'

There was a short pause while Mr. Siddal arranged his ideas.

'Pride . . .' he began.

'What's that?' cried Evangeline.

Something had fallen on the grass quite close to them. She jumped up and searched for it in the gathering dusk. After a few seconds she found it, and brought it to them.

'It's a little . . . where did it come from?'

Mr. Siddal laughed and took it from her.

'It's soapstone, I think.'

'What?' cried the ladies, who had both heard the story. 'Again?'

'We have a poltergeist, apparently.'

'They are generally little girls,' said Mrs. Paley.

'Quite so. And this hotel is full of little girls. I'll give this to my wife. She'll know what to do with it. I'm terribly frightened of Mrs. Cove, aren't you?'

'You mean you think it's the little Coves?' asked Evangeline. 'But they look so meek and timid.'

'Not all of them. Personally I suspect the visionary one with the bad back. Well . . . pride . . .'

'Yes,' said Mrs. Paley. 'Pride. And self-respect.'

'And self-respect. As you say, Mrs. Paley, they are often confused. This is because they give rise, to a certain extent, to the same kind of conduct. Proud people and self-respecting people prefer to sail under their own steam, paddle their own canoes and boil their own kettles of fish. They do not demand help or sympathy. But the motive . . .' he emphasized the word by patting her knee, 'the motive is different. Self-respect regards independence as a social and moral duty. We must not fling our burdens on to the shoulders of other people. We must not inflict on them the story of our woes. But self-respect is not antagonized by sympathy or offers of help. It may feel obliged to refuse them, but it can be touched by the offer and respect the generosity which makes the offer.'

'Yes,' said Mrs. Paley, 'and the proud man is angry with anyone who offers him help.'

'The proud man is humiliated that anyone should

suppose he needs help. The offer is an insult. His motive is not that of social obligation, but a desire for superiority. He always thinks in terms of superiority and inferiority. Help, he imagines, is given by the superior to the inferior, and to offer it to him is to degrade him. If he is obliged to accept generosity he hates the giver. His independence is an indulgence of his own ego.'

Mrs. Paley sighed. And then she thanked Mr. Siddal.

The chimes of Big Ben rang out over the terrace, for Sir Henry was listening to the nine o'clock news in the lounge, with all the windows open.

'And I want to know about patience,' said Evangeline timidly. 'Do you think a person can be too patient?'

Mr. Siddal smiled. He did not often get such a respectful audience.

'No,' he said. 'Patience must not be confused with submission. When we say that a person is too patient, we generally mean that he is not patient at all, but merely submissive . . .'

'Then what is patience, exactly?' she persisted.

'Patience is the capacity to endure all that is necessary in attaining a desired end. The patient man is master of his fate. The submissive man has handed his fate over to somebody else. Patience implies liberty and superiority. Impatience nearly always involves a loss of liberty. It causes people to commit themselves, to burn their boats, to put it out of their power to alter or modify their course. Patience never forsakes the ultimate goal because the road is hard. There can be no patience without an object.'

Evangeline, in her turn, thanked him. To both ladies he had given, though he did not know it, advice on their own particular problems.

'I think it's getting chilly,' said Mrs. Paley, getting up. 'I'm going to stroll up and down.'

They all three strolled up and down the terrace while Mr. Siddal illustrated his thesis on patience by quotations from *King Lear*. But he paused as they passed the lounge windows to listen to a rich voice which rolled out into the dusk. It said:

'Many of you will still be on your holidays or will have just finished them in this beautiful summer sunshine. God bless you all, you and your families. Get all you can of happiness and health and strength out of the sun and the sea and the fresh air . . .'

'Sounds like a bishop,' said Mr. Siddal as they passed out of earshot. 'The news must have been over quickly.'

'I daresay it's the Government,' said Mrs. Paley. 'Well, thank you very much. It's wonderful how you put things. You have always thought it out so clearly. I think it's a pity you didn't go into the Church, Mr. Siddal.'

'So do I,' he agreed. 'I might have been a Dean by now. I'd have liked to be a Dean. Deaneries are generally such nice houses, and very good kitchen gardens. Good fruit trees.'

'I shall never forget what you said on Sunday about innocence.'

'Innocence?'

'How it's the innocent people who save the world.'

Mr. Siddal smiled, but did not commit himself to a sequel on his Sunday subject, which was as well for he was quite capable of taking the other side and proving that innocence is the source of all evil. He could make out a very good case for any side of any question.

After another turn they all went into the lounge where the rich voice was reaching its peroration.

'. . . and so I say to you, as was said long ago: Only be thou strong and very courageous.'

Sir Henry was alone in the lounge. He was sitting beside the wireless and his face looked yellow.

'Who was that?' asked Mr. Siddal.

'The Chancellor of the Exchequer. Broadcasting to the nation after the nine o'clock news.'

'*Was* it? What's he been turned on to tell us this time?'

'American loan. Run out. No more dollars.'

'Well. I'll be . . . whitewashed! I'd rather hear Shinwell. He doesn't quote the Bible at us when he tells us he can't get any coal.'

'I was sure it was the Government,' said Mrs. Paley placidly.

6. Shake Hands for Ever

Hebe's absence at supper was remarked, but it was supposed that she must be sulking somewhere and nobody troubled to go in search of her. They had all finished and dispersed before Bruce brought her back. He left her in the yard, in the car, and went to the scullery door where Nancibel, who had again stayed late, was still washing up.

She was surprised to see him back from St. Merricks so soon, but she would not show her surprise and continued to scour saucepans with her nose in the air.

'Nancibel, I must speak to you.'

'How often must I tell you that I don't want to have anything more to do with you.'

'This isn't about us,' he explained. 'It's Hebe.'

'Hebe? What's she been up to now?'

'I've got her in the car. I want to smuggle her into the house and put her to bed without anyone knowing.'

'I've no use for Hebe. If she's in a jam, let her get herself out of it.'

'Oh, Nancibel, please! Don't be too hasty. It isn't her fault. When you understand you'll be as upset as I am. Come and look at her.'

'What's she been doing?'

'Well . . . she's pickled, for one thing. Passed out.'

'Hebe? No! How disgusting!'

'It's not her fault, I tell you. That kid's been in enough trouble for one day. You know what they're like in this hole . . . Miss Ellis . . . Mrs. Cove . . .'

'I do,' said Nancibel, softening a little. 'Oh well, all right. I'll come. We'll smuggle her up the back stairs. Where's the car?'

'At the stables.'

As they went to the yard Bruce told her briefly what had happened. She heard him out in a stony silence. Between them they got the inert Hebe out of the car and up the back stairs and laid her upon her bed. Then Nancibel spoke.

'I'll undress her and put her to bed,' she said. 'And you can go. Tomorrow I shall go to Sir Henry and tell him what you did, you and Mrs. Lechene. I'll see that Hebe doesn't get blamed. But if you don't go now, at once, and if you say another word, I'll go to Sir Henry at once.'

'I didn't . . .'

'I'm giving you time to clear out, see? If you don't want Sir Henry after you, you'd better clear out now.'

'I can't see that it was my fault. I didn't know she was in the car.'

'There's telephones, isn't there? When you did find out you could have rung him up from there. If you'd so much as threatened to ring him up she'd have sent Hebe back right away, and this would never have happened. Now go, and don't let me see you again.'

Bruce went. In the stable loft he packed his suitcase. Before he left Pendizack he wrote two letters.

The first was to Anna. It said:

Your car is alright. It's in the garage. You taking Hebe
to that house finished me as far as your concerned. I
hope I will never see you again.—BRUCE.

The letter to Nancibel was harder; he re-wrote it several
times and it was late in the evening before he had finished it.

DEAR NANCIBEL,

I'm going to do what you said and get a job as a bus
driver. But not in these parts you need not be afraid
of seeing me about on the roads. Not for a long time
anyway. When I think a bit more of myself, I shall ask
you to think more of me, but not till then.

   I am almost sure I would have left her after today,
and the way she took Hebe off, even if it had not
been for you. It makes me sick.

   Nancibel I love you and you must not be angry
with me for saying so. I have a perfect right to do so,
and it is natural for any man that meets you to love
you, whether he is deserving or undeserving, just as
good and bad together like a lovely piece of music if
they hear it. You are the sweetest and dearest girl in
the world and I am very lucky to have met you, for it
has changed my life, even if you will never look at me
again. I hope you will be very happy. You will probably
marry some nice chap, you have too much sense to
pick a rotter. And you will make him very happy. But
you won't do more for him than you have done for me.

There is one thing she knows about me that may come out. I pinched a car for fun, I meant to return it, but I got in a smash and a cyclist was killed. She knows about it, she got me out of a hole there. But sometimes, if she is annoyed, she talks as if she meant to give me away. I do not think she will, but if she does and it all comes out I would like you to have known first.

Well, that is enough about me. God bless you my darling Nancibel and give you a very happy life. Knowing you has made me sure that there can be a great deal of happiness in the world.

Your loving

BRUCE.

P.S.—I enclose 5/- and my sweet points for the Feast. Friday night, isn't it? I'll think of you all. But don't you think of me unless you can think kindly.

7. Bond or Free?

Gerry had not known that Duff and Robin meant to sleep upon the cliff. He was much put out to find them when he took up the tea basket. Not that he was quite sure that he intended to remain himself for a third night in succession; prudence had suggested to him that it might be better to return to the stables as soon as he had settled his ladies for the night. Affairs between himself and Evangeline were going too far for safety. He must not allow himself to become attached, and he ought to have remembered that before.

Usually it was his first thought, whenever he encountered an attractive girl. He could not sit behind one on a bus without a certain pang of self-sacrifice; for an instant he would see her in a flowered overall, busy at a cooking stove, and then, with a sigh, he would relinquish her. For it was thus that he always imagined a wife, not as a bedfellow or as a playfellow, but as a cook, decoratively preparing his favourite dinner, setting it before him with a smile, watching him eat it, and listening while he talked about himself.

When introduced to a pretty young woman he was always excessively guarded in his manner, for fear that he might raise false hopes. Since he could marry no girl he was able, unchecked, to indulge in the fantasy that all would have been ready to cook for him, if invited to do so. A mild flirtation might have taught him better, but he had never dared to embark upon one for fear of becoming attached.

If Evangeline had been pretty, if she had possessed any of the attractions which made him sigh after girls in buses, he would have taken fright before. But he had begun by disliking her and had grown fond of her in a disinterested attempt to do the poor thing justice. Never for a moment had he visualized her as a possible wife-cook. She had stolen into his heart so imperceptibly that he did not know she was there until faced with the prospect of losing her. His mother, at supper, had casually thanked heaven that the Wraxtons were going on Saturday, and the pang which he then experienced was his first intimation of danger. He could not bear the thought of never seeing Evangeline again. There was a note in her voice to which he had not listened nearly long enough. He had learnt to like it unawares, while telling himself that she was really quite intelligent.

So he toiled up the hill in a mood of melancholy decision, meditating a break. He did not want to hurt her feelings. But while they drank their tea he would drop a hint or two about his position. And, for the rest of the week, he would avoid her.

Before he reached the shelter, however, he was startled by strains of song; Duff's baritone and Robin's lusty tenor were raised in a catch. And all his melancholy evaporated in a gust of anger. How could he drop any hints while those young brutes were roaring their heads off? Was he never to be allowed any intimacies of his own?

Standing still upon the cliff path he silently cursed his entire family. Nor was he inclined to be pleased with Mrs. Paley and Angie for having admitted these intruders. If they had valued him as they ought they would have kept this twilit hour for him, and him alone. Angie had no business to be singing rounds with his brothers; no business to be singing at all. He had never known that she could sing. It was intolerable that Robin and Duff should have discovered this about her before he did. She had a high, sweet voice which toned well with theirs, and as Gerry came round the boulders she gave out the first line of a new catch, singing alone in the quiet summer dusk:

> Wind, gentle evergreen! To form a shade
> Around the tomb where Sophocles is laid . . .

Robin and Duff took up the air. They were sitting in a row on a rock, looking ridiculously pleased with themselves, while Mrs. Paley occupied her usual seat, some distance away, at the end of the headland. The singers did not stop when they saw Gerry; they merely grinned and signed to him to join them. He put down the basket with a bump and stalked off to join Mrs. Paley, from whom he learnt that his intolerable brothers were really intending to stay the night.

'Then I shan't stay,' announced Gerry sulkily. 'I shall go back to the stables.'

But he did stay. He sat down beside Mrs. Paley and fumed for a little while. Then he said:

'I'm in a hopeless position.'

Mrs. Paley nodded. Bruce had sat on the very same spot,

last night, and had used the very same words. He had told her a long story. So was Gerry going to tell her a long story. They could tell her nothing which she had not guessed. And for Bruce she believed that she had been able to do nothing, since it was said that he had gone off up the coast with Anna. It was improbable that she would be able to do anything for Gerry. These people in hopeless positions all seemed to be intent upon their own ruin. She wanted to sit by herself and watch the stars come out.

'I suppose it began when I was born,' said Gerry, mournfully, but settling down to it with a certain zest. 'I . . .'

'Oh, my goodness,' said Mrs. Paley, 'it began ages before that. It began when your father was born.'

'Perhaps it did,' agreed Gerry. 'You see, he . . .'

'I'm sure. But I don't want to sit here all night. Let's skip a bit. Are you quite sure that you want to marry Angie?'

'How on earth did you guess . . . ?'

'Plain as a pikestaff. But are you sure you want to marry her?'

'No. My trouble is that if I did, I couldn't.'

'But that must apply to so many girls. All of them really.'

'Yes,' agreed Gerry. 'I suppose it does.'

'And you can't marry them all. So you aren't in any position, hopeless or otherwise, until you want to marry one in particular.'

'I'd like to be married.'

'I don't wonder. But what has Angie got to do with that?'

'I . . . I like her very much.'

'Umhm?'

'But philandering is no good.'

'I don't agree. I think a nice little philander would cheer you both up considerably.'

'Oh, Mrs. Paley!'

'Don't look so scandalized. It won't get you anywhere, I agree. But it will pass the time agreeably and that's all that anyone in a hopeless position can expect to do.'

'But she mightn't understand.'

'Oh, I think she would. She's in a tolerably hopeless position herself, isn't she?'

The party on the boulders were now singing *Shenandoah*, a sad song at any time and not likely to enliven anybody in a hopeless position. Angie sang the solo lines while the boys joined in the chorus:

> *'Tis seven long years since last I saw you . . .*
> *Away you rolling river . . .*

'And if I philander much longer,' explained Gerry, 'I shall kiss her.'

> *Away! We're bound to go!*
> *Across the wide Missouri . . .*

'And if I kiss her I shall marry her.'

'I thought you said you couldn't.'

'Well . . . I could, if I go to Kenya.'

> *Oh Shenandoah, I love your daughter . . .*

'Then, my goodness,' cried Mrs. Paley in exasperation, 'what is all the fuss about?'

'I'm in a hopeless position.'

Away! We're bound to go . . .

'I can't bear this,' protested Mrs. Paley. 'I really can't. I never heard such a depressing song. Nobody's bound to do anything. We're not black slaves. You take Angie for a little stroll along to Rosigraille, and don't come back until you've made up your mind. Take care of rabbit holes.'

Gerry obeyed her. As soon as *Shenandoah* had been wailed to its last stanza he got up and joined the singers. But his excitement was so urgent that he could not issue the invitation as casually as he wished; he barked an abrupt command at Evangeline.

'Come for a walk.'

She jumped up at once.

'A walk!' said Duff. 'At this time of night? Where to?'

'To Rosigraille cliffs,' said Gerry, seizing Evangeline by the elbow and dragging her away.

'We'll come too,' said Robin. 'No need to run.'

But Mrs. Paley joined them at this point with a counter-attraction, announcing that she had strange news about Mrs. Cove's soapstone. Gerry and Angie escaped while the boys remained to listen.

Robin was much delighted by the poltergeist story and disposed to commend the little Coves. He leant a kindly ear to Mrs. Paley's plans for the Feast and promised his help. But he soon returned to the drama of the soapstone, and while Mrs. Paley made tea he planned further adventures for it.

'I'll get it out of my father, if he's got it now,' he said. 'Oh yes, I'll certainly return it to Mrs. Cove. I know it's hers. Don't worry, Mrs. Paley. She shall find it again.'

'Ssh!' said Duff. 'Listen! What's that?'

A distant bellow had for a moment shattered the quiet dusk. They fell silent, listening, and heard the gurgle of the sea against the rocks far below.

'A bull, somewhere,' said Robin.

It came again, nearer.

'No,' said Mrs. Paley. 'It's Canon Wraxton calling his daughter.'

Presently the Canon appeared, massive against the sky-line, and Mrs. Paley informed him that Evangeline had gone for a walk with Gerry Siddal.

'Then she'll find me waiting for her when she gets back,' said the Canon, sitting down upon a rock. 'I've had enough of Gerry Siddal.'

'Would you like a cup of tea?' suggested Mrs. Paley.

'No. I would not like a cup of tea.'

There was a short silence, and then the Canon opened the attack.

'I should very much like to know,' he said to Mrs. Paley, 'just why you are encouraging Evangeline to behave like this. If you think that you are doing her a service you never made a bigger mistake in your life. She's going to be exceedingly sorry before I've done with her.'

'I hope not,' said Mrs. Paley. 'I hope she'll marry Gerry and get away from you. I hope they're settling it now.'

'What?' cried Robin.

'Umph,' said Duff. 'I thought as much.'

'But he can't,' protested Robin.

'He won't,' said the Canon. 'I won't have it.'

'You won't be able to stop it,' said Mrs. Paley, 'if that is what they want to do. Angie is of age.'

'She's not all there, and you know it. I don't want to lock her up, but I may have to.'

'You can't, Canon Wraxton. There is absolutely nothing more that you can do to Angie. She is free.'

'She shall *not* marry him.'

Mrs. Paley smiled and began to pack up the tea basket.

'I think,' she said, 'that I shall go to bed now.'

The Canon got up and kicked the rock upon which he had been sitting.

'Very well,' he said. 'Very well, very well, very well . . .'

And he gave the rock another kick. The impact must have hurt him considerably. But he continued to massacre his toes against the granite and to repeat *very well* for some minutes after Mrs. Paley and the boys had gone down to the shelter. When at last he went off in the direction of Pendizack he was walking very lame.

'He wants to hurt somebody,' explained Mrs. Paley to the boys, who were shocked. 'So much that he enjoys hurting himself. And now, will you kindly tell me why Gerry should not marry Angie?'

Robin began to explain, but the facts did the whole Siddal family so little credit that he faltered very soon. And Duff said sulkily that he, personally, could manage quite well without any more help from Gerry.

'I can get jobs in the vacations. I've got a scholarship. And there is Father's law library. That's worth five hundred pounds. Gerry seems to think we'd all be sunk unless he runs the whole show. I think he'd much better marry and boss his wife.'

'Then suppose,' said Mrs. Paley, 'you are just a little bit nice to him and Angie about it? It won't cost you anything, and it will mean a lot to them.'

'Nice?' said Duff.

'Kiss her, do you mean?' asked Robin.

'And slap Gerry on the back?' asked Duff.

'I leave that entirely to you,' said Mrs. Paley, with a yawn.

Something disturbed the gulls on Rosigraille cliffs. There was a squawk and a flutter and a chorus of cries, echoing over the water, before they settled on their ledges again. Angie, half asleep in Gerry's arms, roused up and saw the moon hanging over a landward hill.

'We must go back,' she said. 'It's fearfully late.'

'I don't want to go back,' murmured Gerry. 'I'm happy. I've never been happy before. I never shall be again. Let's stay here.'

'But we shall be happy again,' said Angie. 'We shall be happy for the rest of our lives. And if we stay here we shall get rheumatism.'

'I don't mind if I get rheumatism. I shan't get it till to-morrow. And tomorrow we'll know it's impossible. They'll all be against us.'

But they rose from their lair in the bracken and made

their way back along the cliffs towards the shelter, clinging together and pausing often to kiss and to exclaim. The moon rose higher and threw a sheet of silver over the gorse bushes as they reached the shelter. A voice whispered:

'Here they are!'

Two lumps of shadow, couched under a boulder, started up to greet them.

'Sorry,' said Gerry. 'We didn't mean to wake you.'

'We weren't asleep,' said Duff. 'We stayed awake to congratulate you.'

'What?'

'It's what we've always wanted in our family—a nice soprano. We're very much obliged to you, Gerry.'

'I say . . .' stammered Gerry. 'I say . . . but how do you know?'

'We watched you coming back.'

Robin, meanwhile, had bestowed upon Evangeline a cordial hug which astonished her so much that she gave a loud squeak and waked Mrs. Paley, inside the shelter.

'Is that them?' called Mrs. Paley, sleepily.

Gerry hastened in and squatted by her mattress to tell her the news.

'Angie,' he assured her, 'is wonderful. She's marvellous. She's not a bit what you'd think. She's . . .'

He lowered his voice and confided in a solemn whisper:

'Really she's got a very passionate nature.'

Mrs. Paley gave a choked guffaw and wished him joy. He hurried back to tuck his love up on her lilo. Soon they were all asleep save Angie, who lay and watched the moon climb the sky. She was too happy to accept oblivion. This return to a world which had no hostile greeting after all, which showed her, for the first time, a kindly face, had been like an awakening, an escape from nightmare. All her fears and tremors fell away from her. She lay awake, serene, encompassed by her faithful guard.

THURSDAY

1. Too Busy to Cry

Nancibel found Bruce's letter on the kitchen table and read it while she made the early morning tea. It upset her so much that she forgot the tea leaves and carried round pots of hot water to all the inmates of Pendizack. The tears were trickling down her cheeks as she set to work on the lounge.

Even last night her anger against him had been diluted by pure grief, and now she was sure that she would never be able to forget him. Though she had only known him for four days, and though she had so much against him, he had caused her to feel more sharply and keenly than Brian, her first love, ever could. For her emotions, where Brian was concerned, had been expected and comprehensible. He was a nice boy, steady and sensible, and he was refined and he knew how to kiss a person. Whereas Bruce had suddenly opened a window upon some strange region in her heart of which she had not been aware before a wild and troubled territory through which some future Nancibel might travel towards new and nameless horizons. She had felt that life and human beings are very important and that everybody is lonely, and that nobody really knows much about anybody else.

The first pang had subsided, but it had struck a note which persisted in her relationship with Bruce so that in their mutual attraction, their mirth, and their quarrel there was this sharp, strange sadness, and a perception of Bruce as somebody real, somebody three-dimensional and existing on his own, not merely a feature in her landscape. Now he had gone away and she would never see him again; but she felt that she would always be aware of his life going on somewhere, and that reality was as firmly focused in him as in herself.

A lot of bells began to ring all at once. The Paleys, the Giffords, Canon Wraxton and Miss Ellis had all discovered that there was no tea in their teapots. For twenty minutes she had to run up and down stairs, rectifying this error and repeating that she was ever so sorry. By breakfast time she had got so behindhand with the work that she was too busy to cry. She had to leave the lounge half done and rush to the service room to help Fred. Through the kitchen door they could hear a nice shindy going on among the Siddals who were all talking at once. Mrs. Siddal was saying that the girl was a nervous wreck, Gerry was saying that he intended to live his own life, Duff was saying she sings like a bird, Robin was saying why couldn't he leave school at once, and Mr. Siddal was saying that for all he knew his law library had been bombed.

'No,' said Gerry. 'Mr. Graffham wrote about it. He said you'd had an offer. Somebody wants to buy it.'

'Whatever's up?' whispered Nancibel to Fred.

Fred whispered back that the Siddals had lost a library. Neither he nor Nancibel could imagine how they had contrived to do so, for the word conveyed to both of them either a large public building or else a handsome room in a gentleman's house furnished with desks, leather chairs and bookcases.

'Couldn't we find the letter?' Gerry was suggesting. 'The offer might still be open.'

'Couldn't it be sent down here?' asked Robin. 'Then we'd know how large it really is.'

Fred's eyes grew round, and he asked Nancibel if she thought the Government had pinched it for a food office. That, in his experience, was a common fate for libraries.

'You go on in the dining room,' admonished Nancibel, with a glance through the hatch, 'the Coves have come down.'

She herself went to the kitchen to bring the Coves' food and coffee to the serving hatch, where Fred would take them from her. At the kitchen door she collided with Mr. Siddal who was flouncing out to his boot-hole in a manifest rage. His pasty face was flushed and he was muttering:

'I've had quite enough of it . . . quite enough of it . . .'

And Gerry, in the kitchen, was positively storming.

'He wouldn't even have to read the damned letter. If he'd give it to us, we'd deal with it.'

'I don't suppose he could find it,' said Mrs. Siddal. 'There are thousands of letters in the boot-hole. Millions. He doesn't even open them . . .'

'Well, then, we must. This can't go on . . .'

The Coves' tray was waiting on a side table. They were always down first. Nancibel took it to the hatch and made a face at Fred who was standing in the middle of the dining room in a sort of coma. Probably he was still pondering upon the mystery of the disappearing library. Starting to life again he came and took the tray just as the Paleys made their appearance. So Nancibel went back for more food and again collided with Mr. Siddal. This time he was coming out of the boot-hole, and he carried a drawer full of papers. She made way for him to pass her, but the kitchen was not his goal. He went on down the passage towards the boiler room.

'I'm sorry if I'm disrespectful,' Gerry was saying. 'But we must do something. There may be important letters . . . business letters . . . God knows what . . . I'll sort them. But it's time we insisted . . .'

'Mr. and Mrs. Paley,' said Nancibel. 'And Miss Ellis.'

'Miss *Ellis*!' exclaimed Mrs. Siddal, serving out the Paleys' bacon. 'What do you mean . . . Miss Ellis?'

'She's sitting at her table,' declared Nancibel.

'She ought to be in the service room. This isn't her break-fast time. I shall send nothing out to her. Nothing whatever. We seem to be a teapot short.'

'I'm ever so sorry, Mrs. Siddal. Canon Wraxton broke one this morning. Well . . . he threw it at me s'matter of fact, so I had to fetch up another. That's why. It was my fault. I'd forgotten to put any tea in.'

'I don't know what's happened to everybody this morn-ing,' exclaimed Mrs. Siddal. 'How could you be so stupid, Nancibel? Lady Gifford was complaining.'

'I'm ever so sorry, Mrs. Siddal. And I'm afraid the teapot hit a picture on the wall and broke the glass. You know . . . that religious picture of the Virgin Mary with all the cupids.'

Nancibel took the Paleys' tray and set off for the serving room thinking that she would go bats if she stayed in this house much longer. Mr. Siddal was coming out of the boiler room with an empty drawer. If he had thrown all those papers on the boiler fire, she reflected, he would put it out. And there was something awful happening in the dining room. Mrs. Cove was shouting and creating and waving her coffee pot about and asking for Mrs. Siddal to be fetched, and all the Giffords, who had just come in, were giggling.

'It's your great-grannie's image,' whispered Fred through the hatch. 'She's just found it in her coffee pot.'

Batty! thought Nancibel, as she escaped from the ensuing uproar. The Plymouth Blitz was a Sunday School picnic beside this; we all knew where we was going and what we was doing. But in this place the only ones with any sense in them are those little Coves, and they haven't much. Everybody else is bats, including me, wanting to howl myself sick for a crazy boy like Bruce . . .

She flew through the bedroom work and came at last to the Gifford attics where she found Hebe, looking very bilious.

'Not want any breakfast?' she cried. 'Children that don't want breakfast want Eno's.'

'What I want,' said Hebe, 'is to die. Then everybody would be sorry.'

'Not so sorry as you think. They'd get over it after a while and you'd still be dead.'

'Does everybody know . . . about yesterday?'

'Not a soul, ducks, only me and . . . and Bruce. And we'll hold our tongues.'

'Was I drunk?'

'Yes. And it's nothing to boast about. It was disgusting. So we'd better hurry up and forget about it. There's something ever so nice going to happen on Friday.'

As she made the beds Nancibel described the plans for the Feast. But Hebe received the news without enthusiasm.

'I shan't go,' she said languidly.

'Why ever not? It'll be lovely.'

'Everybody is horrid to me.'

'Not the Coves. They'll be terribly disappointed. It's you they want to ask more than anybody. They think such a lot of you.'

'I shouldn't enjoy it. Why should I go to a picnic I shall hate just to please the Coves?'

'Because you'd be a nasty little toad if you don't. There's not much anybody can do for them, poor little souls; but you're the one that can do most, because you're the same age, see? I don't expect they ever had any good times till they met you.'

'I'm supposed to have tried to murder them.'

'Oh rats. Nobody thinks that. It wasn't a bad idea, trying to teach them swimming. Only you acted silly when you chose such a dangerous place. Honestly I think you've been wonderful with them, only you'll spoil it all if you don't go to their Feast. Now you take a big dose of Eno's, Hebe, and wash your face, and you'll feel a lot better.'

'I haven't got any Eno's.'

'I'll find you some.'

Nancibel ran off and borrowed some Eno's Fruit Salts from Mrs. Paley. When she came back Hebe was looking brighter.

'I think,' she said, as Nancibel measured the salts into a glass, 'that a secret society ought to be started in order to give aid to the Coves. They have a lot of allies at Pendizack.'

'The best aid you can give,' said Nancibel, 'is to go to their Feast and make it a success. Here. Drink up!'

'Don't you think it ought to be Fancy Dress?'

'Depends on what they think. It's their party.'

'They've never given a party. They don't know how. They'll want a lot of advice. I've thought of a marvellous fancy dress. Where's Bruce?'

'Gone.'

'Gone? Do you mean right away? For ever?'

'Yes. He went last night.'

'Oh Nancibel! What a pity! He was so nice. He'll be a great loss. To the society, I mean.'

Nancibel turned away and went to make the twins' beds. When all the rooms were done she snatched a moment to slip out to the stables. He had left his loft very neat. His sheets and pillow case were carefully folded and left on the end of the booby-trap bed, ready for the laundry. Perhaps he had guessed she would come for them and wanted to save her trouble.

She sat down on the floor beside the bed and buried her face in the sheets.

Duff was playing his gramophone in the loft next door,

and throbs of music came through the thin partition. It was very sad music, fast and soft, each phrase an exclamation, a whispered protest, like the outcry in Nancibel's bewildered heart. It poured out her dismay at this uncharted world of feeling into which she had tumbled—the pity, the uncertainty, the regret, and all the long vista of experience which must be travelled before she could be old and at peace. It rushed on, just as time rushes on, leaving her too busy to cry.

She could only stay for a moment. Then she gathered up the linen and took it back to the house. Ruthlessly she flung it into the laundry basket, knowing that, when these sheets came home, she would not be able to distinguish them from forty other sheets.

2. Activity in the Boiler Room

Not for years had Mr. Siddal exerted himself so continuously. Within half an hour he had carried every paper out of his room and stuffed it into the top of the coke boiler. He did it all while his family was at breakfast, before they could find out what he was up to and prevent it. Up and down the passage he crept with load after load, and at the eighth trip discovered that the fire had gone out. The mass of paper had choked the draught and quenched the flames.

This was an unexpected misfortune. To take the papers out and relight the fire would be a crushing labour. But it would be nothing to the exertions threatened by Gerry—the sorting, the answering, the decisions . . . After some poking and swearing Mr. Siddal went back to the boot-hole for some shavings in a box under his bed.

A reek of expensive cigarette smoke met his nostrils and he found Anna waiting for him, a very much agitated Anna, with pale cheeks and anxious eyes. At the sight of her some measure of spirit returned to him. For his little window was an excellent spy-hole. People forgot that a habitable room lay behind it. Bruce and Nancibel had forgotten when they carried Hebe into the house the night before.

'Anna! I thought you'd gone to Polly's.'

'So I did. I've just come back. I hired a taxi. My God, Dick! How your room stinks. Do you never open the window?'

'It's stuck. But I don't mind the smell. It keeps intruders away. What do you want, my dear Anna?'

'I'm in a spot of bother,' confessed Anna, puffing at her cigarette.

He grinned.

'We're all in a spot of bother,' he said. 'There's a great hullabaloo going on here. We've mislaid one of the children.'

'Which one?' snapped Anna.

'I've forgotten. I don't believe I heard which one.'

'Hebe?'

'Is that the girl with the cat? I believe it's the girl with the cat.'

'What happened?'

'I really don't know. They never tell me anything. But I heard something about Sir Henry going to the police.'

'Oh Christ!'

He stared at her.

'It's very nice of you,' he said, 'to feel so much concern when you've got troubles of your own.'

Anna took a fresh cigarette from her bag and lighted it on the stub of the old one.

'Where's Antinous?' he asked. 'Why didn't he bring you back? Why did you have to hire a taxi?'

'This is appalling.' She flung the old stub on the floor and ground it with her heel. 'I'm afraid they'll think I'm to blame. You see . . . I took Hebe with me yesterday . . .'

'What? To *Polly's*?'

'Yes. I . . . I was sorry for the child . . . everyone here has a down on her.'

'Preserve me from your compassion, Anna. You'll have an awkward time with Sir Henry. But if you've brought her back . . .'

'But I haven't,' wailed Anna. 'I haven't.'

Mr. Siddal was not very helpful as she told her story. He was provokingly obtuse, so that she had to supply every detail. When she would have welcomed a question he simply stared and said nothing. When she would have preferred him to say nothing he asked awkward questions. But she wanted his help so badly that she was obliged to tell him everything.

Hebe, Bruce and the car had been missed at seven o'clock on Wednesday afternoon, when Anna had remembered her *protégée* and went to claim her from Bint and Eggie. She had not been seriously alarmed, for she had concluded that Bruce must have driven Hebe back to Pendizack, but she had not relished the indignation which would be waiting for her on her own return, should the child's condition have been noticed. So she dismissed her taxi discreetly at the top of the drive and slipped down to discover, if she could, how the land lay, going first to the garage to see if her car was there. It was, and on her dressing table, when she reached her room, she had found the note from Bruce.

'It was very short, Dick. I can't show it to you, because I tore it up. Well . . . I was so angry. But it just said he's gone and he isn't coming back and he never wants to see me again. I'm sure I don't mind. I'm through with him. But nothing about Hebe . . . nothing about Hebe . . . where she is now, I mean . . .'

'Do you think any of Polly's guests could enlighten you?'

'How can I be sure? They all pretended they didn't know. And, of course, I thought she'd gone with Bruce. But one can't be certain . . . well . . . you know what Polly's friends are. You can't trust any of them.'

'Quite so. And you still haven't told me what possessed you to take her there.'

'It was just an impulse. I meant to keep an eye on her.'

'Your impulses fascinate me. I can't help trying to guess. You wanted to shock Bruce, I suppose?'

Anna tittered a little.

'Well . . . perhaps there was that element in it.'

'You like shock tactics, don't you? You use a moral cosh and crack your victims over the head with it.'

'I've no time to go into all that. I've done my duty. I've told you. Now you can do as you think fit.'

'I?' Mr. Siddal looked startled. 'My dear girl, it's nothing to do with me.'

'I mean you can tell the Giffords . . . anything you like. I'm off. Say goodbye to Barbara for me.'

'You mean you're clearing out?'

'Before I meet Sir Henry. Wouldn't you?'

'I haven't your alacrity. You are a one, if I may say so.'

Mr. Siddal laughed, and she said sourly:

'I'm glad you're so amused.'

'So much amused would be better grammar.'

'Just eaten up with spite and malice, aren't you?'

'Too right, as they say in the Antipodes. Where shall you go?'

'I don't think I'll tell you. I shan't be in any hurry to

show up until I'm sure there's going to be no fuss about that child.'

'Very wise. But if she's been murdered it may be years before they dig her up in Polly's garden. Still . . . the hue and cry will die down. You skip off and as soon as you've gone I'll tell Sir Henry what you've done.'

'But Dick . . . I did nothing. The child stowed away in my luggage carrier. I didn't know she was there till we got to Polly's.'

'You didn't mention that.'

'Didn't I? I've only just remembered it. I sent her back at once in the car with Bruce. If he didn't hand her over . . . Sir Henry had better hunt for him.'

'It's all very confusing. Suppose I get it wrong? Perhaps after all I'd better say nothing at all. If you get away quickly . . . nobody saw you come back, did they?'

'I don't think so. What you say or don't say is your responsibility. I'm clear, for I've told you.'

'Have you paid and all that?'

'No. I'll write a cheque now. I'll date it yesterday and you can say I gave it you before I went to St. Merricks.'

She fished in her bag for a cheque book and fountain pen, enquiring:

'How much?'

'How should I know? I don't run this hotel.'

'You let me have the rooms. I believe it's six guineas. I took them for a week, so I'll pay for the week. Say four guineas for Bruce? He had to sleep in a manger. That's ten guineas. No extras. We had no drinks because you don't

327

have a licence in this one-horse bordel of yours.'

'Early morning tea?' murmured Siddal with a sudden flash of business acumen.

'Is that extra? How much? I had it twice; on Tuesday and Wednesday. Say two shillings.'

'Didn't Bruce have any? Didn't Nancibel take any to Bruce?'

'I wouldn't know. But my name is not Cove, and I'll put four shillings on the chance. Ten pounds, fourteen shillings. I think you've done pretty well, for we only came on Monday.'

'Tips?' murmured Dick Siddal.

Anna hesitated, and flushed a little. Then she looked again in her bag and produced ten shillings, which she gave to him.

'That's for Fred. You'll never remember to hand it over, and that's just too bad for poor Fred. Nancibel's tip I'll leave on my dressing table.'

'Because you want to be sure she gets it?'

'Exactly. Here's the cheque. Try to remember to give it to Barbara. Goodbye. It's been nice to meet again, Dick. People quite often ask what's became of you, and now I can tell them.'

She swept the boot-hole with a malicious glance and took herself off, meaning to get out by the back door and slip round the house to her room.

But the back door was no longer accessible. Fred was standing just in front of it, listening to a harangue from Miss Ellis in the boiler room. Luckily his back was turned, or he would have seen Anna.

'Every scrap of this must be taken out and put in the bins. Every scrap!' Miss Ellis was saying. 'The idea! Shoving all that junk on top of the fire. No wonder it's out . . .'

Cautiously Anna tiptoed up the passage and through the baize door into the hall. Fortune favoured her, and she reached her room without meeting anybody.

Her packing took very little time. She put an insultingly large tip upon the dressing table for Nancibel and slipped out to the garage with her typewriter and her suitcases. She opened the garage door, climbed into the car, and pressed the starter. Nothing happened, not even when she got out and cranked the engine.

'Can I help?' asked Duff.

He was going up to his loft to play his gramophone, and had heard Anna swearing inside the garage.

'I don't know,' she said. 'Something's wrong with the bloody thing. Do you understand cars?'

He made a brief inspection and reported that there was no petrol in the tank. Anna's comments on this mishap startled him nearly as much as Polly had startled Hebe, for pretty much the same reasons.

'So what?' she finished, inclined to laugh, in spite of her exasperation, at his shocked expression. 'Don't stand there with your eyes on sticks. Tell me what I'm to do. Bruce has walked out on me. I've got to get to London at once, and I want to get away quietly.'

Duff searched about for a witty and worldly reply. This was the first time that he had ever been alone with Anna, and he had an idea that she expected him to do something about it. But he could think of nothing to say except that there might be a can of petrol in the potting shed from which he could give her enough to get her up to the village. And he led her towards the kitchen garden.

'I've quite a big petrol allowance,' she explained, as she followed him. 'I wrote in and said I needed to drive about the country to get copy for my books and earn lovely dollars, and they fell for it at once. It's wonderful what cheek can do for you sometimes.'

Duff pulled up short and stared down the kitchen garden at a tawny head, just visible through the apple boughs.

'Excuse me,' he said. And then he shouted:

'Hebe!'

'Yes?'

'What are you doing here? You aren't allowed in the kitchen garden.'

'I'm picking lavender,' yelled the distant Hebe. 'Your mother gave me leave.'

'Then she's back,' gasped Anna.

'Back? She's never been away.'

'Your father told me she was lost or something.'

'Oh no. He didn't take the trouble to listen. She was sick in the night, that's all. Woke everybody up being sick in the night.'

'Oh, I see.'

Anna reflected for a while and then said:

'The old sod! Well . . . don't let's worry about this petrol. I needn't really go today.'

She reached up, pulled a ripe fig off a neighbouring tree, and sank her white teeth into it. Duff knew that his mother intended to sell all the figs, but he felt that it would sound childish to say so. He assumed a slight swagger, took a fig himself, and asked why Bruce had gone off.

'He had a call,' said Anna vaguely. 'Fresh fields and pastures new.'

Woods, thought Duff, who had inherited his father's accuracy. But he was impressed by the apparent ease with which Bruce had got away, not gobbled up at all, but free to seek another experience elsewhere. He grew bolder. She was not the kind of woman he wanted; in some ways he found her repellent, but she offered him something which he had never had and concerning which he was exceedingly curious. If he could get away from her as soon as it was over . . . When they got back to the stable yard he asked if he should carry her cases back to her room.

'Where were you off to,' asked Anna, 'when I interrupted you and led you astray?'

'I was going to play my gramophone.'

'Where?'

She gave a wondering stare round the yard.

'Over the stables. I . . . we sleep up there,' explained Duff.

He hesitated, and then added airily:

'Come along.'

Anna looked puzzled, until he indicated the ladder to the lofts.

'Gerry wouldn't approve,' she objected.

'Damn Gerry,' said Duff. 'It's up the ladder and the door on the right.'

'You go first,' said Anna. 'What a wolf you are!'

'You think so?' said Duff, not displeased.

'I'm sure Gerry would never send a woman up a ladder first.'

Duff had never thought of ladders quite in this light, but he managed to return the ball by observing that some women might feel themselves insulted unless given the opportunity.

'Any woman would,' agreed Anna, with a laugh. 'But Gerry doesn't know that. Nor ought you at your age.'

They climbed the ladder and he took her into the large, untidy loft occupied by Gerry, Robin and himself. She looked round her, smiling slightly.

'Almost monastic,' she said.

'Madly austere,' agreed Duff, and then frowned because he was trying to break himself of the adverb since his father mocked him for it.

Gerry, he remembered, had gone out with Angie and Robin had the boat. This *tête-à-tête* could go on for hours before anybody came.

'What's the book?' she asked, picking one up from a packing case beside a bed. '*Steps to the Altar*! Gerry, I suppose.'

'Yes,' said Duff.

'Can one sit on these beds, or do they shut up?'

'No. It's only Bruce's bed that does that.'

He broke off in confusion. Anna sat down on the bed and opened *Steps to the Altar*. An inscription on the title page informed her that it had been given to Duff by his mother on March 5th, 1944.

'What a liar you are,' she said. 'Why did you tell me it was Gerry's? I suppose you made your first Communion in 1944.'

'I was confirmed,' said Duff, reddening.

'Oh, confirmed? What happens when you're confirmed? Do remind me. I thought they only did that to women after childbirth.'

'Oh no, that's churching. You are confirmed by a Bishop. He puts his hand on your head. And . . .'

'Oh, I remember. And if you get his right hand it's lucky, and the left hand is unlucky. I got the left hand, and I was terrified.'

'What?' cried Duff. 'Have you been confirmed?'

'Of course I have. Why not? And vaccinated, and pre-sented at Court. My parents spared no expense over my education. I had a white veil. That I do remember. Why should you think I haven't been confirmed?'

Duff was unable to answer and felt that, altogether, he was cutting a sorry figure. His reputation as a wolf must be slipping. He looked at her doubtfully and wondered what a genuine wolf would do. At the back of his brain a dry little voice whispered that no genuine wolf would waste five minutes on Anna. Wolf does not eat wolf. And while he hesitated, unwilling to see himself as a lamb, there was a sound of steps on the ladder. Somebody was coming up.

'Put on a record,' whispered Anna.

Duff rushed to the gramophone and put on the first record that came to hand. But the machine needed winding and the needle had to be changed. The footsteps creaked up the ladder. Then they turned aside. They went into Bruce's loft.

He started the record. Mozart's Symphony in G Minor sprang to urgent life and throbbed out its muted lamentation. He crossed the room and applied his eye to a small hole in the wooden partition between the lofts.

'Who is it?' murmured Anna, under cover of the music.

'Nancibel.'

'What is she doing in there?'

He did not answer. Nancibel was kneeling by the bed, her face buried, and he thought she was crying. He remembered the jokes in Pendizack kitchen about Bruce and Nancibel. And it occurred to him that perhaps Bruce might not have escaped so easily after all; something of value might perforce have been left behind. Presently they heard Nancibel go away. But the music went on, spinning its swift web of sorrow, fine as gossamer, keen as steel. To resist it was impossible to Duff. He hung over the gramophone and let himself sail away down the current of sound.

Dusty motes danced in the shafts of sunlight from the little windows. Anna's enigmatic smile became a trifle fixed. She yawned. She tapped her foot upon the ground. Duff at the gramophone gave her a reproving scowl, for the noise disturbed him.

Presently she got up and went away. Nor did he try to keep her. She could wait. He was sure that he should not enjoy her as much as he was enjoying the G Minor.

3. Lions in the Path

Gerry and Evangeline were desperately in love. The need for affection, all the frustration of two lifetimes, had merged into a mutual torrent of rejoicing and liberation. Each was, in sober truth, the whole world to the other. Happiness had transformed them. Gerry's spots were rapidly fading, and Evangeline had blossomed into a comeliness which was almost beauty. Her cheeks were pink, her eyes sparkled and her hair shone. Gerry declared that she had already grown a little fatter.

The obstacles which had seemed so formidable when they plighted their troth on Rosigraille cliffs were dwindling and vanishing on a closer inspection. Duff and Robin supported them, and Mrs. Siddal's opposition, though bitter, had been so quietly stated as to seem negligible. As for the Canon, the biggest bogey of all, he seemed to have retreated from the battle. They had plucked up their courage and sought him, immediately after breakfast, but he was locked up in his room and would not answer them. A note for Evangeline, which he had left in the office, explained his attitude.

I leave this house on Saturday. If you want to come
with me you must send this fellow about his business.
If you don't you can stay behind. He can support
you and I wish him joy of it. Marry him, if he is fool

enough. I shall alter my Will. You would have got
the lot as you were the only one of my children to
deserve it. But not now. Not a penny.

'But how can he leave?' exclaimed Evangeline, when she
had read the note. 'Who will drive the car? He can't. His
licence was taken away.'

'That's his headache,' said Gerry joyfully. 'I say! This is a
let-up. It's practically his consent and no fireworks.'

With hearts immensely lightened they ran out to Rosigraille cliffs, in order to live last night all over again.

But twelve hours had changed their mood, and they soon
found themselves talking of the future rather than the present. Evangeline was energetic and practical. It would be,
she said, several months before they could marry, and in
the meantime she had no intention of letting Gerry support
her. She would get herself a job. She had already discussed
the problem with Mrs. Paley, who had told her of a nice
agency in London.

'It won't do for me to stay after Saturday,' she decided. 'Your mother would resent it. Mrs. Paley will lend me
money. I'll go to London and get a job as a cook. Anybody
who can cook can get a job. I'll sell my diamond ring. That
will keep me till I've got a job and give me money to repay
Mrs. Paley.'

'But can you cook?' asked Gerry in surprise.

'Oh yes. I'm quite a good cook. Better than . . .'

Better than his mother, she was going to say. But she
checked herself and substituted:

'Better than you think.'

'Then I wonder you didn't break away before. Oh yes . . . your promise to your mother. I forgot.'

Gerry mused awhile and then said:

'But what *about* your promise to your mother?'

Evangeline thought this rather tactless. She said hastily:

'I haven't left him, It's he who won't keep me any longer.'

'I know. But you'd have married me and left him whatever he said, wouldn't you?'

'Of course I would.'

'Then aren't you a little inconsistent?'

'No!' said Evangeline, sharply.

He should have observed a danger signal, but he knew very little about women. He persisted:

'Yesterday you said you couldn't marry. Today you say you can.'

'I never said I couldn't marry.'

'You said you couldn't leave your father. That implied you couldn't marry.'

'I don't see. I think it's you who are inconsistent. Last night you begged me to marry you. Now you are discouraging me.'

'I? Discouraging you? Oh Angie!'

'You're saying I shall be inconsistent if I do. You're making out I'm wrong. Of course, if you think I'm wrong to marry you, we'd better . . .'

'I don't! I don't! I don't! I only think you were wrong before. I think you were wrong to make that promise.'

'Oh I see. I've got to be made out wrong somewhere.'

'Angie, my sweetest, don't be so angry.'

'Well, why are you so anxious to make me say I was wrong? I don't insist on making you say you were wrong when you changed your mind about whether you could marry.'

'But I have been wrong,' said Gerry. 'Not when I changed my mind. But before. I see that now. Half my troubles were my own fault. I liked being a martyr. Duff and Robin have been so decent . . . they'd have been decent before if they'd had the chance. I never gave them the chance. I preferred to be self-sacrificing and superior.'

'Christians,' said Evangeline, huffily, 'are supposed to be self-sacrificing.'

'Yes. But it isn't right to encourage people to behave badly, just in order to be a noble victim. That's not returning good for evil. It's merely helping them to go to hell.'

'Well, I can't see what good it does you, sitting about and saying you were wrong. Surely we've enough difficulties in front of us, without fussing about that.'

'I'm not fussing. Oh darling! Don't let's quarrel.'

He looked so doleful that she relented and smiled at him. The subject was dropped. But the first edge had been taken off his happiness, for he realized that there were some things which she would never understand. She was a woman, he thought; and women are curiously limited.

So that he was surprised when she said abruptly, on their way back to Pendizack:

'Of course I was wrong before.'

He had been talking about Kenya, and he did not for a moment grasp her meaning.

'My promise to mother was all humbug. I oughtn't to have made it or kept it. I stayed with father out of . . . out of cowardice and morbidness . . . like a sort of illness . . . I wanted the worst to happen . . . I was wicked. I was awful.'

'Then why were you so annoyed when I . . .'

'I couldn't see any point in talking about it.'

'I wanted to know how you felt,' he explained. 'Don't you think it's nice to know everything about each other?'

'Not a bit. If you knew everything about me you wouldn't want to marry me.'

Gerry protested vehemently. This confession had lifted the shadow on his spirits.

'Every new thing I learn about you,' he assured her, 'makes you more sweet and more dear.'

Evangeline smiled. But she decided to hold her tongue about the powdered glass in the pillbox, rightly believing that Gerry would find it neither sweet nor dear. Whatever she had been, she knew that she was now a very nice woman and exactly the right wife for him.

'So we will always tell each other everything,' decided Gerry happily.

'Darling Gerry! I do love you.'

'If only my mother would take it better!'

'Let's go and find her,' suggested Angie, 'and see if there is anything we can do for her.'

They marched cheerfully back to the hotel and into the kitchen where they found Miss Ellis, Nancibel and Fred gathered round Mrs. Siddal, who was lying on the floor with an ashen face and closed eyes.

'Fainted,' explained Miss Ellis.

'Went down like a sack of coals,' said Fred. 'I was in the scullery and I heard a peculiar noise, but I never thought to go and see. Sounded more like a sack of coals.'

'She was laying there when I came in,' said Nancibel, who was splashing water on Mrs. Siddal's face. 'Don't know how long she'd been there. Why should sacks of coal start falling about? You might have looked, Fred.'

'Heart most likely,' said Miss Ellis. 'I'm not surprised. I always thought she was a bad colour.'

Mrs. Siddal opened her eyes and looked at them all with dislike.

'I have fainted,' she informed them, with a certain triumph.

While restoratives were applied she pondered upon this achievement with satisfaction. For it was a proof that Gerry's engagement had really been the last straw. It had broken her down and finished her, so that all of a sudden, while she was rolling pastry, the floor rose up and hit her.

'I shall go to bed,' she told them.

'You'll certainly go to bed,' said Gerry, who was feeling her pulse, 'for the rest of the day.'

'There will be no lunch, and no tea and no dinner,' she continued. 'Nobody will get anything to eat. What you will all do, I don't know. You'd better get Miss Wraxton to cook for you.'

This was meant to spread alarm and dismay. It should bring home to them their utter dependence on her. But Gerry did not seem to understand. He was nodding in a reassuring way.

'Yes,' he said. 'Angie shall cook.'

'And I can show her where everything is,' put in Nancibel.

Gerry put an arm round his mother and helped her to her feet, urging her not to worry about anything.

'I don't worry,' she said coldly. 'I've worried enough. I've decided to leave off worrying. It's everybody else who will have to worry now.'

'Splendid,' said Gerry heartily. 'If only you'll really do that.'

He propelled her upstairs to her bedroom. She sat down upon her bed and delivered a broadside.

'I'm going to give up the hotel. It's too much for me. I can't go on. I did it for Duff and Robin. But I can't educate them without help. So, if you want to get married it's no use my going on. They talk very cheerfully about getting on without you. But they take me for granted . . . that I'll go on working for them. It's me they'll have to do without. Somebody will have to keep me and your father. I've kept you all long enough.'

'You take a good long rest,' Gerry assured her, 'and you'll feel quite different. Angie will stay as long as you like and do all the cooking. And I believe Mrs. Paley will lend a hand, and so will the boys. We'll manage beautifully.'

She said no more but went to bed, determined to stay there until they had learnt their lesson.

4. Miss Ellis to Miss Hill

. . . Well Gertie, four days gone by and I have not finished this epistle—but I must hurry up and finish it now because I am leaving here as soon as I can. I would go today only I have no place to go, only my sister, and I do not want to go there if I can find anywhere else. She keeps writing and writing pretending she wants to make it up. Says would I like a nice holiday at Frinton! I see myself there doing all the washing-up most probably.

Gertie I found a letter. They threw it on the boiler stove but it was not burnt. It quite upset me till I had thought it over. Somebody writing from the Government or something to say this house is not safe, because the cliff might collapse any time especially if it is a dry Summer. Well, this is a dry Summer. I was so upset I went up and packed my boxes. But then I thought you can't trust anything the Government says, always interfering, you can't put up a bicycle shed without a permit. And if it is true, they would have done something. She would not keep her darling boys in a house that was not safe.

But I should laugh if it turned out to be true. Fancy all these people paying six guineas a week for the chance of having half Cornwall fall on top of them one fine day! If some of the guests could have seen that letter I bet there would be a few rooms vacant. For two pins I would tell them just to see their faces. But some people are funny because I did just drop a hint to one woman staying here, it is a big party—4 children—they have all the best rooms. I would have thought she was the sort that could not get out quick enough after what I told her. But no! All she asked was please would I say nothing to her husband. More than asked. Gave me a pair of nylons. Because she thought the said husband might get the wind up and take them all away, so she would have to get out of bed which she has decided not to do, due to some funny business with the police. I suppose she just can't imagine anything unpleasant happening to *her*! Well, I said, it is your look out not mine. For I am going. I only spoke because I thought it was my duty.

I keep writing and writing for jobs but I cannot get anything. I read in the paper about 6 months ago that they could not get enough wardresses for the prisons. So I wrote in about it. The pay is not so good but I felt it was a job I would not mind somehow. Any way it would be me pushing other people about and not others pushing me. But if you will believe me they sent a form for me to fill and one of the things was I had to have reached Matriculation standard at school. Fact! What does anybody want with matric in that job?

This is a rotten world Gertie and that is the conclusion I have come to. I do not mind how soon this house falls down once I am out of it but I expect it is only the Government making a fuss. Will send you my next address when I know what it is . . .

5. Symposium

The plans for the Feast matured rapidly under the belated but vehement patronage of Hebe. Her suggestion of Fancy Dress, discouraged at first by Mrs. Paley and Angie, was received with so much enthusiasm by the Coves that the adults had to give way. She had also lent her paintbox and her Indian ink to the Coves, offering them much advice about the wording and decoration of their invitation cards. She devised costumes for everybody and was much put out when she learnt that Nancibel and Fred intended to appear as Carmen and a Toreador, because she had planned that all the grown-up people were to be characters from Edward Lear. She drew up a programme, a copy of which was to be handed to every guest when he received his invitation card. And she founded a new Society.

During dinner she informed Sir Henry that he was to be dressed as My Aged Uncle Arly.

'I'll make a cricket,' she said, 'to stick on your nose. And a ticket to stick in your hat. Your boots ought to be too tight; it says at the end of every verse: *And his boots were far too tight.* But you needn't. It would be so awkward, climbing the cliff. You must just pretend they're too tight. Walk lame.'

'But what are you talking about?' complained Sir Henry. 'Who is Uncle Arly?'

'A Lear character. Everyone has to be a Lear character. All the grown-ups. Mrs. Paley is going as the Quangle Wangle. Angie has made her a marvellous hat, perfectly huge, with a lot of little animals dancing on top. Nobody knows what the rest of the Quangle Wangle looked like, because the picture only shows his hat. But we think sort of green and skinny, so she's going to wear an old mackintosh of Duff's. Gerry and Angie are Mr. and Mrs. Discobolus. Duff is the Pobble Who Had No Toes. Robin has made himself a lovely nose with an electric torch in it. He's the Dong With the Luminous Nose.'

Sir Henry learnt all this with growing dismay. He had heard the children discussing the Feast at every meal but he had been so much preoccupied with his own troubles that he had not paid much attention, and had failed to realize that a personal appearance was expected of him. His contribution to the funds had been generous and he felt that no more should be required.

Many people at Pendizack thought this, and were now regretting their impetuous benevolence. When first told of it they had offered money or sweet points, supposing that such a plan could only concern the children. Fred and Nancibel might be included, since the lower orders are believed to have a childish turn of mind, but no adult patron of the Feast intended to sit on damp grass, drinking lemonade, in the middle of the night.

Mrs. Paley had been the first convert. She had realized that she must go to the Feast—that patronage was not enough. She must participate as a guest. For the whole scheme was intended to give pleasure to the Coves, and they wanted guests rather than sweet points. To refuse their hospitality would be insensitive and ungracious. She said as much to Gerry and Angie, who had hoped to cry off. She said it to Duff, who was flatly refusing to dress up as a pobble. She convinced them all that they must turn up, just as the little Giffords were now endeavouring to convince Sir Henry.

'But you must come,' cried Hebe. 'Everybody has *got* to come.'

'You don't understand,' said Caroline.

'What don't I understand?'

Caroline glanced across the room at the table where the Cove family was silently eating stewed plums. She leaned towards her father and said in a whisper:

'It's a forgiveness party. To show we haven't quarrelled with the Coves, in spite of yesterday. Hebe is trying to make up for what she did.'

Sir Henry could not hear very well, and her whispering tickled his ear, but he got the gist of it and nodded.

'All right,' he said. 'I don't promise to stay very long, but I'll show up for a bit. Are these brooches you're wearing anything to do with it?'

Every Gifford wore a brooch consisting of a safety pin, a sprig of lavender and a round label with the letters C.C. And he remembered that Fred had worn the same mystic badge on the lapel of his white waiter's coat.

There was a short silence and the twins giggled.

'It's a Society,' said Michael.

'Not another?'

The Spartans had been forcibly dissolved after the catastrophe at Dead Man's Rock.

'You can belong to it if you like,' said Hebe. 'Fred and Nancibel and Robin have been enrolled. The emblem is a sprig of lavender. And the object is something you would approve of. But we can't tell you about that now.'

She rolled her eyes towards the Coves' corner.

'Anyone who is interested in the liberation of oppressed persons can join,' she added.

Caroline whispered once more:

'C.C. is *Cave Cove*.'

'Cav-ce,' admonished Sir Henry. 'Latin. Two syllables.'

'But that would spoil it,' objected Hebe. 'Unless we give two syllables to both words.'

She muttered *cavee covee* under her breath, disliked it, and said, with decision:

'We shall say cave.'

He smiled at her dictatorial air, and then he frowned uneasily. Hebe's character was coming to be a matter of serious concern to him. He thought that she might be going to give a lot of trouble, both to herself and to other people. She needed skilful management. And from whom was she to get it? From Eirene, to whom he should presumably abandon her if their home was really to be broken up?

Why should the children be obliged to live with Eirene when he could not? This question had nagged at him all day, when he was not fuming over the evaporation of the dollar loan, or reading a *verbatim* report of last night's broadcast in four different newspapers. Neither preoccupation allevi-ated the other. No dollar resources could have solved his domestic problem. And after reading a fourth adjuration to be strong and very courageous he felt tempted to fly with Eirene to Guernsey.

He had had no chance to discuss the national news with anyone else, but when he went into the lounge after dinner he found that an animated conversation had broken out, in which even Mr. Paley and Mrs. Cove were taking part. His wife, bored with her bed, had come down in a decorative housecoat to lament the fate of her country. Miss Ellis oc-cupied her customary sofa. Mr. Siddal had shuffled in from his boot-hole. Only Mrs. Paley and Miss Wraxton were ab-sent; they were busy in the kitchen.

An indignant lament was in progress. Everybody seemed to be very angry. They were saying many things which Sir Henry himself had thought during the course of the day, but with which he now began to disagree. For he was a Liberal—the kind of Liberal which turns pink in blue sur-roundings and lilac at any murmur from Moscow.

In Pendizack lounge he inclined to pink.

He sat down beside Miss Ellis who was looking happier than usual as though she, alone, had found something to please her in the news. She said, with a sort of repressed glee:

'They'll have to go short now!'

'Who will?' he asked.

'Everybody,' said Miss Ellis.

'Including you,' snapped Mrs. Cove, who had overheard.

'Oh, I've always had to go short,' said Miss Ellis.

'You'll go shorter now,' prophesied Mrs. Cove.

'That bit,' Mr. Siddal was saying, 'about enjoying ourselves in the sunshine was particularly rich.'

'Perhaps now . . . perhaps *now* . . .' breathed Lady Gifford.

'Not a hope of it,' mourned Mr. Paley. 'They've never lost a by-election.'

'Why should they?' asked Mrs. Cove. 'Most of the voters belong to the so-called working class to whom they are handing out our money. They'll stay in till it's all been spent on nylons and perms and peaches and pineapples. And when it's all gone it won't matter what party gets in.'

'This country will starve,' boomed the Canon, 'and serve it right.'

There was a sigh of assent from the entire room. Sir Henry felt himself slithering leftwards.

'Why?' he asked. 'What has this country done that is so very reprehensible?'

For a few seconds they all gaped in surprise at the renegade.

'This Government . . .' began Eirene.

'Oh I know. Most of us don't like the Government. But why is *this country* so very wicked? People who deserve to starve must surely be very wicked. Mrs. Lechene . . . I've heard you say you're a socialist. Do you think this country deserves to starve?'

'It's not the Government,' said Anna, a little uncertainly. 'Any other Government would be just the same. It's the class war. This whole country is being bitched by anger and spite and intolerance and aggressiveness . . . a new kind of Puritanism . . .'

'Don't you make a rather indiscriminate use of that word?' broke in Mr. Siddal. 'Surely we got rid of the Puritans in 1660?'

'Oh, I don't mean men in funny hats with names like I—am—but—a—potshard—Hawkins,' said Anna, with increasing earnestness. 'I mean Holy Bullies. I mean people who can't live and let live, but have this lust to be pushing the rest of us around, and pretend it's for our good. They think their Holy Cause gives them a heavenly warrant to jump on other people's stomachs. And they seem to run the world now. All the politicians have taken to talking as if they were God's Head Prefects. Look how they quote the Bible at us! Look how they insult anyone who disagrees with them! They might be parsons, insulting people from the pulpit, where nobody can answer back. These Holy Bullies don't want people to agree and settle differences. They want to insult and enrage people and *force* them. Personally, I think it's a great pity we ever left off being monkeys. They don't have these holy ideologies. They only fight over nuts or when they're rutting.'

'And do you really suggest, Madam, that you *have* left off being a monkey?' thundered the Canon. 'I take leave to doubt it.'

'You ask what is wrong with this country?' exclaimed Mr. Paley. 'Let me tell you that this country, and not only this country but the entire civilized world, is being rotted and destroyed by the vicious cry for equality. Equality!

There is no such thing. It's simply an eruption of the hatred of the inferior for the superior . . .'

'Monkeys don't insist that their ideas are God's ideas . . .'

'God,' proclaimed the Canon, 'has only one idea.'

'What is it?' asked Mr. Siddal.

'How limited of Him, when we have so many,' cried Anna.

'. . . we have cosseted and flattered and pampered the inferior masses,' droned Mr. Paley, 'until they really believe themselves equal with their betters. We have told them that they are born with equal rights . . .'

Miss Ellis, properly enraged, broke in:

'What betters do you mean, Mr. Paley? Rich people? Why should they claim to be better than anyone else? What have they got to prove it? How are they different? Does a big car and a mink coat make a person better . . . ?'

'. . . if the people of this country ignore God's purpose in creating mankind, then God will have no further use for them . . .'

'. . . we have allowed every gutter brat to become infected by the idea that he has done something meritorious merely in getting himself born. No matter how incompetent, shiftless, lazy and thick-headed he may be, he thinks he's entitled to an equal share in the country's wealth, an equal claim to its respect, an equal voice in its destinies. Pernicious nonsense! In a just society he would be entitled to exactly as much as he deserves. No more.'

'. . . this country is heading for the scrap heap. Make no mistake about that! We are rapidly sinking to the monkey level . . .'

'But does anyone want a just society?' protested Mr. Siddal. 'I'm sure nobody does. It would be ghastly. Just imagine having to admit that all the top dogs really deserved to be on top! What smugs they would be! And how shame-making for the rest of us . . .'

'. . . Mrs. Cove blames poor people for wanting nylons and pineapples. If the rich didn't have such luxuries they wouldn't . . .'

'. . . far too many people agree with you, I'm afraid, Mrs. Lechene. That is why this country will be scrapped.'

'We're all going to be scrapped anyway, Canon Wraxton. In a Holy War between Democracy and Communism.'

'No, no, Paley! Let us at least be able to criticize our betters! I've only met one duke but I got considerable satisfaction out of finding him a very stupid fellow, and thinking what a much better duke I should have made myself . . .'

'And what is wrong with nylons and pineapples, Miss Ellis?'

'If the rich didn't have them, Lady Gifford, the poor wouldn't want them. It's the rich that set the example . . .'

'. . . a just retribution on a Godless world. Personally I should treat people who admire monkeys as if they were monkeys.'

'. . . no sop to poor human vanity. In a just society the underdog would be allowed no self-respect. He'd have to admit he was at the bottom because he was no good.'

'He did admit it, Siddal, for hundreds of years. Before all this nonsense started . . .'

'I shouldn't mind, Canon Wraxton. We treat monkeys

very nicely. We give them nuts and never preach at them. I wish we were half as kind to each other . . .'

'We exterminate any animal that has become a pest.'

'Exterminate! That's a great word with the Holy Bullies. It wasn't so bad when all that sort of thing was confined to you parsons. You've always had a lovely time burning each other at the stake. But the rest of us used to know that it's uncivilized to lose our little tem-tems and start exterminating anyone who happens to disagree . . .'

'The mills of God grind slowly . . .'

'. . . thinks that nobody is to give him orders, or live better than he does, or understand anything that he does not understand, or work harder . . .'

'. . . grind exceeding small! All standards are lowered. There is a universal moral degeneration. Children no longer obey their parents. The Sabbath is profaned. Chastity is ridiculed. The Churches stand empty . . .'

'. . . till the country is pulled down to the level of the lowest. And no country can survive at that level.'

'If the churches are empty, it's because all the religious people have exterminated each other . . .'

The noise was terrific. It reminded Sir Henry of the London barrage. The Canon had the biggest artillery, but Anna Lechene's boom was quite impressive, and the protests of Miss Ellis were let loose on a rising shriek, like a series of rockets. Mr. Paley's relentless monologue continued, undeflected, droning in to the attack. Mr. Siddal barked intermittently. Lady Gifford's voice was only heard in the occasional lulls, but she had been talking vehemently for some minutes and she now gained a hearing by getting up from her chair, which forced all the men to break off and get up too.

'Money,' she was saying, 'is the root of all evil. Always. I'm afraid I must go to bed now. So tiresome. But I'm under rather strict orders about bed times. And really, you know, if everybody thought less about money it would be quite simple. They think they would be happier if they had more. But that's not so. The happiest people are often quite poor. Did you never hear that wise old story about the king who . . .'

'Yes!' cried everybody. 'Yes!'

For there was a general panic lest they should be going to be obliged to hear again that hackneyed fable of the happy man who had no shirt.

'You try being happy with no dinner!' shrieked Miss Ellis.

Eirene raised her eyebrows and replied with quiet dignity:

'Naturally nobody can be happy if they're hungry. But in a happy country, quite poor people get enough to eat, while in a miserable country, like this one, even rich people can't get enough. We only want money to buy *things*. We can't eat money. Yet people think they want it and ask for more and more wages. And that makes everything so expensive they get fewer things instead of more. The *higher* the wages, the *less* everybody gets. It all comes from love of money. Goodnight! Harry dear . . . will you give me an arm upstairs?'

As the door closed behind the Giffords, Miss Ellis sent up another rocket.

'I never! No I never! She ought to be on the dole. Then she'd find out if money matters!'

'Still, she made quite a point,' said Anna. 'People do concentrate on cash rather than on getting value for it.'

Mrs. Cove, who had not contributed very much to the barrage, looked up from her knitting and said, with a sniff of disgust:

'It isn't money people seem to want, nowadays We shouldn't be in this hole if they did. All they want is less work and shorter hours. Hunger is the only call they'll answer. As soon as their stomachs are full they slack off. They don't want anything that means effort. They don't want higher standards unless somebody else pays. You see . . . you *see* what will happen when all our money is spent. The schools will be the first to go. For years they've educated their children at our expense. When they have to pay for it themselves you won't hear them howling so loud about education. Look at all the waste and extravagance! In my opinion it's sheer laziness that is ruining this country. People hate work. They think it a hardship.'

She sniffed again and held up one grey sock against another, measuring the length.

Nobody took up her point. Mr. Paley, a little ashamed perhaps at his own volubility, had retired behind a newspaper. Anna and the Canon had shouted themselves hoarse. The only comment came from Miss Ellis, who exclaimed that she had never been so insulted in her life.

'Who by?' asked Mr. Siddal.

'By a lot of people. I'm not to ask for higher wages; it's

355

wicked. I'm not to ask for shorter hours; it's wicked. I'm not to think I'm born with any rights at all; it's wicked. I'm not to stand up for myself; it's wicked. If there were more people like me there would be fewer like you, Mrs. Cove.'

'That,' said Mrs. Cove, 'would be a pity.'

Miss Ellis rose, muttering, and flounced out of the room just as Mr. Siddal took up a position on the hearthrug and cleared his throat.

'Don't tell me you are going to start now!' cried Anna.

'I don't see why I shouldn't,' said Mr. Siddal. 'All the rest of you have said what is wrong with the world. Why shouldn't I? . . .'

He broke off to cross the room and look out of the window.

'I thought I heard something fall,' he explained. 'But it was a false alarm. Nothing there. I thought the Pendizack poltergeist had been at work again.'

And he came back to the hearthrug.

'What poltergeist?' asked Anna.

'Didn't you know we had one? It throws things at night out of the top-floor windows . . . little objects of value . . .'

Mrs. Cove sat up abruptly and gaped at him.

'We've heard various classes of people blamed tonight,' he continued, 'for our sorry condition . . . the envious, the luxurious . . . the lazy, the intolerant, and so forth . . . what! Mrs. Cove, are you leaving us?'

Mrs. Cove was bundling her knitting into a bag. With an abrupt goodnight she hastened from the room.

'What a meanie you are, Dick!' reproached Anna. 'Is it really those children who have been playing tricks with her soapstone?'

'I strongly suspect that it is.'

'She'll skin them alive.'

'Oh no! If she does, Paley's wife and Wraxton's daughter, not to speak of Nancibel, Robin and Hebe, will skin her alive. The little Coves can look after themselves. The little Coves are immensely powerful! They have got the whole house in their pockets. They are the Meek, who are going to inherit the earth, and they will feast above our graves. But I, being a sportsman, have a soft spot in my heart for poor Mrs. Cove, that dying gladiator. Now I don't think any one class of individual is to be blamed in this collapsing world. If there wasn't something a little wrong with all of us we could deal with any one pernicious group. But we can't because nobody is grateful enough. Ingratitude! That's what is the matter with everybody. And isn't that because every man, any man, has a completely false idea of what he really is? He will regard himself as an independent and self-sufficient unit—a sovereign state. And in his dealing with the rest of us he imagines he is negotiating with other sovereign states. No wonder the negotiations break down. For by himself he is nothing. Nothing at all. All that he is, everything that he possesses, he owes to the rest of us. He has nothing that is really his own.'

'He has an immortal soul,' stated the Canon.

'Which he didn't make himself. He is simply a creature presuming to negotiate on equal terms with his Creator. If he could ever fully realize what he owes to the rest of us he would be so flooded, so overwhelmed, with humility and gratitude that he would only be anxious to pay his debts, not claim his rights. He'd be the easiest fellow in the world to play ball with.'

'I do not think,' observed Mr. Paley, 'that I owe anything to anybody. What I am, what I have, are the result of my own efforts.'

'You didn't conceive yourself or give birth to yourself. You didn't invent the language you use, and in which the wisdom of other generations has been communicated to you by other people. You couldn't even do a noble deed without some help from us: it was we who first gave you a notion of nobility and anyway you'd need somebody else to do it to. You didn't weave the cloth you wear or grow the bread you eat.'

'I pay for what I have.'

'Do you pay enough? Does anybody pay enough? Has any man repaid a millionth part of all that he has received? Where would you be without us? Did you ever read the life of Helen Keller? Blind, deaf, dumb . . . a soul in prison . . . an intellect frozen by solitude . . . unable to reach us . . . all *alone*! And then . . .'

Mr. Siddal paused, for Mr. Paley had risen with a smothered cry.

'You said?'

'I said nothing,' gasped Mr. Paley, who had grown very white.

'Are you all right?' asked Anna.

'No. I . . . I'm ill . . .' He turned furiously on Mr. Siddal. 'You're talking nonsense. You're talking rubbish . . .'

A spasm shook him and he rushed from the room.

'Now what,' enquired Mr. Siddal, 'can I have said? Why should a reference to Helen Keller give Paley a fit? It's a wonderful story. She found us through the one link left: a sense of touch They used to pour water on her hand, over and over and over again, and each time they did it they spelt out the word on her fingers. At last she understood. It was a message. We were there. She went half crazy. She rushed round the room, snatching, grasping, touching everything within reach, holding out her poor little fingers for more names, more words, more messages. Then the brain could function. Then the soul could expand. Through her finger tips she learnt all that we know.'

Anna yawned, and the Canon, leaning back in his chair, tapped impatiently with his foot. They were now Mr. Siddal's only audience, and they did not encourage him to continue. But he pursued his point, rocking up and down on his heels in front of the fireplace.

'I don't think that man is going to survive. There is this fatal flaw in our construction; a kind of moral imperviousness to a truth which we can perceive intellectually. Reason tells us that we should be grateful. Reason tells us that, if we were, we might be able to cooperate in the pursuit of happiness. But reason can't run the machine. It can only draw up blueprints. Civilization after civilization has gone down into the dust because we cannot manage to be humble.'

'And is that why you hog it in the boot-hole all day?' asked Anna.

'Yes. That's why I hog it in the boot-hole. I am "born but to die and reason but to err". If everybody else saw that as clearly as I do they would all hog it in boot-holes. But you are all very busy and active in the pursuit of happiness and security. A vain pursuit. You are nothing and you can do nothing for yourselves. You might do something for each other, if you really believed in each other's existence. But you don't. Very few people are really able to believe that anybody exists except themselves. Too few. They can never do more than start something which grows a little and then dies.'

'What a ray of sunshine you are,' said Anna, getting up. 'Well . . . I still think the monkeys get top marks. Good-night, Canon Wraxton.'

The Canon did not return her salutation. He waited until she had gone, and then he said:

'Now that we are alone I'd like a word with you, Siddal.'

'If it's about my son and your daughter . . .'

'It's not. I know you count for nothing in this house. No! It's about a cock-and-bull story that was told to me today. I know what is behind it. Somebody wants to scare me out of the place. It's not the first attempt. And I'm asked to believe that the house isn't safe; that the cliffs are likely to subside!'

'Who said so?'

'Never you mind. If you don't know, I shan't tell you. But there's no doubt that my informant was set on by somebody or other. Plenty of people here, I imagine, want to get rid of me. If you know who they are, tell them this: I wasn't born yesterday. They must think of a better lie.'

'Do you mean the Other Cliffs?'

'You know best what cliffs I mean. I was told that you have had a letter from the Government telling you to clear out of this place immediately. Is that true or is it not?'

'No,' said Mr. Siddal. 'Not that I know of.'

'I thought not. I thought you'd admit as much if I nailed you down to it. Very well. Now I know what to think. I wish you a good evening.'

Mr. Siddal sat meditating for some time in the empty lounge. Before he returned to his boot-hole he had an impulse to look into the boiler room. The coke furnace was crackling merrily, and the room was very tidy. There was no way of telling whether all the letters he had left there had been burnt up or not.

6. The Poltergeist

'Seventeen, eighteen, nineteen, twenty,' counted Blanche, as she stacked the invitation cards.

'But there are twenty-three going to the Feast,' said Maud.

'Three are us. Now let's settle who gets which.'

Each card had been decorated by the Coves, who could draw and paint beautifully. They had been busy all day.

Beatrix spread them on her bed, and the three sisters knelt round it, arguing whether it would be polite to give Maud's design of snails to Mr. Siddal. Eventually they gave him hollyhocks and allotted the snails to Robin. For Nancibel they set aside their favourite card, with a border of dandelion clocks, exquisitely done in pen and ink by Blanche, while Mrs. Paley was to have their rival favourite, which had a pattern of shells.

'Rabbits for Mrs. Siddal, the spider's web for Duff, fir cones for Gerry and bracken crooks for Angie. What about Angie's father?'

'Give him the sea anemone I blotted,' suggested Maud.

'No,' decided Blanche. 'That's the worst one. We don't want to give the worst to somebody we don't like. Let's give him the owls. I wonder what he will dress up as?'

'He could change clothes with Fred,' said Maud. 'Then Fred could go as a clergyman and the Canon could go as a waiter. Oh I do hope poor Lady Gifford will be well enough to go. We mustn't forget to put her card on her breakfast tray.'

Their own ecstasy did not surprise them in the least, though they had never enjoyed such a transport before. But they had always believed in it as a natural accompaniment of a feast. So they took it calmly and attended to details. Their costumes had been easily settled. Hebe and Caroline had lent them two cotton kimono dressing gowns in which Blanche and Beatrix were to appear as Geishas. Maud had collected Hebe's slacks, curtain ear-rings, a sash, a red handkerchief and a plastic pencil case which looked like a pistol. No pirate could ask for more.

'Let's go to bed,' said Beatrix. 'Let's go to sleep and make tomorrow come quickly.'

But Blanche objected that now was just as good as tomorrow. And after the Feast was over they would have it to remember for always.

'This time tomorrow,' she said, 'we shall be up on the headland feasting and revelling. Now we are here, thinking about it. Afterwards we shall be in other places, thinking about it. So it will sort of happen for a long time in a lot of places.'

They went to the window and hung out, looking at the solid mass of Pendizack Head, standing out above the sea. The tide was high. They reckoned that it would be high tomorrow when they started for the Feast. They would not be able to cross the sands. The musical procession, the first item on Hebe's programme, would have to wind its way up the drive to the place where the higher cliff path branched off.

They were all still hanging out of the window when their

mother came. Something ominous about her approaching footsteps, as she hurried down the passage, warned them of trouble before she came into the room. A premonitory shiver went through all three. They turned slowly when they heard the door open. She was exceedingly angry, a fact not easily apparent to a casual observer, since it made little difference to her expression, but always discernible to her children.

'Come here,' she said, sitting down on her bed.

They came and stood in a trembling row in front of her.

'Somebody in this room,' she said, 'is a thief. Somebody took my keys, while I was in my bath, and stole my black amber, and threw it out of the window. Which of you is it?'

Anybody could have seen which it was. The blank astonishment of Maud and Beatrix could not have been assumed. Mrs. Cove shot out a steely hand and seized Blanche by the shoulder.

'Why did you do it?'

'I . . . I don't know,' whispered Blanche.

'Who put you up to it?'

'Nobody.'

'Don't tell lies.'

'Nobody else knew. I . . . just didn't want us to have it.'

'You know what happens when you tell lies?'

A gasp went up from them all.

'No . . .' cried Blanche. 'No. I'm not telling lies. Nobody knew.'

'Somebody must have known. You are telling lies. Put a bath towel in the middle of the room and put a chair on it. Put another towel round your shoulders.'

Mrs. Cove rose and went to a drawer for a small safety razor which she used regularly upon her own upper lip.

Beatrix and Maud broke into wails of protest.

'Oh not here! Not here, where everybody can see! Oh Mother! Please . . . please . . . the Feast . . . she can't go like that to the Feast . . . please don't do it till after the Feast . . .'

'There'll be no Feast for any of you,' said Mrs. Cove, turning, 'unless Blanche tells the truth.'

The wails rose to shrieks.

'I am telling the truth! I am! I am!' howled Blanche.

Mrs. Cove took no notice whatever. She took a soap dish from the washing stand and marched down to the bathroom to get a little hot water. The Coves wept hopelessly until Maud, with the courage of the desperate, jumped up and locked the door. A sudden silence fell upon the room.

'She shan't do it,' said Maud. 'We'll lock her out.'

'She'll break down the door,' whispered Beatrix.

'She can't, by herself. It's very strong. And she won't dare tell anyone. It's wicked. It's cruel. They'd stop her.'

'She's our mother,' said Blanche.

'We shall starve to death,' observed Beatrix.

'No. They'll find out. When we don't come to the Feast they'll come and look for us. We shall be very hungry, but we shall have food at the Feast. They will save us.'

Beatrix sighed an assent. Blanche felt too faint to say more. They waited, shivering and still sobbing a little until their mother came back. To her knocks and calls not even Maud had the courage to reply. They let the locked door deliver their ultimatum for them.

She hammered and threatened for some moments until a fresh voice interrupted her.

'Whatever's the matter, Mrs. Cove? Locked you out, have they? Well!'

It was Miss Ellis. Their mother stopped hammering and asked if there was such a thing as a screwdriver in the house.

'I don't know, I'm sure. Not very likely, I should think. But fancy your girls playing you such a trick! Bet those Giffords put them up to it.'

'No we didn't!'

The twins, aroused by the tumult, were peering out of their door.

'If I were in your shoes, Mrs. Cove, I'd leave. Take them away before they learn worse. Even if I had to pay for the rooms . . .'

'Thank you, Miss Ellis. I'm quite able to manage my own children.'

'Doesn't look like it. And if you knew as much as I do, Mrs. Cove, you wouldn't even pay for the rooms. They wouldn't dare make you pay . . .'

'What do you mean?'

'Can't tell you here. Little pitchers have long ears. Come in my room for a minute. You really should know . . .'

Footsteps receded, a door closed, silence fell.

'They've gone to Miss Ellis's room,' surmised Maud.

Blanche, who had been lying on the floor, stirred and sat up.

'It's no use,' she said feebly. 'We can't lock Mother out of her own room. We can't do anything except offer it up.'

'Oh *no!*' cried Maud and Beatrix.

'Then Jesus will decide.'

'I'd rather He didn't,' said Maud. 'We offered up the stray kitten, but He didn't make her let us keep it.'

'He was very sensible,' Beatrix reminded her. 'We saw that, afterwards. How could we have fed it? He made the next-door people take pity on it, and it had a much nicer home.'

'If He'd been even more sensible He'd have let us keep it and sent us food for it.'

'We couldn't have brought it here. Perhaps He knew we were coming here. What would have happened to it?'

'Maud!' cried Blanche. 'Don't you trust Jesus?'

'Not to give me anything I want. He only cares about Kingdom Come, which won't be for millions of years. If I want anything very much I just particularly *don't* offer it up.'

'If we offer it up, nothing bad can happen. Nothing He wants can be bad. That clergyman said so, on Good Friday.'

'I daresay. But something very nasty can happen, all the same,' muttered Maud.

They said no more. Maud was quite right. Their previous attempts to offer things up had never saved them from disaster, though Blanche had insisted that this was because they had never achieved complete indifference to their own wishes. She could not do so now. She could not escape from the hope that Kingdom Come might not require her head to be shaved.

But after twenty minutes of suspense even Maud began to falter. The desperate naughtiness of their conduct became increasingly apparent to all of them.

At last they heard their mother coming back. She tried the door, found it still locked, and called to Blanche. Her voice was changed; it was worried and uncertain.

'Don't be so silly. Open the door, I want to talk to you.'

Blanche tried to get up, but Maud held her down.

'If you'll stop this nonsense, perhaps I'll let you off for once.'

'Don't! Don't! It's a trap,' cried Maud, struggling with Blanche.

'Rubbish!' replied the anxious voice outside the door. 'If I let you off it's because I have other things to think of. I may have to go away . . . to London . . . I may have to leave you here . . . In that case . . .'

'Why should she have to go away all of a sudden?'

'If you want to stay here you must behave sensibly. I can't ask Mrs. Siddal to keep three crazy children . . .'

Blanche threw Maud aside and rose to her feet.

'Will you solemnly promise to let Maud and Bee go to the Feast?' she called. 'If you do, it doesn't matter about me.'

'What? The Feast? Yes, I suppose so . . . I said I'd let you all off, if you'll come to your senses.'

Blanche turned to the others.

'Offer it up! Offer it up!' she exhorted them. 'There's no other help. If Jesus wants us to escape we shall. If not, not. But I must open the door.'

Beatrix and Maud, closing their eyes, began to offer it up.

Blanche unlocked the door. All three children stood rigid, with tightly shut eyes, as their mother came in.

7. Atalanta

It was half-past nine by the old cherry-wood clock in the
Thomas kitchen when Nancibel wearily pushed open the
door. A blast from the radio greeted her and her mother's
voice, asking wherever she had been. All the rest of the
family had gone to bed, but Mrs. Thomas was sitting up
in a mood which swung between indignation and excited
curiosity.

Indignation spoke first.

'I thought this was your half day. I thought Millie Stephens
was going to give you a perm.'

'I cancelled it,' said Nancibel, throwing herself into a
chair. 'I rang up Millie from Pendizack. Mrs. Siddal took
faint so I changed my day and stopped on. There's no hurry
for my old perm.'

'Just what I thought, *just* what I thought. I said you'd
given up your half day again. It's getting too much of a good
thing.'

'Only changed it, Mum. I'll take two days one week later
on. Got a cuppa? I'm dying of thirst.'

'It doesn't do to let yourself be put on,' said Mrs.
Thomas, bringing the teapot from the stove. 'They aren't
grateful. They only take it for granted. And there's such a
thing as being too unselfish. You're only young once. Now's
the time to enjoy yourself. There'll be plenty of giving up

for others later on, without you going out of your way to look for it. When you're married it's never anything else.'

Nancibel smiled as she sipped the sweet, stewed tea.

'Yet you're always going on at me to get married,' she observed.

'Husband and children, that's life,' declared Mrs. Thomas, pouring out a cup for herself. 'It's not much fun, but neither is life much fun here below. What I mean is, Pendizack's not your funeral. Mrs. Siddal has bitten off more than she can chew, poor thing; but that's not to say you have to lose your sleep over it. You can't set the whole world to rights. Do your work you said you'd do, and do it properly, and let her boil her own kettle of fish.'

'Oh, don't go on, Mum.'

They both shouted, for the radio was playing at full strength, unnoticed by either of them. They had become so used to it that they never thought of turning it off. Ever since half-past six in the morning it had supplied an *obbligato* accompaniment to the life of the family.

Mrs. Thomas, having vented her displeasure, turned to a more agreeable topic.

'Oo!' she shouted. 'I forgot. There's a letter for you.'

She took it from the mantelpiece where it had stood all day, leaning against a china statuette of John Wesley preaching in a verdant bower.

Nancibel sat up, eyes sparkling and cheeks flushed. A letter? Bruce?

But it was not his hand, and the postmark was Wolverhampton. She took it and sat hunched up at the table, reading it slowly, while her mother tried not to watch her too eagerly and Geraldo's Band played a foxtrot.

All the Thomas family had been discussing this letter ever since its arrival, for they knew that Brian lived in Wolverhampton, and they had decided that he might be writing to make it up with his old love. But they could agree about nothing else. Mr. Thomas, furious at all the grief which this wretched youth had brought on Nancibel, had wanted to throw the letter behind the fire. Myra hoped that the match might still come off; she had smarted under the reproach of having a jilted sister and longed for a chance to be a bridesmaid. Mrs. Thomas was uncertain; Brian had good prospects, but she had much preferred the look of Bruce. The rest of the family was merely frantic with curiosity, which should have been satisfied in the afternoon, had not Nancibel changed her half day. They had wished to sit up till she got home, but Mrs. Thomas had forbidden it and packed them all off to bed. She thought that she might have more chance to say a sensible word if she got the girl to herself.

'Is it from . . . Brian?' she asked, when Nancibel had finished.

'No. From his father. Read it.'

Nancibel, with a little laugh, pushed the letter across the table and went back to her tea. Mrs. Thomas read:

My Dear Miss Thomas,

You will no doubt be very surprised to hear from me. But I am a plain man and do not think that two

371

young people should spoil their lives for want of a little plain speaking. So am writing to know if your feelings have changed since last year *re* my son Brian.

His feelings have not changed. He has been miserable ever since. He cannot forget you. He takes no interest in anything, he never goes out or takes a girl out, just sits around moping, he does not even take an interest in his food. He says his lifes happiness is ruined since he parted from you. But he says he has not got the nerve to write you after what happened. Though I do not see why you should not make it up if your feelings are the same. I know you are a sensible young lady and have a sweet disposition. You would not let an old grudge interfere with a bright future.

Miss Thomas, I ought to tell you that there has been some very sad changes in our Home lately. My poor Wife passed away in June. So self and Brian are now alone in the Home with nobody to see to us. It is a great comfort to Brian now to know that he did not go against the wishes of his poor Mother. They say a good son makes a good husband. But I am now free to admit that my wishes were not always the same as her's. I would personally be glad to welcome you as my Daughter.

If you have changed it is no good. But if you feel the same a line to Brian would make a new man of him. Or if you feel awkward about that a line to me would greatly oblige and I could drop a hint.

There is the business. It is doing well and he will get it when I retire. There is a good future for him if he will cheer up and take an interest.

With best respects to your parents and your good-self,

I remain, yours sincerely,

A. GOLDIE

'Poor Brian!' said Nancibel, with another laugh. 'First his mum says he mayn't. Then his dad says he may. Did you ever hear anything so soft?'

'What'll you do?' asked Mrs. Thomas.

'Oh, I'll write the old bird. I'll write Sunday. Say I'm sorry his wife is gone and all that, but my feelings are changed, thank you.'

'They are?'

Nancibel took the letter and put it on the dresser behind the communal bottle of ink.

'They certainly are, Mum. If nothing else had changed them, this letter would do.'

'It's a pity Brian didn't write himself,' agreed Mrs. Thomas, doubtfully.

'He's nothing but a spoilt kid. First he lets them talk him out of it and then he moans and groans over spilt milk. I snapped out of it and forgot him. But he's got no guts.'

'Guts! I wish you wouldn't use such common expressions. Why do you?'

'Because I am common, that's how come. Too common for the Goldies.'

'You never learnt such a way of talking from me, or your dad.'

'I know. But we had all sorts in the A.T.S. We had girls with handles to their names, and if I talked the way some of *them* did, you'd turn me out in the snow. Look Mum, the big kettle's on and I'm as dirty as a crow. I got so hot and sticky down in Pendizack kitchen tonight. Can't I have a nice wash down here, comfortable, in front of the fire before I go to bed?'

'O.K.,' said Mrs. Thomas, clearing the tea things.

The unspoken name of Bruce hung heavy in the air between them. Mrs. Thomas was acutely aware that he had not yet been mentioned. Memories of her own youth, experience with other daughters, told her that it is not the boys you hear about who matter. She longed to ask if he had anything to do with this change in Nancibel's feelings, but she dared say nothing lest she should get her head snapped off.

She went into the back kitchen to get a basin, soap and a towel. Nancibel, as if determined to change the subject, launched into a spirited account of the day's doings. She told of Gerry Siddal's engagement, the mystery of the disappearing library, the burnt letters in the boiler, Mrs. Siddal's collapse, Miss Wraxton's competence as a cook, and her own fear lest she should go bats if she stayed at Pendizack much longer.

'It's getting me down,' she declared as she pulled off her clothes. 'Really it is. Every morning I have to drag myself there, and I can't get out quick enough at night. All the spite and the quarrels and the unpleasantness! It's only a few people, but they make a regular inferno for the rest of us. You wouldn't believe so few could do such a lot of harm. Of course Ellis is the worst. Know what she's saying now?' She paused to pin her curls on the top of her head. 'She's going round telling the visitors that the hotel is insanitary. Says the Government says it's got to be closed.'

'Old cat!'

Mrs. Thomas put the basin on a chair in front of the range and filled it from the big kettle.

'If I could catch her at it I'd go straight to Mrs. Siddal, I really would, though I hate tale-telling. But she's just doing it for spite, to crab the hotel, and it ought to be stopped.'

'How do you know she's saying it, then?'

'Fred. That's why I don't like to interfere. He always gets hold of the wrong end of the stick . . . and it doesn't do to accuse a person unless you're quite sure of what you say. If I'd heard it myself it would be different . . .'

Nancibel knelt in front of the basin and began to soap her arms, breasts and shoulders.

'. . . He was collecting the tea tray on the terrace and he heard her talking to Mr. Paley in the lounge. So along comes Fred to the scullery and says: heard the news? This place, he says, has got to be shut down. Mr. Bevin's written to Mr. Siddal . . .'

'Mr. Bevin!' cried Mrs. Thomas. 'Never!'

'He's in the Government, isn't he?'

'Foreign Minister, you silly girl. Got quite enough on his mind arguing with the Russians. No, it's Bevan more likely.'

'I wouldn't know,' said Nancibel. 'Bevin and Bevan . . . I always mix them up myself, so you can't blame Fred.'

She stood up to lather her hips and thighs.

'I don't know how you girls manage to be so ignorant,' complained Mrs. Thomas. 'You're supposed to be so much better educated . . . you learn I don't know what all at school. But you don't read the papers and you don't listen to the wireless and you don't know anything about the country. Now I left school when I was thirteen, but I do take an interest, and I go to the W.I. lectures, and I know the difference between Bevin and Bevan.'

'Be a honey, Mum, and scrub my back.'

'You're nothing but a baby,' scolded Mrs. Thomas, fondly. 'You scrub Dad's back.'

Nancibel knelt luxuriously before the fire while her mother scoured her beautiful white back, kneading shoulders, spine, ribs and hips with the ancient and ritual art of women who have, for hundreds of years, soothed the tired muscles of their men.

'Your dad gets stiff in the fields.'

'So do I get stiff at Pendizack. That's ever so lovely. Go on!'

'But what's wrong with Pendizack?' asked Mrs. Thomas. 'Could it be the well, d'you think? They say wells are insanitary, nowadays.'

'I'm sure I hope not. They'd never have the cash to bring the company water all the way down from Tregoylan. I told Fred to keep his mouth shut and mind not to repeat such a story. But it shows you the sort of spiteful thing I mean.'

Going on all the time. I don't want to let Mrs. Siddal down, but I can't stand much more of it.'

'Want me to dry your back?'

'If you would do! I'm not the only one to feel they can't stand much more of it. We had quite an argument in the kitchen, before I came off, about this picnic tomorrow. The children want it up on the Point, but Gerry, he says we can't lug all that food and drink up there, why not have it on the rocks just outside the garden gate? So then Miss Wraxton said just what I've been saying. She said no, it's got to be as far away from this hotel as we can get, she said. Nobody could hope to enjoy themselves anywhere near this place, she said. And Mrs. Paley said the same. Get up and get out was what she'd been feeling all the week. And it's quite true. You'd never be able to forget all the nastiness there is going on there, or else poor old Mr. Paley would be putting his dreary face out of the window, like a horse looking over a gate, or else Canon Wraxton would rush out and throw something at anybody. Honestly Mum, that place may not be insanitary, but it's something a lot worse. Nobody could be happy inside a mile of it.'

Nancibel stood up, relaxed and refreshed after her massage. She yawned and stretched her arms above her head, filling the little kitchen with her naked glory.

Mrs. Thomas made a sound of agreement, but her attention had wandered back to the letter behind the ink bottle, and the fear that an important decision might be made too hastily. Because, she thought, even if he is a bit soft, won't he be the easier to manage? And the life would be easier, easier than mine, though she won't be getting such a good man as Barny. I would like for her to have something better than I've had . . . Question is: *how* better? P'raps that Bruce . . .

She took the basin into the back kitchen while Nancibel put on an old coat and collected her clothes.

'That chauffeur . . .' began Mrs. Thomas, coming back.

'Oh, he's gone,' said Nancibel quickly.

'Gone? I thought they were staying till . . .'

'He's left that job. Gone off to get himself a better one.'

'Well . . . I call that a bit sudden. Sounds a bit impulsive to me, leaving a good job all of a sudden like that! Nancibel . . . I think you ought to consider seriously about Brian before . . .'

'Oh no, Mum. I couldn't ever. I've outgrown Brian.'

'This Bruce . . . will he ever come back, d'you suppose?'

'He might do,' conceded Nancibel, flushing.

'Well, let's hope, if he does, you don't start finding you've outgrown him too!'

Nancibel pondered.

'I don't think I shall,' she said slowly, 'if he does come back.'

'You'll outgrow the boys on the other side of your face one of these days,' cried Mrs. Thomas in sudden irritation. 'You'll outgrow yourself into an old maid. Twenty years time, when you're wearing the willow, you'll be sorry you went about outgrowing everybody in such a hurry!'

Nancibel laughed and went up the steep little staircase, on tiptoe, to the bed which she shared with her sisters. Mrs. Thomas sighed, turned off the radio, and followed her.

FRIDAY

1. Mr. Paley's Diary

I have had my dream again. I said that I should set it down
here if I had it again. But the memory fills me with such
horror that I can scarcely write.

It was Siddal's fault. He brought it on. If he had not said
what he did, I might have escaped this dream.

I could not shake off the impression for many hours after
I woke. I was alone. Christina leaves me alone now, every
night.

I had gone to bed rather early, after some conversation
in the lounge. Perhaps I had become overexcited, and that
made me dream. Christina came in. She was changing her
shoes. She told me that she wished to remain here until the
end of the month; two weeks longer than we had intended.
There is some trouble here. They say Mrs. Siddal is ill. Miss
Wraxton is to be cook and my wife wishes to help her. It is
no concern of mine, but I have no objection to staying. Nor
am I impressed by that imbecile housekeeper's story. I did
not believe it at all when she first spoke to me. But yesterday, after tea, I went up to the cliffs to examine the alleged
cracks. And now I am inclined to think that there may be
some grounds for it, though I should accept no opinion save
that of an expert. I do not suppose that this jack-in-office
who wrote to Siddal knows more than I do. The cracks seem
to be widening rapidly, and they are sufficiently near to the

edge of the cliff to suggest the danger that the entire cliff face may come down some time or other. I should not be in the least surprised if it did. And in that case I do not see how this building can escape. Siddal, however, must think otherwise, or he would not remain here.

I am quite unperturbed. It is not my habit to scuttle about like a rabbit. My life is not so valuable to me nowadays. I only write of this because I am reluctant to set down my dream.

My dream is as follows:

I do not, generally, attach great importance to dreams. I have had very few in my life, as far as I can remember. But I dislike all dreams intensely. One acts so foolishly in most dreams. They are humiliating and grotesque. It is, however, the horror, the *horror*, of this one which unnerves me.

It is this:

Siddal says he never opens his letters. Perhaps he never opened this one, which would explain why he stays on. I never thought of that. But it does not signify, as I am resolved to stay here.

This is my dream. It is always the same.

I have been asleep. I wake up in absolute solitude. I am suspended in a vacancy which is neither dark nor light. I cannot even see darkness. There is not even darkness for me to see. There is nothing . . . nothing except myself. The fact that I AM is the only fact. There is no other. But not at first. Not at the beginning of my dream. There is something else then. I am smoking a cigar. I can see it, feel it and smell it. I can see the spark of light at the end. It is infinitely precious because it is the last thing left that is not myself. When it is gone there will be nothing. So I smoke it very slowly. I do not dare not to smoke it because it might go out and then I should not see the spark any more. But, however slowly I smoke it, the time comes, *the time comes*, when it is finished. The stub burns my fingers, and I drop it, though I have been resolving never to do so; to allow the burn, since a burn, pain, from that which is not myself, would be better than absolute solitude. But I drop it. The small spark falls like a shooting star and is gone. After that there is nothing, for ever and ever.

Nothing.
I AM.
Nothing
I AM.
For ever.
I AM
    Nothing.

Impossible that this should ever happen to a . . . what shall I say? To an intelligence? *Cogito ergo sum*. But I do not *think*, in my dream. That which is not myself I perceive through my senses. If I should survive my senses . . . what then? Of what, then, should I think? *Cogito ergo sumus ego et non ego*.

I have described my dream, but not adequately. I have not explained that I awake into this vacancy, and that this, my present life, is my dream . . . I am not afraid of dreaming. But I fear to awake . . .

2. Circe

'Branw ll's innoc nt y lids . . .' typed Anna.

She broke off to swear, for the letter e had vanished from her typewriter. For some weeks it had been loose and now it had gone altogether. *The Bleeding Branch* must remain at a standstill until she could find a substitute machine.

There was an old Remington in the office, never used by the Siddals, who could not type, but put there in case they should some day collect a manageress who could. Anna remembered it and set off in search of someone who would give her leave to borrow it. Mrs. Siddal was not likely to be accommodating, but Mr. Siddal might be open to persuasion, and to his boot-hole she repaired. He was not there. Fred, who was scuffling about in the passage, said that he had gone to the stables to find something in the bins. So Anna carried her request to the stables.

The bins were a row of garbage cans which were put in the stable yard on Fridays when a weekly lorry called from Porthmerryn. Some contained true garbage and some clean paper for salvage. But Mr. Siddal had emptied them all into a heap in the middle of the yard, as a preliminary to his search. Cabbage stalks, cinders, tea leaves, coffee grounds, egg shells, and tins were all mixed up with letters and newspapers. Still wearing his old dressing gown, he crawled round the noisome heap, fishing out this letter and that letter, glancing at it, and throwing it down again. Duff, up in the loft, was playing Stravinsky.

'Well . . .' said Anna. 'Are you trying to find something to eat?'

Mr. Siddal said that he was looking for a letter. He was not sure if it existed. And if it ever had done so it might have been burnt yesterday. But it might be in these bins because Fred had, on the instructions of Miss Ellis, removed all the unburnt papers to the bins.

'You've looked at the same one three times in two minutes,' exclaimed Anna. 'Why can't you have some method? What sort of letter is it?'

He was vague. He did not know what it would look like and he asked her to examine a brown envelope close to her foot.

'Not me,' said Anna. 'It's all over tea leaves. Get it for yourself.'

Growling, he reached for it.

'But what would it be about?' she insisted.

He told her. Crawling about and feverishly burrowing under cabbage stalks, he told her about the mine, the cracks, Sir Humphrey Bevin's visit and the Canon's hint.

'I'm quite in the dark,' he complained. 'I'm not quite sure he didn't invent it. But if it's true . . .'

Anna was impressed and suggested that he should write to Sir Humphrey. But he was not content merely to do that. The day, he said several times, was Friday. He could not, at the earliest, get an answer before Tuesday. And in the meantime the blow might fall. He seemed to be quite panic-stricken.

'It hasn't fallen yet,' said Anna. 'One might hope it would stand up till Tuesday. And you're not sure the Canon didn't invent it.'

'But in the meantime where can we go?'

'What does Barbara say?'

'She doesn't know. I haven't told her yet. I thought I'd try to find the letter first.'

'You'll have fun telling Barbara. It would give you less trouble if you opened your letters, wouldn't it?'

'Don't rub it in, Anna. I'm so frightened. I didn't sleep a wink last night. I shan't sleep till Tuesday. Don't you feel it's disquieting?'

'I do, rather. I think perhaps I'll go tomorrow after all.'

'What would you do in my shoes?'

'Say nothing to anyone till I'd heard from Sir Humphrey.'

Siddal sat back on his haunches. He was sweating from his unaccustomed labours.

'Well,' he said, 'perhaps . . . but I don't know how I'm going to stick it till Tuesday. I've searched thoroughly, and the thing is not here. I get a spasm whenever I look at those cliffs.'

'You haven't searched thoroughly,' said Anna. 'There are lots you haven't looked at.'

'I shall die of sunstroke if I stay here,' he said, pulling himself on to his feet by holding the edge of a bin.

And he set off for the house, the cord of his dressing gown dragging over the stones behind him.

'But what about all this muck?' she asked, pointing to the garbage heap.

'Somebody will have to put it all back in the bins. I've done my bit.'

He paused, lifted his voice, and yelled for Duff, whose head presently appeared at the loft window.

'Tidy up this yard,' commanded Mr. Siddal, making off again.

The strains of Stravinsky ceased and Duff came down.

'The filthy old brute,' he said, when he saw the condition of the yard. 'What on earth was he doing?'

'Looking for something he'd lost,' said Anna.

'I'm not cleaning up. I've got to go into Porthmerryn and buy a bald head at the carnival shop. For the Feast.'

'Can you drive a car?' asked Anna.

He could, he declared, drive any car.

'Then would you like to drive me, in mine, to Porthmerryn? I hate driving, and I want to hire a typewriter.'

Duff tried to conceal his glee at getting a car to drive. He seldom did. He was so much pleased that he shed all lupine pretensions until he had got Anna's Hillman up the drive and on to the high road, without grinding the gears. Then, relaxing a little, he responded to her sidelong smile.

'So you're going to the Feast,' she said. 'How funny!'

No place for a wolf, as he immediately realized. He said languidly that it would be a crashing bore but that one couldn't very well get out of it. And, anyway, was Anna not going? He had heard so.

'I found an invitation on my plate at breakfast,' she said. 'Very pretty. So I accepted. The Canon, by the way, tore his up. But after the children had gone out of the dining room.

And old Paley left his on his table with all his empty envelopes. I do think they are a couple of nasty old men. They could have accepted and then cut it.'

'Is that what you'll do?' asked Duff.

'How much fun will it be?'

'No fun at all. Kids' games and lemonade. Madly boring.'

'But sitting all alone in the hotel wouldn't be very gay either.'

'You wouldn't be all alone. You'd have the nasty old men. And Lady G., who is much too ill to come.'

'Oh, well . . . if you can't think of anything better for us to do, I suppose we'd better go. Look out! You nearly had us in the ditch.'

Duff drove a few yards in silence and then pulled up on the grass by the side of the road. He could not impersonate a wolf and drive at the same time. He turned off the engine. The cliff country of small fields and stone walls became very silent. They could hear larks singing. Anna did not ask why he stopped. Perhaps she thought it safer.

'I could,' said Duff, 'think of something better to do.'

'So could I,' said Anna.

'I don't like you,' he told her, abandoning his wolf technique. 'It's only fair to say so first.'

'Oh, but I know that.'

'You don't mind?'

'Not a bit. I get more kick out of it really.'

'More kick if the man dislikes you?'

'Yes. Don't look surprised. So do you.'

Duff laughed excitedly.

'Perhaps I do. I don't mind you knowing what a brute I am.'

'Exactly,' said Anna. 'So I shall cut this picnic. I shall stay in my room.'

'I can't cut all of it. There'd be a row and a hunt for me if I don't show up at the start. We've got this musical procession. But I could slip away after a bit . . . perhaps . . .'

'You'd better make up your mind, for I'm off tomorrow.'

Duff made up his mind.

3. Sometimes Silent, Sometimes Yelling

'Long ago, in youth, he squandered,' whispered Sir Henry to himself. 'Long ago, in youth, he squandered all his goods away, and wandered . . .'

He was obliged to refer to the piece of paper in his hand. Caroline had given it to him with instructions to learn the verses, there set out, by heart before nightfall. For, in a grand *finale* to the Feast, all Edward Lear characters were to recite their own poems. She had warned him that his was rather a sad piece, but he did not think so. The aged Uncle Arly did not seem to have made such a bad thing of his life.

> Like the ancient Medes and Persians,
> Always by his own exertions
>   He subsisted on those hills;
> Whiles, by teaching children spelling,
> Or at times by merely yelling—
> Or at intervals by selling
>   Propter's Nicodemus Pills.

He could have wished that his own life had been half as sensibly spent. But it had all gone to pieces twelve years ago, in a summer like this, at a little seaside village very like Pendizack.

They had had a young nurse who came to them when Caroline was born—a fair, fresh-faced girl whose name he could not remember. She had not stayed with them for long. But she had popped up in his memory at some time during the last day or two. For they had taken her and the baby with them for a summer holiday to a little seaside hotel. The weather had been hot and fine. Eirene was still slowly recovering from her confinement. All day they lay sunbathing on the rocks, occasionally going down to the warm sea for a languid swim. It had been delightful. For he was still deeply in love with Eirene, after eighteen months of marriage with her, in spite of certain trials to his temper. Her sufferings during pregnancy and childbirth had been enough to justify, in his eyes, an egotism and a childish self-indulgence which would surely disappear, now that she was getting well again. He knew very little about women. He had no sisters, and had met few girls during his hard-working youth. He believed that Eirene was a rare and fragile creature, like some hothouse flower, and the brutalities of nature appalled him almost as much as they did her. After nine months of unrelieved misery she had very nearly died. The doctors had not admitted it, but Eirene's mother had assured him that it was so. In his relief at her safety he was shocked that he could ever have felt impatient with her.

Day after day they lay on the rocks. And day after day the young nurse, in a starched uniform, sat by the perambulator on the beach. He could not remember how he first came to wonder why Nanny never went swimming. Perhaps he had seen other nurses, from the same hotel, running down to the sea for a dip. But he did begin to think it strange that a lively girl should be content to sit beside the sea all day without ever going into it, and at last he asked Eirene why it was. Eirene replied, a shade too hastily, that Nanny did not care for bathing.

He might have believed that to the end of his days if he had not subsequently overheard a fragment of conversation on the next balcony to theirs at the hotel. Mrs. Gifford, he learnt, was as hard as nails with that nice little Nanny of hers; she never gave the girl any time off to go swimming with the other maids. She could not even sit beside her own perambulator for half an hour and it was especially hard, because Nanny Gifford was a champion swimmer and had won a silver medal. Mrs. Gifford knew that perfectly well.

Plucking up his courage, he tackled Eirene. He reproached her for lying to him, and he reproached her for inhumanity to Nanny. It was their first real quarrel. And, in a way, it was their last quarrel, for it was the only occasion upon which he had insisted upon having his own way. During the rest of the holiday he had sat beside Caroline for an hour every day while Nanny went swimming. It was in August. Some time before Christmas he supposed that Eirene must have forgiven him, for he could remember a very pleasant Christmas Eve, when, in amity, they had filled Caroline's first stocking. But there had been weeks and months when he had been obliged to live, eat and sleep with a drooping flower. She did not reproach him. She said very little. She simply failed to pick up her strength again, and her mother said all that was necessary.

After that he had been in no hurry to assert himself again. Nor had he ever asserted himself again so effectually, though sometimes he had lost his temper and shouted at her. She did as she pleased. He found it easier to let her do as she pleased when he ceased to love her, which he very soon did. He wrote off his private and domestic life as a failure and devoted all his faculties to his profession. He accepted the fact that his wife was a liar.

He remembered all this, as he strayed round the gardens of Pendizack, conning his poem. And he wondered if he could have taught Eirene to love him by standing up to her. He had grown cold and hard, instead of helping her to cure her faults. And now, when she was manifestly very ill, he purposed to leave her. She would never understand why . . .

> *Sometimes silent; sometimes yelling;*
> *Till he came to Borley Melling,*
> *Near his old ancestral dwelling;*
>   *(But his shoes were far too tight.)*

Sometimes silent, sometimes yelling, he thought, was a very good description of his life with Eirene.

At teatime he took up her tray and found her in a mournful mood, sighing and lamenting because her wretched health had ruined his life. She often said this. He put the tray down on her knees and sat on the bed beside her.

'Your health would be nothing, only a minor misfortune,' he said, 'if we cared for each other.'

'You would love me if I wasn't ill. No woman can hope to keep a man if she's ill.'

'But you don't love me.'

'Harry! You know perfectly well that I'm devoted to you.'

'You don't show it. If you could give me one example of your devotion to me, I'd . . . well . . . I'd feel very differently about all this.'

Eirene poured herself out a cup of tea. He had an impression that she hesitated, not because she did not know what to say, but for some other reason.

'Well . . .' she said at last, 'I could have divorced you, if I'd wanted. And I didn't.'

'What?'

She had taken him completely by surprise.

'Don't bounce about like that. You'll upset the tray. If I wasn't devoted to you I'd have divorced you when I got back from America. I had all the evidence. But I didn't. I didn't even reproach you, though it nearly broke my heart . . .'

'Do you mean Billie Blacker . . . ?'

'I know men have these animal instincts, and you were all alone. I forgave it. Many women wouldn't have.'

'How did you know?'

'Plenty of people knew. Some of my friends knew. Do you suppose they didn't tell me? Why . . . you practically lived with her, for some months, in a flat in Bayswater.'

'Yes. Yes . . . I suppose people did know. It was all so . . . it was in the Blitz . . . life seemed upside down. One had no friends; one had one's own life . . . and the war.'

'Everybody thought I should divorce you. But I said no. I'm devoted to him. I understand him. I always think jealousy is vile. If I wait patiently, he'll come back to me.'

'But Eirene . . . the trouble with us started long before then. It started ages ago, just after Caroline was born. When we had that nurse, you remember? And you wouldn't let her bathe and I . . .'

'My goodness, Harry! Not then! Not that nurse! I never . . .'

'Oh no, no, no! I don't mean I had an affair with that nurse. But we quarrelled about her. Our first quarrel.'

'I don't remember. How you do treasure things up! I don't. I try to forget our little quarrels. You gave me quite a shock about that nurse. For I was sure that warden woman was the first. I told everyone. I said, I know this is the first time he has ever looked at another woman. And that's rather wonderful, if you think of my wretched health . . .'

'To whom did you say all this?'

'To Lulu Wilmott, in Massachusetts. To all my friends there. They thought it was wonderful of me to go back to you and never say a word. They wanted me to divorce you, and stay there. I would have, if I hadn't been utterly devoted to you. I like America. I'd like to live there always.'

'I'm sure you would, unless things got uncomfortable there, when you'd move on.'

He checked himself, ashamed of his own bitterness. But Eirene felt no sting in the taunt. She sipped her tea and said calmly:

'I don't think things ever would get very uncomfortable there, even if there was another war. It's so large. They'd always have plenty.'

The old ire, the need to yell at her, nearly choked him.

'I really don't think I ought to let you bring up the children,' he exclaimed. 'You aren't fit to.'

That did startle her a little. She said sharply:

'Don't talk nonsense! I'm quite able to bring up the children. I've never let my bad health prevent that. I take more care of them than many mothers do who have never had a day's illness in their lives. Look at those wretched little Coves . . . how neglected they are!'

'You aren't fit. I won't have them brought up without any loyalties. I won't have them turned into scum . . . it's a scum that every nation throws up . . . that simply drifts from place to place in search of a full trough. They must be citizens of some country. There must be some community to which they'll stick through good and evil. They're not rats. I won't have them turned into rats.'

Against his will he had raised his voice. It was the old yelling. Eirene lowered hers and spoke very gently.

'I wish,' she said, 'that they would remember not to send me raspberry jam. They know I can't eat it. You might have looked, Harry, before you brought the tray up. And you can't prevent me from bringing the children up, can you?'

'I can take them away.'

'No, really. You can't take children away from their mother unless she has done something wrong. I could have taken them away from you, if I had divorced you. But you can't take them from me. And if you really mean to go away and leave me I won't divorce you. I shall hope you'll be sorry and come back to me one day. I shall always be waiting for you. But you won't see the children till you do.'

There was a tap at the door. Hebe looked in. He waved her away, with:

'Not just now, Hebe. Run along . . .'

'No . . . wait . . .' cried Eirene, holding out her jam dish. 'Just take this down, darling, and ask for jelly instead.'

Hebe approached the bed and presented to Sir Henry a small object like a grasshopper, made of wool and wire, and a pill box with a label saying: *PROPTER'S NICODEMUS PILLS.*

'I made them this afternoon,' she said. 'And Caro is making your railway ticket. Have you learnt your part?'

'What part?' asked Eirene.

'For the Feast,' explained Hebe. 'The Coves' Feast. Didn't you get your invitation card on your breakfast tray?'

'That card? Oh, yes. I wondered what on earth it meant. How could anyone suppose I'd be well enough for that sort of thing?'

'Everybody is invited,' explained Hebe. 'I expect they thought it would be rude not to send you a card, when we are all going.'

'What do you mean? You are all going? When did I give you leave to go?'

Hebe looked dismayed and glanced at Sir Henry for support.

'We never thought you'd mind our going,' she explained.

'I certainly mind. I thought I'd told you not to play with those little Coves. They're not a family I care to have any dealings with. Their mother was intolerably rude to me on Tuesday.'

'Mrs. Cove has nothing to do with it, Mother. She isn't even coming to the picnic. She has to stay at home and pack because she's going to London tomorrow . . .'

'Those children got you into one scrape, when they accused you of drowning them. That is quite enough. I hate to say no to any of your little pleasures, darling, but I really do say it this time. I don't like the idea of this Feast.'

'But, *Mother* . . .'

Sir Henry interposed:

'It's my fault, Eirene. I gave them leave. I had no idea you'd object. And now it has all gone so far, I think you must let them go. It would be an awful catastrophe if we failed the Coves now.'

Eirene gave him a cool stare. He realized that she meant to pay him out for having threatened to take the children away. But she spoke playfully:

'Darling! I know you think I spoil them and that you are the only person who is really fit to bring them up. But you're quite wrong. It's you who can deny them nothing. I'm a great deal stricter really.'

'But, Mother, we must go! We must go!' cried Hebe, who was becoming really anxious.

'No must about it, my precious. I absolutely forbid it.'

'But why? Why?'

'I've told you. I don't care for the Coves.'

'You're wrong about them, Eirene. They're very nice little girls, and we are all rather sorry for them.'

'It's not only the Coves. It's too late an hour for the twins. And none of our chicks have very good digestions.

They'll only make themselves sick, gobbling a lot of trash in the middle of the night . . .'

'It isn't trash. It's lovely things: lobster salad and chicken and ices . . . we all subscribed to it . . .'

'Most indigestible. The little Coves may need to be fed in the middle of the night by public subscription. But my children . . .'

'I suppose,' screamed Hebe, furiously, 'you'd rather we ate tapeworms.'

The altercation came to an abrupt end in a simultaneous gasp from Hebe and Lady Gifford. Sir Henry, turning to reprove Hebe for such an unpleasant idea, was appalled by the expression on her face —the blanched terror and ex-ultation of a child who has gone too far and knows it. He looked at his wife.

Eirene did not ask what Hebe meant. She was the more terrified of the two. She had the jam dish in her hand and was holding it up as if to ward Hebe off. She licked her lips, tried to say something, and put the dish down. Leaning back against her pillows she closed her eyes.

'You'd better go,' he said sternly to Hebe.

But Hebe, though shaking, stood her ground.

'Are we going to the Feast?' she asked, giving him a hard stare.

'Yes,' he said, anxious to end the scene. 'Yes. They can go, can't they, Eirene?'

Eirene opened her eyes for a moment to give Hebe a look of pure hatred. She said faintly:

'Go if you like. But get out.'

Hebe got out with a rush.

'I don't think I want any more tea,' whispered Eirene. 'These scenes are so bad for me. I mustn't get upset. Will you take the tray down, darling, and I'll just relax completely.'

He hardly heard her. He stood at the bottom of the bed, beating a tattoo on the bedrail in time with the words which echoed through his shocked mind:

> On a little heap of barley
> Died my aged Uncle Arly,
>   And they buried him one night . . .

'Will you take the tray away, Harry?'

He pulled himself together.

'What . . . what did she mean?' he asked.

'Hebe? How should I know? Some vulgarity she has picked up. That's what comes of playing with horrid children. Do take the tray.'

He took the tray. At the top of the stairs he nearly fell over Hebe who was crouched there, waiting for him. She said at once:

'You'd better send me back to the orphanage. I'm not your child and I've turned out badly. I'd better go away.'

'We're responsible for you,' he said drearily.

'You can't want me after what I said.'

'It wasn't a nice thing to say. How . . . ?'

But he stopped, feeling that he could not question her.

'I heard Edmée, that was Mrs. Wilmott's maid, talking to another maid . . .'

'Oh . . . in Massachusetts?'

'Yes. Edmée said that was how . . . how people kept thin. She said Mrs. Wilmott was mad at Mother about it and said she was crazy . . . she put on an awful lot, you know, in America. She was getting very fat. And then suddenly she got terribly thin. Edmée said . . .'

'It was vulgar gossip,' he told her. 'Nothing in it. There couldn't be.'

Hebe nodded.

'Did you . . . say anything to the others?'

'Oh, no . . . I never told anyone. Only today . . . I was so furious . . .'

'Forget about it.'

'She won't. You'll have to send me away.'

He knew this was true.

'Perhaps,' he mused, 'you'll do better at school.'

'Perhaps I shall,' agreed Hebe, cheering up slightly. 'Like Jane Eyre.'

He took the tray downstairs and went out on to the sands. So far as he could see this grotesque discovery made very little difference to his position. It merely made him feel more of a fool. It robbed his troubles of any claim to dignity.

4. The Quangle Wangle's Hat

This earthly ball rolled on towards the Feast. That was how a good many people at Pendizack felt. For the seven children it rolled far too slowly and the day seemed endless. But their elders, harassed with many occupations, had no such grudge against time. Evangeline, who was still doing all the cooking, regretted that she had undertaken the manufacture of so many costumes. She did not finish Mrs. Paley's hat until the very last minute and when she ran upstairs with it the children, already dressed, were gathering in the hall for the opening procession.

She found Mrs. Paley struggling into the old green mackintosh which Duff had lent her. It was very tight and the sleeves were rather short. But there was no doubt that it had a skinny look.

'Here it is,' said Evangeline, putting the hat on the bed. 'But how you will keep it on, I can't think.'

'It's a masterpiece!' said Mrs. Paley.

The hat was four feet in diameter. It was made in stiff cardboard. Ribbons and little bells hung from its brim. On the top of it there were two canaries, a stork, a duck, an owl, a snail, a bee, a Fimble Fowl (made with a corkscrew), a Golden Grouse, a Pobble, a small Olympian bear, a Dong, an Orient Calf, an Attery Squash, and a Bisky Bat, all dancing to the flute of a Blue Baboon. Mrs. Paley put it on and immediately it tipped sideways, in a most disreputable way.

'I was afraid it would,' said Evangeline. 'But I've brought some ribbons. If I sew them on, you could tie them firmly under your chin . . .'

She sat on the bed sewing, while Mrs. Paley put on black gloves with pencils in the fingers to make them look like claws.

'I've had the shock of my life,' said Mrs. Paley. 'Mrs Cove has asked me to keep an eye on the children while she is away. She was almost agreeable. Said I'd been so kind to them. Thanked me for the Feast. And *smiled*!'

'I can't believe that,' said Evangeline. 'She couldn't smile.'

'She bared her teeth at me in a sort of grin. Really she did. I wish I knew what she's up to!'

'Oh, but isn't it obvious? She's booked the rooms. She doesn't want to pay and not use them. And why shouldn't she leave the children?'

'One would think so. But Hebe's motto hits the nail on the head. I'm frightened of that woman. As soon as I knew she wanted them to stay, I began to wonder if it was all right for them to stay.'

'Do you think she wants to be rid of them . . . for good, I mean?' asked Evangeline, biting off a thread.

'Yes. Don't you? Haven't you got that feeling, somehow?'

'Yes. But I've nothing to go on— only her manner.'

'I daresay she doesn't quite recognize it herself. But she . . . lets them run risks . . . I don't know. They seem to have had such a lot of narrow escapes. I shall never forget her face when she watched them going down to Dead Man's

Rock. I saw it through the glasses. She did go after them, to stop them; but very reluctantly. She doesn't love them a bit, and I think they are in her way. When she gave me that ghastly smile, I immediately thought: Oh, is it dangerous for them to be here?'

'It couldn't be,' said Evangeline.

'No. It couldn't, could it? Perhaps I'm fanciful. And I don't suppose for a minute that she would consciously . . . it's just that I feel she subconsciously ill-wishes them for some reason. Wants them out of her way. Wouldn't be in any hurry to stop them taking themselves out of her way . . . I wish they were mine, Angie! I wish I could have them for keeps.'

'There,' said Angie, finishing the second string. 'I must run and put on my funny bonnet. Tie it on very tight . . .'

She rushed upstairs to dress up as Mrs. Discobolos. Mrs. Paley had to take the claw gloves off again to tie on the hat. Even with the ribbons it tipped a little, but she was able to secure it by hairpins twisted in the lining and skewered to her head.

While she was doing this she heard her husband come in, but she could not see him, for the huge hat, with its fringe of ribbons, restricted her line of sight. He remained very still and she knew that he was looking at her. Presently he said:

'You can't really mean to make such an exhibition of yourself? What good will it do to anyone? I know you are sorry for these children. But what good will it do them?'

'It'll make them laugh,' mumbled Mrs. Paley, her mouth full of hairpins.

After a minute she added:

'I'm very sorry you won't come. You wouldn't like it, I know. But you wouldn't be more miserable there than you are here, and they would be pleased. So it would cost you nothing, and give them pleasure.'

He did not answer immediately and she felt that he was hesitating. She ducked her head sideways so as to squint at him from under the hat.

'Come,' she said. 'It might take your mind off . . .'

'Off what?' he asked sharply.

'Off . . . whatever it is that's killing you. You won't tell me, so I don't know what it is . . .'

'It's a dream . . .' said Mr. Paley, in a low voice.

A great tumult broke out on the terrace below. The first feasters were issuing to the strains of Fred's accordion.

'I can't hear,' said Mrs. Paley.

'Nor can I tell you,' shouted Mr. Paley, 'while you have that ridiculous thing on your head. Take it off!'

'I can't. It takes hours to fix, and I ought to be going.'

Down below they had begun to sing:

> *The animals went in two by two!*
> *Hurrah! Hurrah!*

'What are you?' he shouted. 'What do you think you are?'

'A Quangle Wangle,' quavered Mrs. Paley.

'A what? I can't hear.'

'I'm a Quangle Wangle.'

'And what may a Quangle Wangle be?'

'I don't know. Nobody knows.'

Mrs. Paley blew her nose under the hat. She was over-come with grief and did not wish to go to the Feast.

'Well?' he shouted. 'What are you waiting for?'

'I don't know. Goodbye, Paul.'

She ducked sideways again to look at him. He had turned away and was sitting in his armchair by the window, his head in his hands. He would not answer.

She got herself and her hat, with some difficulty, through the door.

5. The Last to Leave

A profound hush enveloped Pendizack Manor Hotel. The procession had formed on the terrace and had wound its way, singing, up the drive to the cliff path, since the tide was over the sands. The shouts and music died away and the silence rolled up like a mist.

Mrs. Siddal, lying inert upon her bed, felt it first of all as a relief. The noise made by the children, dressing on the attic floor and shouting from one room to another, had been intolerable. She was glad when they all rushed downstairs.

She was fully dressed, for she was not ill, only tired, and she might be entreated at any time to take up the reins of government again. Some catastrophe would certainly occur which would bring them to their knees. But she would not go down until she was invited. She would not go down while Evangeline Wraxton was in the house.

Her meals were brought to her on trays by Robin, Duff or Nancibel, and they all assured her that she was not needed, that everything went perfectly well without her. She did not believe them. She did not want to believe them. And the excellence of the food they brought her only hardened her heart. Gerry and that girl were very sly; they never came up, they never gave her a chance to shake their confidence. They were happy, down there, lording it over her kitchen, planning their future, and never once thinking of her ruined hopes.

The light faded and the house grew quiet. Her room was always a little dark, for it had no sea view. It was the least pleasant room in the house, which was why she had moved up there; no guest would have taken it. In former days it had been merely a lumber room. The little window looked out on the creek and the menacing bulk of the Other Cliffs, which leant over so close to the house that she got no glimpse of the sky unless she put her head out. She could hear the high tide gurgling into the creek, but she did not hear the noisy departure of the feasters from the terrace on the far side of the house. She merely knew that there was silence, that she was lonely, and that night was falling.

This was the second evening she would spend all alone up here, shut in with her troubles, while the light sank away and shadows on the cliff wall merged into a conquering obscurity. Dusk, in this room, had no soft and lingering tints; it was merely the failure, the death of day. And the silence of this room had no peace, no repose. It was sterile and empty.

She cried a little, and then dozed, until a short, shrill scream jerked her into wakefulness. It was only a gull, swooping past the window, but it left her with a thumping heart and a presage of fear. An overpowering need came upon her to get up, to get out of this room, to see human faces and to hear voices. For a few seconds she fought with it, but the dread, advancing upon her, was too strong. Her pride fell before it. She jumped up and hurried into the passage, where she encountered the same deathly silence. Out there it seemed stronger. She flinched from it aghast, as some wretch, waking to a smell of fire, might peer from his room and meet a wall of stifling smoke. Then footsteps creaked. A door opened. Her panic subsided. For the first time in her life she felt glad to see Miss Ellis. That frog face, peering at her through the crack of a door, was company of sorts.

'Oh!' said Miss Ellis. 'I thought everyone was gone.'

'So did I,' said Mrs. Siddal. 'It's so quiet. Where is everybody?'

'Gone to the Feast.'

And of course that explained everything. She had forgotten the Feast, though Robin had brought up her invitation card that morning, and she had sent her love to the little Coves and her regrets that she was not well enough to come.

'Been a lot of trouble downstairs,' Miss Ellis told her. 'You'll be upset when you get down and see. Well . . . Fred has broken two vegetable dishes. And the way Miss Wraxton is using up the sugar . . . Are you feeling better?'

'Yes, thank you. Has everybody gone? Aren't you going, Miss Ellis?'

'Me? To this picnic affair? No, I'm *not*.'

'But weren't you invited? I thought . . .'

'Oh, yes. I was asked. Along with Nancibel and Fred! Very kind of them, I'm sure. Did you hear the row they made going off?'

'No. I don't hear anything my side of the house.'

'Sir Henry was livid. Well . . . that young Hebe, she'll end up in Borstal if she doesn't look out. There's something about that child . . . something really nasty. What d'you suppose her fancy dress was?'

'I can't think.'

'Nothing.'

'What?'

'Nothing but a pair of paper wings and a bow and arrows. Said she was Cupid. In front of all those boys. So they all had to wait while she was sent upstairs to put something on. So she had the nerve to stick on a nightgown with those wings and say she'd turned into an angel . . .'

'Mrs. Siddal!'

Miss Ellis and Mrs. Siddal turned. Mrs. Cove had come out of her attic.

'I'm glad you're about again,' she said. 'Can you see that my ration book is put on my table tomorrow morning at breakfast? I shall want it. I have to go to London tomorrow, and I like to get my ration book back in plenty of time before I leave. So often in hotels they make mistakes and take out too many points, and don't give you time to find it out.'

'Going to London?' exclaimed Mrs. Siddal. 'Are you all going? I didn't realize . . .'

'No,' said Miss Ellis. 'She's leaving the children. Aren't you, Mrs. Cove?'

Mrs. Cove looked at Miss Ellis. The stifling waves of silence seemed to roll along the passage again as the two women stood gazing at one another. Something passed between them, but they neither moved nor spoke. Mrs. Siddal left them standing there and made her way downstairs to the kitchen, as far away from them as possible.

But it was no better down there. The deadness, the oppression, seemed to have crept into every corner of the house. She could not even manage to be indignant over the fragments of broken vegetable dishes, or triumphant at the prevailing evidence of disorder. Never had such chaos been seen before in her kitchen and her scullery, for the feasters had gone off without clearing up or washing the dishes. But she looked at it all with an indifferent eye, unable to feel that anything mattered very much any more. Lady Gifford's bell, demanding Horlicks Malted Milk, could scarcely shatter the heavy quiet. Its peal left no echoes.

A good thing I'm here, thought Mrs. Siddal languidly. They forgot.

She put on a kettle and went to the dresser for the tin. Here she found something else which had been forgotten—a basket containing four bottles of hock, evidently packed for the Feast and left behind.

A foolish extravagance, she thought, with the same dull detachment. And then a sharp feeling came to her: the first she had known since she left her room. *They forgot*. She was very sorry that they should have forgotten this basket. She felt it as a calamity. While the kettle was boiling she went out on to the terrace to see if any of them were still on the sands. She might wave to them to come back and fetch it.

Nobody was on the sands. The tide was up, and they must have gone by the drive to the cliff path. But she lingered a moment, for the air out there was sweet, after the stuffy oppression of the house, and a fine sunset blazed over Pendizack Point. The fresh air and the sharp colours caught at her heart. She thought that she ought to get out more often.

Somebody came round the corner of the house. It was Dick Siddal, and he was shuffling along quite fast as though in a hurry. But he stopped when he saw her.

'Why, Barbara,' he said, 'are you better?'

'Yes.'

His appearance surprised her, for he was neatly dressed, almost spruce. But he looked very ill and he was breathing heavily.

'Where are you going?' she asked. 'Where were you off to in such a hurry?'

'Oh, strolling . . . strolling . . .'

He looked round him uneasily and added:

'Thought I'd take a turn on the sands, but the tide is up.'

She remembered the boiling kettle and turned back into the house.

'So I started up the drive,' he panted, as he shuffled after her. 'But my ticker isn't too good, Barbara. I was done before I'd got to the first turn.'

'Well, it must be years since you've climbed that hill. Look, Dick. Such a sad thing has happened. The picnickers have left their wine behind.'

She showed him the basket, and he chuckled.

'Poor Gerry!'

'Why poor Gerry?'

'He's the one who'll catch it. He and his Angie. Gifford contributed the wine; Gerry and Angie were to bring it, but they stayed spooning in the passage outside my boot-hole, and forgot all about it. I heard 'em. Cursing the picnic and wishing they didn't have to go.'

'Why? I thought they were so set on it.'

'I expect they'd prefer one another's company undiluted. When it came to the point it turned out to be rather a fag. But they trotted off at last, like good little scouts, and forgot the wine.'

'I wish we could send somebody after them . . . but there's nobody left but Mrs. Cove and Miss Ellis and Lady Gifford. They're no use.'

'Paley and Wraxton are still here,' he said. 'You might try them. Wraxton is writing letters in the lounge. He's writing about his will. He told me so. He means to disinherit his daughter. She'll lose a pretty penny, if he speaks the truth. Perhaps you'd better not ask him. But Paley is looking out of his bedroom window.'

'I might as well ask Hebe's cat to help me.'

Lady Gifford's bell rang again and Mrs. Siddal took up the Horlicks. It was an effort to climb the stairs. The knowledge that the house was really not empty at all, that there were people on every floor, did not raise her spirits.

'Oh . . . it's you,' said Lady Gifford. 'How nice! I was just wanting a little company. Do sit down. I don't see half enough of you. I'd so looked forward . . . Oh, my nice Horlicks! How kind of you.'

'I'm afraid I have rather a lot to . . .' murmured Mrs. Siddal.

But Lady Gifford put out a claw and detained her.

413

'You do too much, you know. I think you're wonderful. But you mustn't turn yourself into a Martha. That's a thing I so often feel, lying here. I want to be up and doing. I get so impatient. And then I think . . . well . . . isn't it *meant*, in some way? If I could get up I might do a great deal, but miss the one thing needful. Lying here I'm just forced to be a Mary, whether I like it or not . . .'

The claw still clutched. But she will have to let go, thought Mrs. Siddal, when she drinks her Horlicks. And Lady Gifford seemed to think the same, for she glanced fleetingly at the cup in her other hand. But her need to talk was greater.

'I always feel that material things aren't really important. Love is all that matters, isn't it? The people one loves . . . and what's best for them. Of course, I've been very lucky. I've been surrounded by love all my life. I was an only child and my parents adored me. And then I married . . . a perfect marriage. Harry is a wonderful husband. So I suppose I just took it for granted that if I gave love I should receive it. I never doubted it. People said, when I wanted to adopt a baby: Isn't it a great risk? I said I like risks. They're *fun*. I loved the little thing. It never occurred to me, for a moment, that my love wouldn't create a return. Everybody had always loved me. But Hebe does not, and it has given me a great shock.'

'Oh, children go through phases . . . Isn't your Horlicks getting cold?'

The suggestion gave obvious pain to Lady Gifford, but still she clutched.

'It's not a phase. There is something abnormal about her. Something which frightens me. And lying here I'm having to face it. It's not only her attitude to me. It's her influence on the other children. That business on Tuesday . . . She is not developing normally. I believe a complete change of surroundings . . . if she went right away . . . right away from all of us . . . began life, as it were, all over again among new people . . . of course, it would be a great grief to us. To me especially, for she's as much my child as if I'd borne her. But, if I felt about Caroline as I do about Hebe, I should do exactly the same thing. I should say: love is the only thing that matters. If I love her enough I'll do anything that is best for her, even to giving her up . . .'

At this point the Horlicks won. Lady Gifford released her prisoner and lifted the cup to her lips.

'Oh, don't go,' she cried, after one sip. 'I do so want to consult you. You're a mother . . . and I feel so lonely tonight . . .'

'Tomorrow . . . another time . . .' promised Mrs. Siddal, escaping. 'I really must . . .'

The forgotten wine was still uppermost in her thoughts. She hurried back to the kitchen to eye the basket and bewail the mishap. Dick was not there, and not in his boot-hole. He must have gone out upon another of his harassed little strolls.

Taking the basket from the dresser she found it unexpectedly heavy, and faltered in a half-formed plan to take it up to Pendizack Point herself. To climb the hill and scramble along the cliffs with such a load would be no light undertaking; she was too tired and too old. They would send back for it. They had not gone so very far away. When the omission was discovered, they would send somebody. They would only have to wait for about twenty minutes. Gerry would be sent. Of that she was certain. It had been his fault in the first place, and in any case it was always Gerry who ran errands for the rest. At any time now she might hear clattering feet in the kitchen passage and see Gerry's worried face coming round the door. *Here's your wine*, she would say to him. He would only be gone for twenty minutes. He would only miss twenty minutes of the Feast. And he had not much wanted to go to it, according to Dick. So that she could not understand her extreme reluctance to let him come back.

Listlessly she began to stack dishes in the sink and to make efforts to tidy the kitchen. But this conviction, that nothing signified, so grew upon her that she could almost have thrown the whole dishes out after the broken ones. Only the basket on the dresser nagged at her with the positive insistence of an urgent task. It stood out, among all these lifeless things, as though it had been illuminated or making some loud noise. It implored her, it commanded her, to go out and climb the hill.

At last she lifted it up again, feeling its weight. A compromise had occurred to her. She need not go all the way. She could take it a little way, up the drive to the beginning of the cliff path, and meet poor Gerry as he rushed back on his tiresome errand. Thus he would be saved some time and trouble. He need not come right back to the house, and the feasters would not have to wait so long for their supper.

But she did not want to meet Gerry just now. Some kind of reconciliation, some tenderness, was bound to arise when he should find that she had taken so much trouble, and she was still angry with him.

'Bother you!' she said to the basket of wine.

She hauled it out of the front door, thinking that she would not go very far. Having climbed as high as she felt able, she could sit down and rest in the cool air until Gerry came. Anything was better than the house. And she stepped out into the drive, just as something shot past her, out of the door, across the drive and uphill into the shadow of the trees. It startled her so much that she gave a little cry. Dick's voice answered her. He came shuffling round the house.

'What is it?' he asked anxiously.

'Hebe's cat. It nearly knocked me over. Something must have frightened it.'

'It's all these mice,' said Mr. Siddal.

'What mice?'

'Haven't you seen any? I never saw so many before. Lots and lots of mice. On the terrace. Where are you going?'

She explained her errand and he astonished her by saying that he would come with her. It was years since she had seen him so active.

'But Dick! You can't get as high as the cliff path.'

'Oh, I might. I might. If you give me your arm.'

He seized her arm and leant upon it heavily. This, with the wine basket, was more than she could manage. She protested. But he clung to her, panting, and together they crept up to the first turn of the drive where they both had to sit down and rest. He kept pausing to listen, and glancing up at the cliffs, in a restless way.

'It's my ticker,' he said. 'It must be in a shocking state. I need a change. Tomorrow I shall hire a car and drive up the hill. I shall go and stay at the One and All. This place gives me claustrophobia. I'll stay up there till Tuesday . . . or Wednesday . . .'

'Oh, plague . . .' said Mrs. Siddal.

From where they sat the house below them was just visible, through the trees. She could now see a faint splash of light from the windows of the garden room.

'There's Anna gone out and left her light on! What a waste! Do turn it out, Dick, when you go back.'

'She hasn't gone out. She's there. I saw her in there when I was strolling around.'

'I thought she'd gone with the others.'

'No. She must have changed her mind.'

So that is another one down there, she thought. All alone. All shut up alone in their rooms, yet none of them at peace.

Having recovered her breath she got up, saying that she really must go a little higher for she would save Gerry nothing if she stayed down here.

'I should think he'd be along any minute now,' she added.

'It's not Gerry that I'm expecting to see any minute,' said Mr. Siddal. 'It's Duff.'

'Duff? Oh, no! Duff never runs errands.'

'What will you bet? Will you bet me the price of my car

up to St. Sody's tomorrow that you don't meet Duff coming back along the cliffs?'

'Oh, yes. But I won't bet the price of a room for you at the One and All. I think that is a silly idea.'

She turned to go, but he exclaimed:

'Wait a minute, Barbara! If I rest here a bit longer I might be able to do another turn. I'm not high enough.'

'High enough? For what?'

'High enough out of this. I keep feeling . . . I keep feeling . . . as if it was all going to come down on me! Pure nerves!'

He laughed uncertainly.

'Honestly, Dick, I can't wait. And I don't think all this climbing is good for you, after years and years of immobility.'

'No. But I think I could get a little higher. I'll rest here and then have another try. I might get all the way, in time.'

'All the way to Pendizack Point?'

'No. To St. Sody's. If I could get up there I wouldn't come down. I should stay.'

She left him and toiled round a couple of steep bends to the place where the cliff path turned off, through a tunnel among the rhododendrons. She had meant to wait here, but it had grown dark and gloomy under the trees, while at the end of the short tunnel she caught a last sunset gleam. So she crept a few yards further and came out upon the open cliff side. Here she could rest peacefully until Gerry came. She thought she could see him coming round the cliff path, but in the soft bloom of dusk she could distinguish nothing very well. Somebody was moving in the landscape.

She put down the basket and peered across the cliff slopes. In spite of the gathering darkness she could perceive a great deal of movement—more than she had ever noticed before in that wild and furzy place. A flicker of white suggested that it might be some unusual activity among the rabbits. There were many of them on the cliffs, but at this time of night they generally stayed in their burrows. Now they seemed to have decided on a mass exodus. White scut after white scut flickered and vanished.

There really was a man coming along the cliff path. He was too tall for Gerry. He looked like Duff. He walked like Duff. But he was bald. Nevertheless he was Duff, as she saw when he got quite close. It was all part of the strangeness which had invaded life and driven her out here.

'Oh, Duff . . .' she said. 'Your head!'

He was very much startled.

'Mother! *Mother!* How did you come here?'

'But what have you done to your hair. You look awful . . .'

He put his hand to his head and pulled the bald wig off. His own yellow hair emerged.

'I forgot I had it on,' he said. 'I'm supposed to be a pobble.'

'Have you come for the wine? I've got it.'

'What wine?'

He had known, she discovered, nothing at all about the wine. Its loss had not been noticed when he left the Feast. They had not started supper, he said: they were playing Hunt the Slipper. He was coming back because he had had enough of it. And he did not look too pleased when she asked him to take the wine for her.

'I can't go back there now,' he said impatiently. 'You've no idea how slow it is. I mightn't get another chance to slip off.'

'I won't carry this basket any further,' said Mrs. Siddal. 'It's very heavy, and I think it was nice of me to bring it this far.'

Duff lifted it up and agreed, with some remorse, that it was heavy.

'Gerry will be chasing along for it in a minute,' he urged. 'They'll find out soon. Can't you wait till he comes?'

'Why should he come? Poor Gerry! When it's not a bit necessary. I do think we are all very selfish to Gerry.'

'Nothing will get me to that picnic again,' he declared. 'But I'll do this. I'll carry the basket to the top of the Point for you, and slip off before they see me. You can take it the last few yards, and get an eyeful of Fred dressed as a Toreador!'

But that, she complained, would force her to join the picnic. And she rejected impatiently his plea that she should do so. It would bore her, she said, quite as much as it bored him. She wanted to go home to bed. They stood on either side of the wine basket, disputing, unsettled. Duff was afraid that she might guess his real reason for returning to the house. She shrank from revealing her real reason for avoiding the Feast, and that she would have fallen in with his plan if Evangeline Wraxton had not been up there. They were growing quite angry when a frightened cry among the bushes startled them:

'Oh . . . oh . . . a snake!'

It was Blanche Cove, who had been hurrying along the path as fast as she could.

'Oh, Mrs. Siddal. Take care! There's a snake . . .'

'It's all right,' called Duff. 'It's only a grass snake probably. There are lots about this evening. They keep slipping uphill across the path all the time. They won't hurt you.'

Blanche appeared, breathless and frightened, in a pink kimono.

'Oh, I was trying to get back to the house without anyone seeing,' she said. 'To get the wine. They've forgotten the wine. We noticed just now and we didn't want any of our guests to know . . . so Fred is keeping them amused while I run back . . .'

'That's all right,' said Duff. 'We've got it here.'

'Oh, Duff! Did you go for it? How kind you are!'

'No. My mother brought it . . .'

'Oh, Mrs. Siddal! Are you quite better? We were afraid you would have to miss it. Now do come quickly because it's really supper time.'

Blanche seized the basket and was quite distressed when Duff took it from her, because she did not think that her guest should be put to so much trouble.

'You haven't really missed so very much,' she told Mrs. Siddal, as she herded them along towards the point like a vigilant little sheepdog. 'Only some games. All the best part is yet to come.'

'But I have no fancy dress,' protested Mrs. Siddal. 'I didn't know I was coming.'

'Oh, that's quite all right, Mrs. Siddal, you can be Duff's

Aunt Jobiska. Oh, Duff . . . where is your lovely head?'

Very reluctantly Duff pulled his wig out of his pocket and put it on. He could see no way of escaping the rest of the Feast, now, without insult to Blanche. He yielded, as everyone else had yielded, to the power of the Coves. He was angry and frustrated, but at the same time he knew that he had had an escape. For if his mother had not met him in the road he might never have remembered that bald pate. He would have descended, wolf-like, upon Pendizack and the expectant Anna in the guise of a pobble. A mistake like that, he reflected, might have such humiliating repercussions as could ruin a man's sex life before it had even started.

6. The Feast

Supper had been delayed rather too long and the genial spirit of the Feast had begun to fizzle out, though all maintained a dutiful pretence of enjoyment. Most of the guests had arrived in low spirits. Gerry and Evangeline were overtired and wanted to be alone together. Sir Henry's gloom was scarcely enlivened by the cricket on his nose. Mrs. Paley concealed a tearful face beneath her hat; Paul's contempt still had power to wound her. Caroline had been struggling with tears all the evening, for Hebe, while they were dressing, had announced that she had done something dreadful and was to be sent away for ever and ever. She would not say what it was, nor would she admit that she minded leaving them. So that Caroline was glad to hide her stricken face under the hood of a sheeted ghost, and Hebe made a very morose angel.

Fred, Robin, the twins and the three hostesses were genuinely happy, and Nancibel's sorrows were so deeply buried that nobody could have supposed she had any.

When Mrs. Siddal and Duff were brought into the fold the whole party was sitting in a ring singing *Ten Green Bottles* to Fred's accompaniment. Nobody much liked this song except the twins, who had suggested it, but there seemed no way of escape from any of its verses. At times the chant sank to a dispirited murmur, and then, under the spur of social conscience, rose to a forced yell. There were moments when Luke and Michael sang alone:

> And if . . . one . . . green bottul . . .
> Should ackserdently fall,
> There'd be five . . . green . . . bottuls
> A hangin' on ther wall.

Karoo! Karoo! wailed the accordion, between each verse.

'Sing up! Sing up, everybody,' adjured Robin. 'FIVE GREEN BOTTLES . . .'

Room was made for Mrs. Siddal beside Mrs. Paley, and the wine was handed to Gerry, who made grimaces of horror and apology.

'It's an awful picnic,' whispered Angie to Duff. 'The best thing we can do is to get tight. Thank heaven for the wine! But the Coves are liking it.'

'The Coves,' said Duff, 'are a menace. They look like white mice, and see what they've done to us all.'

Karoo! Karoo!

> Three . . . green . . . bottles,
> A hanging on a wall.

'Sing up!'

> THREE GREEN BOTTLES,
> A HANGING ON A WALL.

'Sisters ought not to be parted,' said Caroline to Hebe. 'If you go away, I shall go away. Have you got a hankie?'

'No. Blow your nose on your sheet.'

Nancibel sat on a rock looking very beautiful. The Spanish shawl and high comb endowed her with an unfamiliar dignity. For a moment her attention wandered from the scene and her expression was pensive. Then she perceived that Mrs. Siddal had come and her warm smile shone out.

THERE'D BE NO GREEN BOTTLES
A HANGING ON THE WALL.

The penance was over and they might have their supper. All the food was already set out on a white cloth, and Robin had been busy with a corkscrew during the last verses of the song. Beatrice rose, clutching her kimono, which was too large and long.

'And now, Ladies and Gentlemen,' she announced, 'you are invited to partake of a cold collation and to imbibe some delicious hock kindly provided for us by our most honoured guest, Sir Henry Gifford.'

All gathered round the cloth where Evangeline and Robin were pouring the wine into glasses.

'Are the children to have any?' asked Gerry.

'We all need it,' said Duff, firmly. 'Here you are, Nancibel!'

But Nancibel protested that she was Band of Hope.

'This is non-alcoholic,' he assured her. 'Taste it and see. It's white, not red.'

'I wouldn't know. So is champagne white.'

She took a sip and was sure that he was stringing her along. But secretly she was feeling so sad about Bruce that

426

she welcomed stimulant and, after serving lobster salad, she finished her glass. A warm reassurance flowed through her veins. She ceased to mourn the past. A bright future beckoned through the sunset clouds.

He was kidding me, she thought. Lemonade never did this to me. I won't take any more.

But she had to take more, for Maud Cove was proposing a toast.

'Pray charge your glasses,' she cried, 'and drink to the absent but beloved provider of the tomatoes: Mr. Bruce . . . Mr. Bruce . . . oh, dear!'

'Partridge,' said Nancibel, who was the only person to know.

'Bruce . . .' shouted everybody. 'Bruce!'

A pleasant elation was sweeping over the party. Few of them had ever drunk hock before, and only Sir Henry was used to it. Angie had put very little in the children's glasses but enough to enliven them. Caroline and Hebe began to giggle. They took the cricket off Sir Henry's nose and put it in Fred's salad to startle him. Gerry was telling a story and laughing loudly at it.

'She said: "Who met a tarsal?" You did. Didn't you, Angie?'

'You'd think,' said Angie to Mrs. Paley, 'that he'd get tired of that joke.'

'He'll never get tired of it,' said Mrs. Paley. 'Make up your mind to that, Angie. Men have single-track minds. You'll have to live with that joke all your life. He'll tell it against you on your silver wedding day.'

'What joke?' asked Mrs. Siddal, leaning round Mrs. Paley's hat to look at Evangeline.

It was the first time that she had spoken to the girl. Evangeline, swimming in vinous optimism, decided to take it as an olive branch.

'Gerry was telling me,' she began, 'about tarsals and metatarsals.'

Robin, on the other side of the picnic cloth, nudged Duff and made him look.

'Girls are getting together,' he muttered.

Their mother and Evangeline both had their heads under Mrs. Paley's hat, so that nothing could be seen of their faces. But a burst of chuckles could be heard behind the ribbon fringe.

'They're all a bit on,' said Duff.

And Caroline told Hebe that she did not feel as if she was sitting on anything at all.

'We're drunk,' explained Hebe.

'Are we? How do you know?'

'I've been drunk before. Much worse than this.'

Karoo! Karoo!

Fred struck up *The Lily of Laguna*, which Mrs. Paley had named as her favourite tune when asked. It was not, and she had meant to ask for *Pale Hands I Loved*, but had got muddled. The air was taken up with gusto by the whole company.

> *I know . . . she loves me!*
> *I know she loves me,*
> *Because she says so . . .*

'I thought it had something in it about lotus buds,' complained Mrs. Paley.

'Don't let the children have any more hock.'

'Robin! No more hock for the children.'

'I'll have to sign the pledge all over again. I don't know what our mum would say to me.'

'This is a lovely picnic.'

'This is a grand picnic.'

'Where has my cricket gone? Who has taken my cricket?'

'Uncle Arly has lost his cricket.'

'I KNOW SHE LOVES ME . . .'

'No, but Angie, I must tell you a funny story about Gerry when he was a baby. I'd left him in his pram and . . .'

'I've got a wish bone. I've got a wish bone. Mrs. Paley . . . would you like a wish with my bone?'

'No, Hebe. You wish your own wish.'

'Well . . . I wish the Coves could be your children, and you wish it too, and we pull, and whichever gets the wish end . . .'

'It's no use wishing for something impossible . . .'

'SHE'S THE LILEE OF LA . . . GU . . . NA . . .'

The Coves were too happy to sing, too happy to eat. Gravely they circled round the ring offering food and drink to their guests. Without seeming to do so they ruled the Feast and saw to it that everything should be done in a suitable manner. When the twins, who were dressed as Red Indians, evinced an inclination to tomahawk their neighbours,

Blanche put an immediate stop to it by saying earnestly:

'Oh, but we're saving up the *tomahawks* till midnight. It's Nancibel's turn now. She's going to sing about the wicked old dolphin.'

There was a sudden hush and Nancibel looked startled.

'It's ever such an old-fashioned song,' she told them. 'I don't know how I had the face to say I'd sing it. My great-grannie used to sing it.'

'It's a lovely song,' said Beatrix. 'Nancibel sang it to us the day we were drowned.'

'Go on, Nancibel!'

Nancibel lifted her chin and sang instinctively in the sweet, steady tone of an older tradition:

> As I was a walking beside the salt sea,
> A beautiful mermaid appeared unto me.
> 'Oh, where's the young man who will save me,' she cried,
> 'From the wicked old dolphin who wants me for his bride?'

'It's a folk song!' whispered Duff in excitement. 'It's an uncollected folk song!'

> I made her a bow and I took her white hand,
> And I hugged and I tugged and I lugged her to land.
> 'My mother will give you a shawl and a gown,
> If you'll walk to my house in St. Sody Church Town.'
>
> 'Alas, I can't walk for I haven't no feet.
> I've only a tail, as you see, sir, indeed.
> You must carry me up, you must carry me down,
> You must carry me home to St. Sody Church Town.'

430

'A local folk song! And we've lived here all our lives without hearing it.'

> *I lifted her up on my shoulder so high,*
> *And oh, for a mile we were merry and blythe.*
> *But the cliffs they were steep and the road it was rough,*
> *And the maid on my shoulder was heavy enough.*
>
> *And first I must creep and next I must crawl*
> *Till we came to the sign of the Hen and the Owl.*

'*One and All*,' whispered Duff. 'Onen hen oil . . . Corn ish . . .'

> *Alas, my fair maiden, I must put you down,*
> *For it's still a long way to St. Sody Church Town.*

Nancibel stopped abruptly.

'Is that all?' cried the audience.

'No. That's all I can remember. There's a lot more.'

'What happens? Do they get there?'

'No. The wicked old dolphin comes after them and turns them into stone. It's supposed to be true. The stones are in a field just behind our place, and they're called The Man and The Mermaid.'

'I know,' said Robin. 'They're marked on the map.'

A buzz of interest and approval went round the ring, which rather puzzled Nancibel. She had wanted to sing *A Sunbeam Don' Cost Nothun*, but she perceived that the Coves had been right as usual in their choice, and that *The Wicked Old Dolphin* had given pleasure.

And now, after a glance at the programme, Blanche Cove had risen to propose another health.

'Could Bee and Maud and I have some wine?' she asked breathlessly. 'We haven't had time yet, but we want to drink your healths and congratulate you all on being here.'

Glasses were handed to them, and she continued:

'We want to thank you all for coming, and to say how glad we are to see you so happy. We know you did it to please us, but we can see you are really enjoying it. I expect it is the lovely hock.'

'Hear! Hear!'

'So that is a reward for coming, as you wouldn't have got it if you hadn't. We drink to you and we hope that you will all live happy for ever after, especially Gerry and Angie.'

'Hear! Hear!'

'Thank you, Blanche!'

'A lovely speech!'

'A lovely Feast!'

'For . . .'

'FOR THEY ARE JOLLY GOOD FELLOWS,
FOR THEY ARE JOLLY GOOD FELLOWS . . .'

Everybody sang. Everybody shouted. They made such a noise that, for a few seconds, they hardly noticed the other noise which was going on, until all sounds were swallowed up in one shattering, ear-splitting, jarring roar which threw them to the ground in darkness and terror. To some it seemed that the noise went on for a long time; while others maintained, afterwards, that it was all over very quickly. Nor could they be sure that they had not flung themselves down. But there they were lying, in a choking cloud of dust, while the noise subsided in a diminishing *arpeggio* of falling stones . . . skipping pebbles . . . the murmur of waves.

A faint clamour began to rise among the boulders— coughing, sobbing, cries and questions, as they groped about in the dusty haze. All were too much stunned to exclaim loudly until a child's voice rose in a piercing shriek:

'Oh! It's the atom bomb! It's the atom bomb!'

'What is it?'

'What happened?'

'It's the atom bomb!'

'Angie! Where are you? Are you all right?'

'Here, Gerry . . .'

'Oh, Mrs. Paley . . .'

'I'm here, Maud . . . holding you . . . where's Blanche? Where's Beatrix?'

'The atom bomb . . .'

'I've got the twins. Are you all right, ducks? It's Nancibel . . . she's got you . . .'

'Where's Caroline?'

'Daddy . . .'

'It's dust . . .'

'It's the atom bomb . . .'

'Gave me a turn, that did! I thought something must of happened . . .'

'Stop yelling, Hebe! It wasn't! There was no flash.'

'Not any sort of bomb. No blast . . .'

433

'An earthquake . . .'

'Is everybody all right? Is everybody here?'

'Be quiet, please. I'll call over names . . .'

'Be quiet, everybody. Sir Henry wants to call names . . .'

Sir Henry called their names, one by one, as the dust began to clear. All answered. All were safe.

But they could not understand it and still half believed that some kind of enemy had attacked them. For they were accustomed to associate such violent events with an act of man rather than of God. Stunned and terrified they huddled together in a thinning haze of dust until they saw a gleam of moonlight on the sea, and placid waves falling upon a beach; a familiar sight, which might have reassured them, had it been a beach that they had ever seen before.

Gerry and Sir Henry were the first to guess. But they said nothing. In silence they watched the pall of dust subside. As the truth leapt from mind to mind a moaning sigh went through the group. They drew closer together, as if still clinging to that frail, that transient, unity which had so strangely assembled and preserved them. Nobody spoke until one of the Gifford twins, raising his head from the bosom of Nancibel, looked out upon the scene below and asked wonderingly:

'Who did it?'

There was a shout from the hill behind. Little figures appeared on the skyline. People were running down from the village and from the farms. The group on the headland stirred and broke up. They whispered together, giving a name to what had happened. Already it was travelling into the past. Their thoughts turned towards the future.

'We had better go up to the village,' said Gerry. 'To the Vicarage. Father Bott will take us in . . .'

And they moved off, in a straggling procession, taking up once more the burden of their sixteen separate lives.